BENJAMIN

KATHRYN MATTINGLY

Winter Goose
Publishing

Winter Goose Publishing
2701 Del Paso Road, 130-92
Sacramento, CA 95835

www.wintergoosepublishing.com
Contact Information: info@wintergoosepublishing.com

Benjamin

COPYRIGHT © 2013 by Kathryn Mattingly

First Edition, May 2013

ISBN: 978-0-9889049-9-6

Cover Art by Winter Goose Publishing
Typeset by Michelle Lovi

Published in the United States of America

For Taryn Alyse Woodman,
who gave me the courage to seek a publisher
based solely on her enjoyment of Benjamin

CHAPTER ONE

Rafting the Rogue was Rachel's idea. I could see her lean tomboyish form smiling at me from the trail above the river, shouting a greeting not distinguishable over the roaring water. I watched her tanned figure scrambling down the embankment, short honey-colored hair hugging her face. Rachel Milan had been my best friend since high school. I would always associate meeting her with the devastating event of my mother's death. The Milan family had moved into the house next door and Rachel became an angel of mercy in the presence of despair. She made me laugh again, and made grief tolerable.

The men who would join our rafting group soon arrived in an old Ford pickup. They parked it beside Rachel's dusty convertible at the top of the embankment. I could hear their baritone voices above the rushing river as they hauled sleeping bags and backpacks to the shuttle van.

The whitewater company provided tents, prepared meals, and promised numerous whitewater thrills. They also provided our expert guides, Eric and Martin. I had grown up hiking and camping in the lush Oregon woods and was excited about this new adventure. Still, I couldn't help but wonder if it would be more of a thrill than any of us had bargained for, none of us having rafted a wild river before. If nothing else, it would be a testament to our courage, to stay the course for three long days.

Rachel finally reached where I stood, and we embraced in a welcoming hug. We curiously viewed the men who would be joining us.

"Do you know their names?" I asked.

Rachel observed them thoughtfully. "The blond is Daniel Rosselli. Jonathan is the tall dark-haired one beside him. His parents are friends of Miranda's in New York."

"Where is Miranda?" I asked, but Rachel wasn't listening. Her cat-green eyes were focused on the strong current, watching it move downstream to a wide bend in the river. The dry forest gave off a scent of pine needles and wood bark as the morning quickly heated up and I pulled my heavy hair into a ponytail.

Miranda finally arrived and we added her gear to the shuttle van while listening to her tale of taking a wrong exit off the freeway. It was wonderful to see her. Miranda Tanasborne was tall and willowy with exotic features and a soul-warming laugh. I had missed her terribly since moving out of our apartment in the spring, having graduated with a doctorate in psychology.

It was Miranda and her friend Jonathan who had put the trip together. She introduced Robert as Jonathan's law partner, and said Daniel was working on a doctorate in religious studies. It was hard not to stare at Daniel. He had flaxen hair that fell nearly to his shoulders in thick waves. His eyes were some exotic shade of tropical blue, not typical for humans. Cyan to be exact, a primary color used for blending cool tones when painting. All three men looked quite capable of masterfully rafting the wild river, and I was thankful for that.

Eric was the guide who sat at the head of our lightweight raft. He was an excellent coach and we took to it quickly, rowing in unison while making good time all morning. Martin, our other guide, manned the supply boat following well behind us. The day was cloudless and bright, the Rogue peaceful and calm on this beginning section of our rafting trip. We were a pride-filled team of somewhat weary rowers when pulling onto a sandbar for lunch. Everyone reapplied sunscreen and wolfed down roast beef sandwiches, anticipating the thrill of a class four rapid later in the day. Already such expert rowers, surely we would slide easily through.

The first section of river after lunch was exceptionally still, being protected by cliffs on either side. At one point we jumped from the raft and floated through a sheer rock canyon. The chilly water was a welcome relief from the hot sun. Our laughter bounced off canyon walls as we slid through with only our life vests to keep us afloat. Eric wasn't far behind, sitting at the helm of the otherwise empty raft. Martin could be seen in the far off distance with the supply boat.

Floating on our backs we all admired the intense blue sky above the sheer rock walls. I tried to focus on a hawk gliding through the air with his outstretched wings soaring far above me. At the end of the canyon we approached a narrow beach. Pulling ourselves out of the chilly river, we all laid on the sandbar until dried out and warmed up by the sun. It wasn't long until Eric announced it was time to end the calm before the storm.

Rested from our swim through the canyon, we were eager to face the class four rapid. I positioned myself behind Daniel in the raft and listened intently to our guides describe the tricky rowing task ahead. My companions were all quiet as they absorbed their instructions. We looked at one another with confidence before taking off from the shallow beach and heading downstream to our greatest challenge of the trip.

Just as Martin and Eric predicted, our entrance into the shallows before the swirling drop-off steered us sharply to the right. We rowed forcefully to position ourselves correctly for this ride through the fast approaching, tumultuous rapid. But the raft didn't swing back to the left as we hoped it would. Despite our coordinated rowing, we were trapped in the swirling middle. Maybe it was too much adrenalin among us, but despite our synchronized effort we remained dead center, being jerked continually about for what seemed like an eternity. Working diligently to pull ourselves free, first with one side rowing hard and deep, and then the other, we at last broke loose.

Darting quickly from the center of the rapid the rubberized boat tilted out of control. I saw fear in Rachel's eyes across from me and then heard Miranda scream from behind. As if suspended in time I felt the boat flip and toss me high into the air. I inhaled deeply on the way down instinctively knowing I'd be swallowed by the river, and swallowed I was—plunging downward into the bowels of the Rogue.

Wedged beneath rapidly moving water I felt helpless to stop myself from being pummeled by tons of flowing river. How long could I hold my breath? Panic set in and I began fighting my way back to the surface. Surely my lungs would burst before I freed myself. I struggled to remove the life jacket. It was only a deterrent to me now, its buoyancy useless while stuck beneath the strong currents.

For an instant I quit struggling and stared through blurry wetness, my heart beating fast and hard while being held hostage there. Time was of the essence. Had I considered every alternative for resurfacing? Fear of inhaling this bubbly aqua beast that gripped me caused one last gallant effort to break free. Kicking ferociously to rise above the strong current and be among the living left no time for profound thoughts as I quickly ran out of breath. I only regretted my weak slender build. There was no light miraculously appearing except for the sun teasing me from above as I thrashed upwards.

Still my efforts weren't enough. My lungs were burning painfully. I was seconds from inhaling the river and meeting my maker. I hated dying this way. I hated dying at all. I wanted to live. I still had so much living to do. Something gripped my upper arm then, I was sure of it . . . or was it a cramp? Was it God pulling me to heaven? Something was yanking me upwards.

I was suddenly pulled clear from the suffocating river and instantly felt lighter. No sooner had the air hit my face than I sucked in a lungful of it, nearly choking to death as I exhaled, while being deposited on a rock. It was only after clearing my eyes and throat that I dared glimpse who or what had pulled me free from the Rogue.

It was Daniel.

Seeing that I was okay he laid down on the rock beside me.

I couldn't speak at first. The sun was glaring from above and I was aware of sharp sounds, not muffled like beneath the water. The river rushing past made a thunderous roar and moved completely through me, like an orchestra of percussion instruments pounding on my chest. Birds were chirping in the trees on the shore. I squinted through my hair, plastered to my face on either side, and realized Daniel and I were in the center of the Rogue, on a large flat rock.

"Where are the rest?" I whispered hoarsely.

"They . . . grabbed the raft," Daniel answered, breathing heavily. "They're fine, I think. Back a quarter mile . . . or so, I'm guessing."

He sat up and I could see the silhouette of his strong body against the sun. Thank God he was there when I needed him, this angel of a man, who actually looked the part.

"We shot down the river much faster underwater . . . than they did on top of it . . . clinging to the raft," he added tentatively, as if it were a theory he'd come up with and only hoped it were true. So did I. Surely we were the only two who nearly drowned.

I shivered violently despite the hot sun beating down onto my limp flesh and suddenly was grateful Martin kept my camera on the supply boat. This rafting adventure was a short diversion from my graduate studies in graphic art. I was a photographer, and had bought an expensive waterproof camera for the trip. Pointless for it to be waterproof, if lying on the riverbed!

Sitting up slowly, I stared into Daniel's unusual blue eyes. They had such a calming effect. It didn't seem to matter any more that we were on a rock in the middle of a wild river. I felt safe. I hoped our companions were safe too.

"Thanks, Daniel. For saving my life."

"You don't need to thank me, Tori." He studied my face and I wondered if my thoughts were transparent. We had shared something horrific and beaten the odds. Flipping was never supposed to happen and always a death threat when it did.

"I was just in the right place at the right time and did what anyone would do." He smiled at me. "But then again, I guess we were both in the wrong place at the wrong time." Daniel looked over his shoulder to see if the raft was coming.

Why did I agree to come on this trip? How had Rachel squelched my fears about rafting the unpredictable Rogue? I could hear her voice in my head. *There's really nothing to it. By the end of the second day you'll be wishing it would never end. It's going to be fun and the memories will get you through the rest of the summer, while doing all that filing for Professor Cairns.*

I watched noisy seagulls sail across the cloudless sky and then stared into the tons of river rushing by. The Rogue would end its journey at the Pacific Ocean, downstream in the little coastal town of Gold Beach. It had started out as a mountain stream, snow runoff trickling downhill. Where along the way to its destination had this lamb become a lion?

CHAPTER TWO

But upon reflection, perhaps the river and forest
were the only things exactly as they seemed.

"Look." Daniel nodded and pointed toward the bend, where the raft full of our companions was drifting into view. They cheered when seeing us. Eric was in front skillfully maneuvering over to our rock, followed by Martin in the supply boat.

"I guess you're both 'like one' with the river now!" Eric boomed, looking visibly shaken despite his attempt at humor. Rachel and Miranda mauled me with hugs and tears as I climbed aboard the raft. Jonathan and Robert appeared sober and relieved, shaking Daniel's hand and patting him on the back. Once it became clear Jonathan and I were not injured and only wished to press on toward camp for the night, we all began paddling in unison. It felt good to be rowing, to be alive, to be alone with my thoughts as we rounded the bend toward our stopping point for the first day.

Everyone was somber that last hour, breaking the methodical rhythm of our rowing only once, to point at snowy white Egrets perched along the bank. Our private thoughts were surely all the same, trying to understand what had happened and what a close call it was. The Rogue was indeed a force to be reckoned with. In certain places it became tranquil and serene, but for the most part it was exuberant, challenging, and worthy of respect. I thought of it now as something more than just thrilling. It was threatening, if circumstance permitted.

Campfire conversation sizzled with stories of the spill while we devoured Eric's pan-fried salmon and wild rice, suddenly starving from hard rowing and emotional trauma. Someone began a conversation about colleges and occupations. Rachel and I shared how college swept us away from the small Oregon towns of our youth, making us city dwellers now, in Portland proper.

Miranda lived in Portland too, although originally from New York like Jonathan and Robert. She had come for graduate school and fell in love with 'The City of Roses.' Jonathan and Robert practiced law in Portland, having been enticed equally by deep-sea fishing in small northwest coastal towns and a law firm offering immediate partnership. Daniel studied religion in Portland. No one said how he'd met Jonathan and Robert.

What other great adventures would we have during our time on the river, before pulling out at Foster Bar on the last day? We were at least grateful there were no more level four rapids. Jonathan began poking the fire with a tree branch. He stopped for a minute to look directly at me. "Tori is an odd name. Is it short for something?"

"It's short for Victoria. Tori is found conveniently in the middle," I explained. "The nickname eliminates expectation that I will be victorious in whatever I attempt."

"I would say not drowning was quite victorious." Jonathan smiled.

Rachel and Miranda agreed appreciatively.

"I would have drowned, were it not for Daniel plucking me from the river," I pointed out.

"Well, your eyes are intimidating." Jonathan stared at me. "They are quite bold and a striking shade of blue. Very powerful, like your name."

Until that moment I'd always believed my large eyes overwhelmed my face. That they came across as powerful was thought provoking. Power eluded me to be sure, like my name, perhaps powerful in the longer form but a quandary in its shortened version. I didn't know the longer version of myself yet, the one that could go the distance.

I fell silent, not knowing what to say in response, but I liked Jonathan. His smile was infectious. He had a sharp wit that kept everyone laughing, and he rowed with more finesse than any of us.

At some point Daniel and I began to quietly observe each other from across the fire. It was unclear to me what I thought of this odd man. We had nothing in common but nearly drowning, and out-of-the-ordinary eye color. Yet his affect on me was profound. It didn't feel flirtatious, like with Jonathan. It felt more spiritual, if such a word could be in my vocabulary. We knew more than anyone how close we'd come to death and how lucky we were to be alive. We shared what the point of no return feels like, just before it miraculously turns because of unbelievable good fortune, or maybe divine intervention.

After everyone crawled into sleeping bags placed in tents put up earlier, I quietly grabbed my sweatshirt and crept down to the shoreline. I couldn't sleep. Almost drowning had my head swimming with thoughts of my mother, who was killed instantly when her car slid off an icy mountain road and over an embankment. I was fourteen at the time. My father would have found the news of my death an intrusion into his new life, a rude reminder of his former marriage and first kids. Did my sister Eliza regret our drifting apart after Mother died? Eliza left for college right after the funeral but Wil and I became close while living with Grams during high school. Surely we could have made more effort to call and visit these past few years.

I was staring at the star-cluttered sky, trying to shake off these troubling thoughts when Daniel startled me, jumping onto the boulder from behind. I gasped and then relaxed. Here we were on a rock once again. Only this one overlooked the river from the shore, rather than being wedged in the middle of the Rogue.

Almost drowning fine-tuned my senses. The water sounded magnified as it rushed by, and moonlight danced on the surface with intense sparks of light. I keenly felt the heat of the sun still trapped inside the boulder beneath us. Even my sense of touch was ultra-sensitive as his arm brushed mine.

"Couldn't you sleep either?"

"No," he confessed.

The scent of bar soap mixed with wood smoke on his skin was enticing and intoxicating all at the same time. Daniel must have found me somewhat irresistible as well, because he slowly reached out to touch my face, running his fingers along my cheek bone. Finally he drew me near and kissed my forehead. It sent a chill straight through me. Had it not been such a strange day I would have found it odd, getting chills from a kiss on the forehead. The full moon was literally making Daniel's golden locks shimmer. I'd wanted to touch them ever since being stranded on a rock in the river. The hot sun had dried his hair quickly, illuminating the flaxen curls as if he were not entirely of this world, but half hovering in another.

Now in the moonlight I could finally run my fingers through his blond tresses, recalling that moment of sheer gratitude for being rescued. Daniel pulled me closer and kissed my mouth. It made my heart race out of control and reminded me of floating through the air earlier, before hitting the water. Like a dam breaking, there was no stopping this floodgate of feelings pouring out of us. Nestled in soft foliage beside the rock we intermingled silent thought and sensual touch until we dare not stay another minute. While sneaking back to our cold and empty sleeping bags, I hoped no one would be the wiser for how and where we'd spent the night.

At daybreak our two guides could be heard cracking branches for kindling. The sun was barely rising above evergreens on the far shore when they began brewing coffee, enticing us from our tents. I was the first to sit by the welcoming flames licking at freshly split wood. Jonathan soon approached us and began asking Eric questions about what type of whitewater thrills we could expect for the day. Eric laughed and assured him there'd be no more class four rapids.

At breakfast we sat on opposite ends of a fallen tree, drinking strong coffee and inhaling biscuits smothered in gravy. None of our companions sandwiched between us seemed to have noticed our absence from the tents, much to our relief.

Everyone was eager to break camp after breakfast and begin our journey down the river, but I managed to take some impressive shots with my new camera. The early morning sun was already warm and bright as it filtered through Douglas fir trees and danced on the surface of the water. Boldly standing on a rock at the river's edge was breathtaking. It was quite beautiful with sunlight glistening on each little eddy.

Daniel rowed directly in front of me all morning, and I in front of him all afternoon. Memories of lovemaking beside the river made not touching him in the raft difficult. I had no indication as to whether or not it was equally difficult for Daniel, because we barely acknowledged each other's presence until breaking for lunch.

While our companions dangled their feet in the water and savored more roast beef sandwiches, we crawled onto a tall rock formation to be alone. I snapped a few pictures from our perch above the river and told Daniel everything he didn't know about photography. He shared the history and teachings of Christianity. It was intriguing to me how he didn't preach the message of the gospel I'd heard so often as a child. Instead he offered up the most fascinating little known facts about the early Church of Rome.

After lunch, we received curious smiles from our friends, except for Jonathan, who wasn't smiling at all. For the next two days Daniel and I were inseparable, but discreet. Never openly affectionate, never alluding to what became our continual nighttime gathering by the river's edge, where I chose to place my sleeping bag, and where Daniel always came to lie beside me. The intensity of our lovemaking left us sweaty and spent, finally dozing in each other's arms until nearly dawn. It felt as if our very souls were becoming as entangled as our flesh.

Then all too soon it was time to return to civilization.

Our parting breakfast was quite sober. Daniel and I, along with our companions, reminisced about everything we'd experienced. What Daniel and I experienced alone only our eyes disclosed between us. When the rafts drifted slowly past the last bend in the channel at midmorning, I could barely believe our magical time in the wilderness was coming to an end. The water and trees became a blur to me as they passed by. It was as if they were an illusion. But upon reflection, perhaps the river and forest were the only things exactly as they seemed.

At the pullout sight I awkwardly said my last goodbye to Rachel and Miranda, still refusing to share my feelings about Daniel. I felt discussing our affair would make it perfectly clear to me what an absolute crazy thing I'd done, throwing caution to the wind, along with better judgment. I didn't usually fall into relationships as easily as pinecones off a tree, nor would I normally give my heart to someone I barely knew. I didn't wish to examine what exactly happened between Daniel and me. Perhaps the river I nearly succumbed to affected my sanity.

I rearranged the gear in my trunk, and waited for Daniel to say goodbye to me alone. Jonathan and Robert were talking with the guides, obviously waiting for him to see me off. Finally Daniel approached my car. We hugged briefly.

"Will I ever hear from you again?" I asked.

"Of course."

He didn't sound convincing. I'd given Daniel my e-mail address, but he hadn't offered me his, and I had too much pride to ask for it. "Daniel, is there someone else . . . was this time together meant to be forgotten?"

"No, there's not anyone else . . . there's never been anyone else." Daniel stared into the cloudless sky. "I have never felt this way before. I should not have allowed myself . . ." his voice trailed off.

"Are you afraid I'll interfere with your studies?"

"That's not it." He glanced at Jonathan and Robert.

"What then?" I also glanced at them, recalling my conversation with Jonathan on that first night. It seemed so long ago. He saw me looking his way and we held eye contact for several seconds.

I tried to ignore Jonathan's disapproving stare while examining Daniel's odd expression. He was somber, brows knit—no smile. It was as if his mind were somewhere far away and yet intensely focused on the moment. "I love you, Tori. I've never said that to anyone." He looked at me one last time and then walked away.

I got into my car and left, thinking about how I was almost taken by the river only to be transformed by it instead. Yet there was no joy in my heart about it, no peace of mind or excited anticipation. What if Daniel never contacted me? I felt a knot forming in the pit of my stomach as I sped down the hard dirt road. But of course he would. I shrugged off my fear of never seeing him again as I left the Oregon wilderness behind. What I couldn't shrug off was the expression on Daniel's face as he had said goodbye.

It was a look of such total remorse.

CHAPTER THREE

"He has a gift . . . your Benjamin."

Benjamin let go of the sparrow and it faltered for a second as we held our breath, but then flapped its wings and flew away into the blue sky. The little bird made a sharp turn and was soon out of sight. We both jumped up and down on the patio while clapping our hands, relieved and happy.

"That's the second bird this month you've nursed back to health, Benjamin." I hugged my little golden-haired son and ran fingers through his messy curls. "I'm proud of you, Benj," I added, kissing him on the cheek before walking back inside the apartment.

I leaned against the kitchen counter with my steaming mug of tea and observed Benjamin peering off into the sky, his sick pet healed and gone. At eleven years old he was bringing home wounded animals and nursing them back to health, and had been ever since he turned five. He always fell in love with his little pets, and yet he never kept any. Once they were healed he promptly released them back into the wilds of the city.

Benjamin was such a sweet boy, beautiful and smart. His eyes were some exotic shade of blue seen only in the shallow waters of a warm, tropical ocean. They were cyan blue, to be exact, the same shade as Daniel's, with the same dancing slivers of light, and they were always full of questions. Questions he never asked, such as who was his father? Why wasn't he part of our lives?

Maybe it was just my own guilt putting the questions there. Maybe his inquisitive expression only reflected his innocence, his pure heart. And he did have a pure heart. Benjamin was extraordinary. He never cried as a baby, or rebelled as a toddler. He never hit or yelled, or lost his patience. Animals loved him. Everyone in the neighborhood loved Benjamin—big kids, little kids, adults. It didn't matter what their ethnic diversity was—and we had a plethora of cultures and colors on our street. They all saw something in him they admired and respected, something they wanted to protect.

Sitting down at my computer and checking the gallery website again, I realized it wouldn't be long until we could move out of the inner city. I could buy us a real home with a big yard and Benjamin could go to the good schools in the suburbs. I'd finally sold enough Gallery photos for a down payment. Becoming pregnant on the Rogue trip set back my graduate program, but I hung in there, transferring to Portland State and taking classes at night. Now all my persistence and dedication was beginning to earn a decent income from sales at Rachel's Art Gallery.

Next to Benjamin's school picture was our only family photo. I must have been about eleven, the same age Benjamin was now. My father was quite handsome in the picture, and smiling. I couldn't remember him ever being that skinny, or smiling for that matter. Mother looked demure standing there beside him wearing a tight stylish dress, with her long dark hair twisted up and back.

If only my mother could see what I had accomplished. It was my one resounding and impossible wish. She had been the center of my universe as a child, but I was never the center of hers. Being the middle child with classic middle child syndrome by second grade, I appropriately and purposefully chose to go by the middle of my name. I believed in my child's heart victory had not been mine when it came to winning the affection of either parent. I was not as studious as my older sibling Eliza, or as entertaining as our little brother Wil. My only distinction came from inheriting our mother's creative gifts, and that didn't appear to be held in reverence like perfect grades or making people laugh.

My mother was just coming into her own as a renowned sculptor when her car slid off that icy mountain road in the Cascades. I often thought about how few seconds it takes to lose control on a mountain road and not be able to brake in time, or to plunge beneath the Rogue and not be able to resurface in time. She needed a savior that day, a Daniel to steer her to safety, to grab her and wrench her free from death's grip.

I touched the silver frame of Benjamin's school picture, moving my finger up to his cyan blue eyes and the curly golden hair, stopping at the soft yellow glow above his head. Photos of him always reflected light above his yellow-white hair. It wasn't just the hair and eyes that made Benjamin an oddity. It was his ability to heal things. That special gift must have come from Daniel. Why had he never called after the Rogue trip? I had asked myself this question many times, just as I continually recalled every precious moment of our short time together. Despite the endless heartache and unanswered questions for all these years, I thanked God that at least I had our son. Benjamin was a very special parting gift indeed.

There was a knock on the door and Benjamin came in from the patio to answer it. "Hello, Mrs. Gianni."

"Hi, Benji boy. You're just the person I want to see."

"Come in, Maggie, please." I stood from my desk.

"I'm sorry to bother you, but it's my Sarah." Maggie's voice broke and her eyes were puffy from crying.

"Sit down, Maggie. Tell us how Sarah's doing." I led her to the blue sofa with swirling flowers in faded yellows and sat next to her. Benjamin closed the door and perched on the edge of a matching chair. It had been Grams' furniture, worn with age but sturdy and soft, just as she had been.

"Sarah's bad, Tori. Really bad." Maggie unwadded the lace-trimmed hanky in her hand and dabbed at her eyes. She looked older than her forty-five years. Maybe it was the graying hair she pulled back into a tight bun, or all the worry that came with their daughter's cancer. Maggie and Vincent were more surprised than anyone when she became pregnant, after they'd given up. Sarah was their whole world, a petite and sensitive child with soft green eyes and hair the color of light molasses.

"I'm so sorry, Maggie. Is there anything we can do?" I glanced over at Benjamin. We both knew Sarah had cancer. Now a related infection was causing her to spike a high fever. The doctors sent her home from the hospital. There was nothing they could do. She would have to fight it out, or perhaps, quit fighting.

Maggie stuffed the hanky in a pocket of her green print blouse. She always wore loose fitting blouses with generous pockets on either side, carefully sewn on her Italian machine. I watched as she smoothed back a gray hair and looked past me onto the patio. Sunshine from the glass door fell in patches on the hardwood floor. No one spoke or moved as she composed herself.

"She's dying, Tori. I know it. She's slipping away and there's nothing I can do."

Benjamin came and sat on the other side of Maggie, setting one hand on her knee in comfort. I took her other hand and held it.

"She's asking for Benjamin." Maggie glanced at him and her eyes lit up. "She loves you Benji. You're the best friend she's ever had. Will you come with me . . . now . . . to see her?"

Benjamin nodded and then looked at me. I smiled warmly at him. "He'd be happy to, Maggie. I pray you're wrong about her dying, and she breaks this fever," I whispered, squeezing her hand.

Maggie pulled the hanky back out of her pocket. "Come with us, honey." Her large brown eyes pleaded with me.

"Of course I will." Together we walked next door, with Benjamin trailing behind. Once in the Gianni's apartment, we timidly entered Sarah's room. Her father, Vincent, peered up at us with troubled eyes. I hugged his thin frame tightly and his eyes filled with tears as he whispered to me that his Sarah was dying. After patting Benjamin's messy golden curls, Vincent stepped out of the room for a much needed break.

Benjamin sat on the edge of Sarah's wrought-iron bed and looked calmly into her gaunt face. Maggie and I stood on the other side. I couldn't help but observe my son's undeniable peace with suffering. What eleven-year-old would not be squirming by now or awkwardly fumbling with their hands or clothing? But Benjamin seemed to be comfortable with her near-death state. He took Sarah's pale hand into his and touched her hot cheek with the other. Instantly her eyes opened.

"*Benjamin.*" She whispered with finality, as if now everything would be tolerable. "I've missed you." There was the hint of a smile on her face.

"I've missed you, too, Sarah." He paused, carefully moving a stray hair off her forehead. "The sparrow flew away today. She's all healed."

Sarah's face lit up in response.

"You should've seen her, Sarah. She fell for a second and then flapped her wings wildly, fighting it, fighting the fall. Then she flew up . . . up really high . . ." Benjamin glanced out the window and Sarah turned her head to follow his gaze. ". . . made a sharp turn and was gone."

"I wish I could have been there," Sarah sighed.

Benjamin put his hand on her forehead. "You need to catch your fall, Sarah. Like the sparrow. Fight it."

Sarah stared into his eyes intently.

"You can do it, Sarah. Just fly up and away, well and strong."

Maggie caught more tears with her lace hanky and sniffled.

"Benj, we should go, honey. Sarah needs her rest," I said softly.

Benjamin glanced up at me and rose from the bed. He turned to look at her one last time. "Make a sharp turn, Sarah. Okay?"

"Okay, Benjamin." Sarah's green eyes sparkled, full of new strength.

I smiled at Sarah. She was only a year younger than Benjamin, but looked tiny in comparison. "Get well, sweetie. We miss you at our place." I kissed her forehead. "She seems better, Maggie. Really," I whispered into her ear as I turned to go. "Please, call us if you need anything, anything at all. Okay?"

Maggie nodded, and I left, with Benjamin at my side.

Several weeks later I pulled cookies out of the oven and slid them onto a plate. "They're hot, Benj, be careful," I scolded while pouring us each a glass of milk.

"Mrs. Gianni told me Sarah's better." Benjamin took a bite of the warm chocolate cookie while sitting down at the solid oak table, compliments of Grams.

"Really? That's great, Benj. When did you see Maggie?" I sat across from him and set the glasses down.

"Just now. When I got home from school. She was getting the mail." He gulped down his milk and I gave him a thoughtful look.

"That doesn't mean Sarah's in remission, Benj. It just means her fever's gone because the infection healed."

"No." Benjamin shook his head. "She's in remission. Mrs. Gianni said so."

I set my cookie down and studied his angelic face.

"Maggie said Sarah's in remission? Are you sure?"

"I'm sure." He looked at me seriously with his unbearably blue eyes. "Mrs. Gianni says she wants to return to school tomorrow. She wants me to walk with her."

"That's amazing, Benjamin. Really wonderful news." I looked through the patio window and thought about the sparrow, and about Sarah, both free falling to death for an instant, and then suddenly turning sharply away from it.

There was a knock on the door and Benjamin jumped up to see who was there. It was Maggie, grinning ear to ear. I stood to hug her as she cheerfully joined us at the table. We chatted happily about the good news. Benjamin promised to watch over Sarah at school her first day back. Then he left to do his homework and I insisted Maggie stay for a cup of tea.

"It was your Benjamin, Tori, who saved my Sarah. I know it was." Maggie swiped her eyes with a napkin as I set a cup of tea in front of her.

"Maggie, there's no way of knowing that," I said, but I believed my son *had indeed* healed the child. Maggie and I witnessed it together. Sarah's strength began to return the instant Benjamin touched her. The little girl's eyes went from bleary defeat to shimmering hope in a matter of seconds.

"He has a gift . . . your Benjamin. Like that Father Rosselli, at St. Matthew's."

"Father who?" I asked, dropping the sugar spoon and grabbing a napkin to blot tea splashes on the table.

"Father Rosselli. Everyone's heard of him. He's known for healing the sick, and the dying. Especially children." Maggie took a sip of tea.

"I was going to take my Sarah there tonight for his healing mass, but your boy beat him to it." Her whole face lit up from thinking about Sarah's miraculous remission. "They say he's going to be appointed bishop, because of his wonderful healings. The Pope himself is going to have a special ceremony for Father Rosselli, in Rome. This young priest, he comes from Rome originally," Maggie added.

I sat down and nodded my head, too perplexed by Maggie's information to speak.

"Have you heard of Father Rosselli, Tori?"

"No. I mean . . . I'm not sure." I put my hand on my forehead, suddenly feeling flushed. "What's his first name, Maggie? Do you know?" I gathered up the milk glasses and placed them in the sink.

Maggie stood and leaned against the counter. "I can't remember. I'm sorry." She paused. "Are you okay, honey?"

"I don't know. I need to see who this priest is. What time is the healing mass?" I looked into Maggie's questioning brown eyes.

"It's at five." She reached out and took my hands into hers. "Do you think you might know him?"

I took a deep breath. "Maybe. He might be someone from my college days. I'm just . . . surprised that he might be a priest."

Maggie indicated she understood and walked over to the door. "Goodbye, honey. I hope it's your friend. Maybe he can give you some insight into Benjamin's special gift for healing."

I considered the irony of my neighbor's words. Glancing at the stove clock I realized we could make the healing mass if we hurried. I shouted for Benjamin to come quickly while grabbing my purse and car keys. He followed me out the door, asking where we were going. I mumbled something about needing to see someone I knew from a long time ago before he was born. Benjamin didn't ask any questions, and I was grateful, because I was thinking about questions of my own. For Father Rosselli. Could it be Daniel? Was this his mysterious occupation? Is that why he didn't call after our love affair on the Rogue?

Surely not, but I had to see for myself.

CHAPTER FOUR

"I do believe in demons, and that there are
angels among us . . . such as yourself."

I honked my horn to avoid a near accident, and then glanced at Benjamin guiltily. His brows were knit with concern. Vowing to concentrate more carefully on traffic, I willed myself to stop the flood of emotions overtaking me. How often had I tried to examine what went wrong on the Rogue all those years ago? I believed the bond between Daniel and me was much more than physical. So much so that I agonized even now over why he didn't call, didn't look for me during all these years. Could it have been because he was a priest?

Cars honked and brakes squealed again. Benjamin jumped.

"What is it, Mom? Are you okay?"

I glanced at him while chewing my bottom lip. "Benj, this mass we're going to, it's a healing mass."

"A healing mass?" Benjamin looked perplexed.

"Yeah. This Father . . . Rosselli, well, he heals people. Like you heal animals. And Maggie . . . Maggie thinks you healed Sarah." I glanced at him again, nervously.

Benjamin calmly asked, "Do we know him? Father Rosselli?"

"I'm not sure, Benj. But he's . . . like you, with the healing powers. So I want to see for myself."

Benjamin nodded, his flaxen hair moving slightly in the breeze from the window. I parked in the lot behind the Cathedral. Bells chimed as latecomers straggled up the cement steps to the arched doorway. I froze on the sidewalk and stared at the entrance. I could feel Benjamin hovering near my side and it gave me the presence of mind to continue, to follow through with finding out the truth. Was that Daniel in there? *Benjamin's father?*

Grabbing my son's hand I flew up the steps and through the entrance just as the ushers shut the massive oak doors. I let my eyes adjust to the dim light and then inched my way steadily forward until near the middle of the center aisle. Benjamin was right behind me. I genuflected and slipped inside the pew, kneeling as I made the sign of the cross, while Benjamin mirrored my actions perfectly.

After Mother died and I went to live with Grams, we attended St. Luke's every Sunday, missing only once when she was too ill. That Cathedral was small and humble in comparison, but the motions of a mass are exactly the same everywhere in the world. Benjamin and I prayed, sat back in the pew, and observed our ornate surroundings as inconspicuously as possible.

A tremendous pipe organ played a hymn and everyone stood to sing. The acolytes lit altar candles. Priests appeared from side alcoves. I strained to see them, wishing I'd had the nerve to sit up front in the enormous sanctuary. After everyone stopped singing and sat down, several laymen read verses from folded programs handed to worshipers on the way in. An older priest approached the wooden podium and read scripture from a large leather-bound Bible. Everyone stood reverently to listen.

My eyes never left the spacious and intricate altar area, watching every move made by the younger priest in black robes. I couldn't see his facial features well enough to determine if it was Daniel or not, but the height and build seemed right, and whoever it was, he had light hair. The older priest spoke intelligently, his words weighty and measured, but I couldn't concentrate. My mind raced uncontrollably to the past and then anxiously lingered in the present. Benjamin listened intently, his expression one of fascination, soaking up all that was happening like a sponge.

When it was time for communion my heart began pounding. I prayed for strength and took slow deep breaths as I entered the center aisle with Benjamin right in front of me. We followed the procession of worshipers until it was our turn for communion. I didn't have the courage to lift my head and look into the faces of the priests on the way up. I felt weak and shaky, afraid if I did look at them I would surely faint.

Body of Christ, bread of heaven echoed in my ears as we approached the altar. Benjamin knelt in front of me and accepted the host into his mouth, just as everyone else had done. *Blood of Christ, cup of salvation.* He drank from the goblet, still mimicking other worshipers, then made the sign of the cross before circling back to our pew. I knelt and heard the words *body of Christ, bread of heaven,* and looked up into the face of Daniel, his cyan blue eyes showing immediate recognition. I felt a rush of warmth as he set the host on my tongue. Daniel's face drained of color and he wavered slightly, his golden hair shimmering under the lit candles as he caught his breath. *Blood of Christ, cup of salvation.* I drank from the goblet and then stood to face him.

Amen was all I could say in barely a whisper.

Tori emerged weakly from Daniel's lips.

For several seconds we stared into each other's eyes, and then I turned to leave, somehow finding my way back to the pew I had come from.

The rest of the mass was a blur of standing and singing, and special prayers said by Daniel for the sick. His voice was unsteady and trailed off several times, as if distracted from his purpose. Those who wished for hands-on healing approached and knelt at the altar and he touched them, whispering something over each one. After a while the pipe organ played and a final hymn was sung. People filed out of the church and I stayed, truthfully unable to move, with Benjamin waiting silently beside me.

When the last worshiper had left, Daniel sat on the altar steps with his hands neatly folded in front of him. He watched me, as the acolytes put out the candles. I sat straight and still on the wooden pew, my heart racing mercilessly. Benjamin was peering down at the hymnal in his lap, paging through it thoughtfully. After the acolytes left, Daniel stood and walked slowly down the center aisle to where we sat. He held out a hand to Benjamin.

"I don't think we've met, have we?" he asked warmly.

"No, Father. My name is Benjamin." He looked up at *his father*, unknown to him. I observed all of this as if above somewhere floating, my breathing shallow, my thinking labored. I shouldn't have brought Benjamin. Confronting Daniel hadn't occurred to me when I flew out the door to attend this mass. Observing him from afar was all I meant to do, but something had urged me on, urged me forward to communion, and kept me cemented to the pew as others shuffled out.

"Would you mind, Benjamin, if your mother and I walked over there and spoke in private?" Daniel nodded toward the alcove on one side of the altar area.

"No." Benjamin glanced at me, and then leafed through the hymnal again. I stood on shaky legs and walked down the aisle just in front of Daniel.

When I reached the altar, I hesitated. He touched my upper arm and guided me into the alcove, where I stood between two round pillars in the dimly lit space. My mind was ablaze with questions, twelve years worth. I looked at him, my arms folded defensively in front of me.

"Is this why you never called?"

"Yes."

"Who are you, Daniel? *What* are you?" I felt weak from the emotions welling up inside me, and leaned against a wall in the empty alcove. "An angel? A *demon?*"

"Is that what you think? That I'm a demon?" Slowly he walked over to where I stood.

"No. Of course not. I didn't come here to be unkind." I looked at him closely, his white-blonde hair, his chiseled angelic features, still smooth and handsome. "It's just that you . . . overwhelm me with your presence . . . just as you did twelve years ago."

Daniel looked at me intensely with his exceptionally blue eyes. "I do believe in demons, and that there are angels among us . . . such as yourself." He sighed deeply and stared at the pillar beside us. "I'm only a humble priest, Tori. A servant of God . . . a flawed one, I know . . . because you overwhelmed me, too." His expression was vulnerable, pensive. Daniel touched my hair, hesitantly, as if it might break, or maybe he would.

"But there's never been anyone else. You are the only woman I've ever been with."

"Ever?" I couldn't help but look surprised.

"Ever. I have always known I would be a priest. I couldn't let anything get in the way, and so I didn't let anyone be irresistible." He paused, his expression strained. "But you were." Daniel touched my cheek with longing in his brilliant eyes that said perhaps I still was.

How could he have been such a divine lover without *any* experience? Logic told me not to believe him, but my instincts told me otherwise. "So, in a way, I've been *your* demon," I concluded.

Daniel put his hands in the pockets of his robe, purposefully, as if to make himself stop touching me, and glanced at Benjamin, still seated in the sanctuary. I observed our son waiting impatiently on the bench, absent-mindedly thumbing through the hymnal.

"Where is his father, Tori?" Daniel's expression turned to one of torment as he looked back at me and studied my face.

"His father chose not to be a part of our lives." I shrugged. My eyes held his with confidence, for surely truer words had never been spoken.

"He looks just like me . . . with that flaxen hair and those intense blue eyes." Panic clouded his beautiful face. "Is he . . . mine?"

"You forget my eyes are also an odd shade of blue, Daniel. Perhaps not the same shade as yours, but not far from it, and I am sure mine were that exact color as a child," I lied. "As for the hair, my brother's was identical to Benjamin's." My gaze upon him did not waver, nor my voice.

"I don't know whether to be relieved or disappointed." He glanced at the boy again. "He is a handsome lad, confident . . . patient. I bet he's quite intelligent and creative, like his mother."

"He is . . . very special," I agreed.

"You recovered quickly from . . . whatever we felt for each other." He didn't look at me.

"It was love, Daniel. At least for me." I paused. "It isn't right to judge others. Isn't that a house motto around here?" I tried not to sound hurt.

Daniel sighed. I thought he looked like a lost child standing there with his hands in his pockets watching his own child, lost to him forever, for all practical purposes.

"You're right, of course. It's wrong of me to judge you. Especially since I . . . I never called, or came by." He leaned against the pillar beside me. "I wanted to," he whispered. "I wanted to so badly. But I couldn't."

"Why didn't you mention you were a priest, Daniel? The whole time on the river you never indicated you were a man of the cloth."

Daniel looked directly into my eyes, where I saw a hint of the remorse present on that last day of our Rogue trip.

"Forgive me, Tori, but I chose anonymity on the rafting excursion because at the time living up to all that was expected of me seemed over-whelming. I needed a short refuge, a retreat, if you will, from the demands placed upon me by the church. And then I met you, causing me to succumb to the pleasures of intimacy. It nearly destroyed what I knew to be my destiny ever since I was a small boy. That's what loving you did to me."

I nodded my head slowly. "Certainly if I had known, if only you had said something . . . then . . ." my words trailed off.

"Then what, Tori?" Daniel ran nervous fingers through his golden hair. "Would we have felt differently? Behaved differently? I'm not so sure. But I've asked myself many times." Daniel stepped closer, close enough to whisper softly in my ear. *"Do you feel it, Tori?"*

A shiver ran down my spine. *"Yes,"* I responded in a hushed tone. *"But, Daniel,"* I asked, my libido soaring from his breath on my neck, *"if this bond is so strong . . . so special . . . then why did you never call?"*

He had a faraway look in his unusual eyes. *"Because I am what I am."* He gestured with his hands, encompassing the space surrounding us. "And *this* is what I am, what I *must* be."

Daniel delicately intertwined his fingers with my hair, and I shuddered. Reaching out hesitantly, I ran my hands along his cheekbone. Our lips lingered close together and almost met. The strength of our chemistry clearly reminded me of another time and place, and vaguely, of almost drowning in the rapids. Forcing myself to pull away, I ran from the alcove yelling, "Benjamin!"

He flew off the bench and kept pace just behind me as I sailed through the monstrous oak doors, letting the fractured shades of a setting sun stream into the sanctuary on our way out.

CHAPTER FIVE

"I have some strange and exciting news for you, Tori."

Hours later, long after Benjamin went to bed, I sat at my desk and stared out the window onto the street. I didn't see cars and concrete buildings. I saw fir trees and a pristine flowing river. I saw Daniel's unusual blue eyes filled with slivers of moonlight. I didn't hear horns and sirens. I heard water washing over rocks and through reeds along the shore as we lay beside the Rogue, our flesh precariously entangled.

I glanced down at Benjamin's picture on my desk and reached out with my fingers, tracing the light streak above his head. Then I gasped, startled by my own revelation. I opened the bottom desk drawer and rummaged through pictures kept there. Finally I pulled out a small album of snapshots and paged through it.

There it was, a picture taken by one of the guides our first day on the river. I was standing between Rachel and Miranda. Daniel stood between Robert and Jonathan. I stared at Jonathan for a moment, remembering his attempt at flirting by the fire that first night. If only I'd known what he knew about Daniel. I wondered if they'd stayed in touch, and what Jonathan was doing now. I tried not to consider what he thought of me after Daniel and I reached our fateful moment of no return that summer.

I pulled the picture from the album and held it up to the light. Yes. It was there, the glow above Daniel's head. Barely noticeable, looking like a flaw in the film or a reflection from the sun. I pulled out several more pictures from the Rogue trip with Daniel in them. One was of him alone. I had taken it on the afternoon of the last day. He was leaning against a rock, his golden curls perfectly messy as always, his eyes painfully blue, like a postcard of waters offshore a remote island in the tropics. And there was that soft yellow glow above his head.

Carefully I held the picture beside the one of Benjamin. They were obviously father and son, with the same eyes and hair . . . *and halo*. What could not be seen was how they had the same pure heart, and healing powers. Almost as if they were not entirely of this world. I thought of the sparrow, and of Sarah. Perhaps Benjamin and Daniel were more than just mere mortals with a gift for healing. *Could angels actually exist?*

Even if it were true, I could never prove it any more than I could make Daniel leave the church, or Benjamin give up healing every hurt creature that crossed his path.

I shook my head and threw the pictures into the bottom drawer, slamming it shut. Before I could come up with a more reasonable explanation for the oddities of father and son, the phone rang.

I glanced at the clock on the wall. Who could be calling so late? It was almost midnight. It must be Rachel. Only my best friend and art dealer would call at this hour, knowing I'd be up. She was probably still at the gallery where she practically lived among the works of art, checking on each one as if they were her children whose ultimate destinations she needed to fret about. I answered the phone and suddenly felt foolish for my thoughts about Daniel and Benjamin.

"I have some strange and exciting news for you, Tori."

"What?" I thought about how strange and exciting Rachel might find my own news, not to mention incredible, if I had the nerve to share it.

"Someone has bought Benjamin's paintings."

"The doves?"

"Yes, the doves. He hasn't painted anything but Vincent Gianni's doves, that I'm aware of." Rachel didn't sound amused.

I thought about how Benjamin and Sarah loved helping her father care for the many doves he kept. They'd put messages on their legs and release them into the sky for delivering the notes. I'd never inquired to whom the doves flew with their penned treasure secured tightly in a special leg wrapping.

"How can that be, Rachel? They weren't for sale. We didn't put a price on them for the art show."

"But we *did* put a price on them, remember?"

I got up from my desk and walked over to the kitchen window where I peeked out into the starry night. This whole idea of someone buying

Benj's doves was unsettling, as much so as his father's vocation. And then I remembered. We put a hundred thousand dollar price tag on each of Benjamin's three dove paintings. That way they could be a part of the show, but no one would consider purchasing them. I took a deep breath. "We weren't being serious. And who is it that wants to buy his work, anyway, because I don't want to sell the doves. That's why we made up the fictitious price, remember?"

No one was supposed to buy Benjamin's paintings. It was all too much. After just finding Daniel and finding out *who Daniel was,* and now someone wanted our son's doves? My Benjamin's doves that couldn't possibly be let go to a stranger?

"That's just it, Tori. They didn't blink at the price. It was the Zimmermans, that elderly couple from uptown who fund a lot of programs for the arts."

She paused and I didn't say anything as I chewed on my lip and stared into the darkness outside the kitchen window.

"The Zimmermans have been respected art critics in this country their whole lives. They seemed to feel that a hundred thousand dollars apiece for the dove paintings was quite reasonable, considering how profoundly inspirational the pieces are."

There was another pause. Rachel must have been at a loss for words, as was I, to explain why Benjamin's doves had stolen the hearts of the Zimmermans, to the tune of three hundred thousand dollars.

My son had taken up painting in the studio adjacent to Rachel's art gallery. I would leave him with Rachael whenever I had a Saturday photo shoot. He had taken to it as if born to paint. Rachel only wished all her workshop students were as enthusiastic as Benjamin.

It was true the doves were delicate and simply beautiful, dramatically stark against the blue-gray backdrop Benj painted them on. But still, who in their wildest imagination would ever have thought retired art critics would somehow take an inexplicable liking to the work of an eleven-year-old? They were wealthy, and could purchase the work of any renowned artist of their choosing. Why buy these paintings of Vincent Gianni's doves?

"Rachel, I found Daniel." It escaped my lips without consent of my brain, but there it was on my mind, as incredible to comprehend as the selling of Benjamin's paintings.

"What?" Rachel said it flatly, as if she couldn't possibly have heard correctly.

"Daniel Rosselli. He's Benjamin's father, remember?"

"Of course I remember. It may not be our daily conversation over lattes, but it isn't something I'd forget." Rachel sounded slightly wounded.

"I'm sorry, it's just such a shock and all," I admitted. "I'm still struggling with it myself, the fact that I found him after all these years."

"How ironic that he would show up right when his child becomes rich and famous." Rachel was clearly annoyed.

"No. Rachel, listen carefully. Daniel is a priest. I mean a celibate priest . . . of the Catholic Church. And that's exactly what he was on the Rogue trip, except for the celibate part, obviously."

There was dead air for a few seconds, as if neither of us could decide whether to laugh or not, but decidedly, it was nothing to joke about.

"Oh my god, Tori. No wonder he never called. Who told you this? Have you seen him?"

"Yes, I have seen him, at St. Matthew's Cathedral downtown. Maggie told me. She was going to take Sarah to him . . . to his healing mass. He has great healing powers apparently, like Benj. Think about it, Rachel. He's been downtown at the cathedral, right here in Portland all this time. Well, at least I assume so."

"Does he know . . . I mean about Benjamin?"

"No. I lied about Benjamin."

"Why?"

"I didn't go there to tell him he had a son. I just needed to know if this Father Rosselli was the Daniel Rosselli from our Rogue trip. Twelve years ago next month, Rachel. A dozen years of not knowing." I shook my head. "And then suddenly his name comes up out of nowhere."

There was silence on the other end of the phone and then a sigh.

"Tori, I have a check here for three hundred thousand dollars. What should I do with it?"

"That's it? That's all you have to say about Daniel?" I was stunned at her ability to skip conveniently over such a profound revelation.

"What is there to say? It's possibly the only perfect explanation for why a man would vanish after the special bond you had on the Rogue trip."

There was another long pause and then a sigh on my end.

"I'll pick the check up tomorrow and decide how to invest it for Benjamin. College will probably cost that much by the time he's ready to go."

Silence hung between us again, until I continued somberly.

"I know what you mean about Daniel. It's just so unbelievable I didn't *know*, didn't somehow *sense* it."

"Don't torture yourself about Daniel any more than you already have. Things happen in life for a reason, but we can't always know why."

"Thanks Rach, for trying to alleviate my self-inflicted guilt. And thanks for teaching Benj how to paint. You're the best."

"Shush, and go to bed, Tori, it's one a.m."

We said our goodbyes and I crawled into bed but couldn't sleep. My head was swimming between trust funds and healing priests, and the sadness of knowing I would never again lay eyes on Benjamin's beautiful dove paintings that reflected all good things in a peaceful way, just as he did. I tossed and turned most of the night and then all too soon light crept through the window just as the phone rang. I grabbed it off the nightstand and said hello in a hoarse whisper.

"Tori, you sound terrible. Are you okay?"

"Miranda. It's good to hear your voice."

"Have you seen today's paper?"

"No." Great, I thought, what else could happen?

"Benjamin is in it. Did they get your permission?"

I pondered this for a minute. The art show, of course. "Maybe Rachel gave it for me. Is it about his doves?"

"Yes. All about them, and what they sold for."

"I'll probably open a trust fund for Benjamin's college," I said, as I headed straight for the front door to collect my own copy of the paper. I sat on Grams' sofa in the living room and paged through it while listening to Miranda's overtures of concern for Benjamin. She was, after all, practically a surrogate parent along with Rachel in the alternative upbringing of my child. I had fully entrusted my mental health to Andi, as well as Benjamin's. It was a constant balancing act for my dear friend and former graduate school roomy. We had shared many concerns about Benj's wellbeing over the last eleven years, what with having no father, or any male role models except for my brother Wil.

"Tori, maybe I should talk to Benj, you know, just chat with him for a bit. See if he is okay with all this sudden attention surrounding his artwork."

"Yes, of course, Andi. Let's have lunch later this week and I'll leave him with you for a while after. Sound good?"

"Call me if something comes up before we meet. Promise?"

"I promise, Anda Panda." She didn't complain about the smattering of nicknames Rachel and I loved to lavish on her. It was our clever way of doing a hatchet job to her rather serious vocation and outlook on life.

For the next few days the phone rang off the hook. I tried to hide from Benj the fact that these calls were about him. I wanted to keep his life as quiet and unaltered as possible. I was suddenly paranoid outsiders might discover his other hidden talent of healing, and label him some kind of freak. His gift of healing would be even harder to play down than the role of a child prodigy, should word get out.

Several weeks later things had calmed down a bit. Benjamin spent an afternoon with Miranda, who told me he was, as always, unbelievably mature for his age. Benj had always been comfortable with his special healing gift, and the artistic recognition didn't seem to phase him either. None of it had gone to his head. I wasn't surprised, since no one was more matter-of-fact about Benjamin's uniqueness than Benjamin himself.

Not surprisingly, we had begun attending services at St. Matthew's. I felt compelled to observe this man who was the father of my son. Benjamin had his own reasons for wanting to attend with me, as he seemed determined to soak up all he could about the Catholic faith. We hid inconspicuously in the middle of the many worshipers, and I always steered us to the farthest kneeling rail from Daniel during communion.

After a few weeks of this new routine, late one night after Benjamin went to bed, the doorbell rang, and there stood a man I'd hoped to never lay eyes on again. I had not seen him since leaving the university that summer so long ago when doing filing for him both before, and after the Rogue trip. I left suddenly toward the end of that summer, nauseous from the changes in my soon to be swelling womb, and sick with worry for Grams, who'd become quite ill.

That same nauseous feeling swept over me once again as Dr. Peter Cairns stood there in my doorway.

CHAPTER SIX

"You have many years yet to live here on this earth, and I have a feeling whatever you do now will determine the shape of them all."

"Peter." My mouth felt dry suddenly and it was hard to breathe. I couldn't look away from his eyes. They were like two pools of darkness, pulling me down into them, into a cold abyss of bad memories. "It's been awhile."

"Yes it has, Tori. How've you been these last dozen years or so?" His crooked smile was in place as if never having left his face during all that time. He boldly stepped inside my apartment, nearly pushing me aside to do so.

I closed the door quietly and stood against it, glancing down the hall protectively, silently praying Benjamin would not awaken.

Peter's lean frame was still straight and tall, but gray streaked his mustache and dishwater blond hair. Peter had been a professor at the University of Portland, and I had agreed to do filing for him to help defer the costs of my graduate classes. I could do it late at night and at most any odd hours of my own choosing, which made it compatible with my studies. It had been a curiosity to me that Peter was generally always there when I did the filing, regardless of how late I chose to do it.

I would often come at midnight and find him laboring over his research, ready to greet me with a cheerful hello. He was articulate in his manner and dress, and in the way he kept his office behind the old brick psychology building. This would explain why he wished to have his files meticulously updated and organized, an endless job I was only beginning to put a dent into that summer.

He would work quietly for a while and then come and stand near the wall of file cabinets I shuffled through, hoping to engage me in conversation. At times his mood would be dark and philosophical, at other times lighthearted and sprinkled generously with wit or humor. I rarely saw him interact with students or other professors during the busy daylight hours on campus, and when he did it was awkward, as he seemed distracted, bothered really, and not interested in chitchat. I knew from hearing others gossip behind his back that he was quite reclusive, yet he was extremely bright and decent looking in his nerdy sort of way. He always wore tweed sport coats and small round spectacles so stereotypical of a professor.

Our friendship changed considerably after the Rogue trip, as I became the one who was often grim and dark. Peter was determined to extract from me what had happened to alter my disposition. I had become despondent and frightened upon the realization I was not only with child, but the mysterious Daniel had no intention of ever contacting me. At Peter's insistence I opened up, telling every detail of the foolish affair by the side of the Rogue, except for the fact that I was pregnant. This one thing I never shared with him, or with anyone else the rest of that summer or on into fall.

Miranda had graduated with her doctorate in psychology and was overwhelmed with starting her own practice. Rachel was diligently establishing an art gallery. I felt foolish, isolated, and brokenhearted, as if a naïve teenager rather than a grown woman.

One night I became completely overwhelmed by my situation. I sorrowfully missed Daniel, and had no idea what to do about our baby growing within me. I could never abort it, of course, but how would I raise it alone, and how could he never know of his offspring, the product of our love I now questioned ever existed? How could our time together have seemed so extraordinary and yet been so forgettable to him? I broke down and cried desperately as I worked that evening, and then Peter arrived. He held me there by the files where I had crumpled into a pile, and said he wished to marry me.

I was stunned, so inconceivable was it that Peter had these feelings for me and I hadn't known it in all this time. I was so caught up in my own misery and pain I hadn't noticed. I was at a loss for what to say, or how to respond. It was ludicrous of course. Peter was odd in the best of moods, and stranger than anyone I had ever met in his darker moments. I felt compassion for him, but could never love a man with such bitterness toward life, and apathy toward others. At times he frightened me with his nervous darting eyes and somewhat sinister grin.

I had no words for him, my mind on overload already, and so he helped me up and brought me to the pub on the corner, where college students often gathered into the wee hours of the morning. Peter and I occasionally ended a late night discussion there over a cold beer. But this night was different. This night was a night to forget like none other. It still makes my skin crawl and my mind wild with regret over what happened.

We drank our token beer, but then Peter ordered us another. I didn't want another, knowing I was pregnant and should not have had the one I did. I wanted to go home and forget about the new, softer look in his eyes. I wanted to escape the awkwardness of telling him I did not return his feelings. My tongue was tied the entire time at the pub. I was in shock really, and so it was that I let him do all the talking. He tried to convince me of how happy we could be together.

Finally I could take no more and I took his hands into mine and looked him in the eye and told him how much I appreciated his friendship and his concern for me. But I did not love him, and could not marry him. I remember picking up the heavy stein and quickly drinking the frothy beer, washing down these words I had nearly choked on to finally deliver. I was miserable all the more for betraying the child within me by consuming alcohol so foolishly.

The next thing I recall is waking up in my bed, far into the next morning, naked and alone. My clothes were scattered about the floor and my sheets were in great disarray. I knew instantly Peter and I had slept together. There was the obvious residue of his semen, and the scent of him in my bed. I hugged myself subconsciously, wrapping my arms around my naked breasts. Somehow I felt invaded and betrayed, yet surely I was a willing participant, the thought of which disturbed me more than if he had taken me against my will.

I was at first stricken with grief and disgust over my own indiscretion, and then, after sitting there, rocking for several minutes on the bed with the wrinkled sheets gathered about me, I became angry. I reached up and pulled on my dark tangled hair with both hands, and screamed, out of sheer frustration. The ponytail I usually wore was long undone, as I myself had been undone, feeling as big a tangled mess as my hair.

I screamed out in rage against the horror of what I had done . . . first making love to a near stranger beside a wild and scenic river, giving no consideration to safe sex or to anything at all except my need to be with this man, Daniel. And now to sleep with someone I also barely knew, just one month later. This time it was for someone I had little affection for, after drinking only two beers in a pub. And I didn't remember anything at all after that last swig of beer!

What had become of me?

I recalled stripping the bed, showering thoroughly, letting the hot water pierce my skin until it was raw, and then finding a note there on the dresser as I brushed through my damp hair. I picked it up cautiously, slowly, and read it many times before crumpling it severely and tossing it into the trash. It read:

My Dearest Victoria,

I hope that you remember last night as completely as I do.
It was wonderful, and I want to thank you for insisting that I stay.

Love, Peter

Without hesitation I had picked up the phone and dialed home. At the sound of Grams' voice, tears flowed hotly down my cheeks. Not indicating anything was wrong, I asked how she was, and came to find out she had taken a turn for the worse. I told her I would come immediately to care for her, which I did, with no further thoughts of my own distress as I hurriedly packed and headed for the freeway. When I arrived Grams was weak and sipping tea on the back porch, covering herself against the chill with an afghan she had knitted years before. I knelt beside her and laid my head in her lap, and she knew instantly much was the matter with my life.

I remember how Grams stroked my hair gently, her delicate fingers massaging my scalp as if they were the golden combs of angels. I had stared into her lovingly hand-stitched afghan, rich with lavenders and mauves and all the soft greens and blues of an ocean. That afghan was mine now, as were many of her possessions. Eliza and Wil had not wanted any of her things and so I alone had inherited them after her death.

She died that evening in the chair on the porch, but not until we had a meaningful discussion about life, my life in particular, after she shunned any conversing about her own ill health.

"I am old, Victoria," she had said. "My time here is near spent. It is not a surprise, it is just a fact. Now let's talk about you, child." She still called me that, although I was far from being a child any longer, but no doubt acting like one who does not weigh or measure consequences for their actions.

"You have many years yet to live here on this earth, and I have a feeling whatever you do now will determine the shape of them all."

"I am pregnant, Grams," I remembered looking up into her face, and it was her face I saw now rather than Peter's before me, this woman who knew me so thoroughly, to see if any shock registered there. But none did.

"And do you love the father?"

"Yes, Grams, I do. But he is no longer a part of my life."

"Then love the child, Victoria, with all your heart. Love the child for you and for him, and forever. A child has a right to be born, and can never have too much love."

I shook my head, not able to speak through the emotion of it all, tears streaming down my face. We huddled there, me at her side with my face in her lap, and she stroking my hair, for several hours. Grams retelling all my favorite tales from her childhood and early married life, as the sun lowered in the sky and lit up the porch with its last little bit of warmth. And then she retold all the stories about Grandfather, whom we both dearly missed, and of my own antics as a child. It was the greatest peace I had ever known, completely surrounded there by her love, listening to her soothing tone, helping her cross over to a better, eternal life where Grandfather was waiting.

The funeral was on a damp and chilly October morning. My black skirt tugged across my swelling waist. The three days after Grams' death and before her final lowering into the earth were a blur to me. Eliza was at Grams' house, and then Wil. Father did not show at all but sent flowers and a card. All the relatives and friends, and church people from St. Luke's were in and out with food and hugs and memories of this dearly loved woman.

I was distraught, in shock really, being pulled along by an emotional wave that could easily have swamped me at any moment. I confided to

Eliza that I was with child when she asked about my suspicious nausea and exhaustion. Wil was supportive and sympathetic upon overhearing us, but Eliza told me to get an abortion and a job, in that order.

Everyone came and left from the little house on Elm Street, with no elms but rather sprawling oaks hugging the Sienna siding. They drove away after speaking their somber well wishes, following the culminating event of her burial. Wil and I had been the last two standing there at her grave, each with our own private thoughts. My brother and I embraced long and hard before parting, and he made me promise to keep in touch. I said I would visit him at Stanford, where he attended on a partial scholarship. There was a special camaraderie between us, and we felt a need to rekindle it more than ever with Grams gone home to be with the Lord. I managed a smile for my little brother and swore an oath, just as we had often done as children, that I would keep in touch.

When his car pulled away I watched it recede down the road until it was beyond my vision, if not for distance, then for the tears welling up to cloud my view. I had not cried since three days prior, when wrapped in Grams' arms on the porch as she died. But they flowed out of me now. I remember thinking . . . *What am I to do without you, Grams? Where am I to turn? How will I raise this child alone? Mother and Father have deserted me either through apathy or death. Daniel has deserted me for some unknown reason, and you have left me for a place I cannot even fathom, for its joy I do not feel. What am I to do?*

All of this came flooding back when I let Peter into my home this evening, as I watched him walk over and sit in Grams' wingback chair. I slowly gravitated in his general direction and lifted Grams' afghan lovingly from the back of the sofa, while staring into Peter, stroking it, as she had stroked my hair on that day long ago. Tears instantly gathered in my eyes, stinging them with the vivid memory of her love.

"It will be twelve years this coming October, to be exact, since we last saw one another." Peter folded his hands like an open tent and stared into me. His eyes held a sparkle I could not recall ever having seen there before.

"Are you still at the university?" I asked, knowing full well small talk was not the purpose for his visit, although I had no idea what his purpose was.

"No. I have my own private practice now, here in Portland, for these last two years. Didn't Miranda mention it?" He seemed surprised that we had not discussed this.

"Miranda?" My pulse quickened, skipping ahead to the alarming realization that they were both psychologists. Had she discussed my Benjamin with Peter?"

"Yes. Miranda. We've been seeing each other socially."

I slowly walked over and sank into Grams' sofa, still hugging her afghan, trying to extract from it the calming effect of her comforting arms.

"Tori," he continued in a serious tone, "why didn't you tell me . . . that you had become pregnant after our, well, wonderful night of lovemaking?"

I stared at him, hearing the words, but at a complete loss for what to say. Mustering all the romantic charm he could after a twelve-year absence, he continued.

"I was absolutely sick when I discovered you had run home to Portland after our night of . . . ecstasy." He viewed me sheepishly from beneath arched brows and I could barely focus, let alone respond.

"I was frantic with worry, and then learned of your ill grandmother, and I assumed you would return after her death . . . which I heard about from the accounting office. They told me you had terminated your position, and withdrawn from your fall classes."

He stood and awkwardly walked over to the sofa. Sitting beside me, he rested his hand on my knee, making me wish I had thought to put on more clothing before answering the door. I wore only my running shorts and an old university t-shirt, obviously not expecting visitors.

A chill ran down my spine with the touch of his flesh on mine, and I regressed to that moment of complete despair, rocking naked on my bed, clothed in sheets that could only hint of what had happened between them. It seemed inconceivable to me after all these years I still had absolutely no recollection of my sexual encounter with Peter. Yet it affected me as if it were a vivid memory, a decidedly unpleasant one. So much so, that I chose never to dwell on it, fearing what I might recall more than fearing what I did not know. As always, there was the question in my mind of how that night could have happened after only two beers, which were surely not enough to erase all memory of events to follow.

"I can't wait to meet our son, Benjamin." Peter smiled in a rather wicked way. "I couldn't believe it, when I read about him—and that he was *your* son—in the paper. You can understand how that must have confused and excited me."

Feeling a surge of nervous anxiety, I bolted from the couch and walked to the door, which I opened slightly before looking over at my intruder, still seated on the sofa. "No, Peter, you have it all wrong. I was already pregnant before . . . that night. Benjamin is not your child, and I'm sorry to be rude, but it's late and I have an early appointment . . . a wedding to shoot. I am a photographer, remember?" I tried to smile politely.

We stared blankly into each other, our eyes not able to penetrate our thoughts. His I did not care to know, mine were of loathing and regret I did not wish for him to discern. He arose hesitantly, standing stiffly by Grams' antique pole lamp with the rose covered shade.

"Then . . . who? Who is the father if not me?" He looked genuinely puzzled, and equally disappointed.

"That's not something I care to share with you, Peter." My eyes were steady on his, revealing nothing but my desire for him to drop the subject and leave.

He stood frozen there by Grams' lamp, and studied me as if I were an open book he wished to read.

"It must have been . . . Daniel. The one you pined for continually after your chance meeting on the Rogue." He sounded more than a little annoyed, absolutely irritated to be exact.

"No, not Daniel. Someone else. Someone you couldn't possibly know." A shudder trembled through me, knowing the risk for Daniel should Peter ever learn the truth about Benjamin's father.

"It was someone I met here in Portland, before the Rogue trip."

Peter looked skeptical. He was already adding the months in his head no doubt, as I quickly added, "We broke up just before the Rogue trip, and never saw each other again."

"I see." He said this as he walked to the door and I shrank from his form, not wanting our bodies to touch in passing. I prayed he would not sense my distaste for him.

Before leaving he turned to me and our eyes locked again, still blank walls to any real communicating. "I am sorry to have bothered you so late,

Tori. Perhaps we can get together again soon and discuss old times."

"Perhaps, Peter. I am very busy these days, but if you call first . . ." I didn't finish the sentence, my guts churning at the thought of seeing him again. Of course, I had no intention of ever seeing him again if possible. I suddenly wondered why Miranda had not mentioned seeing Peter. I wondered how she could possibly *like* the man. I shuddered again at the thought of them discussing Benjamin.

"Yes, of course. I'll call you and we'll arrange something. I want to hear all about this budding artist of yours!" The sparkle in his eye became a gleam and I knew he'd not given up yet on the idea of collecting dividends from an illegitimate prodigy son. He apparently had no incentive to find me before learning of Benjamin's giftedness, which is odd, given his note about our . . . sexual encounter and his claims of love for me.

I smiled weakly and mumbled something about what a fluke it was that such an old eccentric couple would take a liking to my son's work, paying far more than it was worth. Peter left then, seeming somewhat flustered that his visit was less profitable than he might have hoped.

I stood against the locked door for a full minute, scared and confused, petrified really, as if believing Pandora's box had just been opened, and I was helpless to close the lid on it. Peter was surely a force to reckon with and not likely to give up easily.

CHAPTER SEVEN

"The doves are like love would be if you
could hold it . . . soft, warm, and gentle."

My visit from Peter Cairns the night before seemed unreal to me as I watched Benjamin in the yard fussing over the doves. Vincent Gianni kept them as pets more for himself than for Sarah, who preferred the neighborhood cats to the delicate birds. She sat in a corner of the yard petting an orange tabby and dangling bits of ribbon for it to chase.

I dried the lunch dishes and thought about how the Gianni family was as important to Benjamin as Grams and Gramps had been to me. Every one of my memories with them was like a warm summer shower full of dancing Gene Kellys. Their love had swept over me in the same way watercolors splash onto paper, giving me lavish attention rarely received otherwise. Grams and Gramps added vibrancy to the ordinary, making each day special in some small way. This is what Vincent, Maggie, and Sarah did for my Benjamin, who did not fit easily into his neighborhood and would otherwise have been alone much of the time. Vincent Gianni was in many ways the grandfather Benj did not have the luxury of access to through his birthright.

In part, this may be why Benj was so taken with Vincent's doves, and why he chose to lovingly paint them in Rachel's studio. It was true he possessed an intuitive feel for the acrylics Rach entrusted him with. And the child had an excellent eye for detail. It was clear as to where these talents came from, since my mother was a sculptor of some decidedly profound work, recognized and acclaimed by many in the art world shortly before her untimely death. The smaller pieces she could not bear to part with were now adorning my apartment, giving grace and elegance to an otherwise humble structure filled solely with Grams' aging but eloquent furnishings.

I asked Benj once why he only painted doves. He said it was because he missed them when not home playing with his feathered friends, who lived in elaborate cages behind the equipment shed. Vincent himself had built the cages. Then Benjamin had given me his rather contemplative look that always meant he was going to say something unbelievably mature, and well beyond his years, and what he said was this . . . *"The doves are like love would be if you could hold it . . . soft, warm, and gentle. Their coos are the sound love would make . . . if love could speak. And when they fly . . . they are love in motion."* He made a swooping gesture with his arm, dipping down and flying up and away like the doves often did.

Benjamin went on to tell me how there are any number of poses in which you could paint doves, making them interesting and exciting to put on canvas. I certainly couldn't deny the passion seeping through his brushes, every completed stroke as interesting and exciting as art can be.

Nearly dropping a dish my mind snapped back to the present as a dove escaped from its cage. The latch had not caught when Benjamin shut it, allowing the door to swing open and free the fragile bird. Flying hesitantly around the yard several times, it finally dipped fast and low on its third rotation and headed straight for the clear glass door off our patio. It was only the bird that moved in this half a minute. Vincent, Benjamin, Sarah, and myself stood frozen, watching, waiting, and then there was a tiny thud as it hit the glass and fell to the patio.

It lay motionless on the cement as we all watched helplessly, slowing gravitating toward its crumpled body. Standing there, afraid to touch it, we began sullenly to whisper words of sympathy. Benjamin remained quiet, scooping it up carefully to place in the crook of his arm, and holding it tight against his body. Ever so gently Benj ran his fingers from the tiny head to the tail feathers, but the dove did not move beneath his touch. I placed my two fingers under it, near the fluttering heart that beat faintly like a ticking watch.

"It's still alive, Benj." I looked into his face and saw the same calmness that had always been there when death lingered near, as it often did with the injured creatures brought to this very patio for Benjamin's special loving care. But this time I saw something beyond the calm, steady gaze in my son's eyes. Was it denial? Or defiance? This dove was not a stranger to him, like all the other furry or feathered beasts he'd healed. It was a treasured pet.

But I had not seen this look even with the healing of Sarah, and it puzzled me. Perhaps Benjamin felt directly responsible, having not latched the cage properly.

Tears were swimming in his eyes, and I couldn't remember a time when Benjamin had been so visibly shaken, or at such a loss for what to do. But then it seemed as if it were out of our hands as the ticking beneath my fingers stopped. I glanced at the limp white body in my son's arms. "Benjamin, this bird is dead, honey. You can't save this one. I think its neck was broken when it hit the window. Look . . ." I carefully pointed to the unnatural angle of the tiny bird's neck.

He stared at the dove for several seconds, while behind us Vincent whispered what a shame it was, but that these things happen from time to time. Then Vincent put his arm around Sarah, no doubt thinking of her precarious state of health and how she had all too recently hovered near death. Sarah buried her head into her father's side and cried softly. In the distance I could hear the gentle sounds made by the doves still in their cages, and thought about the love Vincent and Benjamin poured into their care.

Suddenly Benjamin stepped away from us, slowly, and then as we watched, he carefully gathered the dove from his arm and held it in his hands. With the tiny bird lying across his open palms, he raised its body to the sky. Benjamin stood perfectly still, with us standing behind him, afraid to breathe. Was he saying a prayer for his feathered friend, held in his open palms high above his head?

But then something happened that caused me to gasp. At the same time Sarah uncovered her face and sharply turned it toward Benjamin, her long molasses-colored hair flying through the air. Vincent raised a hand to shield his eyes from the glare of the sun and shook his head in disbelief as we all watched the dove in Benjamin's hands begin to flutter its wings in a struggling, shuttering sort of way like a butterfly emerging from its chrysalis.

Soon the small white bird stood erect in Benjamin's outstretched palms. We all stared, gaping and wide-eyed as the dove flew from Benjamin's hands. It soared skyward, swooped ceremoniously into a sharp right and circled the yard, perching on the open cage. Benjamin walked over and gently picked it up. He brought the bird to his face, whispered something, then kissed its smooth cooing head and placed it inside the open door, hooking the latch carefully. Sarah and her father gathered near the cage with Benj, relieved and happy beyond description.

I stood on the patio and wept. For I alone knew the magnitude of Benjamin's miracle healing. I knew the bird had not been in shock and then gracefully recovered. I clearly knew now that my son was no ordinary child. And it scared me. It scared the *living hell* out of me.

On the way to Rachel's studio I questioned Benjamin about the dove incident in as casual a manner as I could muster. "Benj," I said, hesitating, already at a loss for the appropriate words, "that dove . . . it quit breathing there in your arms. It was dead, Benjamin."

"No. Not dead. Just stunned."

"Benj, I felt its heart. It was fluttering at top speed, even for a tiny bird, and then nothing. Absolutely nothing. How do you explain that?"

He looked at me, his jaw set defensively. "It might have quit beating for a second, but when I held it to the sun, the heat stimulated its heart."

I stared at him as best I could while driving. "Benjamin, we both know heat does not make a stilled heart beat again."

He shrugged, watching cars out the window. "I can't explain it. I don't know what happened. It was just one of those things, you know? Like Sarah's cancer going away." He was happy with that non-answer, and I dropped the subject, knowing the dove incident could not be explained in any normal fashion. Did Benjamin understand the depth of his healing gift? Or was he as naïve as he would have me believe?

I dropped him off at Rachel's studio where he was eager to begin painting on a new canvas she had prepared for him. Once he disappeared from view I told Rach about his miracle healing and how just one week into summer vacation he was already bringing the dead back to life. Neither of us laughed. On the way out the door I told her I would be seeing Miranda later, after the photo shoot I was doing on the waterfront.

Rivers and I had a history that did not escape me for inspiration or melancholy moods and I was especially excited about this waterfront wedding shoot. I tried to focus on the bride and the city backdrop of tall buildings jutting up from the banks of the river, pushing everything else out of my mind. But hard as I tried I couldn't stop thinking about Benjamin and the resurrected dove, or Miranda dating Peter. I didn't want Peter with someone I cared about, or to ever see him again. But somehow I knew I would, and it would not be pleasant when I did.

I reached Miranda's office somewhere around nine o'clock, after calling Rach to be sure she and Benjamin were okay. They were making popcorn and watching old movies, and didn't care how late I was.

Andi had left the front office unlocked, as she said she would. I could see her in the back sitting at her desk, with an antique lamp lighting her papers. She spent most of her time in her office. It was cozier than her stuffy, professionally decorated, and routinely cleaned condominium she seldom occupied.

I slipped through her private office door more open than shut and collapsed into one of the wingback chairs hand selected by Rachel. It was covered in little rose-colored flowers with pale green leaves sprawling about. There was another beside it, both facing her enormous oak desk where she slaved over a mountain of paperwork. Glancing up at me she smiled and then continued to diligently sign medical reports.

One of her walls displayed my whitewater photo series of the Rogue trip, used originally as the final project for my graduate program. There were tons of books crammed into wooden shelves on another wall. Beneath the books tins of herbal tea were scattered on a glass table.

Miranda had an awesome view of the boats harbored on the Willamette River, bouncing methodically with the current while moored securely to their rented docks. I walked over for a better look and stared off into the distance, where large flood lamps lit up the pier and surrounding water.

"Hi, Tori darling." Andi put the forms she'd been signing in a neat pile at the corner of her desk and leaned back in her leather chair. It was a beautiful buttery shade of tan and suited her well. Both were exotic and different looking from the moment you laid eyes on them. "What's this urgent business we need to discuss?" she asked. "You sounded pretty rattled on the phone this morning."

"I had a visitor last night."

"Who?"

"Peter Cairns."

"Why would Peter visit you?" Miranda looked genuinely puzzled.

"I was hoping you would know." My throat had become dry at the very mention of his name. How could I ever tell Miranda I loathed the man she was *dating?* I sat back down in the chair facing her.

Miranda crossed her long slender legs. "Tori, I speak with Peter every now and then, and see him occasionally for a drink, but . . . we've never mentioned you, and well, I don't want any more to do with him." She suddenly bolted from the chair and walked over to the window, staring out at the docks as I had done, as if the mention of Professor Cairns made her nervous.

"Peter claims to be seeing you socially. I assumed you were dating. Is that not true?" I asked.

Andi ignored my question. "Why would Peter visit you, Tori? What did he want?"

I had no idea how to ease into it, so I just blurted out the ugly truth. "He thought he was Benjamin's father." I cleared my throat. "Peter read about Benjamin in the paper, and his birthday fit with . . . the one time we slept together." My guts began churning because I hated saying it, or even thinking it, although I still didn't remember it.

"*You slept with Peter?* When?" Miranda paused and then answered her own question. "It must have been sometime while you were still doing graduate work." She had turned from the window and was facing me. "I had no idea. It never occurred to me you had feelings for him . . . but, everyone could see he was crazy about you."

"Andi," I began, awkwardly. "I . . . don't remember sleeping with Peter that night. I'm beginning to think that maybe . . . he drugged my drink. I mean, I never thought of it at the time. Who would ever do such a thing? But according to the morning paper, it's become a fairly common activity these days on college campuses, sadly enough. And so, well . . . I've been putting it all together in my head, when I'm inclined to think about it, which is almost never. It was all so creepy. I have to admit I've spent a lot more time trying to forget the whole incident, rather than try and figure out what happened."

Andi sprang to my chair and kneeled down, reaching for my hand, taking it into hers. She had a deadly serious look on her face.

"Tori . . . I think Peter drugged me too . . . just a few weeks ago."

CHAPTER EIGHT

"It's as if he's taking mental notes of every detail,
letting nothing escape unnoticed."

We stared at one another, Miranda and I, a light bulb going on in each our heads but neither of us speaking, and then she sat in the flower print chair beside me, studying the textured ceiling of her office.

"Here I am this educated professional psychologist and I have no idea what to do about Peter having possibly . . . raped me." Miranda placed her long fingers, with their perfectly manicured nails, on each of her temples and closed her eyes. "I mean, it isn't like I have any proof. I wasn't even completely sure until just now . . ." she looked over at me, ". . . until you indicated he might have done this to you. Oh my god, Tori. How awful. Was this after the Rogue trip?"

"Yes." Suddenly it was such a relief to talk about it. To have a kindred spirit that would understand my loathing. But how I hurt for Andi. Especially since her experience was so fresh, so raw with anger and regret. Although I was not sure that either emotion faded, no matter the course of time. "I was upset about Daniel not calling, and being pregnant," I confessed. "It didn't help that I was all alone ever since you received your doctorate and left to begin your practice. Emotionally I was a wreck. One night I broke down in Peter's office while filing for him, and he consoled me. We ended up at the corner pub."

I paused and shook my head. "I thought for the longest time two beers on an empty stomach had caused me to foolishly sleep with him. I reasoned that changes in my body from being pregnant might have been to blame, and truthfully, I am a lightweight when it comes to alcohol anyway so I wasn't suspicious at first that there had been foul play."

"Victoria, Daniel must have had a very serious reason not to contact you."

"He's a priest, Andi."

Her jaw dropped open but she couldn't speak for several seconds. I could almost see the wheels turning in her head. Everything was falling into place.

"*A priest?* How long have you known this?"

"Not long. I discovered it quite by accident. Just before Benjamin's doves sold for all that money and he was featured in the local paper."

"Benjamin's doves. That's right. I remember now, Tori. Peter did ask me about that . . . about you. The same night . . ." she stopped there for a second, overwhelmed by emotion. "I cannot recall absolutely anything about that night, Tori, after my second glass of wine," she confessed angrily.

I let the silence wrap around us while she took a minute to form the words she needed to say, words to help her understand how it was that Peter left her feeling betrayed and violated.

"I only remember waking up," she continued after gathering her courage, "naked and alone in my own bed, feeling somewhat disoriented. I knew instantly what had happened and with whom, but not *why*. Not what *led up to it*. I did *not* have amorous feelings for Peter, *ever*. *When* did I lead him on? *Where* in the course of the evening did I change my mind about him and give my consent?"

Miranda sat up poker straight. "Tori, I'd had some wine, to be sure, and I have often had sex after an evening of drinking, but only with men I was planning on, or hoping to sleep with. Men I not only remembered being with afterwards, but pleasantly recalled every minute of for many days." She sighed deeply. "I would never consent to sex with a man like Peter Cairns, whom I find strange and somewhat dark. It's hard to believe my standards could be so easily swayed by a little wine, and then to have absolutely no recollection of it." Andi looked at me. "Did you wake up hurting and exhausted, every inch of your flesh tender and raw?"

"Yes," I whispered shakily, her misery invading me, poking and prodding at my own memories from that troubling moment of fully awakening to the realization Peter had not been gentle with his stolen touches. I wanted to tell her the anguish would fade with time. But in actuality, I knew what Peter had done to her would only fester like an open wound that never heals.

"Did my Benjamin have anything to do with why you met on this particular night?" I asked.

Miranda folded her arms protectively in front of her. "Yes," she began, "now that I think about it. I do believe Benjamin was the main thing on his mind when he called and asked if I could meet for a drink, although he didn't mention Benjamin by name. What he had said was, 'you have a client that I wish to discuss.'" Miranda glanced over at me. "He must have put two and two together and realized the young artist I had spoken of in the past was Benjamin, *your* Benjamin."

"How unfortunate he made the connection," I mumbled, more to myself than to Andi.

"I reminded him that I cannot speak about any clients by name, but agreed to meet him down on the waterfront at Stanford's Bar. I arrived before he did and ordered a glass of red wine, feeling confident Peter would have no trouble finding me. We'd met there several times before, and had even sat in that same booth." Miranda shook her head. "I can't believe once upon a time I considered dating the man, until he proved to be a little too strange for my tastes. I did love to pick his brain for opinions about our shared passion of psychology. He was always quite enlightening. Peter is one of the brightest men I have ever met. Of course, he specializes in adults and I work with children, but mental health or the lack of it doesn't deviate much in its definition among humans in general."

Miranda pushed her hair behind her ears. It was wispy and straight but always looked sleek and refined, framing her angular face.

"Sitting there waiting for him, I remembered how Peter almost came on to me the last time I'd seen him. I thought so anyway, but I couldn't be sure. Peter is odd when it comes to women. I've known him ever since we were in graduate school but I've never known him to be involved long term with any specific woman in all that time. I know he isn't gay." Andi laughed. "In fact, I flat out asked him once, to which he replied, no, and then added how relationships were just too tiring for him since he dealt with everyone else's all day long. He was a loner and preferred it that way."

Miranda looked at me. "I felt sure he'd had a crush on you, Tori, that whole year we roomed together. But I knew you weren't interested in Peter." She sighed. "I'm usually attracted to men who are tall and slender but something about Peter has always felt disingenuous to me. He's too slick. His mustache is too perfectly groomed. And his dark blond hair is always smoothed so perfectly back." Miranda collapsed into her leather swivel chair, pulling her legs up under her. "And those dark beady eyes of his are always darting about suspiciously, did you ever notice that?"

"Yes. It's creepy." I shivered. Visions of Peter often made me shiver.

"It's as if he's taking mental notes of every detail, letting nothing escape unnoticed." Miranda shook her head in disgust.

"I know what you mean." All this talk of Peter was making my nerves edgy. "Hey Anda Panda, what do you keep in that cabinet? Are you hiding some vintage wine in there maybe?"

I walked over to her wall of built-in cupboards and looked above the tiny stainless steel sink. Sure enough, there was an arsenal of liquor. I picked out a nice red wine and went snooping in other cabinets for glasses, finding stemmed crystal tucked away under the counter.

Handing a glass of wine to her, I kissed Andi on the forehead and whispered how sorry I was about what had happened with Peter. Then I returned to the cupboards and rooted through them until discovering a tin of assorted chocolates, probably a gift from a client. I opened them and sat on the floor next to Miranda's chair, leaning against her desk while holding the box up for her to choose. She did so carefully, giving full consideration to each one.

Andi took a tiny bite of the chocolate she'd chosen and continued with her recollection of the dreaded night with Peter. "I remember him sitting down and motioning for the barmaid while asking if I had cut my hair. Typical for him . . . being a whirlwind of activity, never seeming focused, yet never missing a thing. I told him it was a little shorter, and requested another glass of wine when the girl came for his drink order."

Miranda and I each chose another sinful chocolate, nearly fighting over the same one, both loving hazelnuts. I nibbled on mine while trying to calm my outrage, washing it down with the smooth wine as my friend continued.

"Peter pulled a newspaper from his briefcase while we waited for our drinks. 'Look at this,' he said, folding the paper neatly and sliding it over to me. I glanced at the heading. 'CHILD PRODIGY PAINTS PROFOUND DOVES.'"

Miranda paused there, too lost in her moment of recall to eat or drink, but I took a rather large swig of the wine and poured myself more.

"I told Peter, yes I know, that's Tori's boy, Benjamin." Miranda looked down at me, sitting there on the floor, getting drunk on her expensive wine. "Of course," she continued, "he would already be aware of that from reading the article. Peter was upset because I hadn't told him you lived here in Portland, or that you had a child. He behaved as if I was totally remiss all this time in not mentioning it."

Andi downed her wine in two gulps and I replenished it for her, opening another bottle from the cupboard.

"That's all I remember," she admitted, "until I woke up naked and hung over with a throbbing headache. And my body felt very used." Miranda hugged her long legs drawn up against her chest, and I saw a flash of my broken self, that morning after my night with this monster, rocking on the bed in the midst of my despair.

We silently finished the second bottle, teary eyed and tortured by our private thoughts as we stared blankly at the stars outside the window. We were both drunk, as Anda Panda slurred her final words about the hideous event.

"I am not ashamed to say I have had some . . . *wild and crazy* nights with some . . . *talented* and . . . *titillating* men," she glanced at me, her eyes glassy, ". . . but I have never felt anything more than a warm glow the day after. Not so with Professor Cairns." My drunken friend was nearly shouting. "I dare not *ever* discover the truth of his exploitation of me, for fear of murdering this deviant man."

With that said, poor little Anda Panda downed the last sip in her stemmed glass. The chocolates were all opened with at least one bite taken from each, and we were beyond despair about this despicable beast that had drugged and raped us. Who else had he sinisterly encroached upon in this manner? After comparing further similarities, Miranda and I discovered he had left her a note as well. Word for word, almost identical to mine.

For the longest time we watched the river ebb and flow under the flood-lights down at the docks. At two a.m. we cleaned up the remains of our feast, and then more sober than not, I returned to Rachel's studio, where she heard my quiet knock at the back door and sprung from the leather sofa to let me in. I could see her through the dim light of a single lamp left lit in the room, her door being half window, divided by little wooden panes, and with no covering. Few people knew of the back entrance, completely surrounded by thick shrubs and a picket fence with a locked gate in sad need of attention for its peeling white paint.

I quietly entered and we hugged warmly, her scolding me for driving under the influence. Then we tiptoed to the adjoining kitchen so as not to wake Benjamin. He was curled up beneath a blanket on the floor in front of the TV neither of them had bothered to turn off.

Once in the kitchen Rach proceeded to make tea, knowing from experience how I craved it on middle of the night trips to get Benj, after an occasional date or a Friday night in Andi's office. She was afterall my shrink, regardless of the fact that children were her specialty. I always felt better after an evening with Anda Panda, discussing Benjamin and life's larger puzzlement, that being men.

I watched Rachel busy herself in the kitchen, while preparing our herbal concoction. It was a wonder she hadn't married and raised a parcel of little blonde pixies like herself. But I knew, of course, why she hadn't. My dearest friend since my mother's death had been in love with a married man for many years, the depth of her devotion spoiling any chance other men might have at getting through to her. Their ongoing affair left them both perpetually unhappy and unfulfilled. But Robert Marsh, Jonathan's law partner from the Rogue trip, had been engaged to another woman on that whitewater adventure, and married her—his high school sweetheart— shortly thereafter.

It wasn't long until he realized his cold feet and wandering thoughts of the little blonde pixie on the Rogue had been more than normal premarital doubts. Twelve years and two children later he was still hopelessly in love with the wrong woman, whom he unwisely chose to stay in contact with, becoming a great fan of modern art. His home was filled with it, as was his law office and all his partner's offices in the thriving practice, where even the reception area was generously decorated in gorgeous modern art originals.

My heart broke for this amazing woman, one of the most practical and capable I had ever met. Rachel was a natural beauty in her sleek athletic way, with an eye for art that was simply uncanny and a passion for teaching it that inspired even the most awkward with paint and canvas. More than anything I wanted her to meet a man to rival Robert. Not that I didn't think he was worthy of her, but he did, after all, have a family that loved him. And she did not. Except for Benjamin and I of course, who considered her as much family as anyone ever could.

"Rach . . ." I began, as she fussed over our tea, not content to swish a bag in a mug as I would do at home, but nursing loose leaves in a china pot while slicing fresh lemon. ". . . do you remember Professor Cairns? I did filing for him, that summer we rafted the Rogue."

She sat down with the bowl of lemon slices in one hand and the teapot in the other. "Yes, of course. You couldn't stand him. You felt he had taken advantage of you." She poured my tea into a china blue cup that matched the pot. It smelled wonderful, like licorice.

"It was worse than that." I floated a lemon in the steaming brew and wondered how to continue, blurting it all out as indelicately as usual. "Peter drugged me that night, I am sure of it. I never had a chance to consent to what happened."

Rachel put her cup down carefully and folded her hands beneath her chin. "You mean, he *raped* you?" Her cat-green eyes searched mine.

"I don't remember it, Rach. So it was hardly traumatic. The part that is emotionally wrenching is *not knowing exactly what in the hell he did, but knowing that he did it*." My hands were shaking as I raised the cup to my lips. The scent of the tea was soothing, and it tasted divine. I was grateful for my best friend's nurturing ways at all the right moments.

"Oh my god, Tori. That's horrible." Rachel hadn't moved a muscle, like a feline slightly tensed and poised to protect her young. She carefully studied my eyes, surely looking glazed and forlorn by this hour of the predawn.

"There's more." I set the cup down, already drawing strength from its lovingly prepared potion. "Miranda was also drugged by Peter, just a few short weeks ago."

"Did he . . ."

Rachel couldn't say it, and I didn't want to hear it, so I quickly answered, "Yes."

After that we drank the pot, two cups each, and I told her all the details of our evil trysts with this insane person who prided himself on understanding the complexities of mental illness. We shuddered to think of how many others might have fallen victim to his drugging and raping scheme. My mind was on overload as I rose to leave, in much need of some sleep, perhaps to help me gain a little perspective on all these new and disturbing events of my life.

Just before waking Benjamin, Rachel handed me one of Robert's business cards and insisted that I, or especially Miranda, whose incident was so recent, at least speak with him about it. She then asked if I was aware Jonathan Davis had returned to Portland from New York, and was once again a partner in Robert's law office. I was stunned at this news, and found myself asking if he had married, although why this would be my first curiosity about him was a mystery to me. Rach smiled and answered no, with an absolute sparkle in her eye, immediately causing me to feel self conscious, if not embarrassed.

Benjamin curled up on the backseat and slept all the way across town while I pondered whether or not to visit Robert, or Jonathan, about Peter. We managed to hit every stoplight red and by the time we arrived at our apartment I had decided not to seek council. Certainly Miranda did not want anyone to know of her recent unsavory experience with Peter.

The last thing I needed was another man in my life from twelve years prior. Two was more than enough at the moment. I went to bed as the sun rose outside my window, trying desperately not to think about Peter, or Daniel, and especially not Jonathan.

Why had he not married?

CHAPTER NINE

I wanted to pull a hidden saber from beneath my porch and run it through his side, piercing his evilness with cold steel.

Saturday afternoon I took a picture of Benjamin and Sarah with butterflies perched all over their bodies. Sitting on a bench in the temporary facility that looked like a large greenhouse, they were delighted with the colorful creatures. The fuzzy winged beauties were especially drawn to Benjamin who wore a red ball cap. He had six different varieties gently flapping their delicate wings on his head. Bright colors were what they liked best.

When Benjamin and Sarah had tired of the fascinating insects we let the teenager in the special zoo t-shirt pick them off ever so carefully. Then we waited patiently to leave the first of the double doors protecting the visiting butterfly exhibit with over a thousand different types on display, fluttering among green foliage and a large variety of brilliant summer flowers ranging from reddish pink to bluish purple. It would not do to let even one of them escape their expensive tropical setting.

This had been our annual trip to the zoo. Every summer we went sometime after school was out, and spent the entire day. Sarah had been coming with us for the last five years. The Gianni family had lived in the apartment next door ever since Benjamin was born. They'd been there for me an endless number of times in which I would otherwise have been alone. Maggie gave birth to Sarah almost a year after Benjamin was born. Having Sarah so late in life did not prevent my kind neighbors from aging gracefully, unlike me, who fought the signs of youth draining from my body with an arsenal of products, and further held it hostage through diet and exercise, weightlifting and yoga.

There was little doubt that the Gianni family was my steadfast lifeline to physical and emotional help. I had Rach and Andi and Wil of course. But they were busy and not always available. Benjamin dearly loved Wil, whom I helped pay for college by sharing my photography money from weddings I shot to support Benjamin and myself, and to pay for my own graduate degree.

Wil went to college late, choosing to travel with a jazz band for several years before settling down to get a degree. He had a knack for numbers and scored so well on the entrance exams he received a partial scholarship to Stanford. His third year he transferred to Portland State, he claims because he hated California, but I think he did it because it was closer to me and Benjamin.

Wil took it upon himself to be like a father figure to Benj, and a wonderful moral support for me. By the time Wil had transferred Benj was a toddler, and Wil was quite fond of his little nephew. In any event, he began his career as an investment broker here in Portland, and has remained, forfeiting his long time dream of moving to New York. Sometimes I feel guilty for being instrumental in the death of that childhood dream, but in truth I am not sorry Wil is here where Benj and I can lavish our love on him.

When returning from the zoo at dusk I told Benjamin he could walk to the corner market with Sarah and Vincent. While he was gone I sat on the porch steps and read the evening paper with a glass of tea from my gallon mason jar. It had been brewing in the sun by my kitchen window all day while Benjamin and Sarah escorted me from one caged animal to another. Sitting there under the awakening stars it was more than a little bit of a shock to see Daniel's picture in the public interest section.

He did look pious in his black robe, with the messy blond curls giving him that shimmering light above his head, as always. The article indicated he was nothing short of a miracle healer, and had a way with people that endeared him to the crowds. He was, as Maggie had said, going to be appointed bishop by the Pope himself, in a special ceremony at St. Peter's Cathedral, in Rome. I thought about the magnitude of this honor for Daniel, and how it could all unravel rather quickly given the sins of his past, and the undeniable reality of our son.

Hearing a car door I looked up and held my breath with a sense of dread as Peter got out and walked over to where I sat. Instinctively I glanced down the street to see if Benjamin was returning yet with Sarah and Vincent, but they were nowhere in sight. I had no idea what to say to this man. I would love to have never laid eyes on him again for the rest of my time here on earth. But I did have an inkling of what he wanted and my heart raced with dread.

"Hello, Victoria," he said, as he stood in front of me, a rolled paper under his arm.

"Peter. What brings you here again so soon?" I asked, hoping to sound pleasant, but each of my words came slow and heavy rather than light and airy as pleasantries would be, because there was nothing pleasant about this moment. I dreaded each additional one he would force upon me with his presence.

"I see you've read about Daniel." He nodded at the paper on my lap, opened to the article and picture of Father Rosselli. Then he carefully unfolded the paper tucked beneath his arm and stared at it. "You didn't tell me your *hero* from the whitewater trip was a *priest*."

I remained quiet, which allowed him to continue. "I did some number crunching, Tori. You know, birthdays and gestation periods." He folded the paper and tossed it on the porch. "And I have determined this child prodigy of yours is either mine, or the priest's."

I stared into Peter's calculating eyes. "I told you, Peter, there was someone else in my life. Someone from Portland I was dating before graduate school."

"I don't think so, *Tori darling*. I specifically remember you telling me there had not been anyone in your life for quite some time, prior to Daniel on the Rogue. It was your own justification for why you fell so hard, and so fast for this man, who apparently didn't return your infatuation." Peter chuckled. "Or perhaps he just came to his senses when returning to his religious duties."

I wanted to pull a hidden saber from beneath my porch and run it through his side, piercing his evilness with cold steel. But alas, I had no hidden saber. My only weapons were my words, and I was not giving in to this despicable creature.

"Daniel is not the father of Benjamin."

"You're lying to me, Tori. There was no man besides this priest, except for me. If he isn't the father, then *I am*."

"Benjamin is not your child," I said adamantly.

Peter pointed to the paper. "Then Benjamin *is* this man's child." His look and tone indicated he understood his accusation could be the undoing of a bishop.

"He is not Daniel's child, or your child," I said flatly as I stood up.

"Then who is the father of this budding artist, Tori? Who is this mystery man?" Peter stepped to the top of the porch and leaned against the apartment building.

"I told you, it isn't anyone you know. And I'd rather not say." I picked the paper up, and folded it. "I'm sorry, Peter, but I really must go. I have a lot to do and it's getting late." My stomach churned while wondering how to get rid of him for good. I also wondered where Vincent and the children were, and then the phone rang.

Wasting no time opening the screen door, I let it slam in Peter's face, as he tried to follow me in. I was relieved to hear Benjamin at the other end, knowing he had arrived safely back at the Gianni home. He wanted to spend the night, and it being his summer vacation, I had no objection. The Gianni family no doubt had extra brand new toothbrushes lying around and sleeping bags galore, because they were always prepared for anything. I knew that he and Sarah would camp out in the living room and watch movies.

Vincent would lay in the easy chair and snore loudly. He never left them alone together at this confusing preteen age, even though they were truly good friends in the most innocent sort of way. Both our beloved children were the odd ones out among the neighborhood kids, who were not comfortable with Sarah's pain and suffering, or Benjamin's special gifts. So together, Sarah and Benj were two lonely children, set apart, and who found solace in each other's company.

I slowly put the receiver down and immediately cringed at Peter's breath on the back of my neck. He had let himself in while I was on the phone.

"Is the little artist not honoring us with his presence this evening?" he hissed at me.

Peter had me pinned against the counter by the phone, and was coiled around me like a snake.

"I want to meet my son, Tori. I want to spend time with him. I want *custody.*"

His last words bit into me, their venom a shock to my nervous system.

"He is *not* your son, Peter."

He took my face in his hands and firmly pressed his lips to mine. Struggling was pointless, but I tried to nonetheless, squirming ferociously as I nearly suffocated in his viper grip.

Nausea swept through me in waves as I became repulsed by his oppressiveness.

When he had given up on getting a response I slipped through his grasp and went straight to the front door, opening it with conviction.

"Get out. And don't come again," I demanded, as icily as possible.

Peter stood stiffly in the arched doorway to the living room. "I will have my attorney get in touch with yours, Victoria. And we shall see about custody rights. I am more than happy to have a DNA sample drawn to prove Benjamin is mine."

Peter smiled that wicked smile of his and then walked over to where I stood.

"You can play your little hard-to-get games, but I know you want me, Victoria. Just like that night when we conceived our child. At first you played hard to get but then you couldn't get enough of me."

"Stop it!" I yelled. Almost adding that he had raped me, but that was one subject I didn't wish to discuss with Peter, not ever.

"Get out of my house!" I shouted, barely able to breathe with him so close to me.

"You can't win, you know. Because if I'm not the father I will sure as hell expose the priest—soon to be bishop—who is. Unless, of course, you want to make a deal." His stare penetrated mine and those dark eyes glistened evilly.

"A deal?" I repeated his words with disbelief. Nothing seemed less savory to me other than making a deal with the devil himself.

"Well, after all, it isn't as if I really *need* to interfere with you and the boy's future. I mean the little bastard has done fine without a father all this time." Peter had dropped his vision from me to his hands, and was examining his fingers.

"I have nothing to say to you, Peter. I don't make deals where my son is concerned. Have your attorney contact mine if you wish. It will be money spent unwisely, as nothing will come of it." I slammed the door and locked it.

So many thoughts raced through my head all at once. How could I keep this man away from my child? Keep him from destroying Daniel's future in the church? Keep him from touching me ever again?

Leaning there against the locked door I had barely recovered from Peter's visit when the doorbell rang. I jumped, my frazzled nerves not able to take much more. Surely it could not be Peter again, I reasoned, peeking out the front window. It was Wil, and I was overwhelmed suddenly by his magical appearance on my porch. I opened the door as quickly as I could, fumbling with the lock beneath my nervous fingers, and fully embraced him before he could take a single step to enter.

"Vic, what is it? What's happened? Is Benjamin okay?"

I cried uncontrollably as he held me and rubbed my back, his chin resting on my head. I loved that about him, his total lack of panic and ability to always comfort me. I thought about how Wil had called me Vic ever since he was a toddler. Our parents had insisted upon my entire birth name of Victoria by everyone, but he was not able to say it and never felt inclined to once he could. I clearly remembered my defiant moment of shortening it to Tori. Wil had looked up at me with equal defiance, and announced that to him I would always be "Vic."

I pulled away finally from his comforting embrace and wiped mascara from under my eyes with shaky fingers. "Peter was here again." It was all I needed to say, for I had told Wil about his first visit, and about everything Miranda and I suspected.

"Okay, that's it. You need an attorney."

I plopped onto the sofa, feeling emotionally spent while Wil paced back and forth across the living room.

"What exactly does this jerk want? Did you tell him you might take him to court for drugging you and . . ."

He couldn't finish the sentence.

"Wil, that happened a long time ago. You know I can't take him to court for that. It doesn't matter now anyway. What matters is that he wants custody of Benjamin." Saying it made me nauseous again, my stomach nearly leaping into my throat. I grabbed a tissue from the box on the end table and wiped a new set of tears.

"I can't believe this idiot would have the nerve to show his face around you *ever again*." Wil frowned and it made his appealing boyish features a near replica of our father in the family portrait on my desk. I decided my brother must have come straight from work because he still wore one of the silk suits I had helped him pick out.

"I'm glad I stopped by to see if Benj is ready for our campout."

"That's right. I almost forgot. He's spending the night at Sarah's, but he'll be back by the time you come for him in the morning," I promised.

Wil had a boat and took Benjamin over to Central Oregon each summer for a boys-only getaway with just the two of them. They would camp at The Cove near a beautiful lake called Billie Chinook, tucked down into a sheer rock canyon. For weeks after I would hear all about the amazing time they'd had fishing and boating.

"I want you to find a good attorney, and get rid of this guy, okay? I don't want him lurking around trying to be a father to Benjamin, the *son-of-a-bitch*. Let him do that test or whatever to prove he isn't the father."

I shook my head in agreement, but Wil didn't know about Daniel. He only knew I'd had an affair on the Rogue trip and then never saw my son's father again.

My brother left with Benjamin the next morning for five days at The Cove, thinking a simple test would solve everything when of course the test must never be done, because Peter might be even more dangerous knowing he *wasn't* the father.

CHAPTER TEN

He smiled briefly, and a glimpse of his warmhearted spirit
hinted of more hope than all the law books on his shelves.

I decided the safest thing for Benjamin would be to see an attorney about a restraining order. I would do anything to keep the twisted Peter from going near my son. I hadn't seen Jonathan since the Rogue trip and I wondered if he and Daniel were still close. I suddenly realized how difficult it must have been to witness the love affair between Daniel and I on the Rogue, knowing of Daniel's vocation. What would he think now, knowing we'd had a child?

When I finally arrived at his office, I couldn't believe how little he'd changed. His dark hair was pulled straight back, but the warm radiating smile was the same. He appeared pleased to see me as we stood shaking hands in his plushy corner office. It was similar to Miranda's, overlooking the boats moored at the city docks below. In fact his office building sat adjacent to hers along the waterfront. I informed him of this as we reminisced about Andi and the rest of our rowing crew from the Rogue trip.

Jonathan mentioned being regretful of not having stayed in touch and I suspected his relationship with Daniel had everything to do with that. Robert entered the office to shake my hand and it felt odd that I hadn't seen him either in all these years, especially since I knew him quite well through Rachel's eyes. I wondered if Jonathan was aware of their secret relationship, but then of course he would be. Robert was far more than a law partner, he and Jonathan had grown up together in New York. Their families were longtime friends, according to Miranda.

Once Robert left, Jonathan politely seated me and then settled into a sleek leather chair behind his massive cherry desk. It was suddenly awkward, being past the rush of re-acquaintance, and Jonathan not knowing exactly why I was there. He only knew Rachel had given me his name and number. I remember thinking it odd that Jonathan had answered the phone himself and then realized it must have been a private number. I felt sure attorneys didn't usually see new clients on the same day of their initial call, and concluded he had made a special effort to speak with me promptly.

I thought briefly about Wil and Benj leaving early this morning, shortly before I dialed Jonathan's number. They had no knowledge of the ominous things I must now confide to an attorney. I felt a sudden rush of gratitude that Jonathan was not just any stranger, who might be excruciatingly cold and clinical about my situation. On the other hand, already having a good measure of respect for him made it difficult to begin this raw exposure of myself. He leaned forward, with his hands folded neatly on the polished cherry surface and began what must have been an equally awkward discussion for him.

"Tori, I have taken the liberty to speak briefly with Rachel and Robert. Only as a concerned friend, mind you, did I seek some explanation for your visit."

I sighed, relieved to have the burden of where to begin over with and grateful that he had taken it upon himself to ease my opening.

"What did they say?" I asked.

Jonathan studied his hands folded on the desk. "They said your son Benjamin was a child prodigy, and showed me the articles about his paintings. I was back east, finalizing details concerning my move west, or I'm sure I would have already known about it. I apologize for being so out of the loop. I would never have left this practice to work alongside my dad in New York had he not pleaded with me to do so his last few years before retirement."

"That's completely understandable. I wouldn't expect you to know." I felt stiff and formal in my gray suit but was glad I had chosen to look professional and reserved. Somehow it gave me the courage to face this dialogue that had to happen if Jonathan was going to try and help me.

"They say Benjamin is a great kid, smart, and I can see that he is good looking . . . like his father." Jonathan looked sheepishly at me.

"Then you know who his father is?"

"Yes."

"How long have you known about Benjamin?"

"Since this morning, when reading the articles pertaining to his paintings. This boy of yours is a dead ringer for Daniel, not to mention the time frame being correct."

"I see. Jonathan, I went to visit Daniel and I brought Benjamin with me, but Daniel doesn't know Benjamin is his."

"He told me of your visit, Tori," Jonathan confided slowly, " but not of your son."

"Then you speak with Daniel still?"

"Yes," he nodded his head. "We've managed to stay close."

I froze. A million questions were poised on my tongue wishing to leap forward and gather up much needed answers about Daniel, but their magnitude prevented even one from escaping my suddenly dry, parched lips.

"Rachel called this morning shortly after you and I spoke, to see if you'd contacted me. The articles were sitting on my desk—placed there by Robert, who knew you were coming. I told her there was little doubt as to who the father was, considering his striking features and the time of birth. She told me that was very perceptive of me, but it wasn't her place to say for sure. How could Daniel not know this child is his?" Jonathan asked, with an exasperated tone, not expecting an answer.

"Protecting his father is one reason I'm here." I didn't quite know where to proceed from there. Jonathan came and sat in the matching leather chair beside mine, apparently not wishing to have a desk between us.

"Is someone threatening to expose who his father is?"

"Yes. Peter Cairns."

"Who is Peter Cairns?"

I smoothed my skirt, not wishing to say what I knew I must say. I then stood and looked out the window as I spoke.

"He was a psychology professor at the University of Portland when I was working on my graduate degree, that summer we all rafted the Rogue."

I glanced at Jonathan, giving him a weak smile. Then I studied the gently moving river water to gather my strength. "Peter wanted to marry me. He was upset I had found someone else on my short vacation, someone I was distraught about not hearing from again."

I paused, and could feel Jonathan's quiet presence in the chair behind me, not moving, perhaps not wanting to break my courage to continue.

"He drugged me one night. I have reason to know this for a fact now, although at the time I didn't know. At the time I thought I had carelessly had too much to drink, and allowed him to . . . anyway, he raped me. I am sure of it."

I couldn't look at Jonathan, so I just continued to stare out the window. "Now he has his own practice here in Portland. He saw the articles on Benjamin and has decided the child is his. He claims he wants custody rights, but all he really wants is the money from the paintings. I'm sure of it."

I sat down in the chair again next to Jonathan, finding strength in my anger, in my near hatred of this man wreaking havoc on my life. Exactly why I was here, I reminded myself.

Jonathan surprised me by reaching out for my hands, taking them into his. They were warm and strong.

"Tori, we have to stop this bastard. You can't give him anything. He'll only want more. And he's obviously dangerous . . . you should never be alone with him." He paused, his eyes focused on mine. "I'm sorry for what this jerk did to you. And you can be sure if he did this to you, he's done it to others."

"I know. He did the same thing to a friend of mine recently, and left her a note almost identical to the one he left me nearly twelve years ago."

"Did you keep it?"

I shook my head no and he did not seem surprised.

"Is your friend pressing charges?"

"No. I'm going to tell you, Jonathan, who it is because I think she would be okay with you knowing. It's . . . Miranda. She and Peter stayed in touch from when we were all at the college together. They were more than associates. They were nearly friends, until now . . . until this."

"Is Miranda okay?"

"Yes. She's as fine as could be expected. It isn't as if either of us *really* *know* what happened, only that *it did*."

Jonathan sank back into the leather chair and sighed. "There must be a way to expose him, press charges, and lock him up."

"No!" I surprised myself by sounding so firm. "He mustn't expose Daniel as Benjamin's father, and this would be his first priority if we found a way to have him arrested."

"I see. So apparently he knew of your affair with Daniel and has read the recent press releases about the bishop appointment."

"Yes."

"Good God. How do we fight our way through this mess?"

"I don't know. I was hoping you would have some ideas . . . that you could somehow help."

Jonathan leaned forward and took my hands again. "Yes, of course, Tori. I can help you. I *will* help you. I'm just not sure *how* yet." He smiled briefly and a glimpse of his warmhearted spirit hinted of more hope than all the law books on his shelves. His next proposal caught me off guard.

"Come to dinner with me next Tuesday night. I promise to have some ideas by then."

I studied his expression, not flirtatious in the least. "Well then, how could I turn you down?" I smiled despite myself.

"I'll pick you up at seven. Okay?"

I gave him directions to my apartment and left, after a brief and careful hug that he initiated. I wondered if he was seeing anyone. And then I reminded myself that getting involved with my attorney would not be wise. That what I needed most was an expert to sort out the messes made by other men, one loved and one loathed, and developing feelings for Jonathan would only be an additional complication in my life.

Nonetheless, I felt the renewing of our friendship was indeed a blessing to come out of this adversity.

CHAPTER ELEVEN

"I am lost, Daniel. How does one find their way out of this maze?"

I dressed for church slowly, changing several times after looking into the mirror and thinking my summer attire was too provocative for a Catholic mass. The thin summer fabrics hugged my body and exposed too much skin. I finally settled on a black cotton dress that fell below the knee and felt conservative enough. Benjamin and I had been attending St. Matthew's for over a month now, and it felt odd to go without him but I was determined to continue the habit, crazy as it was to have this need for seeing Daniel, if only from afar and without his knowledge.

Once inside the cathedral I sat near the back as usual so as not to be noticed by Daniel. At communion time I went to the kneeling station in front of the altar on the furthest side from where he stood. But on this Sunday he surprised me after mass by quietly disappearing through the side alcove of the altar area, only to appear again at the entrance doors where he stood greeting people on their way out. I looked for another exit and not readily seeing one, headed for the furthest corner of the sanctuary to find an available escape.

It was hard not to feel like a criminal sneaking about in the more private corridors of God's house. The hallway I found myself in was long, with a high ceiling and wooden floor. Every step I took echoed down the length of it, making me feel conspicuous. I fully believed I would soon be approached by several men in black robes wanting to escort me out. Nonetheless I couldn't help but glance up at the muted light coming through the stained glass windows that aligned the hall. The faces on the figures were serious and maudlin, as if their threshold for suffering had been reached. Yet there was an inspired mood to the windows that gave you a hint of God's mercy.

I stopped at one point and reached up to touch the face of Mary. I could not resist, as her face alone among them was so peaceful. I wished to have such peace with God, for I hadn't any at the moment. Lost in the warmth of the morning sun fragmenting through the face of Mary, I was caught off guard when someone spoke from behind me.

I turned my head to look at Daniel, knowing it was him I would see, his voice as distinctive as his other features. He had removed his robe and yet still did not look like an ordinary man. He wore casual khaki's and a black polo shirt. Perhaps it was the striking hair, or the eyes, or the reverence in his tone. I couldn't define what made Daniel different from mere mortals. I only knew that he was.

"Why are you avoiding me, Tori?" he asked, his voice echoing in the long hall. "I know you've been here every Sunday since I first laid eyes on you, five Sundays ago."

"You counted them?" I leaned against the wall between emotion-filled windows of colored glass and folded my arms. "How did you manage to see me, way in the back, near the door where I could exit quickly if asked to?"

"Everyone is welcome here, Tori. Surely you know that."

"Surely they are not."

"Who would not be welcome in the house of God?"

I shrugged my shoulders. "Those that would cause others to fall."

"Fall into what?"

"Sin."

"Everyone sins."

I pushed my hair off my face. "I am lost Daniel. How does one find their way out of this maze?"

"I can't let you leave thinking only a chosen few are welcome in God's house." Daniel stepped closer and talked softer. "Did you not grow up with any kind of faith, Tori?"

"I told you my grandmother was Catholic, and took me and Wil to mass with her. I thought it quite beautiful and mysterious. Certainly not something to run from, but perhaps a bit overwhelming to readily embrace."

"I remember that now . . . about your grandmother. Why have you come every week for the last five if it's too overwhelming to embrace?" Daniel looked serious, no doubt concerned for my soul. An occupational hazard, I decided, as he stood there in front of me, making it impossible to bolt.

"Maybe other things in my life are more overwhelming, and I need to believe in something, like these windows. They are a testimony to triumph over adversity. That's what Christianity is, isn't it? A light at the end of the tunnel?"

We stared at each other for a long second, and I had no idea what he was thinking. It occurred to me that I never did have an inkling of what he was thinking, obviously, or I wouldn't have made love to him by the river. And I wouldn't have chosen to give him my heart, had I known his own heart was already filled to capacity with loving God.

"Let's take a walk down 23rd street, okay? I'm starving. I'll buy your lunch."

This invitation threw me off guard completely. I was torn in the seconds it took me to make up my mind. I wanted desperately to better understand my son's father, but I was afraid of losing my very soul to this man.

"Okay," I said, but made no move to exit the hall with my mind and body in conflict over the decision. Daniel smiled and held his hand out for me. Slowly I unfolded my arms and reached for him. He took my hand into his and electricity sparked between us. He hesitated, and then guided us toward the exit. Soon we were on the side street beside the cathedral. Clouds lifted to reveal the warmth of the sun as we walked over to 23rd Street, or "Trendy 23rd" as it was often called because it housed many unique restaurants and specialty shops where college students and young professionals liked to hang out.

We stopped at an outdoor café and sat at a table adorned with heavy white linen. A young girl in jeans appeared to pour us water. Without even looking at the menus placed before us, we both ordered Papa Haidyn's Sunday brunch. It was one of my favorites, having come here often with Rachel and Miranda. I could almost hear their laughter from times past when we would sit at this very table and sip on iced tea, before browsing the quaint little shops along the strip. Sitting here with Daniel was a little disconcerting, considering I had been working, and raising Benjamin, only a few blocks over all these years, not knowing he was right there in St. Matthew's the whole time.

"Tori, if you are so interested in the church, you should take Catholicism classes. It's a great way to learn about the faith."

"When are they, and who teaches them?" I took a sip of water, surprised at my own interest.

"They start again next week. Seven o'clock . . . at the cathedral, on eight consecutive Thursday nights."

"You didn't say who teaches them."

"It depends on how many sign up each time, and which priests are available."

"I see."

"Will you come?"

"Let me think about it."

"Where is that handsome boy of yours?"

"He's with Wil, my brother. They're camping."

Our food arrived, seafood omelets with rosemary fried potatoes. We ate quietly at first, my stifled questions growing with each bite.

"Doesn't it seem unbelievable," I asked when finally finding the courage to speak, "how I've been only a few city blocks away from your St. Matthew's for all these years since the rafting trip?"

Daniel stared at his fork. "Tori, it's more shocking to me than you might think." He looked up, and his unusual blue eyes were slightly clouded. "It almost seems like a cruel joke God has played on me, you being so near all this time. But of course, God doesn't play jokes. Especially not cruel ones. It is my own sin that has caused my pain."

"What pain, Daniel? Surely I haven't caused you pain? I don't remember having the opportunity to reject you, in the end. Certainly I never rejected your passion for me on the Rogue trip."

Daniel looked down at his plate, as if he were gathering strength from the herbs in his food. Then he looked me right in the eye. "I never meant to hurt you, Tori. Had I known you were only a few blocks from the cathedral I could never have stayed away. Maybe that's why God did not reveal your presence to me."

"So, God is my competitor then? As opposed to apathy or regret for a weak moment. Or should I say weak hours on end?"

"I deserve your anger."

"Am I angry?" I put my napkin down and took a deep breath. I didn't realize I still had such anger. I hated not knowing what to be angry at. Fate?

The church? God? The only one I was not angry with was Daniel, but for the life of me, I didn't know why not."

"Tori, I have tried not to think of you for twelve long years, and each and every day of each and every one of them, I have failed."

We stared at each other as the waitress cleared our dishes and poured our coffee.

"Who is Benjamin's father?" Daniel's eyes were more than a little clouded now. Their brilliant luster was tainted with confusion.

"I told you. Someone not able to be a part of our lives." I hesitated and then quickly added, "Someone I met at graduate school, after the Rogue trip."

"I see."

"No, you don't see. I was all alone Daniel. Rejected and miserable, thinking I found true love and discovering I had only been a fool, so I behaved as the fool that I was. Why not? If I couldn't have you, I might as well have whomever else I wanted. And I wanted Benjamin's father. Even though he wasn't available for the long run," I said, those last two statements being completely true.

Daniel's eyes were moist. I was hurting him. That was not my intent. Or was it?

"I pictured you married with two beautiful little girls just like their mother and a doting husband. It broke my heart and healed my conscience all at the same time."

"How sad is that, Daniel? To pretend I could just go on as if we never met? And all the while your God that doesn't play cruel jokes had me raising a fatherless child just down the street from your sacred endeavors. Not that He is responsible for our tryst on the Rogue."

"That's what you call it, a tryst?"

"What would you call it? A secretive meeting between two lovers who have no commitment to each other is a tryst. Isn't that exactly what we were? Secretive lovers?"

"You make it sound so selfish and ordinary . . . the special bond between us."

"Daniel, have you never considered that your feelings for me were nothing more than raging self-indulgent lust?"

Daniel folded his hands on the table. "It wasn't just lust I felt for you. I have dealt with mere lust many times. It was love, combined with desire. I have never had to face the two in one before." He looked up at me. "Or since, until . . . well, you have an effect on me that is hard to explain, even now."

I didn't know what to say. It was what I had hoped to hear. I could feel the anger drain from my body. I was grateful for the public place of this private conversation, because I could run away into the crowd instead of into Daniel's arms. Not that I didn't want to be in his arms, but having the whole city surrounding us at this moment was preventing that from happening, and it was a good thing, because being in Daniel's arms would only cause him to be at odds with his God. With that reality I rose from my seat and mumbled something about wanting to browse through the shops. Daniel stood as I walked away and shouted, "Wait!" But I turned the corner and was gone to him, stepping into a stationery store that smelled of cinnamon and candle wax.

I shuffled through greeting cards until composed enough to walk back to St. Matthew's, and collect my car for the short drive home.

CHAPTER TWELVE

Maybe it was touching the face of Mary and seeing the peace in her eyes.

The rest of Sunday I sulked around the apartment and watched Vincent fuss with his doves in the yard. Maggie and Sarah were off shopping for sneakers, since Sarah had outgrown hers. We had all feared she would never recover from the cancer that ravished her young body, let alone outgrow her shoes. I smiled for Sarah despite my dismal mood. Somewhere in the recesses of my mind I knew God could indeed be merciful. Sarah's recovery was proof of that, yet I did not momentarily wish to sing His praises.

I missed Benjamin and Wil, and planned to make them a batch of cookies for when they returned this evening from The Cove. I decided on sugar cookies, since they take time and I had too much of it. I rolled the dough and cut it into stars and flags for the Fourth of July only one week away, thinking the entire time that it would have been easier to get the sugar back out of the dough than to get Daniel out of my head.

Thoughts of Daniel on the Rogue twelve years ago, in mass these past five Sundays, and at the street café earlier. How could I ever hope to get him off my mind, with our son reflecting every hair on his flaxen head, not to mention the tropical oceans seen within their eyes and this mysterious ability to heal the hopelessly afflicted? For that matter, Daniel had never been more than a thought away for every day of the last twelve years regardless of recent developments.

Benjamin and Wil burst through the door just as I finished icing the cookies. They dropped their gear and grabbed a star for one hand, and a flag for the other. Between sugary mouthfuls they told me about their great camping trip. Later in the evening we had just settled down on the front porch to watch the moon come up when Sarah and Maggie walked through the yard. Sarah's large gray cat was held tightly in her skinny little arms.

"What's the matter with Rufus, Sarah?" Benjamin asked, as they came over to join our stargazing.

"He has a splinter, I think, in his paw."

I stood and examined his front right paw as he meowed, tensing in Sarah's arms. "How did he get a splinter?" I shook my head at the sliver of wood jammed between his toes, not daring to pull on it.

"Following us home," Maggie answered, as Benjamin approached Rufus and examined the tiny piece of wood in his paw.

"Hold him tight, Sarah. I'm going to pull it." Benjamin had his fancy new knife from Wil out of his pocket, looking for the tweezers attachment. He yanked the splinter quickly as Rufus growled long and low. Sarah petted and comforted him until the cat finally wiggled loose from her arms and ran to hide under the thick row of blackberry bushes in the yard.

"That cat's lucky to be alive," Maggie laughed. "He nearly fell off the wooden rail where he got that sliver. Three stories he would've fallen, onto hard cement."

We all marveled at his luck and how strange a cat he was to follow them downtown, tagging along as they shopped today for new shoes. Maggie and Sarah went home after hearing the camping stories from Wil and Benjamin's trip. Shortly thereafter, Benj went to bed, exhausted from all the excitement and too much fun at The Cove. I suspected he had gotten little sleep in the last five days.

Wil and I collapsed on Grams' sofa in the living room and listened to the silence. We had brought a glass of red wine with us from the kitchen, where I ceremoniously opened it in honor of removing the splinter from poor suffering Rufus. His nine lives were surely shrinking to eight left at the most, after his near fall earlier in the day.

"Did you see an attorney, Vic, while we were gone?" Wil asked.

"Yes. I went to see Jonathan Davis. Remember him? From the Rogue trip."

"No, but that's okay. Is he a friend?"

"Yes. We hadn't spoken since rafting the Rogue, but I do consider him a friend and someone I can trust." I was too embarrassed to mention our dinner date for this Tuesday night.

"What did he say?" Wil took a sip from his stemmed glass and looked at me.

I didn't know where to begin. I had kept so much from Wil, and now I knew it was time to come clean. "You know how Benj and I have been going to St. Matthew's lately?"

"Yeah," he answered, puzzled.

"Well there's a reason for that. Not just a spiritual one." I wasn't sure how to continue.

"Vic, what is it? This is Wil, here. You can tell me anything."

"Father Rosselli, the healing priest, the one that is going to be bishop, have you heard of him?" I prayed Wil knew something about Daniel. It was certainly possible. He had been in the news a lot lately between the healing powers and impending bishop title.

"Yeah." Wil hesitated, as if trying to remember what he actually knew. "I read about him in the paper. Do you know this guy?"

"He's Benjamin's father."

There was a second of non-comprehension and then Wil's face became distorted. "Are you kidding? A priest?" He stared at me, an incredulous look on his face. "Vic, no one could make your life more difficult than you do all by yourself."

I sipped on my wine and didn't say anything.

"I'm sorry, Vic." He scooted closer to me on the sofa. "It's just so unbelievable that you would . . . sleep with a . . . *a priest* for god's sake, and not know he was . . . A PRIEST!"

"I'm sorry, Wil. But there is little I can do about it at this point. It happened twelve years ago, and he never mentioned that he was a priest. How could I know? I just fell in love with the man who saved my life. The rest is history."

We were both silent for a minute, sitting side by side on Grams' sofa like lost little children without her.

"Does he know?"

"Of course not."

"What do you mean, of course not? Why not tell him? Maybe he loves you too, and he would leave the church for you."

"That's just it, Wil. I don't want him to leave the church. Daniel is . . . special. His healing powers are amazing. He belongs in the church." I stared at Wil and didn't really see him. All I saw was a long lonely future obsessing over a man already taken, and by God no less. I wanted to light St. Matthew's with a torch and watch it burn to the ground. Then I remembered the Virgin Mary from the stained glass window and felt guilty.

"Does Peter know?" Wil looked worried.

"He suspects. And that's why I can't have him take any tests that would prove him not to be the father. Because then he would know that Daniel is, and he could ruin his chances to become bishop."

"So what? Maybe he doesn't deserve to be bishop. Maybe he needs to be Benjamin's *father*."

"No. You aren't listening." I leaned forward and took his face in my hands. "Wil, it could never work, Daniel leaving the church. He belongs there. And as long as I can help it, he will reach his full potential serving God. I don't want to be a part of messing that up. I could never live with myself."

I let go of my little brother and collapsed against the back of the sofa.

"I didn't realize you were so religious."

"I'm not."

"I think maybe you are, if you're this afraid of God . . . or this supportive of him. I can't tell which."

I left the room out of frustration and began cleaning up the hot chocolate mugs and sugar cookies in the kitchen, nearly shouting, "You don't get it, Wil. It isn't about religion. It's about what's best for Daniel."

"What about what's best for you, Vic?" Wil joined me in the kitchen and leaned against the counter, watching as I washed the dishes.

"What's best for me is to not come between a man and his calling from God," I answered

"I see. Well, a man that would pick God as a vocation over marrying you, doesn't deserve you."

There was a long forlorn meow at the screen door and we nearly jumped out of our skin at the eerie sound and unexpected intrusion. Wil let Rufus in, who had decided to leave the bush he was hiding under, no doubt out of a greater need to eat something. I found a shallow dish and filled it with cottage cheese, which Rufus hungrily accepted. We didn't see Maggie appear at the door until she knocked several times and let herself in.

"I thought our kitty might be here." She watched Rufus while he gobbled down the cottage cheese.

"Yes. And thank goodness Rufus found his way to Benjamin's healing porch for getting his splinter removed," I added. Maggie and I laughed, despite the fact that Benjamin's special gift was anything but amusing.

Wil sat on the floor petting Rufus. "His paw seems fine now, not very tender or sore. What is this about Benjamin's healing porch?"

I sighed. "Nothing really. Benj brings all the neighborhood animals here when they are sick or injured, and does what he can for them."

"Well, that's normal enough for any boy to do. Maybe he wants to be a doctor when he grows up."

Silence hung in the air, thick enough to cut with a knife. Maggie and I were neither one going to offer up our heavy thoughts on the subject of Benjamin's healing powers. And then Maggie spoke what was on her heart.

"Sarah and I saw you today, Tori, when we were shoe shopping, seated there with Father Rosselli at Papa Haidyn's. We would never have recognized him without his robes, but that flaxen hair is hard to miss." Maggie smiled. "We didn't cross the street to say hello. It looked like you were deep in conversation about important matters."

She kept a steady gaze on me and I knew explanations were at least hoped for, if not expected.

"Yes, we did have a lot to discuss." I glanced at Wil, who kept quiet, while continuing to pet Rufus.

"That beautiful little boy of yours, he looks just like the priest. And what a coincidence they both have a gift for healing." Maggie raised an eyebrow.

I sighed, and gathered my courage. "Daniel is Benjamin's father, Maggie."

Wil and Maggie stared at Rufus, as if he could somehow lick away the truth along with the cottage cheese.

"But I had no idea he was right here at St. Matthew's," I continued, "until that day you told me about the healing mass, when Sarah was so sick."

"I know. I figured it all out honey . . . today, when I saw you two together." Maggie shook her head. "That man's in love with you, girl. It's written all over him. Does he know Benjamin is his?"

"No. And I plan to keep it that way."

Maggie sat down at the table, as if the weight of all this information was too much to bear. "I'm not so sure he should be thinking about some grand future in the church." Maggie squinted her eyes. "Messing around with women and all. Getting them pregnant."

I couldn't stand there any longer knowing what kind of thoughts everyone would be sharing, should Daniel and I be exposed. I walked into the living room and sat in the chair by the window where I could stare at the full moon. It looked close enough to reach out and touch.

Maggie and Wil soon left, Rufus running out the door between them. I continued to stare at the moon as if it were a deserted island in the sky, offering me refuge from realities that threatened to consume me. I kept envisioning those nights Daniel and I spent together there by the side of the Rogue, with crickets chirping and the river rushing past. Now we were surrounded by city lights and traffic noise, with the walls of a great cathedral dividing us. I wondered if Daniel ever recalled those dizzying July nights. Surely he must have, for he did say that he prayed each and every day to forget me, and that each and every day he failed.

Thoughts of God had only entered my mind when considering my conscience. It was, after all, not just a one-night stand of unprotected sex with a near stranger, but rather several nights of love making with total abandon, and no desire for accountability to dare creep in until the wilderness was far behind us. I could have easily explained a slip of sanity brought on by emotional trauma from nearly succumbing to the depths of the river, but surely an intelligent God would laugh at my attempt to extend such an excuse to cover the whole trip.

Now I couldn't seem to get God off my mind any more than I could stop thinking about Daniel. Both were only further confusing me. Perhaps it was being in the heart of St. Matthew's and finding it a confusing maze, or looking at the fragile stained glass windows of pain-filled Biblical characters. Maybe it was touching the face of Mary and seeing the peace in her eyes. I could never experience that kind of peace with God, I was sure, until I understood how our creator could allow someone like Daniel to fall completely in love with a woman, and she with him, if their love was not meant to be.

And surely it was meant to be, because it had culminated in the birth of Benjamin.

CHAPTER THIRTEEN

Jonathan gave me a penetrating gaze that bared my soul without consent.

Benjamin kicked the soccer ball around in the street the entire time I was getting ready for my date with Jonathan. The ball thumped outside my window every time he hit it with his fancy footwork. Whenever I peeked at him through the blinds, his look of determination told me he was concentrating on every single move. Benj played on an inner city league with other neighborhood kids. They played at night mostly, under the lights, because the park was used for baseball during the day.

I went to all of Benjamin's games, but forgot about soccer when Jonathan asked me out, not having the presence of mind to think clearly. Vincent, Maggie, and Sarah were going to be at his game this evening as usual. I blushed unexpectedly when asking if they could watch Benjamin for the evening because I had a date.

The men in my life had been few and far between as no one knew better than Vince and Maggie. Thus was the life of an unmarried woman with a child and bills to pay, complicated by a career that was passion driven. The few men I saw were always associated somehow with my graphic design or photography work, since I did a fair amount of local advertising shoots. I had considered marriage with a couple of these men, but did not have that breathless feeling, that merging of the souls I once felt with Daniel, and so in the end, I could not marry them. No matter how hard I tried to convince myself it would be better to settle for comfortable love than to do without, my heart would not listen to my logic.

I peeked through the blinds again, hearing a car door outside the window, and panicked for a second because I was not there to introduce Jonathan to my son. Benjamin knew an old friend of mine was taking me to dinner, but didn't know anything about him. Jonathan soon put my fears to rest as I saw them exchange a few words and shake hands, and then before I knew what was happening, he began kicking the ball around with Benj. From the looks of it, Jonathan had played some serious soccer at one time or another in his life.

I stepped out onto the front porch, where I leaned against the door and watched the two of them spar with the ball. I made no attempt to distract their concerted efforts. I didn't want them to quit. I didn't want my eyes to tear up either, but it was hard to not get emotional, watching Benjamin with a man who shared his passion for soccer. It made me feel guilty for thinking bits and pieces of Wil were enough for my child to feel as if he had a real father. Perhaps I was being selfish passing up all that comfortable love offered to me by good men, who would have gladly raised Benjamin as their own.

It didn't take long for them to notice my presence, while pausing for a passing car. I smiled as they approached me, and hoped my melancholy thoughts were not written all over my face.

"Hi, Tori. You look beautiful." Jonathan paused to smile. "Benjamin tells me he has a game in about an hour." He looked from me to my son, his upper arm muscles and forehead glistening from the soccer activity, which only made him more appealing to look at. He wore casual khaki pants and a polo shirt, and I was glad he came more casual than not, since I decided on a short summer dress and sandals.

"Yes he does have a game soon. Benj is on a city league that plays in the park around the corner. Why don't you both come in for some lemonade? You look like you could use it after all that running around." I opened the door and Benjamin led the way to the kitchen. They both helped with the glasses and ice while I mixed the frozen concentrate with water.

We decided to sit on the back patio in lawn chairs with our lemonade, which Benjamin gulped down in less than a minute, suddenly eager to visit the doves. Jonathan and I watched him cross the yard, and observed his tender interactions with Vincent's cherished pets. He sat on the lawn and held each bird, one at a time, in his lap. Then he replenished their water and seed, speaking softly to them the entire time while they cooed back at him.

"These must be the models for his paintings." Jonathan looked at me curiously.

I smiled. "Benj loves Mr. Gianni, and his doves. When he's not with them, he's usually kicking the soccer ball out front in the street."

"I'd love to see the game, if you don't mind eating a late dinner." Jonathan offered this idea with a look of anticipation. I was pleased to not have to miss it myself, and walked over to tell Vincent we would all come to the park, and Benjamin could go home with them afterwards.

It turned out to be a wonderful way to start a date. We cheered and laughed, and before the game was over, Jonathan was the best of friends with my entire neighborhood. On the way to dinner he told me he went to college on a soccer scholarship, having been a star on his high school team that won state his junior and senior year. This was before he moved to Portland, where he met Daniel, surprisingly enough, on a city league soccer team. My mouth was gaping wide open at the thought of Daniel playing soccer. But according to Jonathan, he was pretty good.

Waiting for our food we relived the game and enthusiastically voiced our thoughts on Benjamin's abilities and stellar performance as if we were doting parents and not a first date. Somehow the subject changed to Daniel, and how he had encouraged Jonathan to start attending mass again, after Jonathan told him about his Catholic upbringing. They soon became best friends.

Jonathan went on to tell me how Daniel was born and raised in Venice, the only son of Timothy Rosselli. Daniel's father was a doctor, famous for his somewhat miraculous healing powers, which obviously ran in the family. Daniel's mother, Alessa, was a student on scholarship at the university where Timothy was studying to become a doctor. She soon became Timothy's private practice nurse, and his wife, giving birth to Daniel within the first year of their marriage.

I found all this quite intriguing while watching the river from the Pilsner room at McCormick and Schmick's on the waterfront. I couldn't say how long we sat there, me with my wine, and Jonathan with his dark ale, telling stories of he and Daniel, while the sounds of others laughing and music playing surrounded us. We shared steamed mussels and fried calamari, and it felt as if we only rafted the Rogue together a week ago, rather than twelve years. Finally we were both quiet with our own thoughts and the bartender cleared the dishes, asking if we wanted another round of drinks. When he brought them, Jonathan stared into his ale and turned serious on me.

"Tori, Daniel tells me you've been attending St. Matthew's, and that you ate lunch with him Sunday." He took a swig of his drink and looked directly into my eyes. "Are you still in love with Daniel?"

I smoothed my hair back and sipped my wine, stalling really, not knowing what to say. I decided to be honest. "Of course I love him. Don't you?"

"Yes. But it's not the same."

"Why not?"

"Because I don't want to marry him." Jonathan gave me a penetrating gaze that bared my soul without consent.

"My feelings for Daniel are confusing at best, Jonathan, if you must know." I looked away from him. "It doesn't matter what my feelings are, even if I could define them. His future is with the church, not me."

"Are you saying you wouldn't marry him if he asked? I mean, if he left the church for you?" Jonathan smiled.

"You don't believe I would turn down such an offer?"

"No."

"Do you think I would marry him just like that, and laugh in God's face?"

"Tori, it's a religion. Catholicism is a vehicle through which one practices their faith. No one has to be a priest. It's just a personal choice."

"And what about his amazing healing powers? Do you think he could use them to their full potential outside the church?" I finished my wine and felt a little tipsy, a little too defensive and indignant.

Jonathan shrugged. "Why does it matter? As long as he's happy . . . as long as you're happy, and Benjamin has a father, *his own father.*"

Now I was the one staring. Looking into Jonathan's eyes told me his heart was not in his words. "You don't believe that. Not really. You know as well as I do Daniel belongs in the church. He is part of the church, and whatever the church is or isn't to you and me, it is *everything* to him."

"Maybe." His eyes sparkled mischievously, and I knew somehow that answer had pleased him.

We left the bar and walked along the shore of the river. Coming upon an empty bench we didn't question our luck and sat down to star gaze. It was a clear night and the breeze drifting off the water was welcome. I asked

Jonathan if he had discovered anything fishy in Peter's past yet. He sighed, taking my hand in his. As if I were a child needing protection more so than as a romantic gesture.

"I don't like to mix business with pleasure."

I laughed. "So this is pleasure then? Going to hot, dusty soccer games on the wrong side of town and giving me the third degree about Daniel?"

"First of all, there is nothing wrong about your side of town. Portland doesn't really have a wrong side. Trust me, I grew up in New York. What I see where you live is hard working people making an honest living and trying to get a leg up on life. From what I can tell most of them are not resorting to selling drugs or stealing others blind. Those dishonest folks have all moved to the suburbs. And secondly, there is nothing I'd rather do than watch the next generation of soccer players learn the sport, with a whole slew of neighbors cheering them on."

"Bravo. Does this mean I can expect a second date?" I grinned despite my wanting to appear serious and make him squirm.

"Only if you let me kiss you."

"Do you mean on this date, or if we have a second one?"

"I mean right now."

"I don't know. Truthfully, I've never been asked that question."

"Is that a yes or a no?"

"It's a maybe."

"That's close enough." Jonathan leaned over and kissed me. All I could think about was how good he tasted, and felt, with his strong arms closing around me. Having certain needs and no one meeting them made me feel vulnerable. The kiss was short and sweet, and left me wanting more. Thoughts of wanting more made me blush, and I was glad for the darkness to recover in as I asked about Peter, partly to calm my escalating libido. As much as I loved being wrapped in his warmth, the thought of bringing him to bed with me later scared the hell out of me for how easy it would be.

Jonathan took his arm back from around my shoulder, as if there was no way to mix romance with his news of Peter. And he was right.

"I have lots of information on the lowlife, thanks to Robert's handiwork." He paused and then added, "Robert's a criminal lawyer. I do mostly corporate work."

"Go on." I was suddenly eager for anything at all to use against the despicable Peter.

"Apparently he was arrested once, three years ago, for rape."

"That's not surprising." My stomach began to churn. "Why isn't he in prison?"

"He was released for lack of evidence."

"Damn him."

"There's more."

"More? What else has he done?"

"Tori, are you sure you want to hear this tonight? I was planning on having you come by my office one day this week."

"I'm sorry, Jonathan, but I have to know everything, right now. I won't be able to sleep otherwise."

"You won't be able to sleep once I tell you." Jonathan stood and walked over to look more closely at the river, across the path from our cozy bench. I followed him and slipped my arm into his. "Okay. I'll tell you everything I know so far, but I need some coffee first," he confessed. "Let's walk down to the Front Street Café."

All the way there I dreaded what I was about to hear.

CHAPTER FOURTEEN

A child has a right to be born, and can never have too much love.

I agreed to buy the coffee, if Jonathan promised not to hold anything back, and so we sat in a corner booth sipping a strong French roast as he began the whole ugly tale of Peter and Mary Jennings.

"According to the official records Robert looked up, and the attorney's documentation he somehow acquired under the table, Mary claimed Peter drugged her while at a pub near campus, where they often discussed his advanced psychology class she took as a graduate student," Jonathan shared soberly.

I couldn't help but wonder if it was the same pub Peter and I visited on occasion, and where he'd drugged me.

"How did Mary know she'd been drugged?" I asked.

"She woke up."

"You're kidding!" I gasped.

"I wish I were, but unfortunately it's true, and according to the records she claims when she began to struggle and scream, he gagged her and tied her arms and legs to the bed with pieces of clothing, and continued to rape her. Then he forced more of the sleeping drug down her throat and untied her. She was out until her roommate found her twelve hours later, about six p.m. that Sunday evening when she returned from a weekend with her parents. Mary was just waking up, and was quite ill. She had a splitting headache and was disoriented."

Jonathan took a drink of his coffee while I stared out the window, teary eyed with horror.

"He is such an evil man," I said, suddenly sick to my stomach. "Why did they let him go? Why wasn't there enough evidence?"

"Because she waited too long, not able to tell anyone the horror of what happened. Her roommate found a note left by Peter, thanking Mary for the wonderful night together. Mary was too traumatized to explain it, and the roommate assumed she was just upset about her indiscretion with Peter. It wasn't until after Mary was dysfunctional for several weeks—behaving severely depressed, not leaving the apartment, sleeping continually—that she broke down one night and told her roommate what really happened. The roommate convinced her to report the incident, so they went to the police station together. Everything I just told you was documented there that night."

The waitress poured us a refill and asked if we wanted to order something. We said no and asked for the check.

"She was a brilliant student, only twenty-two, and very pretty," Jonathan offered up somberly. "Apparently she was quite religious and saving herself for marriage. She had never slept with a man before." Jonathan shook his head with disgust. "I'd love to chain the bastard to a prison wall and let the other inmates rape him at their leisure."

"Where is Mary Jennings now?" I asked, my heart going out to her, hoping she managed somehow to put her life back together.

"She's dead, Tori."

"She's dead? How did she die?"

"It says suicide on the death certificate, but records from the investigation indicate that possibly Peter killed her, to shut her up."

"So, Peter pretty much gets away with everything, doesn't he?" I said angrily.

"He's a very intelligent man, maybe a genius according to some. Certainly he is more than just eccentric and aloof. According to the volumes of testimony Robert and I poured over the last few days, he is one deranged individual. But because he was quiet and mild mannered, had a stellar reputation at the university and a squeaky clean record in general, no one believed him to be capable of such deviant or violent behavior."

"How did he do it, kill her I mean? And how could they let him walk? How could they not know he would keep hurting people?" Tears formed in my eyes as emotion overtook me. Jonathan reached for my hand from across the table.

"Tori, I can't tell you how sorry I am you had the misfortune of being one of his victims. I just thank God you are alive and well. Miranda too.

We're going to figure out a way to get this bastard and lock him away for good. I promise you that."

"How did he kill her, Jonathan?" I asked again.

"She was poisoned, by the same drug he uses to rape women. Her roommate found her dead one day when returning after classes. There was a suicide note written on her computer, still on the screen, but not printed. In it she stated how she fell in love with Peter, but he didn't love her in return, and was ending the relationship. She was devastated and decided to kill herself."

The waitress returned with our check, looking very curious about our heavy mood. All this hideous information had visibly shaken me. We walked briskly down the street, until stopping near our bench again. Jonathan hugged me for a long time without speaking. Then he asked if I was okay and I said yes, so he put his arm around me and told the rest of his disturbing news on the way to the car.

"Once all the evidence was in, and all the statements taken, it was determined she did commit suicide. Even her roommate admitted she spoke about having a crush on Professor Cairns, and might have lied about the rape, out of anger from being rejected by him." Jonathan sighed. "Her mother stated she would never have done that . . . killed herself, because their faith strictly prohibited the taking of one's own life." Jonathan was quiet for minute as we approached the car. Then he leaned against it and continued.

"But the police argued if she was willing to have an affair with her professor, in all likelihood her faith wasn't influencing her decisions at the time, and the note written by Peter, thanking her for the wonderful night they spent together, didn't help convince the authorities it was rape. The university did ask Peter to leave quietly after this event. That's when he opened his private practice."

Jonathan apologized for being the bearer of such bad news. We were silent as we drove to my apartment, mulling over all the misery this man had inflicted and yet was still free. Jonathan walked me to the door and kissed me on the forehead, threatening to take Peter out himself, given the opportunity.

I couldn't sleep. All I could think about was the demented Peter and what he did to this poor Mary Jennings. I wondered how many of us were out there, victimized by this twisted individual. What went into the making of such a monster? Had his parents abused him as a child? Neglected him? Staring at my bedroom ceiling I recalled Peter mentioning, while in one of his darker moods, how his parents were never there for him. His father's business and mother's charity work left him an orphan for all practical purposes, deposited at boarding schools and summer camps. He once spoke bitterly of how they often sent his birthday gifts late, and failed to visit when he was ill. Frustrated with the boring curriculum and endless dull routine of boarding school, he began to act out as a teenager. His parents only threatened to send him to a strict military academy.

One time when I asked Peter why he went into psychology he laughed and said the phrase "charity begins at home" had been a reverse motto for his mother, who prided herself on running the charitable foundations her wealthy family founded, but where was her empathy for him? That's when he decided to quit acting out and become the brilliant student his teachers always believed he could be, in order to get into a good university and receive an excellent education. Why not? His parents were as generous with money as they were stingy with time. This way he could study the human brain, he told me, and perhaps one day have an answer as to why some parents dote on their offspring, and others are neglectful.

Thinking about Peter was depressing to say the least. I rolled over and tried to think about Jonathan instead, but that only excited my libido. No one since Daniel on the Rogue affected me quite like Jonathan did, and I wondered what might have developed all those years ago, had it not been for Daniel saving my life. I needed to sort out my feelings for this man who felt compelled to serve God so sacrificially. Many who served as priests were not interested in women for a plethora of assorted—or sordid—reasons, but this was obviously not the case with Daniel.

It was easy to defend Daniel's passion for God when in the presence of Jonathan, and when *not* in the presence of Daniel. But being with him sorely confused me. And it wouldn't be fair to lead Jonathan on if I could not put my love for Daniel into an appropriate perspective. What *would* I do if Daniel offered to leave his precious church for me? Run to him with open arms? Possibly. No matter how hard I tried not to listen to this selfish inner voice, I could not completely squelch it.

Did I want Daniel to give up God because I craved complete possession of his soul? Had I become my own kind of monster, needing to be center stage in his life because I had not been with either of my parents? My worst fear was that I was doomed to spend the rest of my life pining away for a man that chose God long before our time together on the Rogue, simply because being second best was my only comfort zone.

These thoughts were not contributing to my ability to sleep. I got up and made myself a mug of herbal tea. Then I sat in the living room on Grams' sofa and wished with all my heart she was there with me. I recalled what she said that afternoon, in a chair on her porch, covered by the afghan I was now wrapped up in. *Love the child, Victoria, with all your heart. Love the child for you and for him and forever. A child has a right to be born, and can never have too much love.*

I suddenly felt very sad that Grams would never know my son. And I angrily resolved that I would not let Peter get to Benjamin, or Daniel. I picked up one of the small sculptures from the end table. My mother Arianna had created it. Running my fingers over the smooth surface of the black onyx was something I had done many times before, but never with such a burden on my heart. I wished that I could speak with my mother just one more time. To ask why she carved this particular piece, this woman intertwined with a man, naked and hugging, their expressions blissful and content. Had she known this type of stable, enduring love? Certainly not with my father.

Tears sprang from nowhere and were soon streaming down my face. Was it because I missed her so? Her laughter, her intensity when sculpting? Or because I had never known such bliss and contentment as this piece of art would suggest can exist between a man and a woman? I had only experienced intense love and intense frustration. Perhaps part of me was grieving because Arianna Winslow never really knew who I was, nor I her. I put the sculpture back on the table and fell asleep on Grams' sofa, still wrapped up in her afghan, and feeling somehow cradled in her love. I knew that wherever she was, Grams was watching over me. As to what my mother was doing, I could not be sure.

The next morning I got a call from Jonathan who wanted to know if I managed to get any sleep. I told him at two a.m. I made a cup of peppermint tea and finally dozed off for a while on the sofa. I shared with him what I remembered about Peter's home life growing up, and how that probably contributed to making him the sick man that he is.

Shedding light on this didn't endear Jonathan to him in the least. Instead he pointed out that many people are not so fortunate as to have a close loving family growing up and still turn out to be stellar human beings.

I sighed deeply. "I think maybe Peter is one of those people whom absolutely no one ever took under their emotional wing, not a single teacher or potential friend. More than likely that can make the difference between sane and psychotic."

"Well, our worst psychotic nightmare has just served papers on you for a paternity suit."

"You're kidding?"

"I wish I were."

"How did Peter know you were my attorney?" I asked, dismayed at this turn of events, as if thinking somehow it would never come to pass, despite his ugly threats.

"Maybe Miranda told him. Tori, make sure you are never alone with this man. He has no need to speak with you again unless it is through me. I represent you. Don't let him in your front door, ever. Call the police. Call Vincent."

"What happens now, Jonathan? Now that he is actively pursuing this ridiculous idea about being Benjamin's father?" I collapsed onto a chair in the kitchen, my adrenalin pumping out of control.

"Now I begin to earn my keep," Jonathan said self-confidently, calming my frazzled sleep depraved nerves with his in-control tone. "And we stall for time. Trust me, Tori, I will keep him jumping through hoops, and I will keep you informed every step of the way. We can do this, without involving Daniel, without any real threat to Benjamin, at least for now. Time is in our favor."

I wanted to believe that with all my heart. But where Peter was concerned, things were never in your favor. I called Miranda after taking my morning run, hoping it would clear my head and allow me to think straight. She confirmed Peter had been to her office. She told him who my attorney was, hoping he would contact Jonathan rather than see me in person. She also made it clear to Peter she no longer considered him a friend. Miranda didn't have the nerve to accuse him of drugging her, but did tell him she regretted their night together.

She was livid about his paternity suit, and not really all that surprised by his history with Mary Jennings. It seemed logical to her that Peter would be capable of murder, since rape is a violent act second only to the taking of a life, and she had always wondered why he left his tenure at the university for a private practice in the city.

All I knew is that I wanted more than anything to stop this man from exposing Daniel or exploiting Benjamin, but how does one reason with the devil?

CHAPTER FIFTEEN

"I would never suggest that I understand women, as I barely know any, certainly none well . . . but you least of all."

Thursday evening I asked Benjamin about his latest painting on the way to Rachel's. He told me the flight position of the dove he was working on pleased him a lot. I knew he had been looking in drawing books, of birds and their skeletal structure, to understand wingspan and positions. I could see how much he was looking forward to an evening at the gallery. His whole face lit up just talking about it.

Benjamin and Rachel were kindred spirits in many ways. They loved to simply admire art, and study it. Rachel kept volumes of books in her private studio where she taught her workshops to children and Benjamin painted his doves. They covered every subject from drawing techniques, to the life's work and biographies of artists from each period in history. He would pour over them and ask her many questions about the different types of art, and the artists themselves, when not studying drawing techniques.

I almost ran a stoplight while listening to Benjamin discuss the wingspan of a dove. My son covered his eyes as we nearly took flight through the windshield. This was just one of many minor infractions I was guilty of in the last several days, given the somber reality of Peter's paternity suit. It was wearing on my mind. It hadn't occurred to me that my nervous condition was disturbing my son, until he questioned me about it.

"Mom, why are you so jittery?"

"Am I jittery?"

"Yes. You haven't been okay ever since you went out with your friend Jonathan."

I looked at Benjamin, who was staring at traffic as if he'd need to help me drive.

"Benj, Jonathan is a very nice man. He has nothing to do with why I am so jittery."

"I know. He's a good soccer player, too. The light's turning green."

"I see it. I'm sorry I haven't been myself lately, Benj. I have a lot on my mind."

"Like what?"

He looked at me with those eyes that mirrored an ocean beside an exotic shore. I wished we were on that shore, in that exotic location, far away from Peter. How could I tell him about the threat he posed for us? There was so much happening lately, and I hadn't shared any of it with Benjamin. At eleven years of age, I just wanted to protect him. I didn't want to tell him his father was a priest, soon to be bishop. I didn't want him to know what Peter did to me, and what he had done to others, and could do again.

"Rachel tells me art dealers are looking at your latest finished painting, and the one you're creating now."

Benjamin shrugged. "I know. But we don't have to sell the paintings, Mom. You can keep them. I want you to have them. Really."

"It's not that, Benj. It is true I am sad when your art sells. I feel like a piece of you is taken away from me." I reached over, mussed his hair and laughed. "And looking at your paintings reminds me that you do something other than play soccer."

"I do lots of things besides play soccer." Benjamin's eye lit up. "Sarah and I are building a fort in the big maple tree behind the shed, next to the dove cages. Mr. Gianni is helping us."

We pulled up to Rachel's gallery and I was relieved for more time to think about what to tell Benjamin concerning Peter. He went straight to the drawing books on Rachel's studio shelves while I asked her about the art dealers. Rachel told me they were from London, and were offering to pay a large amount of money for the doves, even though Rach told them as far as she knew, the doves were not for sale. She added they had brought someone along to do an article on Benjamin, and they weren't taking no for an answer.

"Where are they now, Rachel? How long have they been in Portland?" I leaned heavily on the studio door, my head whirling with Peter and Daniel, and the fact that everything could blow up in our faces. Daniel's well-publicized upcoming appointment as bishop, and Benjamin's growing fame as a child prodigy were all fuel for Peter's paternity suit. Peter was like a shadow of doom threatening to expose and humiliate all of us, allowing scrutiny and ridicule to seep in and cause judgment by the entire world.

"I told you when they arrived, remember?" Rachel gave me an exasperated look. "I called yesterday and said they'd been here all morning asking about Benjamin and wanting to see his work, which I had in the back. I mean, his paintings weren't on display. I wouldn't display them without your permission. But I did show them his work. It seemed like a reasonable request, since they came all the way from London. I told you all this on the phone yesterday. Don't you remember?"

I could tell Rachel was nervous. She probably didn't want to blow it with big gallery dealers from Europe, but didn't want to exploit Benjamin, either. She ran long skinny fingers through her short blonde hair and furrowed her brow while studying Benjamin, who was sprawled on the studio floor with several books opened to pictures of birds in flight.

"It's okay, Rach. I remember. I'm just not myself lately. Peter has slapped me with a paternity suit," I whispered, not wanting Benjamin to hear.

Rachel gave me her full attention. "Oh my god," she whispered back. "What are you going to do?" She glanced at Benjamin. "Does he know about any of this?"

"Nothing. He knows nothing. And I want to keep it that way, at least for now. I have to go, Rach, or I'll be late. We can talk when I get back, okay?"

"Okay." She followed me down the hall and watched me leave. I could see her worried expression through the glass pane on the gallery door as I pulled away from the curb. It was a perfect reflection of how I felt. And I hadn't even shared with Rachel yet the history of Peter the monster. I decided to tell her all about what Robert and Jonathan discovered over a hot cup of tea, after my first Catholicism class.

What in God's precious name was I going to do? I had no idea. Maybe God did. If He wanted Daniel to be bishop, He had better have some creative ideas of His own. I prayed all the way to St. Matthew's, exactly for what, I am not sure, other than for a way to derail Peter before he derailed all of us.

When I entered the cathedral I immediately realized there was some type of service going on. I could hear someone praying out loud and others mumbling in agreement. I stood rigidly in the foyer of the massive church and stared all the way down the red-carpeted aisle to the marbled altar area, afraid I might be noticed and cause them all to lose their focus. Daniel was there, praying over someone. There were several people gathered around sniffling and whimpering.

I crept down the aisle a third of the way, not daring to approach any closer, and slid into a wooden pew. I could see now it was a child Daniel was praying over. The young boy was still, lying on the carpeted altar steps where no doubt his loved ones had laid him. There was a small wheelchair off to the side. Daniel was on his knees, with one hand on the child's forehead, while the other held the boy's hand. I could see in Daniel's eyes the same look my Benjamin had when healing his neighborhood creatures. I could hear the same inflection in his voice while asking God to intervene. Goosebumps broke out on my arms as I realized my Benjamin intuitively knew exactly how to heal the animals, for certainly he had never watched his father heal people.

The little boy, who looked to be about five, was very still and limp until he suddenly began to toss and turn his head, moaning slightly. Soon his eyes popped open and Daniel smiled warmly down at him, still praying, only with less urgency. Daniel whispered something to the young boy I could not hear. Afterwards he picked the child up and handed him to a woman who was obviously the mother. There were two men at her side, possibly the father and maybe an uncle. An older woman stood behind a little, dotting her eyes with a tissue, and I thought she might be the grandmother. Carefully they placed the child back into the wheel chair, and talked softly for several more minutes with Daniel. Then I realized they were turning to depart the church and would be walking past me.

The little boy was wheeled down the red carpet by one of the men, and everybody else followed, somberly, except for the mother who stayed behind and continued to speak with Daniel in hushed, serious tones. The adult entourage took little notice of me, but the child and I had looked into each other's eyes down the entire length of the aisle. His were alert and curious, and filled with pain, and yet there was a peace about him. The same peace Sarah had revealed on her face after Benjamin arrived at her sick bed.

I wanted them to stop the wheelchair and let me speak to the child. I could tell he wanted to know who I was and why I was there. My heart went out to this brave little spirit with the pale cheeks and bright eyes—his dark lashes curling thickly like the ends of his brown tousled hair. Soon the mother hugged Daniel and hurried down the aisle to the foyer where the others waited for her. They left quietly, and Daniel became aware of my presence.

The silence of the large cathedral hung between us as we neither one moved. I had lost my desire to approach Daniel about the religion class beginning this evening. Perhaps my hesitation was from uncertainty as to whether or not I should be interfering with Daniel's life at St. Matthew's.

He slowly walked down the aisle toward me and stopped when he reached my pew. "Tori. What brings you here to the house of God on a Thursday night? Surely it is not to see me."

I motioned for him to sit beside me, which he did, hesitantly. "Daniel, I'm sorry I left so abruptly after our lunch. One reason I came tonight is to apologize for that."

"I see. And why else have you come?"

"I've decided to take the Catholicism classes you spoke of."

Daniel was silent. He stared at the altar area a long distance in front of us, and I thought he seemed drained, almost depressed. Maybe the healings did that to him, which prompted my next question.

"Daniel, who was that sweet boy in the wheelchair? Will he be all right?"

More silence, and then he looked at me, his cyan eyes appearing weary. "His name is Zachary Quinn. I don't know if he will be all right. Only time will tell. Tori, the classes were cancelled. It being summer and all, there wasn't much interest."

"I see. What's wrong with Zachary? Do you often do individual healings?"

Daniel sighed, and his vision swept over all of me as if drinking in every detail of my form, but then he locked his gaze on the altar again, its massive marbled presence somewhat dwarfed and humbled from this distance.

"Tori, you show up here after I have come to believe you are lost to me again forever, looking painfully beautiful, and wanting to take our classes.

I would never suggest that I understand women, as I barely know any, certainly none well . . . but you least of all."

"Painfully beautiful? What does that mean, exactly?"

"It means I hurt all over looking at you, knowing I cannot touch you, or have you be a part of my life." He glanced at me. "Yet, I have been miserable ever since you stormed out of it Sunday afternoon. I have prayed you would return, and I have prayed that you would not. Exactly how the last twelve years have gone, only intensified by our recent reunion."

I didn't know what to say to this. I hadn't been expecting such honesty. Until this moment I had not thought much about the pain of his predicament, having focused exclusively on my own. I wanted to crawl into his lap and run my fingers through his golden hair while kissing those pouting lips, but instead I persisted about Zachary, who had stolen what was left of my heart in his short dramatic visit.

"What was wrong with that precious child, Daniel? Can't you tell me?"

"Ignore me then. I deserve as much." Daniel paused. "Zachary has a brain tumor. His only hope is for it to shrink instead of grow, just as I wish my love for you would do."

"Have you ever cured anyone of that?"

"Of loving another beyond all reason and accountability? No."

"Daniel, I want you to tell me this child will not die."

"I am not God, Tori."

"Maybe not. But you are more than what you say you are."

Daniel lifted his head and looked at me. "What do I say that I am?"

"A humble servant of God. From my viewpoint, there is nothing humble about your healing powers."

Daniel sighed. "Perhaps not. But they come at a great price."

"What price? Surely being a priest is a choice, is it not?"

"Tori, I was visited recently by a man named Peter Cairns."

I felt my heart skip several beats. "Peter?"

"You do know him then?"

"Yes."

"Is it true he is the father of your son?"

I stared into Daniel's strange blue eyes, looking quite vulnerable. I wondered if fear and dread showed in mine, as he studied me.

"No. He isn't the father."

"He claims to be. He says he has had to serve you with a paternity suit in order to see his son and be a part of his life. He knows you have been attending church here and wanted me to speak with you, plead with you really, on his behalf to do the right thing and let him see his boy."

I was speechless. I sat back in the pew and stared at the alter, until finding my voice to respond. "And you believed him? Just like that, you decided this stranger who claims to be the father of my child must be, because *you are not?*"

Daniel didn't respond, but his expression showed confusion.

"Has it occurred to you that many men might like to be the father of a child whose paintings have sold collectively for hundreds of thousands of dollars?" I asked, more angry than fearful at this point, concerning Peter's audacity to visit Daniel.

"You worked for this Peter, that summer . . . the summer of the Rogue trip. Did you not?" Daniel still looked confused, but I was done explaining.

I had nothing further to say in God's house about Peter, or Benjamin's paternity. I only hoped that one man would rot in hell and the other would not for their involvement in the matter. Standing somewhat indignantly, I shuffled past Daniel despite my head feeling light and my stomach woozy. He stood and caught me as I tried to slip by him. Holding my shoulders with his strong hands he looked into my eyes, which I am sure showed frustration and despair.

"Let me go, Daniel."

He didn't release me. Instead he pulled me to him and kissed me long and hard. I did not resist. I wanted to, but I couldn't, because my feelings for Daniel were well beyond my control. He had such an effect on me I felt helpless to fight him, nor did I want to. Melting into his arms and becoming one with him was what I wanted, had wanted for a long time. Apparently his own feelings were running just as rampant or surely he would not be so bold as to blatantly sin in God's house.

Every part of my body came alive with that kiss, and ached for his naked flesh against mine again, as it had been long ago beside the Rogue River, but we were not drawn together amidst nature's paradise by near tragedy this time, we were instead reeling against hurt and anger, untruths and half-truths. It did not diminish our inexplicable attraction to one another's very souls.

We both jumped at the sound of a pipe organ and pulled ourselves apart as the chandeliers high above us began to glow softly. A little gray haired woman had begun practicing her hymns for Sunday, and did not see us even now.

I hurried down the aisle and out the door without so much as another glance into Daniel's face, grateful he did not follow.

CHAPTER SIXTEEN

Is free will only an illusion?

Benjamin was painting in the studio when I arrived back at the gallery. I had let myself in with the master key I kept, in case there should ever be an emergency while Rachel was away with Robert. They always went to New York in the fall, Maui in the winter and Rome in the spring. Fortunately for Robert, his wife didn't like to travel with him on business, and although these weren't really business trips, Robert made them appear so. The family did take a vacation every year, usually to Florida where his wife's mother lived, and where conveniently, Disney World was located.

Were it not for their two little girls, I was fairly certain Robert and his wife had nothing in common considering the lack of time they spent together. Robert put in many long hours as a criminal lawyer, rarely getting home before eight o'clock, according to Rachel. His weekends were generally spent researching cases, since court often tied up his week otherwise. Any spare time he had was spent with Rachel in dark out-of-the-way places.

Rachel joined me in the studio and we admired Benjamin's latest painting together. It seemed incredible to me how a young boy could simulate motion with only a few tubes of acrylics and an imagination set in flight. His doves were always white against a stark blue-gray sky, yet the position of the bird in flight, the placing of it on the canvas, the light protruding from beneath the carefully stroked paint, was almost as if from heaven above. It played with your emotions, creating an urge to crawl inside the canvas and be one with God's grace, peace, and hope . . . all there, exposed eloquently through the gentle winged creature soaring upward.

I kissed Benj on the cheek and told him his painting made me cry, wiping a tear as Rachel and I slipped away for a cup of tea in the kitchen.

"I didn't think you'd be back so soon." Rachel turned on her teakettle and rummaged through cabinets.

"The classes were cancelled, due to lack of interest. I guess nobody wants to tie their summer up with the sticky business of theology." I sat down at the table.

After glancing my way several times while fussing with her tea containers, Rachel sat beside me. "What happened at St. Matthew's, Tori? You look really rattled."

I didn't know where to begin. My head was still focused on Daniel's kiss, and my guts were churning from the fear of his effect on me, my helplessness to control myself in his presence. I wasn't a pious person, or even sure where I stood with God—if I stood with Him at all—but nonetheless, completely derailing His plans for Daniel was not something I wanted to be a part of. Or did I? That was the confusing part, the part that had me worried more for my soul than for Daniel's.

"It's just everything, Rach. Has Robert said anything to you about Peter?" I studied her face, but there was no sign of knowledge about the evil predator.

"No. Robert doesn't reveal privileged client information, even when it's a friend of mine."

"He's a murderer. He killed a college girl."

We stared at each other.

"Who? When? Why isn't he in jail?" Rachel got up to grab the whistling teakettle and poured the boiling water over the mesh ball of loose leaves carefully mixed and placed in her blue china pot.

"Because they couldn't prove it. The authorities decided it was suicide, but we both know he killed her, just as surely as he drugged and raped me, and Miranda, and God above knows who else." I told her all about poor Mary Jennings and it took our first cup of tea to wade through the horror of it, and the terror of realizing his availability to strike again.

"Does Daniel know about this paternity suit, and what happened at St. Matthew's to upset you so? Come clean with me, Victoria." Rachel poured us each more tea. It smelled of cinnamon and cloves.

"Well to answer your first question, yes, Daniel knows about the paternity suit. Peter actually came to see him."

"You're kidding." Rachel's eyes were as big as the saucers beneath our ornate cups.

"I wish I were kidding. Daniel seems so hurt by the whole idea of me being with someone else . . . so soon after our affair."

"But you weren't, at least not by choice. He only thinks you were. Why don't you tell him the truth, Tori, and let him decide for himself if he still wants to be a priest? Maybe he'd rather be your husband, and Benjamin's father."

"No. I can't tell him the truth about our son. Don't you see? Daniel might very well choose Benjamin and me over his calling, but he would never be happy. He would never forgive me for coming between him and the church. How could he? Watching him heal that little boy . . . it was so apparent that he must do what he does." I nibbled on a chocolate cookie from the plateful baked earlier by Rach and Benj.

"He could still serve God, Tori, and heal people. The Catholic Church doesn't have a corner on the whole Christian market."

"You haven't seen him the way I have. In St. Matthew's leading a mass, or healing someone. It's his life. When I first discovered him there a couple months ago, he said to me *this is what I am, what I must be.* And I don't doubt it for a minute."

"You still haven't told me what happened tonight." Rachel studied my face while slowly biting her second cookie.

"He kissed me."

"Oh my god . . ."

"In the sanctuary, no less."

"Are you joking?"

"No, and I doubt that God finds it at all amusing."

"I doubt it too." Rachel was still studying me. "What was it like?"

"It was wonderful. And scary, and . . . Rach, I have also kissed Jonathan recently."

"So your date went well." Rachel smiled, as if pleased by this news.

"Yes, considering Peter was our main topic of conversation."

"How was it?"

"How was what?"

"Jonathan's kiss."

I took a deep breath, feeling flushed with all this talk of kissing. "It's warm in here."

"You liked it, didn't you?"

"Liked what?"

"Jonathan's kiss!"

"Okay, yes. It was also wonderful. But different." I paused and stared into my steaming tea. "What am I doing, Rachel? This is my life and I have no idea where I'm going with it. All I know is I can't let Peter ruin Daniel's chance to be bishop. I can't tell him of his son or he will be torn and tortured over decisions made and not made, and haven't we all beaten ourselves up enough over sins of the past?"

"I'm not sure it's your place to make that call for someone else." Rachel leaned forward and touched my arm. "Be careful Tori, not to hurt Jonathan in the middle of all this. I know he's been crazy about you ever since the Rogue trip."

My gaze shifted to the cupboard above my head and eyed the many delicate and distinctively different cups lined up neatly on the shelf. Rachel liked pretty things. Breakable things. She needed little girls to play with. Beautiful little blondes like herself, like Robert's girls, in the wrong house with the wrong mother. Funny how fate can mess everything up, how certain decisions can haunt us forever. Do we truly have a choice in the scheme of things? Is free will only an illusion? Like the lies we learn to live with? Truth was often so much harder to accept than lies. Certainly my everyday reality was not for the faint of heart, nor Rachel's.

"It's funny, Tori," Rachel mused, running her manicured nails over the rim of the fine china cup, "how our lives are so disheveled from one little rafting trip. Almost as if the devil himself had sat among us at campfire and toyed irreversibly with our minds and hearts."

"Would you wish it away?" I asked.

"The Rogue trip? Certainly not. I would rather have pieces of Robert than to never have met him." Rachel's eyes were sparkling at the thought of Robert.

"Me too. I feel privileged to know Daniel, however limited our time spent together." I took a sip of my tea and gazed into the darkness outside the window. "And I thank God every day for Benjamin, despite not always being pleased with our Maker's decision-making."

"Tori, speaking of Benjamin—these art dealers, they mean business."

Rachel put her hand on top of mine.

"Fine. It's okay to sell the paintings." I pulled my hand out from under hers and finished my tea.

"It's not just that. They want an exclusive feature on Benjamin, the child prodigy behind the artwork. You aren't going to be able to hold the world at bay much longer," Rachel warned. "I think maybe your son could turn into a phenomenon. People *need* inspiration, and certainly, Benjamin's paintings are inspiring . . . not to mention the story of his life, Tori, think about it. *Poor fatherless child from the inner city is an artistic genius at only eleven years old.*"

I sighed and folded my arms on the table, resting my head in them wearily, while praying silently for strength to endure this. My child could soon be quite renowned. How would I keep his healing powers a secret? How would I keep his life safe and uninhibited, building forts and playing soccer—especially with Peter lurking about?

Rachel and I agreed we should cooperate with the London magazine. If we didn't, we feared they would write whatever they wished and dig up the information wherever they could.

I spoke with Benjamin about the art dealers from London and the promotional article on the way home. He was fine with everything. Benjamin was more interested in discussing his fort, which several weeks later was up to Vincent's standards for he, Sarah, and Benjamin to sleep in.

They decided their campout would be that Saturday night. It was excitedly discussed around Grams' solid oak table while the three of them cut out pictures and articles for Benjamin's new scrapbook about his paintings. The scrapbook had been Vincent's idea, and I was sorry I hadn't thought of it myself. I was so proud of Benjamin and his beautifully painted doves. I only wished his fame would not invade our private lives.

Having been fearful of everything concerning the discovery of Benjamin's paintings, I had to admit I was pleased with the article done for the magazine in London when it finally appeared. It was impressive to see my son on the cover, but our phone was ringing nonstop again because of an article about it in *The Oregonian*. It spoke about how the Zimmermans had discovered Benjamin. The couple had been respected art critics for the last four decades, first on the East Coast, and later on the West Coast. They had now retired in Portland. Apparently they had some influence abroad as well, since London had taken note of their opinion about my son's newly discovered genius.

I peered over Sarah's shoulder as they cut and arranged the pictures and articles about Benj and the doves from last month, this new *Oregonian* article, and the London magazine spread. We also had pictures I took at Rachel's art gallery of Benjamin and his work when he entered the local art show that brought all this about to begin with. But then something caught my eye in *The Oregonian*, on the page right before Benjamin's latest article. It was a heading with the name Zachary Quinn. Why did that name sound familiar? Of course, it was the little boy from a few weeks ago that Daniel had been trying to heal. I picked up the page and studied it carefully, while only half listening to Sarah and Benjamin planning their upcoming adventure in the fort.

The article was about how Zachary, the son of the mayor, had been prayed over by Daniel Rosselli, *the healing priest soon to be appointed bishop, in none other than Rome, Italy, at St Peter's, by personal invitation of the Pope.* It would seem that five-year-old Zachary's brain tumor was in complete remission, and if it continued to shrink at such a fast rate from his chemo treatments, he might possibly be able to attend kindergarten next month, which was Zachary's one big goal . . . to go to school in September with his friends. I stared at the words on the page and could barely hear Vincent speaking to me.

"Tori . . . is everything okay? You look pale suddenly. Do you know Zachary? Isn't it wonderful he is doing so well?"

"Yes it is. I don't know the little boy, but I was there quite by accident during his healing mass. Do you know him?"

"I met Zachary when I did some tile work for the mayor's house. He was diagnosed while I was working on that project. The family was quite devastated."

I looked up from the article. Vincent was sitting in front of the sun-flooded window. He looked like Moses, with his gray hair and beard. I think wisdom oozed from him in a calm and quiet way. I loved watching him with the doves and rarely thought about his gift for laying tile. His work was admired and sought after, and he would pick and choose his tile-laying jobs to suit his own needs for time and interest.

I wanted to ask Vincent what he thought about Daniel and the healing mass, and if he believed it caused this remission. Then it occurred to me that Vincent probably knew about my history with Daniel, and that he was Benjamin's father. I felt sure Maggie hadn't kept this from him, as they were not the type of couple to ever keep secrets from one another. I also knew Vincent rarely attended mass with her, but was clearly a man of faith—even if a reclusive one.

The phone rang and I lost my opportunity to question Vincent any further. Miranda had been reading the paper and was calling to check out the news about Benjamin. She had also seen the article on Daniel. We discussed both for a while, and then she changed the subject after a sigh and a heavy pause.

"Tori, Jonathan called me and I have been to his office."

"Why?"

"Because he knows about Peter . . . about what he did to me, you told him . . . remember? But that's okay, because if pressing charges will help you and Benjamin, I'm all for it."

"How is that going to help? If Peter has no hope of getting custody of Benjamin, there is nothing to stop him from exposing Daniel as the father."

"Jonathan seems to feel if Peter is in prison, no one will believe anything he says about Daniel."

"You'd be willing to take him to trial for rape, which will destroy your own personal life and hard earned private practice, just to spare me from his nasty threats about custody rights and exposing Daniel as the father if he isn't? That's very touching, Miranda, but I don't need a sacrificial lamb."

"I have a successful practice and a no-nonsense attitude for which I am proud and somewhat famous here locally. I can display a brave front and live down the gossip with little to no permanent emotional damage, or damage to my practice."

Miranda shot this back at me in her best lawyer voice.

I could hear the kitchen scrapbooking crew stomping out the back door and assumed their task was complete. I had no idea what to say to Miranda, but I was suddenly angry with Jonathan. There was silence for a minute across the phone line as we both pondered the awkward position this monster Peter had put us in.

"I kept the note, you know . . . the one where he thanked me for the great time. It matches Mary Jennings' note almost word for word. And yours, but unfortunately, you didn't keep yours," she added, in a softer tone.

There was more silence and then I forced myself to speak.

"Nobody's as brave as you pretend to be when it comes to a rape trial in which you were the victim." I tried to keep a calm steady voice, but I was literally seething beneath it.

"The point would be that we'd done everything possible to stop this evil man." She was still using her attorney tone. Miranda was a consummate professional at keeping her cool.

"How can Jonathan believe that feeding you to the lions will be in the best interest of me, Benjamin, and Daniel? Does he really think convicting Peter of rape will discredit any statements he might make about Daniel? Once a thought is put in people's minds, they don't easily forget it regardless of who said it, or how discreditable they are. And then there are those who will go digging until they've dug up every ounce of dirt they can find, stomping out what's left of our sanity in the process. Not to mention dirtying Daniel's unblemished record for servant of God extraordinaire." I was pacing the floor, and I knew I sounded angry.

"What I know is that someone needs to stop him. Have you thought about how he could rape more women? Maybe kill again? With my coming forward, Jonathan believes he has enough on the guy to put him away. The whole Mary Jennings incident will cinch it, circumstantial, unofficial, off-the-record evidence or not. It's worth a try, Victoria."

Emotion had crept into her voice.

"I can't think about this anymore right now, Andi. Promise you won't press charges before I talk to Jonathan."

"Okay. Talk to him. I'll come too if you want."

"Thanks, Andi."

I had just hung up the phone when it rang again. It was St. Matthew's. They were having a class after all, and it started this evening at seven. Daniel must have given them my name.

I thought it would be rude to decline the offer, not willing to admit to myself that I did indeed wish to go.

CHAPTER SEVENTEEN

"What do you mean . . . exposed with the rest of you?"
Daniel asked, but Jonathan and I didn't answer.

I quickly changed into something conservative for the class at church. I told Benjamin, who was playing soccer in the street with several other neighborhood children, to hang out at Sarah's until I returned. Looking in the mirror one final time, I concluded my long flowery summer skirt was sheer and clingy, but covered me at least, and my blouse had a scoop neck but stopped short of cleavage. Even the most prudish nun would have to admit I was acceptable.

I stopped by the Gianni home before driving to St Matthew's, to be sure Benjamin was welcome. Trying not to think about my annoyance with Jonathan over Miranda, I concentrated on the unusually heavy evening traffic as I drove to the church. Hesitating near the entrance to the cathedral, I realized that I was never sure of what I might discover inside the doors. This time it was choir practice. Harmonizing voices greeted me as soon as I pulled on one of the heavy brass handles.

I stood in the foyer and listened to the beautiful hymn being sung by what were surely angels, their notes floating sweetly in the air with heartfelt emotion. My eyes drank in the heavy oil canvases adorning the walls, each depicting a different Biblical scene, and all of them painted in a dramatic soul-searching way. It was as if the music were coming from within the pictures, driving the actions of the characters painted there.

So mesmerized by the music and art was I, it took great effort to think about my purpose for coming. I forced myself to focus on where classes might be held, and noticed for the first time a narrow hallway to the right of the entrance. Entering cautiously I soon discovered an open office at the far end, past many richly varnished doors, all of them closed tight, and offering no sounds or light from within.

Inside the open office at the end of the hallway Daniel sat behind a walnut desk, reading. I stood quietly at the door, not sure if I should disturb him or not. The room was spacious but cozy with neat rows of old, worn-looking books on several matching bookshelves made of walnut like the desk. A stone fireplace sat between two brown leather chairs, and the fireplace was obviously used quite a bit in cooler weather. I suspected June through August was its only time of rest.

He looked up, as if feeling my presence. The setting sun was seeping into the room from a small window behind him. It bled oranges and purples like the stained glass windows on the opposite side of the church, where I touched the face of Mary and wished for peace with God. If Daniel could not find peace with God, what hope was there for me?

"Tori. You came." He walked over to greet me.

"I didn't mean to invite myself into your office, but the hallway ends here, and I have no idea where the class is to be held. You know the church called me about a class?"

"Please, Tori, come over and sit down. Yes, I did have Sister Margaret call you."

Daniel didn't have his black robe on. He wore jeans and a navy t-shirt. I wondered if he always hung out so casually when not performing some Godly duty. I was glad he hadn't looked this approachable when he kissed me after the healing mass, or perhaps I wouldn't have run away so quickly.

"Where is this class? And how many of us are there so eager to save our souls?" I smiled, but Daniel remained serious as I sat in the leather chair facing his desk.

"Actually, there's only you. I hope you don't mind, but I have some free time on Thursday evenings right now and thought I'd just teach you myself. If that's okay."

"Daniel, that's very generous of you, but I don't know if it's a good idea." I got up and began examining the books on his shelves, reading the titles at eye level.

"Tori . . . I'm sorry, about the other night. I promise to behave like a priest, pious and informative." Daniel stood and walked over to the shelf I was examining. "It's my penitence to myself . . . doing what is right by you."

"Oh really." I looked at him. "And so in a way spending time with me is your punishment?"

"It's more like practicing self discipline, by abstaining from touching you."

"Do you have this problem a lot? Because maybe you shouldn't be a priest if you do." I grinned at him, but Daniel was determined to be somber.

"No. I never have this particular problem, and believe me, I would never make it as a priest if I did."

I pulled a book off the shelf. It was an old leather-bound Bible, and I carefully opened it. The pages were so thin and frail I was afraid to touch them.

"That Bible belonged to my grandfather, in Italy. He was a priest, too. He ended up a cardinal."

"A cardinal? Does that mean your father was born *before* he entered the priesthood?" I wanted to suggest denial and illegitimacy ran in his family, but restrained myself.

"No. It seems my grandfather spent his entire life loving a woman secretly . . . my grandmother. It is rather sad, her having to always live in the shadows, raising her child alone with her lie until my father was old enough to share in the burden of it."

"Your father was a physician, wasn't he?"

"Yes, how did you know that?"

"Jonathan told me."

"When did you see Jonathan?"

"Recently. We've . . . become reacquainted."

"I see." Daniel looked puzzled, as if he didn't really see at all.

I closed the Bible carefully and handed it to him, fearful I might somehow abuse the fragile pages.

"Daniel, about Peter. He . . . isn't Benjamin's father. I did work for him, but we were not . . . we didn't date."

"He seems to feel he can prove it, if need be." Daniel held the book with both hands and leaned his shoulder against the shelf. I thought he looked like a college boy with his casual clothes and flaxen curls, showing no signs of aging since the Rogue trip. I wondered if he still played soccer to keep in such good shape.

"No," I answered emphatically, "he can't prove he's Benjamin's father . . . because he isn't."

"Then why not use DNA samples to back up your statement? He claims you won't allow it."

I sat down in one of the two leather chairs facing the fireplace.

"Tori, there's no reason to let this man harass you and your son. Why not just say who the father is? Why are you protecting him?" He hesitated, and then added, "Is he a married man?"

I stood to leave, not wanting to become upset in front of Daniel, who was looking more hurt than self-righteous, but still his words were hard for me to take. I turned to go when spying Jonathan at the door.

"Daniel, you have no idea what you're talking about."

Daniel turned, startled. "Jonathan. What are *you* doing here?"

"I came to see you about Peter's visit. Rachel told me he had been here."

"Rachel?"

"Yes. You remember Rachel, from the Rogue? I doubt there's much you've forgotten about the Rogue trip, is there Daniel?"

We all stood awkwardly silent, me with a hand on the leather chair, not sure whether to sit back down or bolt for the door. Daniel was at the bookcase looking puzzled, still holding the antique Bible of his grandfather the cardinal, while Jonathan loomed in the doorway as an unapologetic intruder.

Finally Daniel broke the silence. "I do wonder what happened after the Rogue trip to cause all this concern over the boy's father. Surely, Tori, you haven't purposefully kept Benjamin and his father from knowing each other? Can't you see how selfish and unfair that would be?"

"What right have you to judge her? Especially about what is selfish and unfair? Surely, Daniel, you would not be throwing the first stone!" Jonathan sounded more annoyed than angry. He looked every bit the attorney in his gray silk suit as he and Daniel quietly stared each other down.

It was Daniel who broke the silence. "Why is Peter's visit to me of any concern to *you*, Jonathan?"

"Because I represent Tori in the paternity suit."

"Oh really. And how can I be of any help to you with that?" Daniel asked, while placing the cherished book back on the shelf.

I tried not to look at them while seated again in the chair facing the fireplace. Daniel hovered near the bookshelf crammed with hardbound books, while Jonathan remained in the doorway, as if guarding it like some sort of sentinel.

"You can help, Daniel, by not encouraging Peter to pursue this ridiculous paternity suit. Trust me when I tell you he's a sorry lowlife bastard," Jonathan added.

Daniel sat down in the chair next to mine. "This Peter struck me as being well educated and quite intelligent. What point would there be in pursuing custody of a child that could not at least potentially be his?" He looked at me, waiting for an answer.

"Benjamin could potentially be Peter's, from his perspective," I admitted. "But I was already pregnant before we . . . were together."

"Tori, have you bothered to mention that Peter is a rapist and possibly a murderer?" Jonathan asked, in an impatient tone. He finally left the doorway, seating himself behind Daniel's desk.

"A rapist?" Daniel asked with alarm.

Jonathan and I were silent. I knew this moment would have come sooner or later. I could not keep the truth about Peter a secret from Daniel, especially if Miranda was pressing charges for rape.

"Tori, did he *rape* you?"

"I don't remember my night with Peter. It doesn't matter. The only thing that matters is that Benjamin is not his child." I knew my tone was sharp, but this was not a subject I cared to examine with Daniel, and pity was something I wanted from him least of all. It angered me that Jonathan was here divulging this information.

I walked over to face my attorney. "What is this Miranda tells me about a possible rape trial?"

"Miranda from our Rogue trip?" Daniel slowly rose from his chair. "Peter has raped her too?"

Jonathan and I looked at Daniel.

"Yes," we both replied in unison.

I wanted to tell Jonathan, sitting there behind the massive walnut surface cluttered with papers, how worried I was for Miranda. How I didn't appreciate his convincing her to press charges, and how if Peter exposed

Daniel as the father out of revenge, people wouldn't dismiss it as easily as Jonathan might hope. But what I actually said was, "I don't want Andi on a witness stand. Nothing good can come of it."

"It could get the sonofabitch locked up!" Jonathan answered emphatically.

"Or it could cause him to lash out in revenge and Miranda will have put everything on the line just to be exposed with the rest of us," I reasoned.

"What do you mean . . . exposed with the rest of you?" Daniel asked, but Jonathan and I didn't answer.

"Why don't you tell him what you mean by that, Tori?"

"Go to hell," I whispered.

"Telling him would take away all of Peter's power over you," Jonathan added.

"You know why we can't do that. Have you forgotten? Does it mean so little to you how he might not accomplish this thing that matters so greatly to him?" I asked, hoping Daniel wouldn't figure out it was him I spoke of.

Jonathan shrugged. "*You* are my first concern . . . as my client," he added carefully.

We continued to stare each other down as Daniel approached the desk. "If this is something that concerns me, please be frank about it."

I forced myself to look up at Daniel, who appeared to be genuinely troubled.

"Never mind," I said, and then I left, hoping neither of them would follow.

CHAPTER EIGHTEEN

"Why look up a man who chose not to see you again, just to tell him
you had a reason to see him every day for the rest of his life?"

Angry and frustrated, I drove like a reckless teenager all the way home. When I called the Gianni house Benjamin pleaded to spend the night and I let him. After making a cup of herbal tea to calm my nerves, I sat on the front step and listened to the crickets chirping. The August evening was sultry and warm, and watching the clear sky bright with stars helped me gather some inner peace.

I finished my tea and thought perhaps I should go in because it was nearly ten p.m., when a car pulled up. It was Jonathan in his little silver convertible, recognizable for its unique look in my neighborhood. Two-seater sports cars with the top down, shamelessly exposing leather seats, wasn't the norm for where I lived. He turned off the engine and sat there for a minute, looking at me on the porch step. Finally he got out and walked over. He'd removed his jacket and tie, and looked a lot less formal and intimidating. I still wore my long flowery skirt, and was glad I hadn't changed into my comfy running shorts and t-shirt.

"May I sit down?" he asked humbly.

"Hello, Jonathan."

He sat next to me when I didn't object, and we both looked at the stars for a minute, without speaking.

"Tori, I'm sorry if I upset you back there in Daniel's office."

"Did he tell you why I was there?"

"Yes, he did, after you left. I promised him I would convince you to come back for the religious lessons and you would call him to set up a time."

"Did you tell him . . . about Benjamin?"

"Of course not. Did you really think I would?"

"No. I just wanted to hear you say it."

"I told Daniel none of this had anything to do with him. That Peter just wanted the money from the paintings and . . . well, I did tell him Benjamin's father was not a married man. I didn't see any reason for him to think the worst of you. That's all I said about it. I'm not going to lie to him. I think you should be straight with Daniel about Benjamin. But that's your call."

"I can't do that, Jonathan. Don't you see? He would never accept this position as bishop if I told him about Benjamin. He would only feel guilty and torn about his commitment to God, and what good would that do?"

"Maybe he'd be thrilled to have a reason to walk away from his cumbersome responsibilities in the church. Maybe he'd be more than happy to walk away with you into the sunset and raise Benjamin."

"You know Daniel as well as I do. That wouldn't be the case. The church is his whole life . . . by choice."

"If that's true, then why is he so tortured over your return after all these years?"

"I never left. I've been here all along, just a few blocks and several worlds away."

"Did you *ever* try to get in touch with him? I mean, back when you first found out you were pregnant?"

"No. Why look up a man who chose not to see you again, just to tell him you had a reason to see him every day for the rest of his life?"

"Good point." We both admired the stars for another minute, and then Jonathan said, "I think you've finally convinced me there is no future between you and Daniel."

I took a good look at him, sitting next to me star gazing. "Is that what you needed me to do? Convince you I'm not going to mess up Daniel's life? Because I got the impression that's exactly what *you* were trying to do back there in his office."

Jonathan didn't respond, and we were both silent again until he got up the nerve to continue this awkward conversation.

"Look, Tori, it's just that I care about you. And I care about Daniel, and if there's a chance you might actually end up a couple, then I need to know now."

"I've told you all along that my goal here is for Daniel to become bishop."

"I'm just not sure how serious you are about that, Tori."

"What do you mean?"

"If he got down on one knee and offered to give it all up for you, what would you say then? That's what I mean."

I rose to my feet and so did Jonathan. We stared into each other's eyes. His were vulnerable and even a little fearful, causing me to feel less defensive.

"Jonathan, it is my intention to protect Daniel's special calling from God, but feelings can sometimes get in the way of the best intentions, so to answer your question, I honestly don't know what I would do, I mean, if Daniel offered to leave the church for me."

He was silent, pondering my answer, and I felt moved by his obvious dilemma over this. For some reason, I had other feelings standing there so near to him, feelings that made me want to kiss him. Instead I blurted out, "I don't really anticipate that happening . . . Daniel offering to leave the church for me, and anyway, sometimes—like now—I'm even less sure than ever what I want . . . I mean, right now I think I want . . ."

"What?" Jonathan moved closer and touched my face.

". . . you to kiss me." And he did, almost before I finished the sentence. This time it wasn't over too soon. It lasted awhile, and we leaned up against the door and enjoyed kissing until it became dangerously hard not to go any further, so we quit and just held each other until our hearts stopped racing. Then Jonathan pulled out his cell phone.

"What's your number?"

I told him and he entered it into his phone.

"Put my private number in yours, Tori, in case Peter tries to bother you, and no one closer is available."

I grabbed my cell phone from my pocket and put his number in it. "I feel safer already. Thanks."

"Just promise me you'll keep it close and use it if Peter ever comes near you again."

"I promise."

Jonathan looked so serious.

"What if I just want to talk? Can I call then too?" I asked, grinning.

"Please do." He smiled. "You can even ask me out to dinner. I love it when girls do that."

"Really? When's the last time that happened?"

"It's been awhile."

He kissed me on the forehead and then he was gone. I watched his little sports car turn the corner and then looked up at the stars one more time before going inside. I locked and bolted the door behind me, slightly fearful at the thought of another visit from Peter. Laying my phone on the nightstand, I fell asleep feeling relieved to know Jonathan was only a phone call away.

Early the next morning I had a photo shoot at the Old Grist Mill. It was tucked away on the Columbia River, in rural Washington, and they wanted new brochures to advertise their historical site. While gathering up my photography equipment I instructed Wil and Benjamin not to eat the brownies I had made for the soccer party later. They'd been undefeated all summer, and there would be a neighborhood get-together in the park this evening to celebrate. I had unfortunately already planned to do this Grist Mill shoot, and that somehow had turned into a date with Jonathan. We were seeing Miranda after our outing on the river to discuss her possible rape case. Thankfully Wil had offered to spend the day with Benj, and take him to the park later for the party.

Benjamin was so excited about his plans to sleep in the fort with Vincent and Sarah that he couldn't wait to show the tree house to his Uncle Wil, who decided that he and Benjamin should plan their own sleepover in the fort. I reminded them both that Labor Day was next Monday and school started the Tuesday after, while placing some of the cooled brownies in the picnic basket for my date with Jonathan.

"Sleeping in the fort with Uncle Will can be an end-of-summer celebration," Benjamin decided.

"It's okay with me if your Uncle Wil is serious about spending the night in a treehouse." I glanced at my little brother who looked as excited as Benj, and decided little boys never grow up.

Wil grinned. "I do have a favor to ask though."

"Anything for you, little brother," I answered while shoving my gear in a tote bag.

"Can I bring Paige to your barbeque on Labor Day?"

"You mean the Paige from work that you've been dating forever? How long has it been, Wil? Two years?" I asked.

Wil followed me out the front door and watched me cram my tote bag into the trunk of my Jetta.

"That's the one," he answered, helping me lift and arrange the cooler and picnic basket before slamming the trunk shut.

"I'd love for her to come," I told him, smiling. "Are you two finally getting serious?"

Wil looked puzzled. "I don't know. I just think it would be a good idea for her to get to know you and Benjamin better, I mean, we do spend a lot of time together these days, and you're the only family I have, besides Eliza, that is."

I walked around and got into the car. Wil peered down at me from the open window and I smiled up at him. "Are you in love with her, if you don't mind my asking?"

"No, I don't mind. I'm not sure. Maybe."

"Maybe?" I shook my head. "I would think it'd be clear to you after, what, two years of seeing her exclusively?" We stared at each other through the open car window.

"Okay, yes, I do love her. But the thought of marriage scares the hell out of me." Wil watched a car drive by absentmindedly. "Look, Vic, I think I might be ready to settle down and have a couple of great kids like Benjamin, but then again . . ." he quit there as if at a loss for words.

I gave him my exasperated look. "I have no idea what you find scary about coming home every night to a woman who adores you, and wants to have your children."

"Well when you put it like that . . ." he laughed.

"How else is there to put it?" I turned the key in the ignition, dismayed at how our parent's divorce had tainted Wil's view of family life.

"Vic, we need to talk about Benjamin's money from the sale of his paintings . . . how to invest it. Are you busy later?"

"No." I thought about how Benjamin completely dominated Wil's time all morning while I got organized for my photo shoot and picnic at the Grist Mill. Benjamin had shared the new photo album of his growing art career with his Uncle Wil while I cleaned lenses and made tuna sandwiches. Then they were off to see the tree house and the doves. I suddenly had a twinge of guilt for Benjamin's need of a father figure, and a rush of gratitude for how well Wil took care of us both. "Let's talk when I get back later tonight," I suggested.

I put the car in reverse and he waved goodbye as I left. I knew he and Benjamin would find all sorts of things to do on a Saturday afternoon. I wondered if Wil would spend less time with Benj if he married Paige Andersen. But I could only be happy for Wil rather than sad for Benjamin and myself. True love didn't come around that often.

Letting it slip away would be unfortunate.

CHAPTER NINETEEN

He has never taken the time to discover what is out there
beyond his leather-bound books and marble altar.

I sat in my car for a minute and studied Jonathan's home, feeling somewhat out of place in his neighborhood. This was Forest Heights, the most prime real estate to be found anywhere in the city. Million dollar cliff dwellings overlooked the land as if ruling it. Jonathan's home was certainly just like him—architecturally clean, with no unnecessary adornment. It had a strong, solid presence.

His was a traditional three story brick design, with forest-green trim and landscaping that didn't look fragile and hard to maintain. You could easily have put four of my apartments into his house, and yet somehow I didn't feel overly intimidated by Jonathan or his home. Both were inviting and approachable. With this in mind I got out of the car and rang the doorbell, relieved to be greeted by Jonathan himself. I was pleased to discover he had no full time hired help, just a weekly landscaping crew and housecleaning service.

Jonathan gave me a tour of all three stories. I loved the white oak floors with their satiny finish, and the contrasting cherry wood used for most of the trim work. His house nearly pulsated with a strong, calm presence—just as he did. My only comment was that I approved of his carefully chosen pieces of art.

"I'd like to have a photo series here on this wall someday. What do you think?" Jonathan swept his hand over a large area above the fireplace in the front room. "Maybe of something local, and on the river . . . with historical appeal. The old Grist Mill?" We both laughed.

"Well, if there's any hope of that, we need to get there while the lighting is right."

Jonathan took my hint and locked up the house, while I loaded his fly rod and tackle box in my Jetta. He found my CDs in a little black case beside the passenger seat as we crossed the 405 bridge. Approving of my random collection, he made a jazz selection for the player. I commented on how much he was enjoying being chauffeured.

"I never get to relax and watch the scenery," he claimed, "and I almost forgot what a beautiful drive this is."

I agreed with him. Rural Vancouver was full of gently rolling hills and endless green fields. Soon we were on a narrow blacktop road leading to the Grist Mill, which looked the way I remembered it from my childhood, having explored it on several school fieldtrips.

We decided to look through the mill before unpacking the car, both of us suddenly curious about this old landmark building, completely powered by the Columbia River. It sat right on the edge of the riverbank, almost hanging over the side, with water flowing swiftly beneath. Light seeping in the old paned windows created eerie shadows throughout the rough-hewn wooden structure and I couldn't wait to snap my pictures.

Jonathan and I unloaded the car down by the river and laid out a blanket when I had finished the photo shoot. He went fly-fishing and I managed to get some good shots of him with the dense fir trees along the opposite riverbank for a backdrop. After our productive morning of photography and fly fishing, we hauled out the tuna sandwiches from the cooler along with purple grapes, jalapeno potato chips, and a few of the chocolate brownies I'd made for Benjamin's soccer party. Washing it all down with iced tea brewed on my back porch, we talked about our childhoods.

I told Jonathan how ever since I could remember I had admired my mother's passion for sculpting. And then one day I found my own passion for taking pictures. I reminisced about those field trips on a yellow school bus that brought me here without any inkling one day I'd be a photographer, taking note of every shadow and wooden plank.

"It seems ironic to me now," I admitted, "that my mother and I were so much alike and yet I barely knew her. I think she was so caught up in her world of art that there wasn't much left for us children. Eliza and Wil scrambled for what little of her spare time they could manage to dominate, while I held back and watched their interactions from afar. My mother and I were alike in that way—reserved, not your social butterfly—yet she held this amazing energy about her. It radiated out and warmed everything it touched, making her somewhat intoxicating to those near her."

"Then she was exactly as you are," Jonathan commented.

I looked at him. "I'm caught up in my photography, I'll admit, but I try very hard to not let Benjamin feel slighted by it."

"You are a wonderful mother to Benjamin. That's not what I meant."

"What then?" I asked, almost defensively, partially afraid of how I might mirror my mother, whom I admired greatly, but saw fatal flaws in as well.

"The energy, the warmth. You are every bit as intoxicating as your mother might have been. Just ask Daniel." Jonathan smiled.

"Very funny." I smiled back at him. "I didn't mean that her energy won her hopeless love from helpless victims. If it did, she did not speak of such things to me."

"Is that what you think Daniel is? Hopeless and helpless?"

"In a way, you know that he is. Daniel doesn't really understand anything except the Catholic Church. He has never taken the time to discover what is out there beyond his leather-bound books and marble altar. Taking that away from him would destroy his sense of purpose." I shuddered thinking about the power Peter held over Daniel's every aspiration for his life's work in the church. It didn't seem fair that his one small sin of loving me should inflict such irreversible damage.

"My mother loved my father," I said, trying desperately not to dwell on thoughts of Daniel and Peter. "I know she did. It was evident in her face and in her behavior when they were together. But I don't think his love was enough for her. I think it's why he fell in love with his receptionist, because she could give him the undivided attention he craved. Arianna was more in love with her art, and her artist friends. Perhaps one or two men artists in particular." I smiled, and paused, picking a tiny yellow flower at my feet.

"I have no reason to believe they were more than friends," I continued, "but Father was always jealous of them nonetheless, and jealous of the way she would commit to a project with abandon. It depended on where her stream of consciousness was with a piece of artwork, as to whether or not she could tear herself away to spend time with him." I lay back on the blanket and stared at the treetops, thinking about how Daniel was also preoccupied with a passion that consumed him, only in his case it was the church.

"My parents had a solid marriage, and they still do," Jonathan admitted, "but it lacked the passion your whole life has been surrounded by." He leaned back on his arms. "I haven't married, I think, because although I've found women I could have a happy, ordered life with, I just seem to crave something more. Something spontaneous and exciting, unpredictable if you will."

He paused and I could feel him looking at me, as I watched a heron fly along the river. "I'm not sorry I went into law," he continued, "although at one point I considered rebelling against the long Davis line of attorneys. Nonetheless I couldn't have survived in New York, where you go to the same parties and events that your parents have gone to for generations, and listen to the same people talk about the same things each time. The woman you will eventually marry in that setting has certain unwritten expectations for your life, and the lives of your children." Jonathan sat up. He expertly skipped a rock along the surface of the calm water just below us.

"There's nothing wrong with that, mind you, it's just not for me," he added. I need these wide-open spaces and unpredictable clients, who don't know my family name from Adam. I crave the adventure of it, wanting to build my reputation from the ground up instead of trying to maintain it from the top down. And I'd prefer a woman who hasn't already picked out the schools our children will go to," he concluded.

We watched the high silky clouds slither into new formations. Both of us were quiet for a minute, basking in the sun and pondering our own thoughts about the things that had formed us, until Jonathan began playing with my hair—running his fingers through it. Finally he kissed me in a way that was tender and slow, just like our day by the river. It scared me, this kiss. Feeling so comfortable in Jonathan's arms. I sat up in a panic and announced we should take a hike down by the river, my heart pounding wildly in my chest as I gathered up the remains of the picnic.

"Okay. Can I bring my fishing gear?" Jonathan helped me fold the blanket and we put it in the car with the lunch cooler.

"Sure. Are you hoping to find the perfect fishing hole, glistening with trout that can't wait to nibble on your handmade lures?" I asked teasingly.

"You bet. Every true fisherman's dream. That and a pretty girl to come along and make fun of his search for this elusive fishing hole."

We both laughed. I led the way down to the river, bringing one of my cameras secured around my neck on a thick strap. Jonathan brought his fly rod with a few lures tucked in his pockets. The water was rushing in spots but quite calm at certain points along the trail. We spent the rest of the afternoon lollygagging along it, wading into the cool stream at shallow places where the current was sluggish. I watched Jonathan fish while picking flowers on the shore, and he gave me a few lessons in casting a line that brought us both to tears for laughing.

Time had gotten away from us and the sun was already setting as we crossed the 405 bridge on our return trip to Portland. Colors of raspberry and tangerine bled into the high feathery clouds above us while softer tones of melon and peach hung over the Willamette River. Shimmering lights began to dot the skyline, illuminating tall buildings jutting straight up from downtown Portland in the near distance. I drank it all in, this dramatic ending to a perfect day on the Columbia.

When Jonathan and I reached Jake's Seafood restaurant, Miranda was already waiting for us at a table by the window. Suddenly my Columbia River adventure seemed long ago.

I had visions of rape trials and headlines bearing not just the names of Miranda and Peter, but of Daniel, Benjamin, and myself as well.

CHAPTER TWENTY

How much worse will it be in court, with all those gawking strangers looking for a cheap thrill at your expense?

Miranda and I hugged, and spoke about our day. I gave the highlights of the photo shoot at the Old Grist Mill, and she informed me of the sales I had missed by not shopping with her. Jonathan ordered a bottle of wine and some appetizers. He then brought up the subject of Peter, wasting no time getting around to why we were all there.

"Miranda, did you bring the note from the night Peter Cairns drugged you?" he asked, sounding very much like an attorney, and not the laid back man I had picnicked with a few hours ago.

I studied my sleek exotic friend, all crisp and fresh looking in a white summer dress with her silky hair pulled up in a simple chignon. She handed Jonathan the note from her purse. It was in a plastic zippy, probably put there under Jonathan's instructions. He took it from her carefully and placed it in his shirt pocket. The waiter brought our wine and I almost inhaled my first glass, upset by Miranda's note from Peter, which conjured up flashbacks of a similar note I had received from him myself.

I poured another glass of the merlot and tried not to listen to their discussion about the dreadful Dr. Cairns. Our appetizers arrived and I realized how hungry I was, having worked up an appetite hiking the river. Concentrating on butter clams and stuffed mushrooms, I paid little attention as they went over the particulars of whether or not they had a solid case against Peter. When they finished debating the issue I interjected my thoughts, perhaps a bit bluntly, due to my wine consumption.

"Please," I looked from one of them to the other and back again, "tell me that you don't believe this is the right thing to do. You barely have a case, Miranda. You stand to lose everything for nothing."

"Tori, we have a solid case," Jonathan answered confidently. "I would never let Miranda go through a trial like this unless we did."

"Peter drugged her at the beginning of the summer," I protested, "and it's almost fall. There couldn't be any real evidence of the rape . . . no semen anywhere, no marks on her." I watched Miranda squirm uncomfortably, and hoped she was beginning to realize how this would feel in a courtroom full of strangers.

"Miranda wants this man put away, so he can never do to anyone again what he did to both of you," Jonathan patiently explained. "I agree with her, Tori. Even though there is a chance Peter will expose Daniel as Benjamin's father, I firmly believe people will think he is simply crying wolf. Who is going to listen to a convicted rapist?"

The waiter collected our menus and took our orders. When he had left, Miranda further explained her decision to prosecute.

"Tori, honey, listen to me. Mary Jennings is dead because of this man. Whether he killed her or she took her own life, either way it's his fault." She glanced at Jonathan as if they shared a secret. "Robert has found information on other college women who made complaints about Peter, but the allegations were never investigated."

I looked at Jonathan. "Are you sure about this?"

He nodded affirmatively.

"There have been several women from his classes," Miranda continued, "that have died of drug overdoses. We have no proof that Peter was involved, but worst case scenario is that Peter might have raped and killed more than just one or two women during his tenure at the college, not to mention possibly before and definitely after. I am proof of the latter, of course."

Our dinner arrived and I ate my shrimp linguini hungrily despite being at odds with my dinner companions. Jonathan seemed to enjoy his steak regardless of my irreverence for his professional opinion. But Miranda only toyed with her scampi. I couldn't be sure if it was not having my approval for their plan that made her melancholy or the fear of what it would entail for her.

"Tell me about this solid case you have against Peter," I asked, unable to keep frustration from my tone.

Jonathan looked at Miranda, who put her fork down and folded her hands. "We have a semen sample, and skin, and hair we can prove is Peter's," she said somberly.

"How could that be?" I asked, surprised.

"I had ripped the sheets off the bed that next morning and stuffed them into a bag that I intended to put outside in the recycling bin . . . and never did."

Miranda and I stared at each other for a second.

"I couldn't bear to think about what happened, let alone touch the bag I'd thrown into a corner of the garage. And then there is the note . . . it matches the note Mary Jennings had . . . and the waitress remembered me from that night in the bar. She asked Peter if I was okay when he could barely hold me up as I stumbled out the door . . . according to her. And she did think it seemed strange, because I'd only had two glasses of wine."

I pushed my plate away and looked at Jonathan. "Proving the semen is Peter's doesn't mean it wasn't consensual sex. And the waitress can't prove Miranda hadn't been drinking before she came to the bar."

"True, but we have surveillance video from the restaurant that clearly shows Miranda quite coherent one minute, and suddenly very lethargic the next. You can't clearly see Peter drug her drink, but the video does show when it might have happened. The camera footage catches their upper bodies and facial expressions, not the wine glasses on the table, but Peter is obviously reaching in his pocket at one point, and shortly thereafter is nodding for Miranda to view something on the overhead TV in the bar."

"That doesn't sound like enough evidence to convict him," I noted.

"I agree. But it is one more piece of the pie and the best part is the parking lot video that has Peter picking up a passing out Miranda before she hits the pavement, and only minutes after the suspicious scene where he might have drugged her drink, with Miranda cheerful and alert shortly beforehand."

I nodded, feeling less apprehensive but still skeptical.

"My neighbors thought it odd for me to have a strange car parked out front all night." She looked at Jonathan, as if for approval on her testimony. "I always have guest's park in the garage, and they never leave until after breakfast. My nosy neighbor across the street observed Peter sneaking out around five a.m. This same neighbor knocked on my door at ten that morning, after I suspiciously didn't leave for work as usual by seven thirty. He told Robert, who's been investigating all this for Jonathan, that I looked very ill and acted disoriented when I spoke with him for a minute at the door. I don't remember this neighbor coming over. I must still have been pretty out of it." Miranda paused there and took a drink of water with a shaky hand. "I do remember stripping the bed in a screaming fit of rage and stuffing the sheets into a bag, and then throwing it into a dark neglected corner of the garage."

Jonathan and I were silent for a few seconds while Miranda composed herself. I wondered if he was as concerned as I was about her ability to pull this trial off without eroding her dignity beyond repair.

"Foul play might be considered due to skin samples from the sheets," Jonathan continued. "It isn't usually considered normal to scratch your sexual partner. The Spanish woman who cleans Peter's office will testify that he had a nasty scratch on his face, on what would be the day after Miranda's rape. The cleaning lady doesn't like Peter, who is always rude to her. She's happy to comply." Jonathan sighed, knowing how our good fortune with a key witness was grim nonetheless for subject matter. "And there is the suicide note left by Mary Jennings," he added. "Even if we can bring up Peter's sexual history of leaving similar notes as admissible evidence, it would only show that psychologically he is a bit dark. It would not prove him to be a rapist. However, the suicide note written by Mary Jennings uses suspiciously similar phrases and aligns a little too coincidentally with the love notes."

Jonathan seemed confident in his ability to pull all the incriminating puzzle pieces together.

"Look at you, Andi," I said pleadingly. "You're a wreck, and from our quiet little conversation among close friends. How much worse will it be in court, with all those gawking strangers looking for a cheap thrill at your expense? And let's not even mention the press . . . or Peter's lawyers, who will make it their goal to drag up your entire sexual history and prove that you were asking for whatever you got, whether you remember it or not."

"Tori, I also have video from the condominium complex where Miranda lives and it shows Peter arriving and leaving in his car, with a slumped-over passenger, which he carries into the apartment." Jonathan took a drink of water and I thought perhaps he was mentally building his case as he spoke. "It shows Miranda leaving in a taxi that afternoon, walking slowly and dressed in sweats, as if she were home ill from work for the day. The video shows her returning in her own car an hour later."

"Even if you have enough evidence to convince a jury, it is not going to be a cake walk in that courtroom. I dare say what unfolds in there could cause all of us to doubt ourselves more than the jury might. That will be the goal of the defense."

"Okay, yes. It will be difficult," Miranda had to admit, "but it will be worth it to get Peter locked up, where he can't hurt anyone else ever again . . . including me or you!" She tossed her napkin on the table, as if throwing in the towel on what was left of her pride.

I glanced from Andi to Jonathan, my feelings of despair somehow not alleviated. I was afraid for Miranda, and how her career might be forever destroyed by this trial, and if Peter should win, well, I shuddered to think what her state of mind would be then. As for me, I felt ashamed at suddenly wanting to give Peter the money from the paintings so he would simply go away—far away, never to be heard from again.

"Do what you think is best, Andi." Standing to leave, I encouraged Jonathan to stay and talk to Amanda awhile longer. He agreed with me, and said he'd take a taxi home.

While driving back to my apartment I banged on my steering wheel with a clenched fist, screaming out in anger about the horror of it all . . . my Anda Panda agreeing to a rape trial that might destroy her emotionally, if not her career, and Jonathan was aligned with locking Peter up too, if at all possible. I wanted to hate him for not discouraging Andi from doing this, but I couldn't, because in my heart I knew they were both right.

Once I entered my apartment I collapsed on Grams' sofa next to Wil, who was watching an old horror movie with the lights out and a large bowl of popcorn on his lap. I asked him if Benjamin was sleeping in the tree house with Vincent and Sarah as planned. He assured me they were squared away in the little fort with their sleeping bags and flashlights, plus an arsenal of snacks and games. Fortunately Wil was too engrossed in his movie to notice my anxiety.

I snuggled up next to my little brother and nibbled on the popcorn, letting my mind get lost in the make-believe monsters on the screen, rather than think about Peter Cairns, who was surely a more frightening monster than anything make-believe.

CHAPTER TWENTY-ONE

My only hope was to somehow outwit him, and thus far,
Peter had unfortunately been far more clever than I.

Wil ejected the movie when it was over and startled me by speaking. His deep voice reminded me strangely of Father many years ago. I didn't want to move a muscle, nestled safely next to Wil in the dark on Grams' sofa. I felt like a child again, needing a parent to lean on. Truth be known, I couldn't remember ever having leaned on my father, but surely this is how it would have felt.

"Vic, you're awfully quiet."

"I guess."

"I bet you drank your fair share of wine at dinner. That would explain why you're so relaxed."

"Sometimes it makes me want to dance." I dug my bare toes into his side.

"Oh, don't I know it. I've spent a few evenings with you like that." Wil grabbed my feet and began to tickle them. I laughed uncontrollably and begged him to stop, grabbing pillows within my reach to throw at his head until finally he quit.

We both fell silent for a minute.

"Benjamin had a great time in the park," Wil finally offered up. He looked over at me lying there in the dark. "What did you decide tonight? I mean about Miranda and the rape trial."

"She's going through with it," I said flatly.

"How do you feel about that?"

"I feel scared and frustrated," I admitted.

"Are you going to testify?"

"They won't ask me to."

"So you're not going to help."

"I *can't* help," I said defensively.

"Can't or won't?" Wil prodded.

I got up and walked to the kitchen. Once there I started banging things around to make a cup of tea.

"Vic." Wil walked up behind me and leaned on the counter. "I'm sorry. Let's not talk about the trial. Let's talk about investing Benjamin's money."

"I can't think about that right now, Wil." I didn't look at him as I picked out a mint tea bag and tossed it into a heavy white mug.

"What do you mean you can't?"

"I mean I need to have that money available, in my savings account." I studied the stainless steel teakettle, as if that would make the water boil sooner.

"Why?"

"It's none of your business why."

"Don't even think about giving that money to Peter. Do you hear me, Vic? Do you have any idea what a bag of worms that would open?"

I turned to stare at him.

He stared back at me.

"You would never have peace of mind again, Victoria. He would hold you hostage emotionally for as long as you could both get away with your dirty blackmail. And the people you're trying to protect would never agree with what you're doing," he added, adamantly.

"You aren't Benjamin's father. There isn't any way you can possibly know what lengths a parent will go to in order to protect their child," I shouted.

"That isn't fair, Victoria. I love you and Benjamin as much as I could love anyone," Wil said emphatically.

Why was I purposefully hurting Wil? Did I want him to give up and leave? Perhaps somewhere inside I knew if he hung around long enough he would talk some sense into me, and stop my plan to protect Benjamin and Daniel from Peter by simply paying him off.

The kettle emitted steam as I answered him.

"That may be true, William. But you have no say in this. You're only my little brother. Not my husband. Maybe you've unwisely invested too much time into *my* life and not enough into building *your own*."

These insensitive comments had the effect I was hoping for. The look in

Wil's eyes before he stormed out told me he would not be returning soon. I didn't touch the tea. I went straight to bed without undressing and cried myself to sleep.

In the morning Benjamin came barging into my bedroom in order to announce that he hadn't slept a wink in the treehouse, and was exhausted after a terrific night of stuffing himself on sweets, playing board games, and owl-hunting all over the neighborhood with Mr. Gianni and Sarah.

The rest of the week went by in a whirlwind of back-to-school shopping. After each trip Benjamin and I sat in the yard, exhausted from our hunt for sales. We watched fat brown squirrels hide nuts in the gnarly oak trees across the street, and drank newly-squeezed cider fresh in at the corner market.

Summer was over.

My cell phone lit-up with Jonathan's number at least twice a day but I chose not to answer it. I listened to his messages asking me to please return his calls. One message in particular stopped me cold in the NIKE store, where Benjamin didn't notice my distraction, so enthralled was he by all the soccer gear. I sat down hard on a chair in the shoe department as my attorney explained via voicemail that Peter had been arrested on charges of possessing illegal drugs, breaking and entering, sexual abuse, and rape. Jonathan and Miranda had thrown the book at him.

As the message played my mind was suddenly full of high-pitched choir hymns, muffled beneath the sound of churning Rogue water. I didn't know if I was losing my sanity or trying desperately to hang on to it, but I listened to the retelling of Peter's arrest too many times to count. Each time my heart would race and my stomach cramp while my ears suffocated me with Catholic hymns and rushing rapids, ultimately drowning out the words of the message.

I still hadn't told Benjamin anything. He could wake up one morning and find out who his father was on the front page of the newspaper. How could I prevent Peter's wrath from taking that direction? I had to fight a strong desire to visit him in the county jail. Reassure him I had no part in it. Beg him to be quiet. Offer him all the money from the paintings and then some. Jonathan specifically told me on several of the many phone messages not to try and see Peter at the county jail. He must have known I would impulsively want to do exactly that.

I asked Vincent and Maggie if anyone had come to see us each time Benjamin and I returned from our daily mission of school shopping. Apparently Jonathan stopped by several times, but Wil not at all. Saturday was fast approaching and what was I to do with no Wil to sleep in the treehouse? How could I explain to Benjamin that I had run Wil off with wicked words born of my devilish plan to appease the demonic Peter?

When Saturday finally arrived it was Vincent who saved my fall from grace by offering to sleep in the fort again after Wil called Benjamin and apologized for not being able to make it. Something about a last minute decision to drive to Seattle and meet Paige's family. I baked chocolate chip cookies and felt sorry for myself because Jonathan didn't drop by all day, and quit leaving messages I never returned. By dusk I had packed enough food and drinks to sustain four people in the treehouse for a week. Maybe it was guilt, or perhaps nervous energy.

Sarah opted not to stay with them this time and so it was just Vincent and Benj. By nine o'clock I had showered and collapsed on the sofa to watch my favorite comfort films, the type where you can get lost in the characters and know the dialogue by heart. Perhaps summer was over, but it was still quite warm. I wore only a tank top and nylon running shorts in an effort to stay cool. The window was wide open but presented no breeze to enjoy on this muggy night with barely a crescent moon.

The back screen door creaked open as the first movie ended.

"Benjamin?" I wondered what I could possibly have forgotten to pack, but then maybe he only needed to use the bathroom. There was no answer. In fact, there was no sound at all. Had I heard the screen door creak? Yes, definitely. I knew that sound in my sleep, and I wasn't sleeping. I glanced into the darkness behind the sofa in the direction of the kitchen. Then I looked at the small oak table in front of me and impulsively reached for my cell phone.

"Benj, is that you?" I tried to sound nonchalant, but the fact was my heart began beating wildly in my chest. With one click my cell phone lit up. I scrolled to Jonathan's number, holding my breath, afraid to move. Staring at his name I swallowed my pride and without hesitation gently touched the screen to dial it. Not a second later a hand closed around my mouth and an arm encircled my neck. The phone flew out of my hands and slid across the hardwood floor.

Peter whispered in my ear as my heart jumped into my throat. "Did you think I was still locked up, Victoria? In jail, where your little whore of a friend sent me with her pack of lies?" He tightened his grip on my neck and I could barely breathe. "Why else would you leave the door unlocked, you stupid little bitch? Haven't you ever heard of bail?"

My cell phone rang and we both jumped. "Who did you call, Victoria? Someone to keep you company?" He chuckled under his breath and my head throbbed from lack of air. "Well never fear, little girl. I can accommodate your every desire. Remember? Perhaps you don't. But this time you will."

The cell phone quit ringing and for one tortured second it was silent with only the sound of Peter's heavy breathing on my neck. The landline in the kitchen started ringing. First it was loud but faded fast as I began to lose consciousness. Peter removed his arm and yanked me up from the sofa. I sucked in a lungful of air as he dragged me to the kitchen, hoarsely whispering instructions at the same time. He placed his hand back over my mouth as he spoke. "Answer it, Victoria, and tell whoever it is you are on your way out the door and will call them back tomorrow. No funny business, do you hear me? Or you and that kid will both be headlines in the morning, one way or another."

He picked the receiver up and held it to my ear. Slowly he removed his hand from my mouth. I could hear Jonathan's voice and it choked me up, making it hard to speak.

"Hello? Tori, are you there?"

"Yes . . . Jonathan."

Peter jerked my arm, the evil gleam in his eye sharp and penetrating. "I . . . was just on my way out. I'll call you back tomorrow." Peter set the receiver down and chuckled under his breath. "Very well done, my little brunette vixen. Now if you scream I'll strangle your pretty neck." He was still holding me tightly against him, and put his arm back across my neck. We were both sweaty and breathing hard. I couldn't clear my mind to think. It was all I could do not to collapse under my legs of jelly as he dragged me back into the front room, lit only by the crescent moon outside the window and blank glow of the TV waiting for me to eject the movie.

Peter whispered in a husky voice as he dragged me, "I'm going to teach you a lesson, Victoria, and then if you come clean about me fathering your bastard son, worth millions of dollars before he's done painting his stupid little birds, I won't ever have to teach you another one."

He brought us to the front door and pushed me against it. "That bitch Miranda doesn't have a case," he hissed, while looking at the cell phone on the floor. "I strongly suggest you encourage her to drop it, or I might have to teach her a lesson, too." For an instant he carelessly loosened his grip on me to snatch up the phone. It was the only instant I needed to push backward with all my might, causing him to let go of me while falling to the floor. I ripped open the front door and raced into the night with every ounce of strength I had left. My legs nearly buckled beneath me midway across the lawn, but I miraculously recovered and shot for the street with ample adrenaline to fuel my flight. Screaming *help* at the top of my lungs I was suddenly glad beyond words to be a disciplined runner, three miles every morning or evening depending on my schedule of events for the day.

Nonetheless I could hear Peter's feet behind me.

"Help! Someone help me," I screamed, while trying to focus on solid footing as I sprinted in darkness.

I knew from the strength of his body against mine for the last twenty minutes that his tall lean frame was in good condition, and he was probably also a runner, as almost everyone in Portland was.

My only hope was to somehow outwit him, and thus far, Peter had unfortunately been far more clever than I.

CHAPTER TWENTY-TWO

"No one can know what a madman will do."

I headed for the apartment complex across the street, stumbling somewhere along the side of the building, with the slit of a moon and scarce streetlights nowhere near. Peter's footsteps got louder, and I could hear him breathing as he tried to fall on top of me but only landed at my feet. He grabbed my legs as I screamed and struggled. I finally slithered out of his grip, from being wet with perspiration. Crying *stop* repeatedly I hoped someone would hear my hysterical outbursts.

Once free of him I again took flight, rounding the corner of the apartment complex and slipping under a nearby house porch. I knew this was possible because I had sat on this porch many times with Julie Watters, who kept her canning jars beneath it. I helped her retrieve them once for making jelly, after she and I had picked ripe blackberries from our yards. I tried to concentrate on breathing slow and steady, and quiet, by thinking about berry picking and making jelly. Meanwhile my heart was jammed in my throat and short of suffocating myself I could only silence my breathing so much.

Peter ran somewhere near the porch and stopped. He nearly choked inhaling thick night air. Beads of sweat broke out on my forehead, while lying there beneath the cool, damp porch. And then he sprinted forward, having apparently chosen a direction in which to pursue me. After several more minutes I crawled out cautiously, convinced he would not return to this area. Carefully I stood and took a deep breath before doubling back to the apartment, hoping to lock myself in and call Jonathan. Weary with fear and exhaustion, I ran into the street without looking and was blinded by headlights. Brakes squealed and a car barely stopped at my feet. While covering my eyes from the glare of the headlights I heard a car door slam.

"Tori? Is that you?"

Before I could answer, Jonathan pushed hair from my face and I saw that it was him, thinking I had only dreamed I heard his voice, it being so engrained in my subconscious from his messages played over and over all week. Upon the realization he was truly there in the flesh and blood, I collapsed in his arms and lost any hope of composure.

I barely remember him placing me in the car and walking me into the apartment. We were sitting on the sofa together as I told him all the traumatic details of Peter's visit. I wouldn't let Jonathan call the police, convincing him that Peter would expose Daniel out of spite. Peter really had no motivation to lash out at anyone but me, because I was the only one who could give him what he wanted—paternity rights to a child worth a fortune, in Peter's twisted mind. Miranda had a private detective to prevent Peter from getting near, should he have any thoughts of a simulated suicide.

"Tori, the only reason I am not calling the police is because you don't want to be involved with Miranda's case. I understand that you never reported anything and only suspected he had drugged you years later. I realize you want to stay neutral now to help prevent him from involving Daniel. But I don't like it. Not at all. I hate that he is going to get away with this."

Jonathan was quite annoyed with himself for not thinking to get me a P.I., too. He called one to come and watch the apartment as soon as we determined the police would not be called. I wouldn't let him leave my side long enough to make me a cup of tea. I begged him to spend the night and he agreed I shouldn't be alone. Peter's car was nowhere in sight and we assumed he had returned to it and left, but that didn't mean he wasn't watching us now, perhaps waiting for Jonathan to leave so he could finish what he had begun.

I calmed down after a while, and left the safety of his arms to take a shower. Jonathan made a pot of chamomile tea while the hot steamy water cleared my senses. Reappearing damp but somewhat calmer, he and I discussed what to do about Peter while I sipped the tea.

Jonathan was going to have Peter followed so we'd always know where he was. He wanted me and Benjamin to move in with Rachel, but I didn't want to do that with Benjamin beginning school in a few days. What was the point to any of this if I couldn't keep Benjamin's life normal?

"Tori, I didn't know he'd been released on bail. I'm so sorry I couldn't warn you." Jonathan shook his head. "Damn him. I should have figured he'd come straight for you. What was I thinking?" He peeked through the blinds, probably looking for the detective to show up. "I can't believe the man made bail. He has one hell of a lawyer to get out on rape charges. All the evidence being circumstantial has played a large role in the judge's decision. The other charges are not so serious as to prevent bail, without a prior record." Jonathan let go of the blinds and looked at me apologetically. "I am so sorry, Tori, that I didn't think about him coming here."

"No one can know what a madman will do. I didn't think of it either. I'm not the one who arrested him on rape charges, so why would he come looking for me?"

"He probably came here to get you to talk Miranda into dropping the charges."

"Yes." I nodded in agreement. "That's exactly what he did."

He continued to look at me, as if it was a pleasure to do so. I suddenly felt self-conscious, as I hadn't put on any makeup and my hair was combed, but still wet from the shower.

"Tori, why didn't you return any of my calls?"

"I don't know." I smoothed my wet hair back and gave him eye contact. It was the least I could do after being so evasive all week. "I guess I needed to get used to the idea of the trial and all. I didn't realize the news of Peter's arrest would affect me as much as it did."

"I see." Jonathan stood there, not moving.

"No. You don't see. I'm scared, Jonathan. Petrified that Peter will ruin Miranda's career, if not her wonderful sense of self, and Benjamin's hope for a normal life by revealing who his father is. And then there's Daniel. No ordinary priest mind you, but one with great healing powers and a chance to be bishop. Perhaps a cardinal someday. I feel the least I can do after being his one major sin is try and protect him from the consequences of it."

"You're not responsible for Daniel's behavior on the Rogue. Why can't you see that? And Benjamin is a strong kid. He can survive this, especially with you to help him through it."

"No. Somehow I must protect them from this demon. Peter is the only thing standing in the way of what they need to accomplish. We both know if it weren't for Benj's paintings and their worth, Peter wouldn't be pestering me for custody. Purely out of greed he has surfaced to derail all the goodness Benjamin and Daniel have to offer, and Miranda could be destroyed as well in the wake of his plan."

He came and sat beside me on the sofa.

"Tori, you wouldn't let Peter blackmail you?"

"No. Peter is insane. There would be no appeasing him with any amount of money," I lied.

Jonathan kissed the top of my head and pulled me close to him on the sofa. I had thrown on a cotton tank top and running shorts, hoping to make our night together not any more difficult for either of us by wearing my flimsy silk pajamas. I tried not to think about how good he smelled and made every effort not to remember how sweet his kisses tasted, but lying in his arms I could not ignore his strong body. I found everything about him arousing. Somehow I knew Jonathan loved me, although he hadn't mentioned it. But then, I hadn't either, and it was suddenly so clear to me that I loved him too. I couldn't understand how that escaped my attention, until now, and I didn't try to analyze being in love with two very different men at the same time.

Lying there in the dark on the sofa neither of us could sleep. It was apparent by our shallow breathing and tenses bodies. Finally we reached out for one another and connected in a tender kiss that seemed to never end until Jonathan stood and lifted me in his arms, depositing me on my bed, and him beside me. We pulled the covers back and our clothes off while kissing intermittently, and made love by the glow of the streetlamp just outside my bedroom window. My memories of Daniel on the Rogue could not rival the passion Jonathan and I shared in the remainder of that night.

By the first light of day he kissed me goodbye and left silently to spare Benjamin's discovery of our night together. I watched the little silver car turn the corner and thanked God for His selfishly hording Daniel. Were it not for God's obsessive need of him, I might never have known the less complicated and completely amazing love of a man like Jonathan, who somehow made me feel more protected in the last few hours than any army of angels might from above.

I lay back down just as the cell phone rang. Glancing at it sitting on the nightstand I saw that it was Jonathan and I wondered what he must have forgotten.

"Hello?"

"Tori. I already miss you."

I laughed. "Is that why you called? To tell me you missed me? Or did you forget something?"

"Yes."

"Yes what?"

"I did forget something. I forgot to mention that I love you."

There was a pause as I savored his words.

"Jonathan, I love you too."

"I know."

Another pause.

"Tori . . . I'm only a phone call away. Don't hesitate to contact me for any reason. Even if you just need to debrief some more about Peter's visit."

"Okay." I smiled into the phone, wishing he were still there next to me, naked under the sheets.

"What are you doing tomorrow? It's Labor Day, you know."

"I have no idea. Wil was going to come and bring his girlfriend Paige, but they went to Seattle instead."

"Would you and Benjamin consider spending the day with me?"

"We'd love to."

"I'm having the partners and their families, including Robert and his wife, and their little girls. Would that be uncomfortable for you?"

I suddenly realized how we never spoke of it, but obviously Jonathan and I were both protective and cautious about the long time affair of my best friend Rachel and his partner Robert.

"No. It wouldn't be uncomfortable. But thanks for asking."

"I'll pick you up around noon."

"We'll be ready."

"Tori?"

"Yes?"

"I've wanted to make love to you for twelve years. And it was completely worth the wait. Have a wonderful day and I will see you tomorrow." He hung up.

I didn't know what to think. I was stunned really. But I didn't have time to dwell on it. Benjamin came crashing through the screen door and I could hear him putting things in the fridge from the cooler. I threw on my robe and went to help him. Over pancakes I told Benj we'd be going to Jonathan's tomorrow for Labor Day and he seemed pleased. He asked who the guy was in the car out front.

I peeked through the window and smiled. I told Benjamin it was some-one who would be watching us for a while because of Aunt Andi's trial. It seemed like a good time to explain it to him, so we had a long talk about Peter and Miranda and the rape trial. I left my association with Peter com-pletely out of it, other than having known him in graduate school. I used that for an excuse as to why he might want to speak with me about the trial, but emphasized how important it was that we have no contact with Peter. I wished with every fiber of my being it were really that simple.

Jonathan picked us up in his Land Cruiser. It was silver like the little con-vertible. Benjamin loved it. They talked about skiing all the way to Jonathan's house because this was the vehicle he used when heading to Mt. Hood for that very purpose. As we pulled into his neighborhood he told me how this barbeque was something his law firm partners held each Labor Day. They rotated homes for the event, and it was at Jonathan's home this year because he was the newest partner, in a sense, having just returned from practicing with his father in New York the past couple years. He planned to consider it a house warming too, having just bought the home a few months ago.

There were four partners: Remington, Marsh, Davis and Lowe. Chase and Alexa Remington would be there, but had teenagers who opted to do something different for the day. Robert Marsh, I already knew, was coming with his wife Claire and their daughters Bronwin and Emma, who were eight and ten. James and Brianna Lowe were also planning on attending the annual event. They were quite young, and James was not a full partner yet. He was Chase Remington's nephew fresh out of law school.

I felt somewhat nervous, knowing full well Jonathan would not be introducing Benjamin and me to his partners unless he was quite serious about our relationship. Miranda said he generally did social events with the partners solo, at least he had before he left, and then while practicing with his dad in New York. He dated women discreetly, she offered up, and was never in any long-term relationships that she knew of. Miranda got all her information through the gossip chain comprised of other mutual friends—the Tanasbornes and the Davises having been close for many years.

Of course I already knew Robert, mostly through the eyes of Rachel. I had seen pictures of his little girls because they attended the art workshops Rachel held at her studio every summer. There would be a showing of the work the children created and a group picture of the participants hung on her studio wall for each year of the summer workshop. She loved Bronwin and Emma, and it broke her heart how they were also very fond of her, and had no clue about Rachel being in love with their father, and he with her.

We parked in the garage, next to the little silver Mercedes, and Jonathan gave us another house tour for Benjamin's benefit. More exciting to Benjamin was a tour of the backyard, which sloped steadily downhill to a rushing creek at the bottom. We crossed a footbridge leading into the woods on the other side of the creek, and followed a natural trail of sorts for about a mile upstream. The leaves were already turning and small creatures looked busy with preparations for the rainy season inevitably on its way, although this day was promising to be quite warm and dry.

Benjamin and Jonathan did all the talking, on subjects as diverse as how to catch crawfish in the creek and where to find the tender chanterelle mushrooms in these woods. I watched their interactions and it warmed my heart at how aligned they were for mutual, if not minor interests. Somehow the subject changed to boats and there was a discussion about Jonathan's cabin cruiser docked on the Willamette, just down from his and Miranda's offices. Benjamin pleaded with me to go boating this evening after Jonathan generously invited us to come when the barbeque was over. I had no objection to their plans.

We headed back to the house in order to be present when guests arrived and Jonathan taught Benjamin how to bait little pieces of raw bacon on a string, for dangling in the creek with the hope of snaring crawfish. He ran off to try it out and we began arranging appetizer trays, prepared by Jonathan's part-time housekeeper earlier. She'd also made some side dishes and a dessert. It was fun setting things up for the party together.

We had just opened a bottle of wine and taken one sip when the door-bell rang.

CHAPTER TWENTY-THREE

"Are you made of flesh and blood?"

The first guests to arrive at Jonathan's house were Chase and Alexa Remington, Chase having started the law practice solo and being the eldest of the partners. He looked distinguished, with graying hair around the temples. Alexa was eloquent, and they made an attractive couple in their casual designer wear. Both seemed surprised but pleased to meet me, and admitted they had no idea Jonathan was seeing anybody.

Robert and Claire arrived next with their beautiful little blonde girls, who stood carefully at their father's side until spying Benjamin down at the creek. They begged to join him and were allowed to do so with specific instructions not to fall in. Soon they were skipping down the hill with their long French braids flopping behind them. They knew Benjamin from the art workshops. After several minutes you could hear their little girl shrieks of delight as Benjamin pulled a rather large and active crawfish up on his string, attached firmly to the bacon at the bottom of it.

Jonathan became busy distributing drinks and doing other host duties as we heard the doorbell again. I offered to let James and Brianna in, introducing myself somewhat awkwardly. I admired their youthfulness and liked them immediately as we laughed about how Jonathan managed to avoid ever mentioning a girlfriend, and here I was, a true surprise typical of any good attorney. I had felt that Chase and Alexa were slightly more protective of Jonathan, and seemed subtly concerned about how I would fit into his life.

Robert's wife Claire was the only person at the party I felt compelled to avoid.

She was a tall, boyish looking woman with narrow features and straight black hair cut dramatically off at the chin. Some saw her as perfect fashion model material, with her painfully thin body and reserved aloofness. But

I sensed her to be insecure and unhappy. It was hard to understand why Robert married her in the first place after having met Rachel on the Rogue, but it was easy to see why he couldn't put his feelings for the confident, warmhearted Rachel behind him.

It was a stressful afternoon of asking intelligent and thoughtful questions that were not prying and answering questions of the same type. Especially concerning Benjamin's father, my history of never having been married, and the particulars of my relationship with Jonathan. I hadn't recently practiced vague half-truth answers on any of these topics. As the afternoon wore on I began to feel familiar with everyone present and was relaxed by the wine and bright sunshine peeking through the maples near the large redwood deck. Jonathan announced that he would be barbequing salmon shortly, but then the doorbell rang again and our host looked surprised.

"I wonder who that could be?" Jonathan asked, as he walked inside to answer it.

My heart skipped a beat when he reappeared with none other than Daniel standing beside him. "I didn't think Father Rosselli was going to make it, but there was a change of plans." Jonathan gave me an apologetic look. Daniel was already shaking hands with the men and smiling at the women. He seemed to know everyone and I felt perhaps he had been at other gatherings of this particular group. He looked at me and said hello, a bewildered expression in his eyes.

Sitting on the other side of the deck he was soon holding a glass of red wine that Jonathan had poured for him, and discussing the softball tournament apparently they had all played in quite recently. I decided that must be the main reason a priest and four attorneys would be so friendly and familiar with one another. Jonathan no doubt recruited him for their team knowing what a wonderful athlete he was beneath those healing robes. Today Daniel sported his casual attire that belied any celibacy restraints, or other pious restrictions.

"Victoria, I read where Peter Cairns was arrested recently. Are you planning to testify in Miranda's trial?" he asked of me, despite every member in the firm behind Peter's trial being present and accounted for, making the whole subject entirely awkward. No one knew I had any association at all with Peter Cairns, except for Robert, which caused me to be additionally mortified at Daniel's indiscretion. I wondered if maybe he was lashing out in some way, distraught over my recent involvement with Jonathan. Surely he had no idea exactly what that involvement was, unless instinctively he had figured it out.

"Dr. Cairns was arrested? The psychologist, Dr. Cairns?" Claire asked, sounding surprised and displeased about this news at the same time.

"Yes, why? Do you know Dr. Cairns?" Robert asked, looking directly at Claire, who was seated next to him on the wrought-iron bench.

"Not really." Claire paused. "I have a friend who sees him." She glanced at Robert, and then looked quickly away. "Why was he arrested, for god's sake?"

"Rape, Claire." Robert stared at his agitated wife. "You actually have a friend that sees this animal?"

"He does have quite a rap sheet," one of the partners piped up. "I skimmed the file sitting on Robert's desk."

Jonathan stopped fiddling with the grill he was heating for the salmon. He looked thoughtfully at Claire, as if wondering what she could know about Peter, and I wondered the same thing right along with him. But then he glanced at me and made an obvious attempt to end the subject and move on by saying, "You know, this is Robert's and my case. We probably shouldn't talk about it." He added, "I think the subject of Peter Cairns would only spoil everyone's appetite for this salmon, anyway."

"Who did he rape?" Claire asked, with a look of unbelief, as if she had not heard Jonathan.

"This man has a history filled with innuendoes and probabilities for having drugged, raped, and killed more than one woman," Robert answered her.

"It is such a difficult thing to understand how anyone can be so purposefully evil," Daniel commented. He wasn't speaking to anyone in particular, with his eyes focused down the hill at the children catching crawfish.

Everybody mumbled in agreement, except for Claire, who had left to refill her wine glass, causing the case of Peter Cairns to be tactfully dropped as Jonathan had suggested. Daniel excused himself to join the children and take a look at their catch.

Chase, Robert and James were discussing politics while I helped Alexa and Brianna bring out the side dishes to accompany our salmon.

I was happy to volunteer when Jonathan asked if someone would go fetch Daniel and the children. When I arrived Bronwin and Emma were watching the bucket full of squirming crawfish with gleeful disgust. Daniel and Benjamin had crossed the footbridge and were exploring the other side of the creek.

The girls asked if they could bring the bucket of crawfish up to show everyone. I laughed at how fascinated they were by the fruit of Benjamin's labor, telling them they could indeed haul the bucket up the hill to show everybody. Sitting on the bank of the creek I could feel the coolness of the water rushing gently past while observing Benjamin with Daniel. They were so obviously father and son to anyone taking the time to really look . . . same hair, same build, same gait. Benjamin was but a small replica of Daniel. And of course, there were those cyan eyes.

I wondered if they would figure out their true relationship to each other. I wondered even more how they could not. I felt such a peace about the day, being there in the sunshine, in the backyard of a man that loved me enough to include me in his barbeque with the revered partners of his law firm. I wouldn't have cared if Daniel and Benjamin ran back across the footbridge to scold me for not telling them they are father and son. I would have been relieved that they had figured it out. I would have laughed my fool head off and thanked God for taking their fate out of my hands.

But it was truly only a daydream of the most whimsical kind. There would be nothing simple or joyous about such a revelation beyond the first several moments. The complexity of it would only grow like a cancer until it crippled them both, and they became like crawfish in a bucket. Not able to escape the critical eye of everyone who would gawk at them . . . Benjamin for being the son of a celibate priest in line to become bishop, and well, Daniel for his rather large indiscretion. And then there were the unusual healing powers they both possessed. Before all was said and done the two of them would be a freak show for the whole nation to ponder and judge, if not the world.

The thought of it scared and saddened me. I couldn't let that happen.

I yelled across the creek for them to come and eat while dusting off my khaki shorts. After hiking back up the hill I went straight for my stemmed glass and refilled it with red wine, noticing Claire had single-handedly consumed a whole bottle since arriving. I knew it was Claire because the other women present drank only white wine, and the men had opted for microbrews.

By the time we were all eating salmon Claire could barely function. Robert seemed more annoyed than concerned, but was as gentle and helpful with her as possible, encouraging her to eat and not drink anymore. They were the first to leave, just after fresh Oregon strawberries sliced over homemade cheesecake.

Robert almost had to carry Claire out the door, supporting her heavily all the way to the car. Bronwin and Emma giggled and yelled goodbye to Benjamin after helping him return the crawfish to the creek. They climbed in the backseat, their French braids unraveling and their jean shorts muddy from playing down by the water.

The other partners left shortly, and then only Daniel remained. He had gone back down to the creek with Benjamin. Jonathan and I cleaned up the remains of the food and sat on the deck, wondering if we should join them or let them be. But before we had made up our minds, they came bounding up the hill to us. Benjamin was holding something small and furry in his arms. It was a baby raccoon.

"Look what we found!" Benjamin held the tiny creature out for me to examine. It couldn't have been more than a few weeks old.

"Should you be handling it? I mean, won't the mother reject it now?" I asked, knowing they could not put it back for that very reason.

"It truthfully shouldn't be alive. We fear a dog or some other animal that wasn't especially hungry has toyed with it," Daniel informed us.

"It looks pretty feisty to me," Jonathan commented, observing Benjamin barely able to contain it in his arms.

"Perhaps now. But when we found him, the little creature was barely breathing until Benjamin revived it," Daniel shared, looking at me, and then at Jonathan. His expression revealed feelings of confusion about what type of relationship Jonathan and I really had, and about this half grown child who healed the raccoon. There were many questions in his troubled eyes. I could only guess what those questions were. Was this his son, or just a huge coincidence? Was I in love with Jonathan? Was I *sleeping* with him?

His tortured look sliced into me while Jonathan left to find a cage in the garage for the distressed animal. Benjamin had gone with him, leaving me alone with Daniel. I stared back into his pain-filled eyes for several seconds and then headed for the creek without a word. I couldn't bear to face him . . . but he followed me.

"Tori, stop. I need to speak with you."

I kept walking until I reached the water swiftly moving over and around an assortment of rocks. It pooled in some places, remaining still for crawfish homes and green water frogs that occasionally chirped at us. Daniel sat beside me on the bank in the thick grass. He was silent, but I could feel the heaviness of his burden, expressed in the lines of his forehead as I glanced at him. It hurt me to be the cause of his anguish. I looked back into the stream, gurgling and rushing along, oblivious to the late afternoon sun angling off its wetness and glistening with sparks of color.

"Who is Benjamin's father, Tori?"

I could feel Daniel staring at me. "Why must you know?" I asked, refusing to look into his face.

"Is he my son?"

His question dug into my soul. "Do you wish him to be?" This time I looked at him. His eyes reflected terror.

"Stop toying with me, Victoria, and tell me who his father is."

"Why does it matter to you?"

Daniel ran his hands through the messy blond curls and then stared into the creek. "It matters because I cannot be bishop if this is my flesh and blood."

"Are you made of flesh and blood?" I asked.

"Why are you so cruel to me, Tori? What have I done but love you?"

"Your love is fleeting at best, Daniel. I am only a reason to go to confession. A distraction from your purpose. And rest assured, you *will* be bishop. Benjamin is just a normal child with a knack for consoling hurt creatures," I adamantly answered, and then added, "The raccoon was probably more frightened than injured. It just appeared nearly dead, playing possum from the shock of it all."

I tried not to think about how Daniel was doing the same thing. Pushing away his instinctual need to be loved by me, and by his son, so he could serve God completely. Could he truly ever push God away in order to love *us* completely, placing Him in the shadows and corners of his life where we were now?

I was convinced that he could not.

I stood to leave as Jonathan reappeared on the deck with the caged raccoon and Benjamin beside him, calling us to come and see.

"Daniel, don't make me tell you who Benjamin's father is. I don't care to share that information, as Benjamin himself doesn't know." I looked at him as he stood to come with me. "I'm sorry if I've been unkind to you. I don't mean to be."

"Nor I," he added before I could say another word. "Come to class Thursday, will you? My office, seven o'clock."

I studied his face . . . searched his eyes. He returned my intense gaze. What did he hope to accomplish with the Catholicism classes? I could not be sure, but I felt his intent was more than the saving of my soul. Perhaps possession of it was what he ultimately wanted. Which made me think of Peter. I was instantly ashamed for considering a parallel between them.

"Yes. I will be there," I answered hesitantly, not sure it had been a wise request—and even less sure I had given a wise response.

CHAPTER TWENTY-FOUR

God help me, I had no idea who this child before me really was,
but that he was his father's son, to be sure.

Daniel and I walked up the hill together in silence. He said goodbye to Jonathan and Benjamin after one more look at the baby raccoon. We dropped the wild animal off at a Fish and Game Center. There was a nice lady on duty feeding other stray creatures brought there for similar reasons.

Thinking it would be fun to spend a couple nights on the cabin cruiser, Jonathan packed a bag and stopped by the apartment for us to do the same. We shopped for food and supplies en route to the marina, excited and happy to finally arrive at the peer.

"It's going to be a beautiful sunset," Jonathan commented as we unloaded our supplies. I had my camera and hoped he was right about a colorful conclusion to the Indian summer day. Before we left the dock I was obsessed with snapping shots of the boat, harbor, and water. Everything in view of my lens was a photo opportunity until Benjamin and Jonathan begged me to stop and join them on the front deck. Once the sun had passed the prime of its brilliance, all fractured by the strung-out puffy clouds, I put my camera down.

It was a warm night, not unusual for early September in the great Northwest, but being on the water we did need lightweight jackets up on deck once the sun had set. Lots of boats were anchored in the harbor on this holiday weekend and it was quite festive. Benjamin and I were standing at the rail soaking in everything we saw and heard, inhaling the slightly fishy scent from boats that unloaded their catches for the day earlier at the docks. Jonathan went below to fix a snack and insisted we not help.

I felt as if in a dream, standing there feeling the subtle sway of the boat, watching the lights of the city and the other mariners. The day had been full of new experiences and new people. There was a lot to think about, but as always, my thoughts drifted to Daniel and his concerns earlier at the barbeque about Benjamin. I wasn't prepared for my son to quiz me here and now on that very subject.

"Father Rosselli said I can call him Daniel," Benjamin offered up without glancing at me. He seemed focused on the water directly below, shimmering from the boat lights, and occasionally revealing fish rising up enough to be seen for an instant.

"Do you want to call him Daniel?"

Benjamin shrugged his shoulders. "How long have you known him . . . Father Rosselli?" He still did not look at me.

"A long time, Benj. Since before you were born. Why do you ask?"

"Is he my father?" This time he looked up, and we studied each other's eyes. I felt mine stripped of any façade that might hide the truth, so taken aback was I by the question. But surely I must have known it was coming, how could I not have?

"Why do you think he is your father, Benjamin?"

He shrugged again and looked out over the water. "It's just a hunch."

I felt he believed it to be more than a hunch, and feared losing his trust if I did not tell the truth. "He doesn't know, Benj, that he's your father. He has suspected, but I lied to him."

Benjamin nodded his head slowly, watching the lights dancing over the choppy surface of the river. "Because he is a priest?"

What was I to say? That I didn't know, at the time, Daniel was a priest? That answer would only make his father look worse in his eyes. And I couldn't know for sure if it would have made a difference anyway. It was a question I asked myself too many times to count, and never with a clear answer as to whether or not I would have done things differently, had I known.

"Yes. And more importantly, Benjamin, he wants to be bishop. The church is his life. I . . . well, I was only a diversion from his goals." I paused there, not sure of what else to add. But surely more needed to be said to this boy on the brink of adolescence. "Love is a hard thing to understand, Benjamin. We don't choose who we will love. Love chooses us. And when it does, it can be a very hard emotion to control."

"He still loves you." Benjamin looked up at me. What did I see in his eyes? Was he pleading for me to tell Daniel the truth so that he could be with his father, a father he needed now more than ever? Daniel was the one person who could help Benjamin understand exactly who he was. *God help me,* I had no idea who this child before me really was, but he was his father's son, to be sure. I saw the longing in his eyes to live the dream I too had longed to live every day until now, until my night with Jonathan. Only then had my dream dared to change. Daniel, Benjamin, and myself being a family no longer clouded my every thought.

"How do you know he loves me?"

"I just know."

"Did he say something?"

"Not really."

From this abstract conversation I decided Daniel's misgivings over what was transpiring between Jonathan and myself earlier at the barbeque must have been apparent to Benjamin.

Jonathan returned on deck with a large tray of goodies. Peanut butter crackers and milk for Benjamin, cold crab and shrimp with dipping sauces and wine for Jonathan and me. My mood was sullen despite trying hard to be light and cheerful. It was disconcerting to have Benjamin make these profound inquiries of me, straight out of the blue, asking difficult and disturbing questions unasked for all his eleven years, until this moment.

I felt an omnipresence about the changing season, knowing full well my life, and Benjamin's, were about to evolve in as drastic a way.

Milestones had been made this summer in my discovery of Daniel, and in my new love for Jonathan. And now that my son had figured out who his father was, there was no turning back to the innocence of his youth, nor my dreams of the past. I couldn't help but wonder what Daniel was thinking. Could he push the truth of Benjamin's belonging to him out of his mind? What misery such truth would cause him, I could not imagine. But it would be great misery indeed, with the bishop title not far off competing with the chance to be a father to this incredible child.

Jonathan noticed my preoccupation with something other than the stars emerging by the dozens right before our very eyes. He left me to my quiet mood and pointed out the constellations to Benjamin. They spent several hours together exploring the boat, Jonathan answering all his questions and explaining things that were fascinating to an eleven-year-old. Before he went to bed in a cabin below he had learned how to tie several different kinds of knots, and how to read the instruments on the control panel.

"I told Benjamin we could do some fishing early tomorrow morning. He was pretty excited. I just checked on him and he's out like a light. All the fresh air on the open water, and his hard work catching crawdads earlier, I guess." Jonathan laughed.

"It has been a fun day," I admitted.

"I hope it wasn't hard having Daniel there. I had no idea he was coming. He told me last week he wouldn't be able to make it unless the nuns at St. Matthew's didn't need him to help with their Labor Day festivities." Jonathan shook his head. "It seems odd he chose my barbeque over the church picnic, especially considering the words we had in his office recently."

"Maybe that's why he came."

"Maybe." Jonathan hesitated before continuing and I could feel the question on his mind piercing the darkness. "What did Daniel say to you, down by the creek?"

"He keeps asking if Benjamin is his."

"I see. Forgive me, Tori, but he would have to be a fool to believe your lie. The resemblance between them is striking. I'm surprised it wasn't obvious to everyone there today."

"Maybe it was."

"No, I'm sure no one suspects, except Daniel himself."

"And Benjamin."

Jonathan looked at me. "Has he said something to you?"

"He knows, Jonathan."

"So you told him then?"

"No, I only admitted the truth when he confronted me with it. I felt a lie would be inappropriate, considering the lack of doubt in Benjamin's eyes. If I had blatantly lied to him he would never have trusted me again."

"And what if there had been some doubt? Would you have lied then?"

"I don't know. All I know is that lying to him would have had greater negative consequences than the truth. It's hard to say what guides us when dealing with matters of the heart."

"Where does this leave us, Tori, right now at this moment?"

I didn't answer him. I reached out to touch his face, as if that could take away the confusion in his eyes. And I think perhaps it did, replacing the wondering with longing. We kissed tentatively, as if examining our feelings, the strength of which led us down the stairs to Jonathan's cabin below. I stayed with him until predawn, and then slipped down the narrow hall to the cabin where I had placed my things the evening before. It was not a moment too soon, for shortly thereafter I heard them climbing up the stairs to the deck, where they hoped to catch a few hungry perch.

I showered and made coffee, familiarizing myself with the galley while the boys were hard at their play. I brought a cup to Jonathan and some hot chocolate for Benj. Watching the sunrise through various lenses of my camera, I began snapping pictures of my two fishermen on deck, and those across the way, before sitting against the mahogany railing. Drinking in the quiet morning I studied the ebb and flow of the water in the harbor. It lapped against the sides of the boat in a soothing pattern, disturbed only by an occasional cawing seagull flying overhead, or the gleeful sounds of an eleven-year-old who just caught a fish.

After proudly presenting me with a bucket of small quivering perch, the somewhat rumpled looking sailors returned to the cabins below for a hot shower. I fried the perch in a pan, after cleaning them in the sink, and made scrambled eggs for an accompaniment to our fresh breakfast. Any fresher, in fact, and it would still have been breathing. Jonathan was impressed with my fish cleaning skills, something I learned from boating and camping with Wil.

We took a cruise down the Willamette, and set the sails for a nice easy wind, allowing for a lazy ride adrift on the calm waters. The sun rose high and hot as was promised by the weather forecast. Still, a noticeable change in the air filled our heads with foreshadowing, like a wave of premonition floating past us, bringing an edge of discontent to our silence. The three of us soaked up this shared solitude on the open river for several hours before returning to dock the boat and get a good night's sleep. We'd be heading back to the city tomorrow.

After breakfast we secured everything on the boat and packed our bags. The harborside shops enticed us to enter as we walked along the riverfront to Jonathan's vehicle, each with a duffel bag or backpack over our shoulders. I volunteered to watch our things when finally a tackle shop lured Benjamin hopelessly inside to examine the depths of its treasures. Jonathan tagged along to explain the mystery of each carefully crafted item for the sport of fishing. They returned to find me basking in the sun on a bench overlooking the harbor. Benjamin couldn't wait to show me the various sharp, shiny items in his sturdy new tackle box, compliments of Jonathan.

"I hope its okay, but we couldn't resist the great buys in there today, it being the end of the season and all." Jonathan looked apologetic for his spoiling of my son. I smiled my approval and gave Benjamin money to buy us a cold drink and hot pretzel from the vendor nearby since it was nearly noon by now.

"He starts school tomorrow," I sighed. "I'm going to miss him."

"Tori, I've been meaning to talk to you about that."

"About what?"

"Benjamin starting school."

"What about it?"

"Well, I just think with everything going on right now, it might not be a bad idea for you and Benjamin to move in with me."

"Move in with you?" I looked at him somewhat puzzled, a bit surprised at the offer. Jonathan ran sweaty hands through his hair, as it had become quite warm . . . warm enough to match this subject.

"Yes, move in with me. Think about it, Tori. Peter has been to see you once already, and surely his unpredictable behavior will only become even more of a concern as the trial gets under way." We both thought about this, watching Benjamin in line behind two teenagers at the vendor cart.

"I have to admit I've been concerned about our safety. I realize the rather tough-looking man in the plain Chevy outside my house is an expensive luxury." I looked at him apologetically.

"It doesn't matter what he costs. I will gladly pay him for as long as necessary. That's not the point." He reached over and took my hand into his. "I want you near. I want to see that you are fine, every night when I come home. And I want to have you somewhere far away from that easy access neighborhood. Penetrating where I live would be much harder and riskier for Peter."

I nodded my head. "What about Benjamin's school? I don't want him to change schools. Sarah needs him."

"I don't know why he couldn't still attend his regular school. When I explain the special circumstances, the district will not make him transfer to the one in my neighborhood. I could drop him off every day on the way to work."

"And I could pick him up after school," I added.

We looked at each other through shaded glasses, amazed by our plan put instantly in place.

"Jonathan?"

"What?"

"We need to have separate bedrooms."

"Of course."

"I mean it isn't as if Benjamin hasn't figured out how we feel about each other, but still . . ."

"I completely agree. We will explain to him about needing to shelter you from Peter, and we should caution him about Peter too, while we're at it."

"That's a good idea."

Benjamin was ordering when Jonathan walked over to help carry the drinks and pretzels. I watched them standing side by side—one blond and the other dark, but despite their different coloring, no one on the peer would have doubted they were father and son.

And for one indulgent instant, I wished that they were. I wished Jonathan and I had been the lovers on the Rogue trip, had married shortly thereafter, and had spent the last twelve years raising our son through an endless parade of weekends just like this.

But that was then, and this was now, and in the end, now is all we have. I remembered what Grams used to say when the wishing got out of hand. *If wishes were horses, Victoria, we would ride through the night.*

Indeed we would.

CHAPTER TWENTY-FIVE

*He looked up slowly, his expression not registering
surprise so much as curiosity.*

We all three discussed moving into Jonathan's home on the ride back to our
place from the boat excursion. I carefully explained to Benjamin how it was
a matter of safety, since Peter was out on bail.

"What about Sarah?" Benjamin asked.

"I don't mind taking her too," Jonathan answered, without hesitation.

"And I can bring her home from school. As long as Vincent and Maggie
don't object," I added. None of us said it, but we all knew they would be
happy to have her avoid the school bus.

"Mr. Gianni is depending on me to care for the doves," Benjamin said
seriously.

"Why don't you work out something with him while we're there today,
Benj. Maybe you could care for them a couple times a week, while I water
plants and collect the mail."

Benjamin agreed to that, and seemed okay with moving into Jonathan's
house despite these concerns. He helped me pack up our necessities once
we arrived at the apartment. Afterwards he ran off to see Sarah and speak
with Vincent about the doves.

Jonathan and I walked over sometime later, after loading everything
we'd need into the car. We explained what was happening in as un-alarm-
ing a manner as possible. Vincent and Maggie were visibly worried nonetheless, not having previously known about the connection between me,
and the Dr. Cairns written up in the paper on rape charges. They knew
Dr. Miranda Tanasborne was my close friend, of course, but not that I had
known Peter in graduate school.

While Benjamin and Sarah were checking on the doves, I explained how
I had been one of Peter's victims all those years ago, and of his recent visit. I

felt it important to warn the Gianni family in regard to how dangerous this man truly was. That way they could protect themselves against his possible intrusion into their lives, should he attempt to reach me through friends and neighbors.

Benjamin and I spent our first night at Jonathan's house as if we had always lived there. Benj explored the woods and creek even more thoroughly than he already had, after rules were established to ensure his safety. Jonathan and I read the paper on the deck while grilling shish-kabobs—collaborated on after rummaging through the kitchen.

Benjamin had chosen the bedroom overlooking the creek. It was at the far end of the hall from my guest room and Jonathan's master suite. I thought it truly a blessing to have Benjamin at the other end of the house, when needing Jonathan's strong arms to hold me that first night. I wasn't sure if it was a nagging insecurity caused by my recent visit from Peter, or my newly discovered feelings for Jonathan that gravitated me to his bed. Whichever the case, Jonathan was happy to have me, and so I stayed until dawn. Upon returning to the guestroom I couldn't sleep. I kept thinking about what I needed to do later that morning.

Over scrambled eggs and toast I told Jonathan I'd be spending the day at Rachel's studio. I needed to show her the pictures I took from the weekend and get her opinion on which ones to blow up and frame for the gallery. In truth, there were other pressing matters to take care of first.

After Jonathan and Benjamin left I mustered up the nerve for my outrageous plan. I was going to visit Peter and offer him the money from Benjamin's paintings. It was a desperate act on my part, but something I felt I must do, for fear he would try to catch me off guard again, or simply go to the press out of spite. I was grateful that he was a greedy man. You wouldn't think a practicing psychologist would want for money, especially since Peter's parents had been wealthy. No doubt his parents had washed their hands of him after the Mary Jennings scandal and dishonorable exit from the college. It wasn't like they'd ever cared about him to begin with. According to Miranda his private practice was not thriving as hers did.

I knew Jonathan was having Peter trailed in order to keep him from harassing anyone, or fleeing his trial date. Getting around the person trailing him would be a challenge, but I was determined to make it happen, and happen this morning. I was also aware Peter's phone had been tapped. I did not have a cell number for him, but I convinced myself he would not touch me in his home, knowing full well he would be completely accountable for any altercation between us on his property. I just needed a way to get in, to get past Jonathan's private investigator, without being recognized.

I ran some errands downtown while gathering the nerve to visit Peter. Soon the morning was almost spent and I decided it was now or never, as lunchtime was fast approaching. I drove by his house in an older suburb of Portland, tucked away in a quiet middle-class neighborhood of unobtrusive homes. It was unsettling to have his surroundings appear so normal, a place where peaceful coexistence was the standard. A neighborhood where social agendas did not generally cater to mayhem and various manias of the insane, whose deviant escapades often resulted in violent acts of rape and possibly murder.

Driving slowly down his street, I spied the plainclothesman in the generic Ford sitting near the front of his home, and as luck would have it, Peter was backing out of his driveway. It would be even better to meet him in a public place I decided, smiling at my good fortune. I circled the block and fell in behind the white Ford, following Peter's little black sports car. I soon discovered that Peter's destination was a locally run deli two blocks away. The private detective began playing with his phone after he parked in a lot across the street—probably catching up on e-mail. He appeared in no way concerned with whatever it was Peter planned to do inside the deli. I parked several rows away and took a deep breath before having the nerve to follow Peter inside.

My heart racing, I kept reasoning with myself that Peter was quite harmless in a public setting. In fact, he prided himself on looking as normal as possible to the outside world. This was exactly why so many people were appalled at the accusations about him in the local paper. Miranda had been quite shocked by his following of supporters, and was even more shocked by the suspicions of many that she was lying about the rape.

Once inside the deli I stood near a shelf stacked with fresh baked breads. There were long crusty baguettes and round loaves of dark rye, sour dough rolls and flaky croissants—all for making sandwiches. The room was comfortably full of patrons. They stood in a haphazard line to order their lunch items at the counter. Small round tables were scattered about for those who wanted to eat on the premises.

Peter sat by the window and was reading a small paperback novel. I mustered up the nerve to walk over, telling myself that Peter cannot possibly hurt me in this public place, all the while picturing my sweaty body under the damp porch, feeling scared out of my wits. I somehow crossed the cluttered room and found myself eerily standing before him. He looked up slowly, his expression not registering surprise so much as curiosity.

"Victoria. I see you've come to your senses and have quit running from me."

I sat across from him, not sure my shaky knees could have stood much longer. "I'm here to make a deal with you, Peter." *A deal with the devil*, I thought to myself, the realization of it only adding to the sweat breaking out on my forehead.

"How sensible of you. And what about Miranda? Have you talked some sense into her, too? Is she going to drop her lame charges against me?"

A young girl delivered a deli sandwich to Peter, who took a large bite and waited for my reply.

"I will gladly give you the money from the paintings, Peter. If you remain silent about my son's paternity, I will give you any additional funds he may incur from his artwork as well. I would only need a forwarding address to send it to."

In truth, I was only interested in buying more time before deciding exactly how to deal with the entire dilemma.

"Are you implying I should take the money and run?" Peter laughed. "Perhaps to the ends of the earth?"

"It wouldn't be a bad idea. Remington, Marsh, Davis, and Lowe are excellent attorneys. You might otherwise find yourself . . . indisposed . . . for quite a long time."

What I really wanted was for him to be shot down in cold blood like the rabid animal he behaved as, before getting very far away on the money.

"That Miss-High-and-Mighty friend of yours doesn't have a prayer. No evidence, no case." Peter pushed his plate away with disgust. "She must be crazier than those messed up kids she sees to believe this trial has a leg to stand on."

"Perhaps." I glanced out the window at the unmarked Ford in the lot across the street. I never thought such an average everyday sight as that would steady my heartbeat. "Peter, where and how would you like your money?"

He glanced around to be sure there was no one listening. "I want cash, Tori dear. *All of it* in cash."

"Okay. I can do that. When and where should I deliver it?" I asked, trying not to look frightened or nervous, being so near him, making a pact with this deviant.

"I am able to easily escape my dimwit buddy here any time I wish," he said matter-of-factly, nodding at the generic white car outside the deli window and across the street in the empty lot. "I need only leave out my back entrance and cross through the shrubbery to catch a bus one block over. I have done this several times already to visit my office downtown, as I have several clients I don't wish for my idiot friend in the Ford to know I'm seeing."

"How very clever of you. But then, I have never doubted your cleverness." I tried not to sound as if I despised him. "Does this mean you want me to bring the money to your office?" I inquired, trying desperately to fake a business-as-usual demeanor, all the while silently questioning my sanity.

"Yes, I think that would be perfect, and of course, mums the word about your not-so-celibate lover." His face lit up from the amusement of mocking me. "Although I still believe that, quite possibly, your Benjamin carries the blood of my own genius in his veins rather than that sappy priest's." Peter's eyes were literally glowing with conceit.

I shuddered, hoping not visibly, and was overcome suddenly by weariness, emotionally and mentally drained from being in Peter's ominous presence. I wanted nothing more than to get far away from him as quickly as I could. Standing to leave, I glanced out the window one last time, hoping the sight of Jonathan's P.I. might steady my weak knees.

"Exactly two weeks from today, *Tori darling*, at precisely noon, I will see you at my office." He gave me a no-nonsense look, the humor gone from his expression. I nodded and left quietly, my head swimming with guilt, regret, and relief all mixed together.

With my hair tied back and mostly under a ball cap, I raised the collar on my over-sized jacket and wondered, walking back to the car, if I looked inconspicuous or stood out as overwhelmingly suspicious. The hardest part was not glancing at the white Ford to see if Jonathan's detective had noticed me.

The rest of the day I spent in Photoshop on Rachel's state-of-the-art gallery computer, grateful she was out somewhere delivering art to clients. I didn't feel up to facing her, afraid I would admit what just transpired, never having been successful at keeping secrets from her. I busied myself with attempting to transform my photos from our outing on Jonathan's boat into an impressive showing of harbor prints for the gallery, but the layering effects I was aiming for were going painfully slow. Finally it was time to pick Benjamin and Sarah up. They talked about their first day of school, nonstop, all the way to the apartment complex. Once we arrived, they hurriedly jumped out of the car, claiming to be famished and knowing Maggie would have warm cookies waiting for them.

I sat quietly behind the wheel, with the late afternoon sun streaming in through the windshield, and thought about how fleeting Benjamin's carefree days of childhood were. As fleeting as these hot, dry days of Indian summer. I did not wish to glimpse into his future for a hint of where it all was leading. I had a hard enough time dealing with the present, and keeping it as unencumbered by the past as I possibly could.

Finally I visited our apartment and gathered up more things we might need. I watered the plants again, although we had only been gone one day. My main goal was to avoid Maggie, who would surely raise an eyebrow at my sullen mood and the obvious guilt I saw in the hall mirror, where I stopped to scrutinize my reflection. I wanted to see what a self-serving traitor to the cause of justice would look like staring back at me. But all I saw reflected there was a tan, composed woman with large, deep-set eyes the color of a Montana sky—as my father used to say. I had to take his word for it, never having been to Montana.

It occurred to me how I was truly no different than Peter for being other than what I seemed. With this depressing knowledge weighing on my mind and heart, I drove to Jonathan's in silence, Benjamin preoccupied beside me with a new art book from the school library. After helping unload our things from the car, he ran off to play in the creek, and I tried to busy myself with arranging and rearranging our things in an attempt to avoid Jonathan until dinner.

My guilt kept growing until I could barely breathe from the weight of it, wishing I were not doing such a traitorous and selfish thing as to scheme in the aiding and abetting of a criminal. I couldn't shake the reality that Jonathan had taken us in to protect us from the very man I was now consorting with. I was making a mockery of Jonathan's justice. But I reasoned that Benjamin did not have the church to protect him, or to hide behind, as Daniel did.

He only had me.

CHAPTER TWENTY-SIX

"Did He not make man to love a woman?"

Dinner was spent on the deck watching the sunset. It was surely one of the last warm evenings to grace our presence. Dark brisk evenings of mid fall would soon chase us indoors. I quizzed Benjamin about his first day back at school, while trying to suppress my nagging thoughts about having spent the day bribing Peter. After dinner Benj ran off to catch crawfish down by the creek, and I told Jonathan about my upcoming Catholicism lesson with Daniel.

"Do you think having these lessons with Daniel is wise?"

"Don't you trust me?" I asked, knowing I did not deserve his trust.

"Now that Benjamin knows Daniel is his father, you're giving him false hope. And you might be giving Daniel false hope, too. At least, I pray to God it's false hope," Jonathan added.

We stared at each other for a second and then I shrugged. "Are you honestly thinking I'd drop everything and run off with Daniel?"

"I'm thinking that I don't know what you're thinking, and that scares the hell out of me," Jonathan admitted.

I wouldn't look into his eyes, because I was afraid of what truths might be revealed there, one of those truths being how I *needed* to see Daniel. Especially now that Benjamin *knew* and we were *here*, and I loved Jonathan. I needed to see if my love for Daniel was still real, or if it had vanished into the night with Peter when I was rescued by Jonathan, and fell into this love affair with him, unlike anything since the Rogue trip. I needed to face exactly what Jonathan wanted me to avoid. My feelings for Daniel, and whatever they were now, as opposed to whatever they were then.

I cleverly changed the subject and eased the tension mounting between us. Later, in the middle of the night, I completely chased his fears away by wrapping my body around his and making sweet love to him. Memories of my night with Jonathan lingered in my mind as I stood in Daniel's doorway, and observed him behind his desk. The blond hair was ruffled, the collar on his shirt askew. It was a light blue button down with the sleeves rolled up, and when he glanced at me, his eyes appeared brilliant in the melding of them with that shirt. My heart raced, so taken aback was I by the troubled look on his angelic face.

"Tori. I didn't think you would come."

"Then you didn't forget?"

"Of course not." He put his pencil down and closed the ledger he'd been writing in. "I prayed you would not show. And I prayed that you would. Mostly, I prayed for my own redemption . . . because I fear you just may be the death of me."

I leaned on the doorframe, afraid to enter, afraid to cross the line into his space and then into his life and into his being forever. A part of me so wanted to consume him and all that he was and had been and would ever be. And I hated myself for these feelings, stronger at this moment than ever. Perhaps because he looked so lost, or because he looked so good. Or perhaps, because I believed that I was not so good, especially after my visit to Peter yesterday.

Daniel stood up. "Are you going to come in?"

Slowly, I walked over to the fireplace, still cold and damp and fireless, but I knew it would only be a matter of time now until it would burn hotly. It was as imminent as the healthy green leaves dying crimson, burnt orange, and golden yellow, and soon thereafter, falling to the cold hard ground.

Daniel sat in the chair beside me. We sank into the worn leather of the generous and sturdy furniture, quietly watching the hollow, blackened fire pit.

"Are you living with him then?" He did not look at me, but continued to stare at the ash stained firebricks.

"Yes. For protection . . . against Peter." I looked at him and wanted nothing more than to join him in his chair, curling up in his lap, and taking his head into my hands while kissing his perfectly formed lips.

"I see." It did not sound as if he did. And then he added, "Are you sleeping with him?"

My heart skipped at least one beat, and my throat became dry. "Is that a proper question for a priest to ask a Catholicism student?"

"Not at all. It isn't proper to feel about you the way I do, either. But that would be the bigger issue, wouldn't it?"

Daniel sounded more on edge than I had ever heard him. I was worried about such despair in his tone. I was even more concerned about the compassion it brought forth in me, gushing out in great quantities that somehow piqued my lust for him beyond belief.

"I am so sorry, Daniel, that I have been such a curse to your ministry and all that you wish to accomplish. I just keep spoiling your perfect relationship with God and the church. Like a fever that refuses to break."

Daniel looked up with a startled expression. "No, Victoria. You mustn't feel responsible. Were I a stronger servant, you would be no threat to me."

"I see. A stronger servant, or a stronger man, or a stronger *what,* Daniel? How much stronger would God expect you to be, if you truly are only a man? Did He not make man to love a woman?"

He just sighed. There would be no answer from him, of that I was sure. Slowly he picked his Bible up off the table beside him and flipped through the thin pages to a particular passage where he stopped, and spoke while staring at the print. "Tori, I promised to be your teacher this time, and I need to keep that promise."

"Fine. Teach me then, all about your cruel God that will not allow you to love me."

"I can *love* you, Tori. I just can't *have* you."

"Can't have me? That sounds so possessive . . . like something Peter would say or think. It is what he did, actually. He *had* me, as if I were nothing more than flesh to steal."

"Don't be cruel, comparing me to this man, *Benjamin's father.*" Daniel stood and walked to the only window, peering out as if a refuge from reality awaited him there, just beyond the glass.

"Is that what you believe?" I stood too, and gaped at his back, unable to comprehend such a misconstrued truth.

"Isn't it obvious?" He turned to face me, with a faraway look. "The strong, slender build and blond hair, and his instincts about the nature of things. He has quite a gift for psychology . . . now with small hurt creatures, but eventually perhaps like his father . . . he will be a brilliant doctor."

He paused there and focused on me. "Benjamin has an amazing mind, like Peter, only because of your influence he is even more good than his father is bad."

I wanted to shout at him, run up and shake him, screaming, *You have blond hair and an amazing mind! You are his father, healer of man and beast, as he is, and not entirely human, as he isn't . . . is he . . . is he?*

I suddenly realized I was shaking.

Daniel crossed the room in one fell swoop, and wrapped his arms around me. "Tori, I'm sorry. I know how hard it is for you to believe that Peter is Benjamin's father, after what he did to you. But it has to be faced. *You must face the truth.* Nothing can change it, no matter how much you wish it away."

"Is that what I'm doing?" I whispered into his soft blue shirt. "Wishing away the truth? You would know all about that, wouldn't you, Daniel?" I wanted to tell him the truth more than ever, just as I *wanted him* more than I ever had.

"Peter has been here again, to speak with me." Daniel rested his chin on the top of my head and told me this with a heavy sigh, either not hearing or not listening to what I had said. I pulled away and looked up at him.

"Really? And what did Peter want this time?" Without waiting for a reply I walked over and fell into the chair again, exhausted from the heavy truths I bore alone.

Daniel sat beside me in the other brown leather monstrosity, well suited for the overbearing piety of a priest's den. "He wanted to know about the Church, actually. About religion and faith. All the things he should be concerned with, lest he burn in eternal damnation."

"Does that excite you? The thought of saving his miserable soul?" I did not temper my sarcasm.

"Saving every single soul is a worthy ambition, Tori. Your hate can only hurt *you*, not *Peter*."

I despised his logic, thinking Daniel's truisms were more annoying than his relentless need to be God's perfect servant. "What specifically did Peter ask you?" I demanded, staring at the partly burned candles in heavy brass holders on the mantle above the fire pit. It was impossible for me to believe Peter didn't have an ulterior motive for his questions about Daniel's faith.

"Besides the philosophies surrounding John 3:16 . . . *For God so loved the world, that he gave his only begotten son, that whoever believeth in him should not perish, but have everlasting life* . . . he wanted to know about the history of the church. And specifically about my personal history, his curiosity piqued by the recent news surrounding my impending bishop title."

"Your *personal* history?" My worst fears were realized in that instant. I knew what Peter was up to, and it escalated my desire to pay him off and get rid of him.

"Yes. I told him where I grew up in Venice, where I studied in Rome, and about the history of the cathedral where I served, until coming here to America to continue my studies." Daniel looked over at me, and I at him, both of us aware that we had spent many hours on the Rogue discussing these very things about Daniel's past. Only he had omitted the part where he served as a priest, indicating merely that he *attended* the small cathedral near *Campo di fiore.*

"Did he ask about your healing powers?" I shuddered, knowing full well the answer to my question.

"Yes."

We stared into each other's eyes, the unasked questions between us falling into a vast valley at our feet, for it was the *gift of healing* we could not face, or deny. It was this performing of miracles that made Daniel whatever he refused to confess to, and made his son undeniably his, no matter how completely he tried to avoid this truth.

I put my face in my hands, overwhelmed with it all. Peter knew. He knew my son might be more than just a child prodigy, that he might very well be a conundrum the world could never accept with open arms, unless sheltered within the mysteries of the church. It was dangerous information for such a deviant mind to play with. I could only be thankful he didn't know *for sure*. He knew nothing, to my knowledge, of Benjamin's healings.

I was not aware Daniel had kneeled in front of my chair until he pushed my hair back gently, and pulled my hands away from my face. "What is it, Tori? Why are you so disturbed by this man, Peter? I know he wronged you once, but you say you don't remember it. And he can't hurt you now. It is my understanding that Jonathan has him watched every second. And if justice is served, he will be behind bars soon enough."

I studied the pure cyan hue of those extraordinary eyes. "Burning in hell will be his only true justice."

"Hating this man will destroy *you*, not him. You must forgive him, Tori. You must admit he is Benjamin's father and move beyond it. The boy deserves to know the truth. Peter's sins will not be visited upon the son."

"And how can you be so sure? Heredity is a predisposition to many things, no matter how much we may want to ignore that fact." I stared at him intently, wondering if he had even a vague idea of what I meant.

Daniel ran his fingers lightly down my neck. "Tori, I could mentor Benjamin. I could have him work beside me here, in the church, and teach him about . . . his spirituality, his faith in God."

He knew. I decided at that moment *he knew* and all of this was just a charade, a cover for his purpose to become bishop and have Benjamin too. "How generous of you to take such an interest in my son, *the son of a genius* as you say, who just so happens to also be a rapist and possible serial killer, in the hopes of saving Benjamin from the same demonic future with God's help, no less."

"Tori, even if I didn't take him under my wing, Benjamin would be fine. But he has shown an interest in the church and I want to help him if I can. The boy is very important to me . . . because *you* are very important to me."

I heard his words, but they were not registering. Only in the fact that he was deluding himself more than he was reassuring me. It was the tone, soft and vibrant, and the eyes, clear and perfect. His hair . . . I wanted to run my fingers through his irreverent curls . . . *he was so close.* And then he was quiet as he studied me. And soon thereafter his lips were touching mine and we were somehow hopelessly entrenched in this very hungry, lingering kiss. After which, I didn't chose to run away for once. With his face just inches from mine, he further cajoled me with a plan I felt for certain had been thoroughly plotted long before this moment.

"Tori, come with me on my retreat next week."

"Your retreat?"

"Yes, at Mt. Hood. There is a cabin, a house really, very quaint and comfortable. It sits directly at the foot of the mountain, with a breathtaking view. The church owns this retreat home. It's called Rosewood. I am going up Monday, alone, and will be undisturbed for five days, completely. There are no phones, no deliveries."

"And what would we do at Rosewood together? Study religion? Maybe fast? Pray?" I kept my tone innocent, despite knowing full well these were not his intentions.

"I love you. And I *know* that you love me. Don't pretend otherwise. Don't torture me, Victoria. I need you. I can't bear the thought of living without you any longer. Of never being with you ever again."

"And how do you then propose to live *with me*, if as you say, you can't bear the thought of living *without me*?" My eyes did not avert his.

Daniel stood up in frustration and stared at the books on the far shelves. "Are you in love with Jonathan?" he asked, his attention seemingly fixated on the neatly arranged rows of books.

"Yes." I couldn't think of a reason to elaborate.

"Is there no hope for me then?" He looked at me, masking any hurt he might have felt by that response. Certainly, he didn't look surprised, and I believed this desperate attempt to hang on to whatever it was we didn't really have was spurred in part by that knowledge, already known by him, obtained through his recent observations.

"I don't know what you mean by hope."

He kneeled before me again and took my hands into his. This time when he looked into my eyes there was determination there . . . to accomplish what, I could not be sure.

"Victoria, come to Rosewood. Monday evening." He handed me a card with the address and directions, obviously printed up for visitors who planned to stay there. "You owe it to yourself to be sure your love for . . . someone else, is genuine. We owe it to ourselves to see if moving on is even a possibility, because if it is not, if we are destined to be together . . . then we are fools to fight it. And we are wrong to hurt others," he reasoned.

"It's too late for that. Others will already be hurt," I said emphatically. We both knew I meant Jonathan, but I couldn't bring myself to say it, or to ask him if he was thinking of leaving the church for me, and for Benjamin. Did he even know what he was thinking? I thought not, and that perhaps this is what Rosewood was all about.

"Please, just think about it. Don't say no." He closed my hand around the card. "Eight o'clock, Monday evening. Tori, you will not want to leave. It is so beautiful and peaceful there by the mountain. Come prepared to stay for the whole five days."

He stood up, and just in time, as a nun knocked on the open door while peeking in at us. I came to find out she was the Sister Margaret I had spoken with on the phone once. Daniel introduced us as old friends, and then I excused myself, indicating a need to pick up my son. He was at Sarah's waiting for me.

The drive there went quickly, so dazed was I. Confused and disturbed by my fickle feelings and behavior. I did not like this person I was becoming. Why was I making deals with Peter, whom surely would one day know the devil himself intimately, if he didn't already. And how could I allow myself to be tempted by Daniel? I knew he was chosen by God as a gifted healing servant, here to accomplish something far beyond what a mere mortal could accomplish. Most of all, why was I deceiving Jonathan in this way, by succumbing to both the devil and the divine, strictly out of weakness for one and fear of the other?

I felt as if poised to throw away my only chance at happiness with someone who, try as he may, simply could not save me from myself.

CHAPTER TWENTY-SEVEN

"He interprets his love for you as a weakness to indulge,
not a strength to embrace."

I did not come to Jonathan in the night, and because he stayed late at the office and then worked out at his club, I did not see him until morning. Vincent picked up Benjamin, claiming to have an early morning tile-laying job. Whether this was true or not, I knew that he wished to help with the carpooling. It allowed Jonathan and I to linger over coffee and discuss what we had been avoiding.

"I missed you last night." Jonathan did not elaborate, but I knew what he meant.

"I missed you too."

"Really? Then why did you stay away?" he asked, skeptically.

"Because I knew you weren't pleased about my appointment with Daniel. And I wasn't sure you would welcome me." It was the truth, but I also felt guilty for having been so drawn to Daniel, for realizing the attraction between us had not subsided with my love of another man.

"I could never reject you. I love you too much. My fear is that your love for me is secondary to your obsession for Daniel." He let go of the morning paper he was holding and folded his hands on the table, as if bracing himself for my response.

I didn't know what to say. At that moment, looking at him there across the table from me, I loved him more than I had ever loved anyone. Because I understood him, as much as any woman can understand a man. He was not like Daniel, who was a frustrating mystery, a riddle that could not be solved, a temptation that could not be explained or denied. That was all I knew for sure about Daniel, that perhaps he truly was merely an obsession. But how does one stop obsessing? How does one tear such an obsession loose from its hold on their soul?

"Tori, your silence is killing me. Has Daniel won then? Are you going to live your life in stolen moments with him? Or has he at least offered to leave the church for you?"

"I love you, Jonathan, more now—after my visit to Daniel—than I ever have. I don't know what to say to convince you of that."

"Say you'll marry me."

Now I truly was speechless, and I just looked at him, no doubt with an expression to equal my bewilderment.

"I mean it, Tori. I want to wake up with you every morning for the rest of my life, and I don't want you in the next room. I don't want you even an arm's length away, which is as close to Daniel as you can ever hope to get." He stood up and walked over to the window, looking out at the sun already warming the trees beyond the creek. "I don't believe for a minute he is not scheming to keep you in his life, and out of mine. You must realize any commitment he makes to you will never be more than minimal. He interprets his love for you as a weakness to indulge, not a strength to embrace." He looked at me, sitting there staring up at him. "I don't tell you that to hurt you, Tori. And it's just my interpretation. I could be wrong. God knows I might not be as objective about Daniel as I have deluded myself into believing I am."

"I thought you and Daniel were good friends, Jonathan. I thought you loved him like a brother." I was disturbed by their sudden jealousy of each other, and mortified that I had caused this deep rift now gaping between them.

"We *are* friends. We've always had a lot of common interests. Unfortunately, you are one of them. Maybe I should never have acted on my feelings for you."

"I'm glad you did." I stood up and put my arms around him.

"We can go ring shopping whenever you wish, that is, if you decide you want to spend the rest of your life with me."

I didn't answer him. Instead we began indulging in a passionate kiss, but it was interrupted by a phone call. Peter somehow escaped the P.I., which completely changed the mood of the moment. I almost told Jonathan how it was that Peter did this, but realized I would also have to confess my interactions with him at the deli. I decided not to say anything, and he left soon thereafter, still on the cell phone with the P.I.

I finished getting ready and headed nervously for Rachel's, under strict instructions from Jonathan to be very careful. He was going to have someone meet me there and guard me until Peter was found. The P.I. who lost Peter was now headed for Miranda's office, to keep an eye on her. Jonathan feared what Peter was capable of. He had a clever way of making it appear that all his victims were suicidal, and had taken their own lives. But he and Robert had determined after their extensive investigation that the doctor was as much a serial killer as a rapist with his mysterious drugs.

Once at Rachel's I tried to concentrate on completing the boating pictures, using the oversized computer in her office. It was Friday, and Rachel was teaching a morning art class at the community center. She especially looked forward to it because Robert's girls, Bronwin and Emma, were in the class. I knew she would be back soon because their private school started at ten a.m. on Fridays, supposedly to give all the over-achievers a chance to take enrichment classes.

I was looking forward to a talk with my best friend, over her fine china and exotic tea, both fetishes that had grown to be quite calming to me. I was hoping she could sooth my jumpy nerves. It made me impossibly edgy, knowing I could have prevented Peter's evading the P.I. by telling someone he was sneaking out through a back escape route. But that would have been incriminating myself. One minute I was being righteously indignant about this demon and the next I had somehow become a co-conspirator in deceit.

When Rachel finally walked through the door, I blurted out the news of Peter's disappearance.

"Has anyone talked to Miranda?" Rachel looked instantly worried.

"Yes, Jonathan and I have both spoken with her. We called as soon as the news came in from the P.I. this morning. That same private investigator is with her now. And the plainclothesman out front is watching me."

"I wondered who that was parked in front on the street. I almost told him he'd be towed if he left his vehicle there unattended." Rachel dropped her big oversized school bag and large sketchpads on a bench in the hall and headed straight for the kitchen, with me following, telling her all I knew in a nervous frenzy.

"The investigator came in to check the back entrance, instructing me to keep it locked. He also checked all the windows and said to keep my cell phone handy, in case I needed to call him. He programmed my phone while giving all these instructions."

"I see." Rachel sighed. "Well, I need some herbal tea. This whole situation is down right spooky." She busied herself with filling the kettle and choosing the teapot and cups we would use.

"How was class this morning?" I asked, trying not to think about Peter, out there somewhere unattended.

"It was fun." Rachel stopped fussing for a minute and looked at me standing there at the far end of the counter.

"You know, Robert's girls are both quite talented. Bronwin has a wonderful sense of design and color. Emma is just plain bold with her ideas. She has quite an imagination." Rachel laughed, as if recalling Emma's work. Then she became serious. "But Robert picked them up. Claire never came for them, so they called their father. It was odd seeing him there with his girls. I never see him with Bronwin and Emma. I only see them with Claire."

"I met Claire at Jonathan's barbeque."

"What did you think of her?"

"I thought she was . . . self absorbed. Not very friendly."

"That sounds like Claire all right. Exactly the way she is when dropping the girls off and picking them up." Rachel put the ball of loose tea in the pot. "I often wonder if she knows about me and Robert, and if that's why she's so cold. But truthfully, I think she's not the least bit aware or even concerned about what Robert's doing. She seems to have her own agenda and it completely consumes her."

"I think she knows Peter," I offered up.

Rachel didn't respond to that, other than giving me a serious stare. She turned off the whistling teakettle and poured steaming water into a pale yellow teapot. Then she brought it to the table with two matching cups.

"Tori, why do you think Claire knows Peter?"

I shrugged. "It's just a hunch. She got terribly nervous when Peter's name came up at the barbeque. Daniel mentioned the trial and she appeared flustered almost immediately."

"What was Daniel doing there?" Rachel looked surprised.

"I'm not sure. Jonathan wasn't expecting him, although he'd been invited. The church always has a big get-together on Labor Day and Jonathan assumed Daniel would be attending."

"How *is* Daniel?" Rachel had that steady gaze upon me, that scrutinizing look that saw right through to my inner thoughts.

"He . . . wants me to spend time with him."

Rachel raised an eyebrow, but didn't look surprised really, just concerned. "What does the good man of God want you to do, exactly? Meet him somewhere, just the two of you?" She took a sip of tea.

"Rachel, how could you know that he wants to . . . be *alone* with me?" I laughed, a nervous, self-conscious laugh, somewhat taken aback by her intuitive nature.

"Tori, you forget, I live continually sandwiched between reality and non, between the sunny side of my every day life as a gallery owner and art teacher, and my stolen moments with a man that belongs to someone else. Sometimes I feel as if I am nothing more than a cool, lush shade tree, a temporary refuge from the searing sun, more of mirage than a mortal. And I don't mind. I have never regretted it. But you must ask yourself if you are willing to be a mirage, lurking about in the hidden corners of Daniel's fame and glory, secretly defying the sanctity of the church.

I slowly sipped my tea, watching the steam rise from the cup. I didn't have an answer. I didn't have a clue as to what, if anything, I wanted from Daniel short of his soul, which I couldn't have.

Rachel sighed. "And what about Jonathan? Have you told him of Daniel's proposal for a lifelong tryst?"

"I didn't say that Daniel had offered such a thing." We stared at each other, a knowingly, who-is-kidding-whom stare. "Actually, I told Daniel that I love Jonathan, and it's true."

"I bet that didn't discourage Daniel in the least."

"Rachel, you're incorrigible."

"But I'm right, nonetheless."

"Okay, then, yes. He does want me to meet him at Rosewood Monday evening, and stay the week."

"What is Rosewood?"

"It's a retreat house owned by the church, up at Mt. Hood."

"I see."

"No, you don't see. I have no intention of going." We stared at each other again, and I wondered if the uncertainty I felt was reflected in my eyes. We drank our tea in silence for a while, both lost in our own thoughts and then I laid the pictures before her of the boating weekend. I had almost forgotten about the two dozen eleven-by-fourteen photos I stacked at the far end of the table earlier for her to view.

"These are beautiful, Tori. The soft shadows and the sunset melting into the water . . . I could get lost in them." She shook her head while staring at a photo of Jonathan and Benjamin fishing off the side rail. "He would make a wonderful father for Benj, wouldn't he?"

"Jonathan has asked me to marry him."

"And what did you say?"

"I haven't given him an answer yet."

She looked up, studying my expression, which I kept as neutral as possible, not wishing to reveal my confusion. And then I changed the subject. "Daniel thinks Peter is the father of Benjamin."

Rachel laughed out loud. "You're kidding!"

"I only wish I were. Peter has been to see Daniel again, and has been making inquiries into his background."

"Really?"

"That's not good, Rachel." I stood up and walked to the window, having managed to upset myself. "He is only prying into Daniel's past to discover any other secrets that he can, especially now that he is fully aware of Daniel's unusual healing powers. There is no telling what he would do with privileged information about the source of these healing powers. I wouldn't put it past him to blackmail the church, if only to delight in the power of it."

"Maybe, but he doesn't need any more information to blackmail *you* than he already has." Rachel stood to put the cups in the sink. "Have you thought about that? About how you have all that money now from Benjamin's paintings and the promise of more to come?"

I averted my eyes, my nerves nearly jumping in my throat over the word blackmail, especially since it was me initiating it, *not Peter*. Thankfully the phone rang before I could spill my guts and shock the hell out of Rachel, who believed me to be a much better person than I had recently become. She answered it on the first ring and did a lot more listening than responding.

I studied Rachel's body language as she lowered her head, nodding it slowly, as if the person on the other end could actually see her response. Sitting down hard at the table she said yes several times, and then goodbye. Rachel clicked the phone off and gently placed it on the table. I stared at her sitting there, while leaning against the window with my arms folded, clutching myself in a way, bracing myself for whatever that phone call was about. I knew it was nothing good. I knew I would somehow pay for my sin of bribing Peter and then being silent about his devious behavior of eluding the P.I.—sneaking out to his office in order to visit clients, he said, *clients he didn't want anyone to know about.*

"Who was that, Rach?" My voice cracked, filled with the same fear I saw in her expression.

"It was Jonathan." Tears formed in her eyes and began to trickle down her cheek, but she wiped them away with shaking fingers.

"What did he say?" I asked, feeling myself turn pale. "It's Peter, isn't it? He's done something . . . something terrible, he's killed someone, hasn't he?"

I came and sat beside her at the table.

"No one knows if Peter has done anything. No one knows where Peter is. But Claire . . . well, she's dead. Oh my god, *Robert's wife is dead!*"

I swallowed hard, and then barely found my voice to ask, "*Where?* Where did they find Claire?"

Rachel tried to compose herself, handing me a tissue from the box on the counter and using one herself. "They think, well, it *looks like* she committed suicide . . . in *Peter's office.*"

"No!" It was all I could say, but not all I could think. I knew I had caused her death. My silence surely killed her. *Surely it did.*

"Jonathan is on his way here. He doesn't want either of us to leave."

"I bet not," I said, and to myself I added, *I bet he knows.* He knows I have seen Peter. How could he not know? This P.I. would have told him every detail of every minute of Peter's surveillance. I was fooling myself to believe I had successfully escaped his notice. Why hadn't I considered that before? What was I thinking, sitting there by the window in the deli, glancing out at the man in the unmarked car, believing his presence was a comfort to me even though I also believed he knew nothing about my presence? *What was I thinking?*

And that's just it. I wasn't thinking. Not clearly anyway. I hadn't ever thought clearly where Peter was concerned. And now someone was dead because of it. *Claire was the client he didn't want anyone to know about.* Claire was seeing Peter as a patient. Claire was dead . . . Robert's wife, Robert who had done all the extensive investigating into Peter's past. *Robert didn't know.* He couldn't have known Claire was seeing Peter. No one knew. *I could have prevented her death.* How was I going to explain that to Rachel? Or to Jonathan? Or to Robert? Or to Bronwin and Emma? How could I ever tell them how sorry I was?

Or expect them to forgive me when I could never forgive myself?

CHAPTER TWENTY-EIGHT

There is only one God, Tori . . . and He lives in all of us.

Jonathan arrived shortly after his phone call with the news of Claire's death. Rachel went to let him in when the doorbell rang. I sat frozen at the kitchen table, staring out the window where fall leaves were dying a brilliant death, and winter felt a little more imminent every time one fell from a tree.

Perfect weather for a funeral I thought, wondering suddenly when the funeral would be. There was a sharp wind off the gorge that could slice right through you now in early morning. At least the cold breeze would be a reminder amidst the grief of it all that we were still alive. Those of us standing at the graveside would only have the warmth of our tears to ward off the chill. I was so lost in the perplexity of this coming event that I didn't notice Jonathan slip into the kitchen chair next to me.

"Tori? Are you okay?" he asked, looking at me wearily, as if he had lived a lifetime in the last two hours since I saw him.

"Yes, I'm sorry," I sighed. "He killed her, didn't he? Peter killed her and made it look like suicide, just like he always does. How many more times do you think? Until he is finally stopped once and for all?" I wasn't really expecting an answer, since no one could predict how many more times Peter would kill until he was killed himself, or stopped, at least.

"We don't know. She might actually have committed suicide. Claire was a troubled woman, not well at all mentally." Jonathan paused there, as if unsure of how much to say, or what to ask. And ask he would, because I knew he had questions for me, concerning my visit to Peter. How could I have thought he didn't know about that escapade from the moment it happened? One cell phone call from the perceptive P.I. is all it would have taken to inform him. Why didn't he say anything then? Why didn't I?

Rachel was crying quietly. She sat at the end of the table and looked at me strangely. I realized how calm I was. Not emotional, not reacting in any way at all really, just staring out the window in order to avoid her questioning eyes.

"How's Robert doing?" she asked, meekly. "How did he find out? It couldn't have been long after he picked the girls up from art class." A fresh set of tears began streaming down her face.

"The medics called right after Bronwin and Emma phoned their father to pick them up. They identified Claire by the things in her purse, and called Robert to tell him she'd taken a bottle of pills in Peter's office. They didn't say she was dead."

"What kind of pills?" I asked curiously.

"Whatever they were, the prescription was in her name. And the note didn't line up with Peter's typical notes of the past." Jonathan and I looked at each other, sadly hopeful that she had actually killed herself, rather than Peter having done it. But truthfully, either way, he was no doubt responsible for her death in the end.

"Why? Why would she kill herself in Peter's office?" Rachel demanded.

"Well, according to the suicide letter, she was having an affair with Peter." Jonathan paused there, and we all glanced at one another. "When she discovered his past involvement with drugging and raping women, she decided she too had been his victim." He paused again and we all stared at our hands, or the table, dazed and unbelieving. Jonathan stood up and walked over to the window. "She claims that Peter was treating her for an obsessive-compulsive disorder, by hypnotizing her."

"How did that make her a victim?" Rachel asked.

"According to the letter she left, neatly written in long hand and carefully propped against the computer monitor on Peter's desk, she desperately needed his sessions to alleviate her symptoms, so she saw him twice weekly. Before she realized what had happened, he'd made her completely dependent on him in order to function normally without the return of her obsessive-compulsive behaviors. He claimed to have fallen in love with her and made it clear he wanted to have an affair. She knew Robert would question it if she continued to spend so much money on her hypnosis therapy, since he didn't approve of this type of treatment. So she and Peter became lovers, and she quit paying. But then felt trapped into having sex with Peter in order to get the hypnosis she had grown dependent on."

Jonathan sat back down at the table. "The only way out, as she saw it, was to kill herself."

"Why didn't she take drugs for her symptoms? Obviously she was taking some type of drug if she overdosed with a prescription in her name." I was mortified and feeling perfectly miserable for any part I might have played in her demise by not telling anyone of Peter's escape route from the P.I.

"Apparently Peter had her convinced that nothing short of the regular hypnosis could help someone with symptoms as serious as hers, even though she was still taking drugs. She had seen other doctors but no one had ever alleviated her symptoms as much as Peter had. She was convinced that no one else could. Essentially, she couldn't live with knowing what kind of man he really was, and the things that he had done to her and to others, and yet she couldn't live a normal life without him."

"Whatever made her think she was living a normal life?" I asked. "Tied to Peter for hypnosis and paying for it through sex?" No one answered, because we all knew Claire's illusion of normal was partly to blame for her death.

"I feel so bad for Robert." Rachel smoothed back her short honey-blonde hair that always looked slightly untamed . . . sort of like she was, prowling about her large kitchen or the well-equipped studio and art stuffed gallery, every nook and cranny of her life oozing free expression and unlimited boundaries. Rachel was anything but fenced in, or codependent. And she was the sanest person I had ever met. How could Robert be involved with two women who were so completely different in every way possible?

"So you believe she committed suicide? That Peter didn't kill her?" I asked, wondering which was worse, really, but selfishly, I needed to believe Peter didn't do it. Otherwise, I played a role in her death by not telling anyone how Peter needed to see clients he didn't want anyone to know about . . . *clients like Claire.*

"I don't know. It's hard to say." Jonathan folded his hands on the table.

"Why is it hard to say?" My voice was rising, and Rachel looked at me, startled. "I mean, damn-it, Jonathan, you just told me she was desperate! You just recited every best reason in the world to kill oneself, straight out of her suicide note!" Now they were both staring at me and I realized that I was truly shouting. I stood up and walked over to the counter, banging cabinet doors until I found a glass, pouring water in it from the tap. I drank shakily, gulping it down in frustration.

"What's the matter, Tori?" Jonathan asked too calmly. "Are you mortified that you hadn't considered Peter planned to kill again? This time to avenge Robert, who did all the investigating for his trial? Or perhaps only to shut Claire up because she knew too much?" I turned to look at him, to look into his eyes, to see if he knew I had visited Peter at the deli *and he did*. Staring right back at me he added, "Are you feeling guilty, like perhaps you allowed him to do it—by not ratting on his escape route from the house?"

"Tori? What is he talking about?" Rachel looked anxiously from Jonathan to me.

I sat back down at the table and stared at him. "Why didn't you say something . . . about my visit to Peter?" My eyes filled with tears that spilled over, not out of grief for the pathetic Claire, but out of spite for the even more pathetic me.

"He told you of his escape route, didn't he?" Jonathan was still calm.

"Yes."

"Because that's how you were going to get the money to him, wasn't it? The blackmail money for Benjamin's doves you said you'd never consider paying Peter just to shut him up? You were going to meet him at his office, weren't you?"

"Yes." I completely broke down now, and Rachel was beside herself.

"What are you saying? When did you see Peter? Jonathan, when did she see Peter?"

"She met him one day at the deli by his house. She wanted to pay him off for his silence. I'm surprised you didn't think of that yourself, Rachel. As determined as our Tori is to keep Peter quiet, you must have considered that she would try to see him, regardless of what she may have said otherwise." Jonathan sighed. "There didn't seem to be any reason to confront her about the visit, but I was wrong. I should have interrogated her. If it had been anyone else I would have. But I wasn't thinking clearly." He looked at me. "It's hard to think clearly when you love someone so much it hurts. You want to do everything possible to protect them. That's why you saw Peter that day, to protect Benjamin, and Daniel, at all costs. And that's why

I knew about it and didn't say anything, because I was trying to protect *you* at all costs."

Jonathan was on the verge of breaking emotionally. "And that's why if Peter killed Claire, God help us, we are both partially responsible." He slammed his fist on the table. "Because we could have stopped him." He paused and shook his head. "If I had only confronted you about that day, you would have told me everything. And we could have saved Robert's wife."

"But, we don't know that Peter actually killed Claire," Rachel interjected. "And truthfully, it sounds like the poor thing did herself in." We both looked at Rachel. "You said yourself that this death wasn't much like the others." She studied Jonathan.

He composed himself and responded carefully. "No, you're right. It doesn't have the same set up at all."

"And why would he kill her in his own office?" I added, wondering how smart that would be, especially for a genius like Peter.

"We have to face the fact, though, Peter is nowhere to be found. He could have cared less where he killed her, if he had no intention of ever getting caught." Jonathan shook his head in frustration.

"Then why make it look like a suicide? And such a convincing one at that?" I asked.

"And why tell the truth about their relationship? No one would ever have had to know, without the suicide letter," Rachel added. "And you said yourself it was in her own handwriting."

"All true enough," Jonathan admitted. "But remember that Peter is a complex individual. He may be up to something more than meets the eye here. Only time will tell, and let's pray that somehow he slips up and gets caught, soon. We are doing everything possible to narrow his opportunities for escape. Airports and train stations have been alerted. Every measure is being taken to get him into custody."

The phone rang and Rachel answered it. We watched her reaction and knew immediately that it was Robert. Quietly we left the kitchen to give them some privacy. I grabbed the stack of pictures on the table from the boating trip and Jonathan asked if he could see them. I handed him the photos as we sat down on the bench in the hallway near the door, because I sensed Jonathan had things to do and would be leaving soon.

He looked at the pictures in silence. I didn't know what to say. I wanted to apologize for the visit to Peter, but the words wouldn't come. Instead I asked about the funeral arrangements and recalled my images of it earlier while watching the turning leaves outside Rachel's kitchen window. Now all I could see flashing before me was a beautiful corpse with pale skin and dark hair. Red lipstick would complete that dramatically sweet, troubled face in the satin lined box.

"Robert said Claire was Catholic, just as he was. He'd already called Daniel, since they neither one had attended mass for a long time and he was the only priest Robert knew. Daniel was with him when I left."

"Is Daniel going to do the service then? At St. Matthew's?" I asked.

"Yes. Early next week."

We were both silent again.

"These pictures are terrific." Jonathan said this after a painfully long period of time in which he studied each of them carefully, with me viewing the photos over his shoulder, barely breathing, afraid to touch him.

"Thanks," I responded uncomfortably, knowing neither of us were finding much joy in photography at the moment.

"I should get going. Robert needs me."

"Do you think he'll come to see Rachel, I mean, before the funeral?"

"I doubt if he'll have a spare minute between her family coming in from Seattle, and attending to Bronwin and Emma, and his own family coming from New York. Besides all that, the investigation into her death will be exhaustive." He hesitated, and then added, "You'll be questioned, Tori, about your visit with Peter."

"I will?"

"Yes. There's a photo the P.I. took, and the visit is recorded in the records he kept."

"I see."

"I'm sorry." He looked at me for the first time since we had sat down in the entryway. "I know how difficult that will be for you."

"What can I tell them? I mean, for why I was even seeing him in the first place?" I didn't want to talk to the police or anyone else about Peter. Not ever. I stood up and began pacing there in the hall, feeling rather desperate and alone.

"I would recommend the truth," he answered sympathetically.

"You know I can't do that, Jonathan," I said, somewhat irritated.

"Then you will have to think of something on your own. I can't help you lie," he responded.

I stopped pacing for a minute and looked at him. "What do you really think? Do you believe she killed herself?" My eyes were tearing up again.

"I honestly don't know, Tori, but I pray to God she did. I don't think I could live with myself otherwise."

I smiled, despite tears streaming down my face. "That's ludicrous, Jonathan. If she did kill herself, according to her own faith, she will not see heaven for it. Is that what you really want?"

"I don't believe that," he answered quickly, and I could tell he meant it. "I think God would have to be merciful to a woman that suffered as much as Claire did. Not only from her illness, which consumed her at times according to Robert, but also from her bondage to Peter, who literally drove her to such a desperate act. He and he alone should rot in hell for her death, regardless of whether she took the pills herself, or he force fed them to her." Jonathan stood up, and handed me the pictures.

"Yes, I agree, in theory at least. But Daniel might disagree. His God has clear cut rules for these matters."

"His God? There is only one God, Tori . . . and He lives in all of us. I believe in what my heart tells me, more so than in Daniel's rules."

"I wish I could be as sure about everything as you are."

"Let's stay on the boat this weekend."

"The boat?" My head was thick with so many things I couldn't think clearly. But I looked at the picture on the top of the pile in my hand, and it was of a beautiful sunset on a peaceful sea. I longed to be there, on the boat in the harbor.

"Yes, it would be the best place for you and Benjamin, away from all of this. We could use the solitude, and the time together to gather our thoughts. There won't be many more weekends warm enough, or dry enough for staying out on the boat, there in the harbor." He looked hopeful.

"I'd love to."

Jonathan stepped forward and hugged me, tightly. He ran his figures through my hair and whispered into my ear. "It's going to be okay, Tori.

We're going to catch this bastard, I swear to you. I won't stop until I find him and put him behind bars for the rest of his life."

Then he left, and I watched him speaking to the P.I. in the car out front before getting into his own vehicle and speeding away from the curb. He was either angry or in a hurry, or both, but on a mission at least to stop Peter.

Before Peter could strike again.

CHAPTER TWENTY-NINE

The whole truth was that half-truths were quickly becoming a lifestyle for me.

When Benjamin got home from school I told him we were spending the weekend on Jonathan's boat. He immediately went to his room where he stuffed his duffel bag with everything an eleven-year-old might imagine needing for this two-day event. Jonathan and I also began to pack, somewhat somberly. I purposefully did not tell Benjamin about Claire. I was going to do that once we arrived at Harbor Place down by the docks, over fish and chips.

The sunset was gorgeous as we drove beside the river, deep purples and blood reds to rival even the most brilliant turning leaves in the trees along the shore. Early autumn was a bittersweet, melancholy time to depart this earth. All the lush green summer leaves were dying a dramatic eye-catching death. It seemed appropriate for Claire to pick such a poetic preseason to orchestrate her demise, if indeed it was of her design. How climactic to overdose in Peter's office. What a poignant ending to the struggle within her own mind, to end everything where she received the very treatments that gave her the will to live in the first place.

These heavy thoughts nagged at me as we climbed aboard the sailing yacht and unloaded our supplies for the weekend. After unpacking we took a stroll past the cafés and art shops on the waterfront, choosing an outside table overlooking the river for our dinner. Jonathan and I ordered fresh steamer clams and crab legs, while Benjamin had deep fried halibut and French fries dredged in mountains of ketchup. We watched the lights from the city begin to twinkle over the water. It was chilly when the sun went down, and we were glad we thought to bring our jackets. Harbor Place became quite busy with the onset of evening. There was music and laughter everywhere. People were standing about talking, eating at the outdoor tables, or browsing through shops.

I decided not to put off the subject of Claire any longer.

"Benjamin, something very sad and tragic has happened to Bronwin and Emma's mom."

He looked at me, waiting for an explanation.

"She . . . died . . . unexpectedly this morning." I wasn't sure what else to say, even after having this conversation a million times in my head.

Benjamin just stared at me. "How did she die?"

I looked at Jonathan, who gave no indication he wanted to help explain.

"Well, they think perhaps she took her own life. She swallowed a great deal of pills, and left a letter telling us as much, and why she did it," I explained.

"She committed suicide?"

"I don't know, Benj. There is a possibility that she was murdered by Peter. The same man Miranda is taking to trial." I cleared my throat and looked out at the water, trying not to tear up from the enormous guilt I felt at having perhaps played a role in allowing Peter access to Claire.

Benjamin looked confused. "Why would he kill Bronwin and Emma's mom?"

Now I really was at a loss for words. I just gazed passively at my sweet, innocent son. What could I say? Fortunately, Jonathan decided to help me stumble through it.

"Benjamin, Dr. Cairns was treating Mrs. Marsh for a mental illness, but he was also abusing her as he has many women. That might be why she took the bottle of pills, or perhaps Dr. Cairns forced her to take them so she could no longer be a threat to him by possibly telling others of his abuse, which would further incriminate him regarding Miranda's trial."

Benjamin looked concerned. "Dr. Cairns has hurt lots of women, not just Aunt Andi?"

I took a good look at my son, who at almost twelve was no longer a child in so many ways. He deserved complete answers, just short of knowing I might have prevented Claire's death, if indeed it was Peter's doing. What would Benjamin think if I told him I'd been bribing Peter with money from the dove paintings, when I learned of his escape route from the P.I.? Looking at life through my son's eyes made me feel ashamed.

"Yes, he has hurt many women," I admitted.

I was afraid of what Benjamin would ask me next. I was suddenly aware that he had wanted to ask more about Peter all along, and perhaps I should have told him the whole truth from the beginning. The whole truth was that half-truths were quickly becoming a lifestyle for me.

"Is that why Jonathan is paying someone to keep Dr. Cairns away from you? Because he wants to kill you, too?"

Jonathan answered for me. "It's a little more complicated than that, Benjamin, but basically . . . yes, Peter is a dangerous man, and we don't want to take any chances."

Benjamin carefully observed Jonathan, and then me again. "Did he drug you, and rape you, like he did Aunt Andi and those other women?"

I sat back in my chair and took a deep breath before answering. "Yes he did, Benjamin. In graduate school, before you were born."

Benjamin looked out over the water, absorbing that information. I somehow knew it wasn't a surprise to him, and that he'd only drawn this out of me to verify what he'd already concluded. Still, it must have been a bit of a shock to hear the words.

"Did he drug and rape Bronwin and Emma's mom?"

"We don't know," Jonathan admitted. "Possibly. What we do know, according to the suicide note, is that Peter was taking advantage of her illness by forcing her to do things she would not have chosen to do otherwise."

"I hope they catch him, and charge him with murder and then execute him," Benjamin announced, angrily. Then he switched gears entirely in his thinking and asked, "Who is going to care for Bronwin and Emma?"

Jonathan answered the question about Bronwin and Emma for both of us, as I too was wondering who would keep the girls.

"Rachel is going to pick them up from school and stay with them until their father is home from work."

We fell silent while considering this new development, and then Jonathan elaborated. "Rachel is quite fond of the girls, and they like her, too. So, she has offered to be a nanny of sorts, except they will be coming to her studio, rather than Rachel going to their home."

I observed Benjamin's reaction. He looked pleased and said, "They always talk about how much they like Aunt Rachel and her art classes, and how their father rafted the Rogue with her a long time ago. That's how they met."

"Yes, that's right. That's also when I met your mom," Jonathan admitted.

"Father Rosselli was on that trip too, wasn't he?" Benjamin asked.

"He was." Jonathan glanced at me, just as he had that last morning, when pulling out at Foster Bar. It was the same look of dismay and concern.

How could so much have happened, and yet in many ways, so little have changed since then? Robert and Rachel were still challenged by a river, for the river of life was continually dividing and reuniting them with all its ebbs and flows. Daniel and I were still tempting the very fate we feared would consume us with regret. Jonathan and I were still unsure of where we stood. Miranda was still taking wrong turns off the freeway, only this time it was Peter she'd taken a wrong turn with. He was far more dangerous than any rapids we had faced.

"Daniel wants my painting," Benjamin informed us as Jonathan signed for the check. We both looked at him, puzzled.

"Your painting? The one you just finished?"

Benj nodded as we began walking toward the boat.

"When did he tell you this?" I asked.

"When he came by Aunt Rachel's studio to see it."

"He came to the studio?" I leaned on the railing beside the walkway, too stunned to keep moving.

Benjamin stopped in front of me.

"I'm going on ahead to get the fishing gear in order for tomorrow morning," Jonathan informed us, leaving Benj and me for a little alone time.

"Why didn't you tell me Daniel had been to see you?" I asked.

"I don't know. I haven't had a chance really." Benj leaned on the rail beside me and studied the water below us. "He came by Thursday, when I was finishing the painting. Before Aunt Rach took me to Sarah's for dinner."

"Daniel never mentioned he'd been to see you when I saw him for class that night," I commented.

"He wants to buy it. For a fair price."

I was more than a little surprised that Daniel would visit Benjamin and offer to buy his artwork without mentioning it to me.

"I didn't think priests had any money. Does he know how much a fair price for your work *is* these days?" My attitude was undeniably defensive.

"Daniel says the church has tons of money, and they love to invest it in art. And, he says that *my* art is of special interest to them."

"Oh really." I raised an eyebrow and took a long look at this beautiful, pale, lanky child with the same full lips and flaxen curls as his father. Then I scrutinized the ebb and flow of the river tides as if any power I had over my son's destiny was being washed out to sea with the undercurrent.

"Let's join Jonathan," I suggested.

Jonathan was drinking wine, with his legs dangling over the side of the boat. He was admiring the lights of other boats dotted across the river, anchored in every which way between the dock and the far shore. I joined him on the open deck, but Benjamin was more interested in examining fishing gear below in the galley.

Finally alone, he asked me about my interrogation this afternoon by the Portland police. I leaned on the railing, trying to recall exactly what I had said.

"I told them I wanted Peter to drop the paternity suit, and that's why I had been there to see him."

"Did they ask why Peter thought he might be the father of your child?"

"Unfortunately, they asked lots of things I didn't wish to answer, but I gave them as little information as possible, as pleasantly as I could manage."

We fell silent for a while and I sipped the wine Jonathan poured me. The stars were out and there was a full harvest moon just now rising above the trees across the river. Jonathan seemed especially melancholy and I knew it was because he felt responsible for Claire, and for not interrogating me about my visit with Peter.

I was having a hard time releasing my own guilt from not offering up the information Peter shared with me about his escape route. Part of me wanted to believe that Peter had nothing to do with Claire's death other than driving her to it. I wondered if I would ever know for sure, and also wondered where Peter was. I had no doubt the despicable man would return for his money. I shared these thoughts with Jonathan, who agreed there was a very good chance he was hanging around, waiting to retrieve his cash.

We both decided to wait and devise a plan for that event when it got closer, neither of us being in a frame of mind to stress about it now. There were just too many other cumbersome events to get through at the moment, like the funeral, and the ongoing investigation into Claire's death.

"Robert and I were supposed to go on a fishing trip in Alaska this week," Jonathan announced, while staring at the moon. It had risen high enough to light up the whole river as far as you could look in any direction.

"And instead you're going to watch him bury his wife. That's really sad, Jonathan. Can you reschedule?"

He sighed. "No. In fact, I'd like to go. I need to get away for a few days. A change of scenery would do me good. And the plane doesn't leave until after the funeral on Monday. It's a quick trip. I'd return on Saturday." Jonathan paused for a few seconds, and then he added, "I was thinking maybe Benjamin could come in Robert's place."

I didn't know what to say. All I could think of, was, *why this week of all weeks?* It was the same exact time as Daniel's retreat. Was God playing some kind of joke on me? Was this a test? If I failed it, was I going to rot in hell with the likes of Peter? I actually laughed out loud.

"Why is that funny, Tori?" Jonathan looked puzzled.

I got control of myself. There was no way to explain. So I didn't try. "Benjamin loves to fish. You know that. He'd be thrilled. He's never been anywhere to speak of, so this would be a great adventure."

"I would take good care of him."

"I'm not worried."

"You would really let him do this?"

"Why not? I trust you completely. It would be a great experience for him."

We went to bed after that, each to our own, exhausted and weary from the day's events. My last thoughts were of Claire at the barbeque, flitting about like a cornered rabbit, her delicate body twitching and restless. Did she take those pills to end her misery?

Or did Peter end it for her?

CHAPTER THIRTY

*And whatever it was he so desperately needed to fulfill him
that Claire couldn't give, Rachel could, and she did.*

Jonathan, Benjamin, and I cruised up the river on Saturday and down it
on Sunday, stopping wherever we wished to fish along the way. We gave no
heed to whether the fish were biting. None of us had much to say and were
mostly quiet, breathing in the crisp fall air and relishing the warm after-
noons. Fishing was surprisingly good, considering we had no plan other
than dumb luck. Benjamin became quite an expert with all the particulars
of the sport. You might say he took to it like a fish to water.

By Sunday afternoon Claire's sudden death was ancient history and
Peter only a bad dream. We were telling silly jokes and laughing at them
or at nothing at all. Our skin was dry and our lips chapped from the chilly
mornings and relentless northern wind. But our spirits were soaring with
the seagulls, sailing effortlessly on the crest of the constant breeze. It was
exactly what we all needed. The wide flowing river and the vast open sky
seemed gigantic enough to minimize the significance of all the Peters in the
world, who would surely get their just reward in the end.

We returned to land refreshed and ready to help Robert put Claire to
rest, something she never had on earth. Robert had insisted the funeral
happen quickly, for the sake of his daughters. I had to admit it was the best
way to minimize gossip and endless attention drawn to the Marsh family.
Claire's history with mental illness was well documented, the prescription
she overdosed on was in her name, and the suicide note was not suspicious,
so there would be no official investigation. Case closed. The hard cold earth
could swallow up her body, while leaving gaping holes of guilt in those who
loved her.

Perhaps now she would finally be free of her mental torment, and human
tormentor. Jonathan and I both vowed to track Dr. Peter Cairns down and

bring him to justice. We could only pray that we'd have grounds to charge Peter with murder, either Claire's or one of the many others. Several had happened in the recent past, soon enough to be dusted off and brought forward with proper evidence. Robert was quite gifted at turning up evidence through the scantiest paper trail, and his personal motivation had just skyrocketed. We were more than refreshed, we were eager for the hunt.

I called the Gianni family when we returned to Jonathan's house Sunday evening and arranged to have Benjamin come home from school with Sarah on the day of the funeral. I told my trusted neighbors I would be attending Claire's service at St. Matthew's, and burial at Mt. Calvary. Part of me didn't want Benjamin at the funeral because Daniel would be presiding over the services, and I was annoyed with Daniel's unmentioned visit to my son. Thankfully Benjamin was eager to tell the Gianni family about his fishing trip to Alaska, which would begin only hours after Claire's ceremonious departure.

Jonathan and I decided we would pick Benjamin up together after the funeral and I would ride to the airport with them. It would seem odd staying at Jonathan's without him while they were gone, but he persuaded me it would be safer at his house than at my apartment.

When the day of the funeral came Jonathan and I sat together in a very crowded St. Matthew's, full of especially sad and restless mourners for Claire. Their anger and disbelief lingered in the air, its potency thickly mixed with the sweetness of funeral flowers. I had never seen so many varieties and elaborate arrangements. The colors were as rich as their mingling scents.

I couldn't help but think the entire service reflected Claire completely. The ambiance of her personage was everywhere . . . in the confused mourners, and the bold vibrant flowers, in the eerie ache of the hymns painfully executed by the huge pipe organ. Trauma was as much a part of this event as it had been a part of her. The sadness here for her parting soul was a desperate hollow echo for answers . . . about her death, as well as her life.

Bronwin and Emma sat in the front row with their father, looking dazed and confused, but no more so than Robert. Gazing at the girls broke my heart. They were two little visions of beauty poised for years of recovering from whatever their mother was or wasn't. They neither one looked like her in the least, except perhaps for their long fragile bodies. They both had honey-blonde tresses hanging down their backs in loose natural curls. Completely in contrast to Claire's poker-straight ebony locks.

Even now not a hair was out of place as Claire Marsh lay in the blue satin-lined box, where she looked every bit as beautiful as I had imagined she would in Rachel's kitchen, a regular Snow White straight out of Grimm's Fairytales. She fit the tragic role perfectly. One could only hope Bronwin and Emma's lives would be as dramatically different from their mother's as their hair coloring.

Jonathan and I were several rows behind Robert and Claire's family, by the aisle, where we had a perfect view of Daniel as he read the 23rd Psalm.

> *The Lord is my shepherd; I shall not want. He maketh me to lie down in green pastures: he leadeth me beside the still waters. He restoreth my soul: he leadeth me in the paths of righteousness for his name's sake. Yea, though I walk through the valley of the shadow of death, I will fear no evil: for thou art with me: thy rod and thy staff they comfort me. Thou preparest a table before me in the presence of mine enemies: thou annointest my head with oil; my cup runneth over. Surely goodness and mercy shall follow me all the days of my life: and I will dwell in the house of the Lord forever. (Psalm 23)*

It made me dizzy sitting there among the crowd of mourners, who were mostly strangers to me, but for the fact that everyone from the Rogue Trip some dozen years past was present. Rachel and Miranda sat together, across the aisle from us. We glanced at one another often. They had the same intense look on their faces that I felt surely was reflected in mine. Jonathan was oblivious to everything except the actual mass. He took each word and gesture to heart, as if concentrating on this event would be the only thing to get him through it.

Several times during the proceedings Daniel's vision rested on me, and it then seemed an enormous second before he spoke his next word. The high mass was laden with unsettling mystery to those unschooled in Catholicism. It was filled with poetic chanting that echoed our uncertainty about Claire's salvation, and perhaps our own. Not in the words so much as the tone and inflection that seemed void of hope and joy. The entire ordeal was, at the very least, a dreadfully serious reminder of our fleeting mortality.

Halfway through the mass Emma was given a warm smile and a nod by Daniel. She walked stoically up to the podium to read an essay written at the start of this school year. It was about her summer vacation.

"This summer my mother, my sister, and I traveled to Italy. I will never forget celebrating my ninth birthday in Rome."

She hesitated there and glanced at her mother in the open casket. Somewhat teary-eyed she continued with a delicate, if not vulnerable, voice.

"Mother was very funny in Rome. She would laugh among the vendors, admiring their jewelry and fine things made of leather. We would hurry down the narrow cobbled streets, and then stop to buy pastries and cocoa. Mother liked the cappuccinos, with lots and lots of cream that she would allow us to pour and carefully stir. Then she would let us each have a sip. Winnie and I did not ever want to come home."

She paused and looked at Robert for quite a long second, before returning her gaze to the single sheet of lined school paper.

"Except Father wasn't there. And we decided, Winnie and I, that we would miss him too much if we stayed forever. Mother liked to barter with the artists in the Piazza. She would give all her change to the gypsies. And make us look at art until we would whine and beg to eat pizza in the café by the hotel. One time the waiters let us have two scoops each of the gelato behind the glass counter. Gelato is Italian ice cream."

Emma looked at Bronwin and they both smiled. Then she cleared her throat and continued reading.

"I will always remember this vacation, because my mother was so happy. Winnie thinks it was the home-brewed wine in the unlabeled bottles Mother bought from a shopkeeper in the Piazza. I think it was walking to the market place each day for fruits and vegetables. Mother always got fresh flowers, too. And she would let Winnie and I pick them out. It was a very fun time, and it was what I liked the best about my summer vacation."

From the carefree surface of the words one would think they had been a close, happy family. But beneath the lighthearted phrases volumes were left unwritten about Robert's perpetual absence and Claire's dependency upon others to care for the girls. They had an entourage of traveling nannies and various private tutors for tennis and piano, painting and dance, and whatever else the days could be filled with. I glanced at Rach and Andi, whose thoughts were the same, I knew, by their facial expressions.

Bronwin, who was nearly Benjamin's age, read a poem next. She passed her sister midway down the altar steps as she walked up to the podium. I couldn't help but notice the dazed, lost look shared between them. My eyes began to fill with tears as I remembered that lost feeling after my own mother's death. The adolescent stood tall and straight, as her sister had before her, despite a painfully pale face and near trembling voice as she recited her poem.

Mother made me tea
with lemon once
when my throat hurt.
She'd play Chopsticks
on the piano
in rounds with me.
Mother was beautiful
and usually sad
except in Italy.
Wine made her laugh
and we'd dance
sometimes for hours.
I wish we'd stayed
in Italy longer
and Father had come.
I'd view endless art
to have her back
and dance again.
I hope Mother's watching
from up in Heaven
with God's angels.

It was a sweet and sad commentary on their young lives, filled with only fleeting moments of their mother's nurturing. Reflected in lemon tea and rounds of Chopsticks on the piano. One glance across the aisle to Rach and Andi told me we were all on the brink of breaking down emotionally over Claire's distant and disturbed life. The closing hymn brought no relief from the cumbersome feeling sucking my breath away . . .

Amazing grace,
how sweet a sound,
that saved a
wretch like me.
I once was lost,
but now am found.
Was blind,
but now I see.

I needed fresh air. I longed for that steady breeze and wide-open sky on the river, where everything felt balanced and the elements were all you had to deal with. Raising the right sail, using the right lure. It was simple and pure. Nature was honest and real with no illusions or pretenses. You could face those odds and beat them.

On the way to the cemetery one glance at Jonathan told me he was somewhere else mentally. Probably planning a way to slap Peter with a murder charge when he approached me for the blackmail money. But we both knew it would not be that easy. We would have to stay one step ahead of him. I had no doubt he would come calling earlier than planned, expecting me to pay in full.

Before I had time to become frightened over the prospect of Peter surprising me again with an unannounced visit, we were winding around Mt. Calvary. Old garish tombstones were sunk haphazardly into the side of the hill. Some threatened to tumble right onto the twisty narrow road, as if to grab the mourning people passing by in their slow moving vehicles and push them into the soft, sinking earth. I envisioned us being swallowed beneath the plush grass, no one the wiser for our detour.

Jonathan opened the door for me and together we walked passed car after car, parked tailgate to hood, all for Claire, to ceremoniously bid her a final farewell and watch Robert, Bronwin, and Emma put a flower on her casket. There was not a cold wind off the gorge as I had considered, sitting in Rachel's kitchen. In fact, there was no breeze at all. The air was still and dry and the colorful leaves shown like paintings in the distance. The entire scene was too postcard perfect, just as Claire had been to the casual observer. And now here she was, proving the perfect fall day to be far from it, as we focused on her dismal decent into the earth amidst the brilliance of Mother Nature in all her glory.

I stood beside Rachel and Miranda, and thought about what an illusion life was, as there was no indication of Rachel being a major player in Robert's life. And yet she was. The distraught and weary husband stood only inches from the oblong box that held his wife of almost twelve years. The mother of his two girls, the woman he married upon returning from the Rogue that very summer. Never believing for a minute his feelings for Rachel, having blossomed on that trip, would not subside or fade with time. Until one day he realized his second thoughts had not been wedding jitters, but an intuition he should have listened to.

How much did that play a part in Claire's unhappy condition? Did it even make a difference? Was she doomed to live a life of mental instability regardless of the circumstances surrounding her marriage? If so, then having Rachel was a godsend for Robert. Perhaps indeed, she had been exactly that. And what she would be now, only time could tell. Being a wife was entirely different than being a lover sandwiched in the shadows of non-reality, where the lovemaking was heated but the discussions were not. Because essentially, the only decisions being made in stolen moments of time were where and when to meet, not how to live.

I listened as Daniel finished his scripture reading with Genesis 3:16-19, which was more profound and appropriate than anyone standing there listening would have liked to believe. Yet each of us fully understood it was everything life is all about, a formula each of us must follow whether we wish to or not, whether we believe it or not, whether we even know it, or not.

Unto the woman he said, I will greatly multiply thy sorrow
and thy conception: in sorrow thou shalt bring forth children;
and thy desires shall be to thy husband, and he shall rule over

*thee. And unto Adam he said, because thou hast hearkened
unto the voice of thy wife, and hast eaten of the tree, of which
I commanded thee saying, Thou shalt not eat of it: cursed is
the ground for thy sake: in sorrow thou shalt eat of it all the
days of thy life: Thorns also and thistles shall it bring forth to
thee; and thou shalt eat the herb of the field; In the sweat of
thy face shalt thou eat bread, till thou return unto the ground;
for out of it wast thou taken: for dust thou art, and unto dust
shalt thou return. (Genesis 3:16 –19)*

Robert, Bronwin, and Emma each laid a single red rose on the dark
mahogany casket, and Claire was lowered into the grave. Robert tossed a
handful of earth on top. Daniel closed his Bible and hugged Robert, who
had broken down, finally, after all this time of putting up a brave front for
the world. A façade having begun long before Claire's death. But now it was
over, all of it. The pretense of happiness, the pretending of normalcy, the
constant preparing to lie and cheat. The stolen moments of deceit.

I looked at Rachel, who had also fallen apart emotionally, probably as a
direct result of Robert's breakdown. She was being comforted by Miranda,
and observed curiously by others near, who had originally perceived her to
be a somewhat distant friend of the Marsh's. Now, I was sure, they wondered exactly what role she had played in the lives of this family. But I only
wondered what role she had yet to play. Perhaps one day she would be
Robert's wife. Why not? Bronwin and Emma were quite fond of her and
certainly being a best friend, soul mate, and lover need not exclude you
from the realm of wife and mother.

I watched Daniel depart with Robert, and then Jonathan took my hand,
whispering that we should leave now for Robert's house. I looked up into
his face and saw only tension there, a distance in his eyes told me he was
focused on not letting any of it penetrate. Not the pain of potentially having played a part in her death, or the suffering of those who loved her, or
the misery of those who tried and failed.

Perhaps I was being too harsh. In all probability Robert had indeed loved
Claire. But in the end love alone wasn't enough. Maybe it was more about
need. He needed something Claire couldn't give him for all her beauty and

intellect, and everything that made her uniquely Claire.

And whatever it was he so desperately needed to fulfill him that Claire couldn't give, Rachel could, and she did.

CHAPTER THIRTY-ONE

Our love was as real as it gets, but as invisible as we could make it.

Robert and Claire's house was quite large with many rooms that were spacious and sparsely furnished, just as their marriage had been. The cathedral ceilings and two-story windows made each room light and airy, but the elaborate cherry wood trim and walnut floors gave a feeling of warmth. Oversized leather furniture filled the floor space nicely in the front room. It was contemporary in design, as were the many works of art hung here or there, or placed about in the form of clay, or glass sculpture. My senses were pleased but confused when observing the modern lines of each piece, yet somehow the overall affect was restful.

The house and its furnishings drew you into its personality, just as Claire and Robert had done as a couple, whereas individually they were like the undefined lines of their own modern art. Fortunately their home held a lot of people, and it was filling to capacity as mourners arrived from the cemetery. Caterers busied themselves with arranging food trays. They placed silver coffee urns and stacked china cups on the island counter in the very center of the large kitchen. The mood was especially somber, despite the beautiful surroundings and appetizing food trays.

I watched as Rachel entered the front door. How odd it must have felt to be in Robert's home. Her pained expression made me hurt for her. Hurt for having to face the part of Robert she was not a part of, hurt for knowing she may have played a part in Claire's unhappiness, possibly even her death. Hurt for his little girls that she loved dearly and had no right to love at all.

Yet I had no doubt she would wish Claire back to life in a heartbeat. Because that was who Rachel was . . . good, kind, thoughtful, never demanding of Robert, never complaining of her second place in his life. If Claire were to suddenly appear from heaven wearing a flowing gown, like a risen sleeping beauty with her full red lips and ebony hair, and inquire of

Rachel as to why she was there, Rachel would apologize for having loved Robert. She would beg Claire's forgiveness, and express sincere regret for the tragic end to her desperate life. Because Rachel's heart was among the purist I had ever known, weak though it be for Robert's open arms whenever he required it.

I spoke with Rachel and Miranda briefly, having arrived together, and eventually gravitating to my familiar face. It felt wonderful to embrace them, hugging first one and then the other as sisters in crisis, the cause of which was one atrocious man, Peter. I couldn't remember a time when we were all wearing black for the same event, and I hoped there would never be another occasion that called for it.

Rachel wore a simple but eloquent dress that clung to her slender form while Miranda looked tall and sleek in her clingy silk suit. I wore a fitted sleeveless dress that was conservatively mid-calf in length. Black was everywhere, on every mourner, as if gloom itself had determined the dress code. I couldn't help but notice Daniel enter the room, still in his priestly robes. Robert entered just behind Daniel. Rachel's eyes began to tear up and Miranda tried to distract her with conversation.

"Have either of you heard anything more about Peter? Has he been found?"

We both looked at her, happy to look away from Daniel and Robert and all that they represented in our lives, none of it simple or easy, or even justifiable at the moment.

"I know he's still at large, or else Jonathan would have gotten a call on his cell phone," I offered up solemnly.

We all saw Robert glance our way as I answered, and I could feel his agony. He almost seemed as if a small boy, the sandy hair falling loosely on his forehead, the tight muscular body tense in this uncomfortable situation. Written in the creases of his furrowed brow was a need to swoop over and envelop Rachel, so that he might melt into her loving warmth. But outwardly he could not let his guard down for even an instant, lest the world know his true vulnerability.

Instinctually Miranda guided Rachel toward the kitchen, claiming a sudden need for food and being famished from all the emotional strain. I stood my ground and waved them on with a smile, saying we would catch up to each other later. They were no sooner out of sight and Robert approached me, with Daniel still at his side. I hugged Robert tightly and told him how very sorry I was about Claire. He patted me on the back to acknowledge the sincerity of my words.

"Tori, I just spoke with Jonathan. He still has no information on the location of Dr. Cairns. Be very cautious. This man might not have fled the area at all. He may be waiting patiently for an opportunity to confront you."

"I know. But don't worry about me, Robert. I'll be at Jonathan's house, and even though he'll be gone for a few days, he has a security system. And he's going to have his friends on the police force patrolling the area. I have their number in my cell phone."

Robert looked more like a concerned lawyer than a grieving spouse. He seemed to have put his wife's death at arm's length and returned to his comfort zone of legal work and catching bad guys.

"Where is Jonathan, anyway?" I asked, realizing I hadn't seen him since we arrived together from the cemetery.

"He's out in the yard checking in with his P.I.s. He's thinking Cairns hasn't left the area, but feels he won't bother you until he knows you've got his cash. It wouldn't do him any good to approach you until you have the money. He knows you're not going to get that cash out of the bank any sooner than you have to, which means he has to hang around until the date you both decided to meet on. The man's not stupid."

Robert glanced about the room, and I knew he wished with all his being it were empty and he could hide behind the Cairns case and not have to speak to anyone else about Claire. I could see in his eyes that his heart was sealed off and he had put his troubled marriage into a dark corner of it, not penetrable by anyone, including himself. He would forever store his guilt and self-loathing there in that untouchable part of his most vital and least understood organ.

Hugging me again briefly, Robert moved toward the kitchen. I hoped Rachel and Miranda were no longer there, filling it with their beautiful but disturbing presence. If I was sure of anything on this ill-conceived day it was that Rachel and Robert did not want to confront one another face to face while among the many mourners, some of whom must already be partially suspicious of their relationship.

Daniel had not followed Robert to the kitchen and we were suddenly alone in this room full of people and could no longer ignore it.

"The service was beautiful, Daniel. You did a great job, even if I have nothing to compare it to since Grams' death, some twelve years ago."

"It always saddens me when someone with so much living left to do departs from us prematurely, especially in such an unsettling way."

"Do you think he killed her?" I asked.

"Possibly. I actually would prefer to believe she did not take her own life."

"Then you think if she truly committed suicide she will not enter heaven?"

"Why is it, Tori, that everything you say is so black and white? Even I, as a priest who studies these things, cannot bring myself to judge her. Only God can do that."

"Is Robert going to be okay?" I asked, knowing Daniel would have some insight into his guilt and how he was handling it.

"I think so. He is no longer in denial, at least, about whatever he and Claire were, or were not." Daniel paused, hesitant to ask me something.

"What is it, Daniel?"

"Rachel . . . and Robert. They've been good friends ever since we rafted the Rogue, haven't they?" He studied my expression.

"Why do you ask?"

"Because I sense something in Robert whenever she is near. Something more than friendship."

"What is it you are sensing? That he loves her? How does one sense that?" I asked, while scanning the room for familiar faces, Jonathan's namely, but he was nowhere to be seen.

"I can't define it really, but there is something there. Something very real that he is trying to hide, like you are now."

I looked at him sharply, somewhat stunned. "What are you saying, Daniel?"

"I'm saying that you love me. You do love me, don't you Tori? I can feel your love. I can see it on your face. Don't try and deny me this truth, *because I need you.*" He barely whispered it, and we both glanced about instinctively, but no one was paying us any mind.

"I don't think that has ever been in question. Your love for *me* is what I find questionable, at least whether or not it can compete with your love for God. Or even if it should." It was always frightening to be this close to Daniel, because I couldn't ignore the way it made me feel, which was aroused. It was exasperating to have this connection to him, because he was such a mystery. It wasn't what I knew about him that scared me. It was what I didn't know, and more to the point, what I wasn't sure I wanted to know.

We were both glancing about the room more than at each other during this out-of-place conversation. Our bodies were as close as they had ever been in public, and yet our privacy felt less threatened than in an empty room. There, strangers might wander in and expose what we were hiding so well among this crowd. In a way, we were no different from Rachel and Robert. Our love was as real as it gets, but as invisible as we could make it.

"Tori, are you coming?" Daniel asked, ignoring my comments about his love for me competing with his love for God. Perhaps he was wise to not respond to that.

"Coming where?" I asked, knowing exactly where, and also *why*.

"To Rosewood. Tonight. I know you can, and that Jonathan will be out of town with Benjamin," he answered calmly.

"I don't fully understand why you wish for me to come, Daniel. You've never really said," I pointed out, feeling more like we were bartering for power than setting up a love affair.

Claire's mother approached us, her eyes swollen and stricken with disbelief. She thanked Daniel for the wonderful service. They chatted briefly and I introduced myself, consoling her as best I could for not being someone who really knew Claire, except from a distance. Then she left and we were ignored again. Daniel looked carefully into my eyes, and I could see the begging in his.

"Tori, come to Rosewood, and I promise you will not be sorry. It will all be clear to you—why I want you to come."

I didn't answer, nor did I have an opportunity, as we were interrupted the instant he concluded his proposal. Claire's father, looking as miserable as one might expect, had approached Daniel to speak of his daughter, now gone forever. I glanced about for Rachel and Miranda, or perhaps the return of Jonathan if he had even set foot in the house yet. But I saw none of them, and then to my surprise, I did see a couple of familiar faces. But not faces I would have expected.

It was Vincent and Maggie Gianni walking through the door. And then I saw Sarah, between them, just short enough not to be noticed at first glance. But there was no Benjamin. I glanced at my watch. Surely Benjamin would be with them by now, school having been out for nearly an hour. They were glancing about, looking serious and concerned, panicked really. They were not mourners, of course, never having met Claire. Why were they here? What had happened? *And where was Benjamin?*

I nearly shouted across the room to them, "Vincent I'm over here." He turned his head in my direction, as did Maggie and Sarah. We made our way to each other through the unsuspecting crowd until I was standing directly in front of Vincent's tall familiar form. I reached out for him. Taking his arm and wrapping my fingers around it, I looked up into his soft gray eyes.

"Vincent," I glanced at Maggie and paused for half a second, "why are you and Maggie here? And where is Benjamin?" Their expressions were filled with a dread that made me shudder. I glanced down at Sarah, quietly crying, and knelt in front of the undersized girl who looked all of eight for her ten years. "Sarah, honey, what's the matter? Does it have something to do with Benjamin?" And then realizing in that instant that it most certainly did, I cried out softly, "*Oh my God*, what has happened?"

"Benjamin . . . he's . . . gone. With that . . . that man . . ." Sarah began to cry uncontrollably as these words sank into my heart.

I pulled her to me and stroked her head as a small crowd gathered around us. Whispering into her hair I asked in a near choking voice, "*What man, Sarah?*" But I already knew *what man.*

"He said his name was . . . *Peter,*" she answered, nearly frozen with fear. We clung to one another, hugging tightly, our faces buried in each other's hair. I heard the hushed murmur of those mourners surrounding us and felt the familiar touch and scent of Rachel and Miranda, who were gently pulling me away from Sarah. I looked up into the face of Jonathan whose shocked expression took my breath away, and then he was guiding me through the crowd and I was glancing back for Sarah, whom I did not want to lose track of. For she alone held the magic answers for making any sense of this.

I soon realized vaguely that we were in a bedroom with a high ceiling and walnut furniture, not contemporary at all but more like solid, well preserved antiques. The bed was a four-poster monstrosity from a past era. I absorbed all this in an instant, and was keenly aware of those present without a glance to be sure. Rachel and Miranda were there, along with Jonathan, Vincent, and Maggie. Sarah was present of course, and for a hovering second Robert appeared at the doorway but then disappeared and was soon replaced by Daniel, who was let through like water parting for Moses. It occurred to me while observing Daniel being hastened to my side that everyone present knew him to be the father of Benjamin. Whether he was willing to admit it to himself, or to his God, the fact remained written all over his stricken face.

He sat on the bed near Sarah, who stood in front of the chair I had collapsed into. It was an ornate, antique cane rocker, with swirling wood on either side that looped around and around, similar to how my head was spinning. It sat in the corner of the room beside a window wall that looked out into a late afternoon sun. Eerie shadows fell on my mismatched family of loved ones standing or seated throughout the large bedroom, waiting for Sarah's details about what none of us might ever have imagined could happen.

Benjamin had been kidnapped.

CHAPTER THIRTY-TWO

It just didn't seem enough for me, at the moment,
to kill only one of him . . . and only once.

"Tell me what happened, sweetie," I whispered, "from the beginning."

Sarah glanced at Vincent and Maggie, seated on the bed. Then she looked into my eyes, timidly, her crying temporarily stopped. Anyone walking into the room at that moment could have heard a pin drop on the highly polished wooden floor.

"We . . . we were walking home from the bus stop," she began, "and this man walked across the street toward us. He had been leaning against the streetlamp, like he'd been waiting there for us."

Sarah's courage seemed to falter as she recalled the disturbing events of her afternoon. She suddenly became silent, looking pale and unable to speak. I patted her hand and whispered, "Everything is going to be okay, Sarah. Just tell me what happened."

She began again, slowly. "He was tall . . . and dressed nice. He didn't look scary, you know?" I nodded, indicating I understood. "He smiled and put his hand out to shake Benjamin's. We stopped to talk to him, because he wasn't weird or anything like that."

Her eyes were searching for approval, and I told her that of course someone dressed so nicely would not appear to be a threat at first.

"He said his name was Dr. Peter Cairns and asked Benjamin *Do you know who I am?* and Benjamin nodded. Then he said something . . . something I didn't know about Benjamin." Her eyes were panicky, questioning.

I smoothed her collar down, and tried to soothe her with a calm and steady voice. "What, Sarah?"

"He told Benjamin that he . . . that he was his father. And he asked Benjamin if he knew he'd been trying to make it *legal,* so he could spend time with him, and get to *know* him. Is it true? Is that man Benjamin's father?" Sarah asked, with dread in her tone.

I glanced at Daniel, who looked away from me and out the window, and then at everyone else, whose faces were filled with concern. Finally I looked into Sarah's confused and frightened eyes. "No, Peter is not Benjamin's father. What did Benjamin say to him?"

"He said . . . *If I agree to be your son will you promise to stay away from my mother, to never go near her again?* Why did he say that?" Sarah studied my face, needing to understand.

"Peter and I do not agree on who Benjamin's father is, and he is taking me to court over it. But that's another story. What happened next, honey? You mustn't leave anything out that might help us determine where they went."

"That man, Peter, he smiled. He said he would stay away from you, and that Father Rosselli would be there as comfort for your loss . . . you'd have each other at least and maybe that's how it should be." Sarah broke down there and began to cry uncontrollably. Silent tears fell like rain down my cheeks as we hugged tightly and Sarah spoke to me between choking sobs. "Benjamin told me . . . everything would be okay. That . . . he was going to go with Dr. Cairns and I needed to tell you . . . not to worry. He said he would be fine, and Father Rosselli could have his painting . . . as a gift for becoming bishop."

Daniel looked at us then, no longer able to stare out the window in a dazed manner. There was terror in his eyes. My own vision began to blur as everything sank in and I realized Peter didn't want ransom money. He wanted the source of it. He wanted Benjamin and his unpainted paintings, his unhealed healings, his yet undiscovered and untapped ability to make Peter rich and powerful.

I looked away from Daniel's troubled eyes as someone burst into the room, and then I saw that it was Wil. Jonathan came in behind my brother, having obviously located him for me. Sarah and I hugged one more time and then she returned to Maggie. I stood and met Wil halfway, embracing him tightly and whispering weakly, *Peter has Benjamin, Wil. You were right all along. I should never have tried to reason with him. And now he is gone, Wil. Benjamin is in the hands of that maniac . . .* " and then I collapsed into Wil's strong and loving arms, his expression filled with all the pain I felt. It was the last thing I remember before passing out and the first thing I recalled upon awakening, in Jonathan's guest room with Rachel seated beside me on the bed.

"Welcome back, kiddo." Rachel looked into my eyes, and smiled.

I glanced about the room and at first I wondered why I wasn't at my apartment but then I remembered that Benjamin and I had moved in with Jonathan to be safe from Peter. That plan had obviously been false security. "Did they find Benjamin? Is he here? Can I see him?"

Rachel took my hand and patted it. "No honey, not yet."

"Did Jonathan bring me here?"

"No. It was Wil who brought you. And that's been four days ago." Rachel picked up a bottle of pills off the nightstand. "Jonathan's doctor has been here every day to check on you. He's a personal friend of Jonathan's." Rachel rattled the bottle of pills she held. "These are to calm your nerves and help you rest. You've been so out of it we've barely gotten food and water in you."

"What happened? I mean, after Wil came and I passed out?" I sat up slowly, my head aching and heavy, and Rachel handed me a glass of juice from the tray near the bed.

"Wil carried you to the car and you regained consciousness about the time he sat you inside. Then you became hysterical, wanting to run off and find Peter and Benjamin yourself." Rachel paused, smoothing my hair back off my face. "It wasn't pretty, Tori. You were absolutely losing it. A full-on breakdown if I've ever seen one."

"Jonathan left you in Wil's hands," she continued, "as he and Robert dashed off to pick up any leads they could find from the scene of the kidnapping. He left instructions to bring you here, call the doctor on the number he gave us, and to not leave your side. So Miranda and I have taken turns being here with you, and Wil's been in and out over the past few days checking on you. Jonathan calls about every four hours, and only comes home long enough to eat a late dinner and sleep."

Rachel smiled weakly. "He comes in here when he finally gets home about eight or nine at night, and just sits next to you and holds your hand. Tori, the look on his face makes me want to cry. He loves you that much. His eyes are full of nothing else, but his love for you."

I tried to focus on what she was saying, but all I could think about was how I'd lost four days. Peter could have taken Benjamin anywhere by now. "Rach, is Miranda here?"

"No, but she will be soon. She comes right after work and we eat together."

I was afraid to ask my next question, but asked it anyway. "Do they know anything? I mean, about where Peter has taken my Benjamin?"

"I don't think so. But Jonathan probably wouldn't tell me anything even if he did know. And I've quit asking. It depresses him so to talk about it."

Miranda popped her head in the door and looked surprised to see me awake. "Welcome back, honey." Her eyes teared up and she walked over slowly, asking Rachel when did I become coherent, as if I'd been a rambling idiot the entire time and I hoped surely that could not be true. It was obvious she wanted to see me alone and Rachel was relieved to let her, knowing Miranda was a psychologist and could check to see if my sanity had really returned. I wasn't sure that it had. But I wouldn't share that with Andi, or how my reoccurring fantasy since waking up only minutes ago was to load a semi-automatic and unleash it on a room full of Peters. Actual Peters, not other evildoers like him. It just didn't seem enough for me, at the moment, to kill only one of him . . . or only once.

When we were alone I finished the juice and Miranda helped me stand. I told her I wanted to take a shower and wash my hair, and she helped me gather everything I needed in the adjoining guest bath. Then she left me and I could hear her talking to Rachel about bringing me a hot meal. I felt tired despite having slept for four days, but at least I felt human again. Rachel and Miranda sat with me while I nibbled on roasted chicken. Somehow my stomach was not as receptive as my head for the food. All I could think about was Benjamin.

When I was finished forcing down tiny bites of the food, Rachel took the tray and left me alone with Miranda. I leaned my weary head against the bedpost and told her what I had wanted to say since awakening several hours ago.

"Andi, I remember." It felt strange to say the words, but even stranger to know, finally, what had happened.

"You remember . . . what?" But her eyes told me she knew exactly what it was I remembered.

"What happened, with Peter. When he drugged me, and . . ." I didn't finish the sentence.

"I know. I was afraid that's what you meant. But I had to be sure."

"When I awoke, it was right there . . . on my mind. All mixed up with the funeral, and Benjamin's face the last time I saw him."

"Tori, it's better to know. Nothing is more frightening than *not knowing*. The mind can play cruel tricks, and torture us more than the truth sometimes."

"Why, Miranda? Why do I remember?" I asked, desperate for her professional explanation.

"It's hard to say. The brain is a complicated organ. But I do know this, you spoke of your trauma with Peter all those years ago frequently while laying here agitated and restless the past four days, despite the mind-numbing drugs we gave you."

"What did I say?"

"You spoke as if you were there again with Peter, begging him to stop his advances," Miranda explained. "Maybe the drugs he gave you didn't put you completely out, but your mind blocked everything that had happened. It's something the mind does as a safeguard, so we can function normally— it suppresses the trauma."

"My recollection of it isn't any worse than my imagination had envisioned, thank God, for my imagination is vivid enough," I admitted.

We were silent for a minute and then Andi tried to reassure me. "I'm so sorry, Tori, for what's happened. Peter taking Benjamin like this. But at least you know he'd never harm him, and Benjamin is more than just bright, he is very wise. He'll be okay, Tori, until we can find Peter and get him back."

"We? Who is we?" I began to feel agitated, too agitated to hide it from Andi. Between recollections of Peter touching me, *hurting me*, and thoughts of Benjamin with that monster, I was sorely afraid I might lose another four days to drugs and darkness. But I was determined to be well, for being well was the only way I could find Benjamin. And find him I would.

"Jonathan and Robert, and all of their many resources are working on this around the clock," Andi added. "Not to mention the spiritual realm, as Daniel is beside himself and has withdrawn into a holy state of prayer. He has become a total recluse in that sanctuary of his, on his knees to the God who denied him the privilege of fatherhood in the first place.

"I fear denying his God in the first place is what got us into this mess."

"What do you mean by that, Tori?"

I wanted more than anything to jump from the bed and pace the oak floor scattered with tapestry rugs sporting rich fabrics and intricate designs. But I felt too weak to even try. "I mean I should never have defied Daniel's God."

"You speak of God as if He were only Daniel's. It isn't Daniel's God. *He is everyone's God.* Daniel and his Catholic church cannot patent the universal concept of God. And what do you mean by *defying Daniel's God* anyway?"

"I mean that had I told Peter to forget about blackmail and paternity suits and to go ahead and expose Father Rosselli for the adulterer that he was—can you be an adulterer to God?—well, anyway, surely none of this would have happened and perhaps Claire would still be alive. Damn me. I've screwed everything up. And I've lost the most precious thing of all in the process. *Benjamin.*"

I crawled awkwardly out of bed despite my better judgment and stood peering through the window, trying not to collapse under my weak limbs. Miranda sat there on the bed watching me with worry all over her, as I made a gallant effort to project an image of clarity and strength.

"Andi, I think I know where he is, and you're going to help me get there."

"That's ludicrous, Tori. You can't go *anywhere*. You've just had an emotional breakdown."

I put my unsteady hands on her shoulders. "Miranda, you of all people should know that I must first face, and then conquer my fears in order to overcome them."

We stared into each other's eyes. It felt like swords were drawn in battle.

"Well, I have faced my worst fear," I continued, trying not to falter in any way, "and I am still standing. Now I am going to conquer it. *With God as my witness* I will track Peter down and bring Benjamin home."

I let go of her and sat heavily on the bed.

"Victoria, I can't let you leave this room, let alone this city. And where do you think Peter has gone, anyway?"

"Do you swear not to tell anyone?"

"Yes, of course," Andi whispered. "Confidentiality between patient and doctor was part of the oath I took, silly."

"He has gone to Rome."

"Why do you think so?"

"Because Rome is the source of whatever Daniel is, and of the church and its secrets to bear, and it would be Benjamin's heritage as well. And what better place than Italy to value the paintings of a child prodigy? That is, if the church doesn't solely covet them itself."

"You're not stable enough to go anywhere, Tori. You could have a relapse at any moment, a full-on anxiety attack. You're not well. You need time to recover, lots of rest and quiet. You must let yourself heal."

I pulled my legs up under me, while leaning against the pillow, trying not to let the room spin—trying to sound strong and confident.

"Andi, you more than anyone should understand the personal vendetta we alone share against Peter. You must help me do this. I can't ask Rachel. She's been through too much lately with Claire's death and her own guilt. And now she'll be helping with his girls. Bronwin and Emma need her full attention. Not to mention Robert. And I don't want her to have to keep this from him. *I don't want her to know.* I don't want anyone to know, except you. Because anyone else would come looking for me, and that would not be helpful. In fact, that could be disastrous."

Miranda put her hands on my shoulders. "I'll drug the hell out of you and strap you to this bed before I will let you go to Rome anytime soon."

I didn't answer, knowing how stubborn she could be.

"Promise me one thing." Her tone had become gentle but serious. It was her doctor voice, I realized, and I had grown to love her soothing wisdom when spoken as Dr. Tanasborne.

"What, Miranda?"

"Promise me you'll let yourself feel worthy of Jonathan's love."

"What do you mean?" I asked, puzzled.

"I mean that you feel this obsessive need to have Daniel's complete devotion, when he isn't capable of giving it. Just as your parents weren't. And you are hell bent to feel unworthy of someone who *is* capable of giving you complete and total adoration. Think about it, Tori. I know it's years of therapy in a nutshell, but promise me you'll try to understand what I am saying. Don't blow your one chance at true love without at least examining why you are driven to possess Daniel, *if only as his possession*."

I lied and said, "Of course I'll think about it. I need to rest, Andi. I'm suddenly very weary." I slid down into the bed and closed my eyes. Miranda kissed my forehead and informed me that she wouldn't be far away if I needed her. I watched the door shut as she left the room and immediately sprung from the bed. Pacing at the foot I began planning my newly conceived trip abroad, and suddenly the fuzziness began to clear from my head. I felt a dull ache with the return of serious thinking, but it was a good feeling.

I stopped dead in my tracks for a minute and stared at the nightstand. It had a bottle of pills sitting on it. Reading the label I decided these were a sedative and I would surely need that considering the race of my heart and near destruction of my nerves while contemplating my quest and the magnitude of its importance. I determined that I'd cut them in half so as not to completely obliterate my ability to think clearly. Surely half a dose, taken only when needed, would prevent me from becoming hysterical in a foreign country and allow me to make do with this one nearly full bottle.

I grabbed my suitcase from the closet and began opening drawers ever so stealthily, giving utmost attention to what I would and would not need, because I knew one suitcase was all I'd be able to manage as I snuck away into the dark, where I might possibly need to outrun airport terminal police, or whoever else Miranda and Jonathan might send to track me down and drag me back to this sickbed. Hiding the packed piece of luggage in the closet I then riffled through my handbag to be sure all my credit cards were there, and adequate ID. Thankfully my passport was in the front zipper compartment of my suitcase, where I always kept it for safekeeping.

I had no sooner crawled between the sheets, exhausted, when Wil knocked on the door. He came in and looked at me, smiling at my revival. I somehow found the words to speak what I had been meaning to say for a long time now.

"I'm sorry, Wil, for everything . . . for not listening to you, but mostly, for hurting you. Please forgive me."

"It's okay, Vic. I forgave you the minute I left that night." He sat carefully on the bed by me, and sighed deeply. "My only regret is that I stayed away in order to try and make a life for myself. And I did. I asked Paige to marry me. But we can't tie the knot until Benjamin comes home. I need him to be my best man."

"He will be, little brother. He'll be home in time for your wedding."

And I prayed with all my heart I could keep my wits about me long enough to accomplish this difficult task, as broken as I appeared to be, even to myself.

CHAPTER THIRTY-THREE

But then, miracles do happen, and sometimes we get to
witness them at the hands of an angel, whether seen or not seen.

I decided to start in Venice where Daniel was born, and see if Peter had approached Daniel's mother, Alessa Rosselli, who was still located there. Perhaps she would share with me the secrets of Daniel's lineage, and how the mysterious healing powers played a part in it. Whether Peter was in Venice or not, what Alessa had to say might be key to understanding my son better.

If I found no sign of Peter and Benjamin in Venice, I would move on to Rome, where Daniel's history and connection to the church would surely be a calling card for Peter, not to mention that Daniel himself would soon be in Rome for his ceremony to become a bishop.

On the plane I thought about Miranda, who ever since my collapse was behaving like a doting mother fretting over a sick child. I deduced if she ever had children, this is the Miranda they would experience. Not the sophisticated, consummate professional she prided herself on being. I had left her a note, of course, in the brown leather tote she only used when making an overnight trip. This way she wouldn't find it too soon, but soon enough. I had pleaded shamelessly in the note for her understanding and forgiveness at slipping away in the night.

As soon as my five a.m. flight left the ground, exhaustion crept in. Miranda would think I was heading to Rome. I could only hope changing my plans and spending time in Venice first would prevent anyone from catching up with me. Surely they would check Rome first, and then be looking elsewhere when I finally arrived. Several times my eyes would shut and then pop open, wondering if it had all been a dream, slipping down the hall and into the garage where my car was not heard backing out. I suspected it wouldn't be since I never heard Jonathan come home each evening until his cheery hello resounded from the hallway.

Thankfully Jonathan had been away for the night gathering evidence against Peter, where exactly no one knew for sure. Rachel had said Robert was spending time with his girls before returning to work. They were in Hawaii. I knew Jonathan must have insisted he could handle everything himself until Robert retuned and Rachel was available to watch his girls, rather than hover over my sickbed. I didn't want to think about what Jonathan would do when Miranda told him I had run off in the dead of night. I wondered if either of them would ever speak to me again. I guess it didn't matter. If I found Benjamin, surely they'd forgive me. If Peter got to me before I got to Benjamin, well, then it would be time to meet my Maker, who surely would have a great deal to say to me. I had a few things to say to Him as well.

I decided it might have been divine intervention that got me a ticket on this plane. The clerk had said it was because of a last minute cancellation, and wasn't it my lucky day? I had smiled at her and didn't say anything because she couldn't possibility know just how lucky it was. I even secured lodging from a website on my laptop while waiting for the plane to load, half expecting Miranda to barge through the terminal door at any second and drag me back to my sickbed.

After convincing myself there was no way they could apprehend me at my connecting flight, thoughts turned to Peter and how I had brought an arsenal of documents to render him helpless in proving his rights to Benjamin were legitimate. This comforted me as I fell into a deep sleep. The stewardess had to wake me upon landing. It was slightly surreal, tiptoeing through the terminal looking for guards who might be alerted to snatch me up. I gave the attendant eye contact when taking my ticket, for fear this would cause alarms to go off, but none were heard as I scampered down the carpeted runway to board the plane of my connecting flight.

Upon arrival in Venice a taxi brought me to the *pensione* where I'd made reservations. Never having been in Venice before, I found everything out the taxi window charming. It resonated of Daniel. If I were not fighting panic over possibly never seeing my son again, I would truly have been enchanted by this first glimpse of the city.

After checking into my room at the small Inn, I began to walk the streets. Venice had a scent in the air all its own. It smelled of pastries mixed with a salty breeze off the Adriatic Sea. The gently flowing waterways calmed me as magically as the little blue pills. After browsing through a few local art galleries and clothing shops, I sat at an outdoor café and sipped on an espresso. I fully believed the serenity of this city had absorbed all the way to my inner core, and would never allow so much as a seed of anxiety to escalate beyond a manageable point during my visit there.

Once I returned to the Inn I ordered room service while plotting my plan of action, until I fell asleep sprawled across the soft bed, my laptop still on and map of Venice spread open. I hadn't taken any blue pills since having an espresso at the outdoor café. It must have been the unhurried Venice lifestyle that calmed my inner storm and allowed my good night's sleep.

The next day was spent tracking down the Rosselli family by talking to local patrons in shops and cafes. It wasn't long until someone knew of the family who had a son that was a priest in America, and they confirmed to me that his wife Alessa, Daniel's mother, still lived in Venice. How ironic that I had heard this first from Jonathan rather than from Daniel, who was never in a mood to disclose information about his family, other than sharing about his grandfather the cardinal in reference to the old Bible with the thin, yellowed pages.

On this second day after my arrival I truly wished I was a native, so enthralled was I with the many waterways to gaze upon and dream beside, and small bistros that offered fresh seafood and handmade pasta. But most importantly, I was strong again, and rested. My mind was clear and focused. I no longer had mild anxiety attacks causing clammy hands and shallow breathing while fumbling for half a blue pill in my purse. I had even managed to convince myself it was just a matter of time until I hugged my half-grown son to my aching chest, filled with a heart beating solely for that moment. Best of all, I had located Alessa.

I stood facing the door of a home among modest but quaint row houses and stared at the fresh flowers clenched in my nervous hand. I was about to speak with Daniel's mother. See her, face to face, this woman who had raised a son not much different from my own Benjamin in many ways, making them different from other children in the same ways.

She answered my knock with a warm smile and I recognized Daniel's heart-shaped face and milky white skin immediately. Alessa was a small woman with poise and charm to match her son. I introduced myself as a friend of Daniel's while she delighted in the flowers. She invited me in graciously, soon disappearing around the corner of the kitchen to fetch a vase of water. I sat on the emerald-green sofa and admired the many charming family photos adorning the pale rose-colored walls. Some were of Dr. Rosselli and Alessa when they first met and were married, a few were of Daniel as a child, and several displayed the three of them together.

My curiosity got the better of me and I had to take a closer look by timidly approaching the heavy framed portraits of all different shapes and sizes. Daniel's father, not surprisingly, had the same white-blond hair and slight halo above his head. Could it really be the reflection off the hair causing this oddity? Alessa's hair was wavy and brown in the pictures, as soft and warm as her beautiful smile.

Looking at the photos I couldn't help but wonder, who were the real angels among us . . . those born with unexplainable yet undeniable gifts of mysterious origin, or those who stood by them regardless of the cost? Surely it had been difficult being married to the good doctor, equipped with more than an education to cure his patients. This was a man whose father had been a cardinal in the Catholic Church. It wasn't like you could visit aunts, uncles, and cousins for Sunday dinner, at least not on the Rosselli side of the family.

When Alessa returned she encouraged me to continue my scrutiny of the pictures. I was pleased that her English was so articulate, and complimented her on this as she set the flowers on a table by a window overlooking the narrow cobbled street. Alessa insisted on preparing a pot of tea and brought it on a tray with hot, crusty cinnamon toast for what turned out to be a delightful midmorning feast. I had been too nervous to eat breakfast, and didn't dare hope Alessa would be so receptive and genuinely pleased about my surprise visit.

"Daniel writes every week. Like clockwork I can expect his letter in the Thursday morning mail. He always was a very disciplined child, a creature of habit and routine." Alessa smiled, thinking about him, and gave me a warm glance. Her delicate hazel eyes were sparkling, and I wondered if the cyan-blue of Daniel's and Benjamin's had been as vivid in Dr. Rosselli.

"Does he ever mention anyone outside of the church? Jonathan Davis perhaps, or my son Benjamin, of whom he is quite fond?" I asked, guessing that he might, tears instantly forming in my eyes, as I remembered the true purpose for my visit.

"Oh, yes, indeed. And you too, dear. Daniel admires your photography. He's sent me several for gifts. Are you okay?" Alessa reached out for my hand.

"Yes, I'm fine." I couldn't bring myself to tell her yet about how Benjamin might be somewhere in Venice. Obviously, Peter hadn't been to her home, at least not with my son . . . but perhaps alone. I didn't want to alarm Alessa by seeming too unstable, or eager for personal family information that perhaps she coveted as much as Daniel did.

"Come, I will show you the gifts of your work he has sent." Alessa stood and we walked together down the narrow hall and into a sunny bedroom with three photos from my wildflower series on the wall. I had sold them through Rachel's gallery, just as all my work was displayed and sold through Rachel. It surprised me more than a little that Daniel had purchased and shipped these photos. I had no idea he visited Rachel's gallery before his trip to see Benjamin's work, let alone to buy *my* work and send it to his mother. Why had my best friend Rachel never mentioned it? But of course, I knew the answer as soon as the question formed in my head. Rachel would never purposefully stack the odds in Daniel's favor with me, knowing the erroneous state of living daily in a partial lie.

We returned to the sofa in the front room and I gathered up my nerve for inquiring about Peter. "Mrs. Rosselli, have you had any other visitors lately interested in Daniel?"

"Please, call me Alessa," she insisted. The tiny, attractive woman thought for a few seconds before answering. "No, not for many months. Not since the priests from Rome were here to talk about Daniel's appointment to be bishop," she shared frankly.

"I see." We sipped our tea in silence for a minute. I felt suddenly overwhelmed to be in the presence of Daniel's mother. Something about this small feminine version of the mysterious man behind the sacred robes was both comforting and disconcerting. Perhaps it was the understanding in Alessa's eyes. I somehow believed this gentle woman knew more about me than she had so far revealed.

"My son Benjamin," I started, and then paused, overwhelmed by what all that encompassed past and present, and how it related to her in ways I had never dared think of. "He is eleven, nearly twelve." I paused again, and smiled at Alessa. "But sometimes I think he is many years beyond his actual age." I became silent, too distraught to continue, and sat as if frozen, willing the emotional struggle within me to subside, while Alessa handed me a tissue from her pocket and patted my knee.

"It's okay, Victoria. I know all about your Benjamin." We looked into each other's eyes and I drew strength from hers. I forgot about wanting to search for the little blue pills in my handbag. "How is the boy?" she asked, her expression worried.

"He's been . . . kidnapped."

"Oh my goodness. When did this happen?" Alessa took my hand and began to squeeze it, upset by my disturbing news.

"It will be a week tomorrow. I was hoping, well, that maybe the kidnapper had come to you for information about Daniel. Because, it all has to do with . . . Daniel . . . in a way."

"You mean because of the healing powers they share?"

"Yes." I looked at her curiously.

"Daniel told me." Alessa hesitated, perhaps needing to form her words carefully. She still held my hand protectively in both of hers and I felt calmed by it. "He has grown quite fond of your Benjamin. I'm sure he has expressed this to you?" Alessa looked as if she certainly hoped he had. "Who, Victoria, do you believe has taken Benjamin? For it sounds as if you know."

I looked her straight in the eye, somehow sensing she would have heard this name before. "Dr. Peter Cairns."

"Oh, dear Lord!"

"You know of him then?" I asked.

"Yes. Daniel has written of this Peter, and how he has harmed perhaps many women. He is determined to show him how to find the grace of God, and concerned about his interest in our family history." Alessa looked thoughtful. "I suppose this Peter could be a threat to Daniel if he decided to exploit him, by exposing the secrets of his family for profit. This is not uncommon when people are assigned very responsible tasks in society. Their private lives are threatened to become public knowledge." Alessa glanced out the window and a shadow of dread crossed her intelligent, sweet face.

"Is there something in Daniel's past he doesn't want exposed?" I asked, innocently enough.

Alessa redirected her attention to me. "It's not that. It's more a matter of him wanting to protect my privacy, and that of our whole family here in Venice. Not have me or anyone else bothered due to his new popularity in America, or sudden fame, for lack of a better word in your language."

Alessa reached out for me and we hugged tightly. "I am so sorry my dear for what has happened to your Benjamin. What can I do? What can I tell you that may help him to be found?"

"It would help if I knew what family secrets Peter would want to dredge up for profit. The story behind the healing powers, for one."

Alessa folded her hands in her lap. "There is nothing to hide, Victoria. It is a great gift that comes with a great price. Life is about balance, no? Daniel's father, my Timothy, was a doctor, as I am sure you are aware. He used his healing gift through his profession. But the Church of Rome felt that Timothy had missed his calling as a spiritual leader, and they never let him live in peace. Always the guilt haunted him, always the belief he had let God down in some way."

"Did they know Dr. Rosselli's father was a cardinal?" I asked.

Alessa's half smile indicated her lack of surprise that I knew this.

"That is one reason, my sweet Victoria, why Timothy chose not to protect himself, and his gift, within the sanctity of the church. My Timothy did not wish to live a lie as his father the cardinal had done before him, hiding Gina, the woman he loved, in the shadows of the church steeple, and so he avoided any leadership within the church."

Daniel suddenly seemed a lot like his grandfather to me. Wanting his cake and eat it too. Wanting the shining glory of the bishop title and the warm arms of his lover in dark shadows at the same time. But that was unfair of me. That would be judging him. Who was I to say that accepting his calling from God and the church, while embracing his passion for healing the otherwise hopeless of their afflictions, wasn't a great sacrifice in and of itself?

Alessa poured us more tea. "So that is why my husband hid his healing powers behind his vocation as a doctor."

I nibbled a buttery piece of cinnamon bread, digesting this information, thinking of Rachel hidden away in the recesses of Robert's need for her, and of Gina, hidden away by the very visual cardinal. Alessa's husband Timothy, however, had chosen to use his gift as part of a profession often at odds with the Church. Difficult as it was, outcast as he felt, still the sacrifice was made to properly honor the woman he loved, and the son they eventually conceived—Daniel. Could it have been any less torturous, in the end, to be an honorable family man but an outcast of his faith? Perhaps observing this nemesis for his father is what caused Daniel to embrace the church rather than try to work around it.

I suddenly felt strangely bonded to this woman I only met hours ago. It was a difficult parting for both of us. I promised to keep in touch, and keep her abreast of the situation. Just before leaving I asked about Daniel's childhood, and if he had healed small animals continually, like my Benjamin.

Alessa nodded and said, all the time. Once, he made a newborn kitten, suffocated by its young mother lying upon it, rise again to suckle milk beside its siblings. Shocking, she had said.

But then, miracles do happen, and sometimes we get to witness them at the hands of an angel, whether seen or not seen.

CHAPTER THIRTY-FOUR

It was time to beat Peter at his own game,
and make one last phone call in case he beat me instead.

On the train from Venice to Rome I could think of nothing but my visit with Daniel's mother. It was as if I had known her for a lifetime. So warm and comforting was her gentle spirit that I dared to consider feeling closer to her after one afternoon than to my mother in all our years together. Alessa Rosselli and I alone understood the awe and confusion of having a son who touched kittens and birds in such a way as to turn their stillness into movement. She also knew Daniel and I were hopelessly intertwined in ways we could never fully admit or deny, just as she knew Benjamin was her grandson. Of this I had no doubt.

Watching trees fly past on the train I realized how pieces of this puzzle we call life never fully come together, but have moments of clarity at least, that allow us to feel as if our spirit is soaring up over canyons in a cloudless blue sky. I remembered a Bible verse from my childhood, while sitting there somewhat impatiently and being gently tousled by the moving train. It was something about how we see through a mirror dimly in this life, and how clarity only comes after death. I could only wonder what that clarity might be—exonerating or condemning. For clearly it could only be one or the other. Perhaps how we dealt with the hardest moments of our lives, rather than how we handled the easier ones, would be key to exoneration verses condemnation.

That made me think of Daniel, for surely even angels, if he were indeed such a thing, would have to suffer consequences for their actions. Daniel was undoubtedly more selfless and compassionate than he was selfish and weak. As far as I could tell, I was the only Achilles heel Daniel had. Daniel's love for God and the Church, and for the needy souls he healed, was unconditional, just as Jesus Himself loves without boundary or restraint.

Perhaps his love for me was no different. Perhaps I finally understood why, despite his oath of celibacy, he would welcome me into his bed. He was not driven by lust alone, but by complete and total love.

In welcoming a lifetime of stolen moments, I could see us still finding comfort in each other's arms as elderly, weary warriors, having fought the good fight but having lost this one battle of the flesh. The fact that Daniel had a need for intimacy was something a merciful God would surely forgive. The bigger question was whether or not I could be that lover in the shadows, never having more than a forbidden morsel of him. One thing was evident; our unsanctioned love would defy selflessness, self-sacrifice, and a desire to mirror all worthy traits laid out clearly in scripture as causing abundant joy and peace of mind, neither of which I would ever have.

Finally the train reached my stop and I took a taxi to Campo di Fiori where I stood staring at the small unassuming cathedral with its tall steeple and arched entrance. I carefully touched the large handbag at my side with all the documents claiming Benjamin to be my son. Nervously, I took a deep breath. The morning sun flooded my face and enticed me to further linger outside the church. I closed my eyes and prayed that my Benjamin would be inside. That by some miracle my theory would be correct, and Peter would have brought Benj here to be watched over by the priests, while he weaved a blackmail web worth more money than all the paintings he could ever hope the son of an impending bishop might paint.

After my silent prayer I glanced at the people in the open piazza shopping among the many vendors there. It could have been an oil painting. Rows of seasonal produce reflected all the colors of autumn against the bright fall sky. To the sound of patrons bartering for rutabagas and plump tomatoes I opened the heavy wooden door and entered the marbled foyer, pulling my suitcase behind me and hoping no one had thought I might come to the church where Daniel first served.

Slowly my eyes adjusted to the dim lighting. The candles on the altar far down the red-carpeted aisle flickered in the breeze from my entrance. I could almost hear the dancing wicks sizzling in the quiet sanctuary. Stained glass windows aligned the sidewalls with richly colored, detailed drama of Biblical characters, whose facial expressions reflected my pain and anticipation. Several worshippers were poised on kneeling benches at the foot of each mahogany pew. They prayed with such concerted effort that my presence was all but unknown to them.

I wanted to invade the private quarters beyond this vestibule, and diligently search each nook and cranny of those hidden places housed within this landmark cathedral until finding Benjamin. But my stomach was churning, and my head felt light. I wished I had taken one of the blue pills before coming. I pushed my suitcase up against a back wall and barely made it to a highly polished pew before nearly passing out, my heart and head both throbbing.

Kneeling in conformity with the few scattered worshippers, I prayed diligently for the miraculous appearance of my son. Despite having some issues of not forgiving a God that would allow my own human father to abandon us and take my mother's life too soon, I still believed in the power of prayer. I could thank Grams for that. Because of her I knew God had a plan for our lives if we would only trust enough in Him to follow it. She never gave up on me, never scolded or lectured about why my skeptical attitude might be the death of me. She was my steadfast bridge builder, despite the wall I hid behind.

As I prayed there in the last pew, arms folded, head down, I asked God to take the walls away. I was ready to cross the bridge. I told God I was on His side. Whatever it would take, I wanted to be on His team. His goodness was so perfectly reflected in Daniel and Benjamin I could not doubt for one minute that God's game plan was all we needed to give meaning to our lives.

Feeling calmer after bearing my soul to my Maker and asking forgiveness for my stubborn defiance these past few years, I devised a plan for speaking to the priests, who were surely here somewhere, ready to serve those in need. I could only hope they would be as truthful with me as I planned to be with them. The scrapbook of Benjamin's budding artistry fame was in my large oversized handbag. I even had pictures of Peter and the article about his impending rape trial. But on the other hand, Peter had managed to bring Benjamin all the way to Italy with a fake passport. If he could do that, no telling what type of other documents he had paid for in an effort to prove his paternity. All of this weighed heavily on my mind as I watched an altar boy enter the small, lavishly decorated sanctuary from a side alcove.

The boy had a reverent posture, and wore a white satin robe with a black sash as he fussed with the consecrated elements of the Eucharist, placed on the altar in gray marble containers. He was measuring and pouring as if their meaning were more scientific than spiritual. Biblical characters dominated religious paintings hung in this sacred area, while dozens of burning wicks on dedication candles reflected off the gold inlaid frames.

The candlelight accentuated the alter boy's light hair, causing it to glow softly. It occurred to me that this half grown boy looked like my Benjamin, although I could only see the back of him, and it was from a distance, as I was kneeling in the last pew. A surge of warmth suddenly began to rush through me. I wondered if truly I had lost my sanity. Could this be Benjamin, who seemed so comfortable with his task, as if having been born and raised in this very cathedral? Could God have answered my prayer?

He finally turned, glancing about the room as if taking inventory of who was there. His gaze rested on me. We neither one made any effort to move or speak, as if overcome by disbelief. The last seven agonizing days were over. Not seventy days or seven years, as I had feared with dread, but only seven long suffering days.

Benjamin genuflected to the crucifix hung high upon the center wall behind the dozens of lit candles and then walked quickly down the aisle to where I was now standing, ready to embrace him. He returned my hug tightly, and then we sat together in the pew. In whispering voices we assured one another that we were fine, hugging again for a long time without speaking, our eyes filled with tears of joy when finally we pulled apart. Benjamin quietly filled me in on his past week, and then he nodded to a door near the front of the cathedral. I followed him down the outside aisle and through an opening that left the main sanctuary, right where I had envisioned myself boldly invading earlier on a desperate mission to recover my son.

Once inside the inner chamber of the old building Benjamin took my hand and nearly pulled me down the narrow hall, claiming I must meet someone in the study at the foot of the stairs. We descended the half flight of tiled steps and felt the coolness of the basement level as Benjamin knocked gently on the door. *Come in* was heard from the other side. Benjamin opened it, and stood at the entrance. I looked over his head and saw a priest behind a huge desk. His books and papers were stacked neatly about, his black collar stiff and straight beneath an angular, pleasant face.

"Please, come in, Benjamin, and tell me who you have brought with you." He stood and gestured for us to enter the dimly lit room, where we sat in tall ladderback chairs placed in front of the massive desk. The priest extended his hand to me as Benjamin told him that I was his mother. I was grateful the Italian clergyman spoke English. It would make everything easier.

"Really?" Father Mario looked surprised. "Well, if you have come to collect Benjamin, I am not at all sure that I can help you."

"And why is that, Father Mario, considering I am a single parent with sole custody of this child, who was kidnapped just last week, making you look rather suspicious to say the least." My heart was nearly in my throat as the Father and I stared one another down.

Father Mario proceeded to tell me how Benjamin's father claimed to have no rights in America as the natural parent, because he never knew about the child until many years later.

"That isn't true," I responded, " in as much as Peter is not the father."

The priest looked at me with interest, his dark, bushy brows furrowed.

I began to pull documents out of my oversized bag and placed them on the desk for him to examine as I explained that Peter claimed to be the father, knowing full well that he was not. Benjamin sat quietly beside me and exchanged glances occasionally with Father Mario, whom I was sure had a lot of questions for Benjamin. He was a soft-spoken man with unusually good English skills—well beyond my expectation, considering how native-born Italian he looked.

After nodding his head politely and listening intently to my explanation of the last seven days, including a brief rendition of Peter's sordid history, Father Mario turned his attention to my son.

"Benjamin, why have you never mentioned this Dr. Cairns was not your real father?" His look was one of partial reprimand, but I sensed a mutual affection between them.

"I don't know." Benjamin glanced at me. "I was afraid Dr. Cairns would hurt my mother if I didn't cooperate with his plan."

"I see. And what was that plan, exactly?" Father Mario asked.

"He wanted me to be his son. At least, for everyone to believe I am."

Father Mario gave Benjamin his full attention. "Why, Benjamin, do you think Dr. Cairns wanted everyone to believe you were his son?"

"I think, because I paint."

"Because you paint?"

"Because my paintings are worth a lot of money."

"Indeed they are. And so, you think he wants to profit from your talent?"

"Yes. And . . ." Benjamin didn't finish. He sat back in the chair, having been perched on the edge until now. He played with wax that had dripped onto his fingers and hardened there, while arranging candles on the altar.

"And what, Benjamin?" I asked, not waiting for Father Mario's response.

"Nothing," he answered, still focused on his waxy fingers.

"Oh, I think there is something more, Benjamin. Please, share your thoughts with us," Father Mario pleaded.

Benjamin shrugged. "I think he wants to know more about how I heal animals, and how . . . how Father Rosselli heals people."

"Father Rosselli?" The tall slender priest eased forward in his chair. "Do you mean Dr. Timothy Rosselli's boy, Daniel, from Venice?"

"Yes, that's who he means," I answered for Benjamin.

"Do you know Father Daniel Rosselli, in America?" Father Mario looked from me to Benjamin and back again.

"Yes, we do," I answered. "I have known Daniel for twelve years, to be exact."

Father Mario's eyes lit up, as if a light had gone on in his head. "Of course, Portland . . . St. Matthew's. You are from Portland, and that's where Father Daniel is located."

We were all silent for a moment, as I allowed this new information to settle in, seeing that Father Mario appeared somewhat overwhelmed by the news. Finally he scratched his head and folded his hands on the desk.

"Benjamin, let me see if I understand all of this correctly."

Benjamin looked up at him respectfully.

"Dr. Peter Cairns has brought you here, kidnapped you, not because he believes he is your father and wants to protect you from an overbearing mother that will not allow him partial custody, but because he wants to profit from your paintings." He paused there and Benjamin nodded in agreement. "I dare say he wants to profit from your healing gift as well, should there be an opportunity. Or perhaps I should say, when that opportunity presents itself, and it will present itself. The potent gift of healing that you obviously possess could easily be misused for financial gain."

Benjamin looked puzzled. "You believe I possess such a healing gift, as great as Father Daniel's?"

"Yes, I believe that you do." He looked at me as if he had done the math, not to mention adding up the attributes, physical and otherwise, possibly concluding that Peter was messing with something much bigger than kidnapping. He was messing with the appointment of a bishop, and not just any bishop at that.

"But I only heal animals. I have never healed a person," Benjamin protested, not willing to believe what he always suspected, for surely he suspected his powers were beyond his understanding, or control. I had observed this struggle within him over the dove incident.

"Have you ever tried, Benjamin, to heal a person?" Father Mario asked inquisitively.

Benjamin stared at him somberly. "Once, I prayed for Sarah, and her cancer went into remission."

"Well then, you see?" Father Mario smiled. "And that is only the beginning, Benjamin. Healing Sarah was done without full knowledge of your potential. Think what you can do once you know what you are capable of."

We all sat pondering the magnitude of this information until Father Mario suggested that Benjamin return to his chores, and then to his canvas and paints in the study. Benjamin seemed grateful to be excused. He hugged me before leaving and I almost hesitated to let him go, but thought better of being a clingy mom. The last thing Benjamin needed was an emotionally disturbed mother in this tense situation.

As soon as Benjamin had left Father Mario turned his attention to me.

"We have to stop this Dr. Cairns."

"Yes we do," I agreed, and then changed the subject. "Father Mario, Why is Benjamin here? He has told me that Peter dropped him off to be mentored by you and another priest, and that he is learning how to do certain tasks, but that he gets to paint in the old study and use your supplies."

"Yes. I paint as a hobby. I have always dabbled in it." Father Mario stood up and walked around to the front of the desk. He sat in the chair Benjamin had occupied only moments ago, and looked me straight in the eye. "Ms. Agostini, I recognized your son, Benjamin, the minute I laid eyes upon him. When Dr. Cairns first walked through the door of the vestibule."

I looked at him curiously. "You recognized him?"

"From the cover of *Art Today* . . . the magazine."

"I see," I replied, but truthfully I could not imagine the odds that someone such as Father Mario would recognize him from the cover of the upscale London publication.

"I felt honored to meet him, and told Benjamin and Dr. Cairns this. The doctor had become immediately at ease and asked if the boy could stay with us while he furnished the apartment he'd found and began his medical practice in earnest."

"Did he," I said, obviously annoyed at the mere idea of Peter showing up with my son and asking anything at all concerning him.

"Yes. I believed him to be who he said he was. A father struggling to claim his rights as such. Relocating here in Rome, in order to protect his son from a domineering mother that wished only to have him paint continually for profit."

I raised my eyebrows at the genius reversal of truth Peter was using, making himself the victim of *my* domineering behavior and selfish greed. "Has Benjamin been happy here?" I asked, although I could clearly see that he'd been well taken care of and as for his mental state, he seemed as focused as ever.

"Yes, Benjamin has taken to his new environment like a fish to water, I believe you say. Father Ralph and I have been pleased to have a replacement for the young lad lost to us recently, swept away by soccer stardom. In the end, sports won over his religious devotion."

We both smiled. And then a seriousness set in so deep it could almost be felt in the damp air with each measured breath we took. Father Mario leaned forward in the ladderback chair and put his hands together as if praying, but he looked at me rather than up to God.

"This child of yours, Benjamin Ross Agostini, he is very special."

I didn't say anything and we both considered the truth of it for a few seconds until he continued. "I am not going to ask the significance of his middle name. Or the heritage of his healing powers and highly unusual blue eyes."

Again he paused. The silent communication of our mutual stare spoke volumes.

"But I must tell you," he continued, "that if Dr. Cairns knows as much as I fear he knows, then having him arrested now, right before Father Rosselli is appointed bishop, might prove disastrous."

"What is it you want from me, Father Mario? That I leave my son with Peter? That I pretend he is indeed the boy's father, entitled to Benjamin's earnings from his artwork?"

"No, of course not." He stood in frustration and walked back around the desk to his worn leather chair, collapsing into it as if at a loss for where to go from here.

I stood up, eager to leave and find Peter. "Father Mario, I must see Dr. Cairns, and I wish to see him now. Do you have an address for him?"

"Yes, but is it safe to visit this man who has taken your child?" he asked, surprised I would want to.

"Don't worry about me. I'll be fine. But promise you won't let Benjamin out of your sight. And if I don't come back for him, you must contact Father Rosselli about Benjamin. And never let Dr. Cairns near him again."

"I can do that."

"I want you to swear an oath on your Bible."

We studied one another, and then Father Mario scribbled an address on a piece of paper. He gave it to me and reached for his large black sacred book of scripture. With his right hand on it he prayed for God's protection to watch over me, and Benjamin, and Father Rosselli being anointed bishop, where in such a revered position he could touch many lives, and do much good work for the church. Lastly he prayed for mercy, for the misguided soul of Dr. Cairns, and for the carnal sin of Father Daniel Timothy Rosselli, come to visit him in the flesh, as a small replica of none other than himself.

I left quickly, petrified that if I did not pull this off and deal with Peter once and for all he would somehow prevent Daniel from becoming bishop in just a few precious days, or worse, steal the Catholic Church blind so as not to interfere with the sacred appointment. Or he might snatch Benjamin again, right out of God's very house. Who knew what innocent Roman women he would drug and rape for sport? He had to be stopped, and I didn't trust that the Italian *polizia* had the necessary motivation to see that justice would be served. Nor could I leave to fate whether or not he would be returned to the American court system, or that justice would prevail should his trial ever happen. No indeed. I had decided when fleeing in the middle of the night that nothing short of death would stop me from dealing with Peter Cairns myself.

Now I only hoped that I wasn't foolishly going where others had gone before me and failed, only to fail as they had. For certainly of all the women Peter had harmed, those who retaliated did not live to tell about it. I did not dwell on this as I stoically planned my course of action.

It was time to beat Peter at his own game, and to make one last phone call in case it was Peter who walked away victorious.

CHAPTER THIRTY-FIVE

*When all was said and done, Daniel might be willing
to sacrifice everyone and everything in order to be bishop.*

"Miranda, I've found Benjamin."

There was silence on the other end of the telephone.

"Miranda? Are you there?"

"Oh my god, Tori. Where are you? Everyone is in a panic!"

"I'm here at the little cathedral in Campo di Fiori where Daniel first served as priest, and Benjamin is here too. I suspected it might be where Peter would bring him, as a catalyst for his little game."

"Have you called the *polizia*?"

"No. I haven't any proof that he's done anything wrong. His false custody documents probably look more legal than my genuine ones. I'm going to visit Peter and try to convince him that his plan won't work, whatever it is."

"You're going to confront him? That's crazy talk, Tori. You know how dangerous Peter is!"

"I must see him. I must make one more effort to try and reason with him," I said, not wishing to allude to the fact that I did not plan on being reasonable.

I paused and there was dead silence.

"Tori, why don't you just grab Benjamin and run? I mean it. Why not just head back on the first plane and not bother with the *polizia* or Peter either one?"

"I have to do this for Daniel," I said, and added, "besides, what would prevent Peter from trying to take Benjamin again if the law never catches up to him? And so far, outrunning the law has not even been a contest for Peter."

"You're not going to see him alone are you?" Miranda asked, and I could almost see her mind racing, planning, scheming to call the Venice police . . . firemen . . . army . . . and anyone else she could get to track me down and stop me.

"Of course not, silly. Only an insane person would see Peter alone," I lied. Or was I lying? I didn't feel very sane. Judgement, calmness and the ability to reason seemed to be eluding me more each minue. "Two of the priests here are coming along, and they do after all have God on their side." I glanced into Father Mario's office while standing stiff and determined in the hallway. He was bent over his desk writing something, looking incapable of hurting anyone, even a monster like Peter. As for God, so far He seemed to be content to let us all fend for ourselves.

"Be careful, Tori. If I were there I would not let you do this, you know that, right? Despite how many priests you are taking with you."

I didn't respond and Miranda gave up on that subject.

"Daniel and Jonathan have left for Rome to search for you, although their millions of phone calls have gotten them no trace of your whereabouts."

"Is Jonathan worried Peter will play his hand sometime before the ceremony?" I asked, trying to shift the focus off me.

"Yes. But he isn't nearly as concerned about that as he is about you being there *with* him. Doing something foolish like you're getting ready to do, *right now*."

"Don't worry about me, Andi. But if something unforeseen should happen, promise that you and Rachel will take good care of Benjamin."

There was silence again.

"Promise me, Miranda. I'm counting on you."

"I promise. Of course. You know how much I love Benjamin, and you, Victoria, despite your nearly causing me an untimely death by heart attack when discovering your cold and empty bed. Now you promise me you'll call as soon as this little trip to see Peter with heavily robed men at your side is over."

"Yes, I will call you."

We both paused again.

"Andi, I have to go."

"Tori . . . be very careful."

"I will. I promise."

We hung up and I leaned against the thickly plastered wall, willing myself the strength to face Peter one more time—alone. I would agree to sign the paterinty papers he no doubt had in his possession. Peter always covered all his bases. He probably was anticipating my visit, knowing me distubingly well. My stipulation would be that he could have all the money Benjamin might ever make off his art in exchange for me having total custody. Of course, I had no intention of letting that happen—his extortion of Benjamin's profits from his paintings—but for now it would have to do as a convincing argumet. At least it would buy time. It would also take away his power to hurt Daniel. He could hardly accuse Daniel of being the father of Benjamin if I signed paterinty papers indicating Peter to be the dad.

After a couple of deep breaths I reentered Father Mario's study. We exchanged looks of concern. "I'm going to see Peter now," I explained. "If I'm not back in two hours, call the police and have them come to Peter's apartment."

Father Mario nodded, a grim expression on his face. He seemed to be at a loss for words, at least he made no effort to talk me out of seeing Peter. More than likely his urgency to protect Daniel and the empending bishop ceremony was as important to him as it was to me. I asked again for his verbal commitment to protect Benjamin from Peter. He nodded, slowly, and said *may God be with you* as I headed for the stairs. The nun in the vestibule, seated at a little desk in the corner, gave me directions to the address Father Mario had scribbled on the paper. Then she stood and excused herself, disappearing into the dark recesses of the cathedral.

I observed the scarce items on her desk and saw a shiny letter opener beside some mail as yet unopened. It had an ivory handle and gold tip—long, slender and pointy. Shoving it into my oversized bag I exited quickly, before I could examine my thoughts about stealing from a nun, to possibiliby injure a lost lamb that would never find redemption if dead before redeemed. But then, the lamb was more like a ferocious tiger, and no one could fault the possible need to defend myself against his strong desire to hurt me.

I decided to walk, since it was only a few streets away. The warmth of the sun flooded my face as I left the cathedral and made my way to the open market, past a few bistros and clothing shops along the narrow street. I could hear busy vendors and bartering customers as I reached the open *piazza* filled with fresh cut flowers, leather goods and jewelry, silk scarves, and other assorted items of interest. Farmers were selling produce and fishermen their catch of the day.

Sitting down at an outdoor bistro near the marketplace, I ordered a slice of pizza and iced tea. I did not wish to see Peter feeling as weak and squeamish as I did at that moment. Looking up to read the street sign on the corner I realized it was the street on the address. Father Mario had said the *pensione* he'd recommended to Peter was very nice and not expensive.

I thought about what I would say to Peter, and how I had no way to protect myself from him, other than a stolen letter opener stashed inside my oversized bag. I would make it clear that Father Mario and everyone else at the cathedral knew where I was. As did Miranda, who would tell Jonathan. Not that threats of the whole world knowing I had come calling would stop Peter from doing as he pleased. That's what scared me. I thought of Grams and how she would often say to me . . . *brains will only get you so far, Victoria, and luck always runs out.* I needed Peter's luck to run out and prayed that it would.

After hurriedly finishing my pizza, I paid the bill and left. Heading down the proper street I rushed past tourists and locals nervously looking for the address scribbled on my paper. Several times I entered shops and asked where this particular *pensione* might be, in broken Italian, pulled straight from my purse-sized dictionary purchased in Venice. The last shopkeeper pointed across the street and said something unrecognizable to me, but by his grin and gesture, I believed it to be the *pensione* I was looking for.

Standing outside the brick building, I gazed up at flower boxes overflowing with white wisteria. Fear and dread began to creep into every part of me. A surge of indignant and outrageous anger replaced the dread as I thought about Benjamin, there at the cathedral, and how Peter had stolen him, had stolen more than just this child from me. He had taken my peace of mind, and nearly my sanity at this point. I thought about all the other women he had drugged and raped, and how some of them were dead now—if not at the hand of Peter, then indirectly. Either way it was clearly his fault.

I climbed the stairs and knocked firmly on the door marked number seven. When Peter opened it, I was completely taken aback, even though I had anticipated and even hoped he was there. He stared at me as if a ghost, and said nothing. I too was quiet, not having summoned the nerve yet to speak. Finally he grinned devilishly, and in his most appealing voice, welcomed me to come inside. I hesitated briefly and then entered, standing just inside the door instead of just outside it. Somehow I couldn't find the courage to actually *leave* the doorway.

"Please, Victoria, come and sit here in the front room." Peter motioned lavishly for me to lead the way, and finally, hesitantly, I did. I stood for a while as if frozen in time and space but then somehow mustered the presence of mind to sit down on a periwinkle-blue sofa. It had a matching chair, which Peter sank into heavily. Looking through a pair of tall narrow windows behind him I saw the white wisteria spilling over their boxes. One window was slightly opened, causing the lace sheers to dance lazily in the breeze.

"How clever of you to find me already." His voice was rich and joyful, as if this was a game of chess and he was poised for a checkmate. I didn't answer as I studied him. Peter's dark blond hair was slicked back with a gel of some sort. His shifty eyes were nervous but not agitated, looking darker than ever against his gray turtleneck. I realized in this odd moment that I had never seen Peter without sporting corduroy pants. The ones he wore now were a charcoal color. He was literally dressed like doom itself, all in gray.

"Tell me, how did you do it so quickly . . . figure out where I was?" he asked, chuckling under his breath as if amused somehow. I felt a shiver tingle down my spine as I drank in this picture of him sitting there, in front of the window, his dark presence against the lacey white sheers flitting in the breeze.

"It was easy, Peter. Where else would you bring Daniel's child, but to where Daniel would be?"

He laughed out loud this time, as if not able to contain himself at my playing right into his hands. "So then, you admit your bastard child is the priest's!"

"What are you scheming, Peter?"

"Why, Tori darling, that hurts. Whatever makes you think I am scheming something?" he asked, pretending to look wounded.

"You know this child is not your son, and you also know there isn't any way you can sell his paintings, not without the proper authorities figuring out who you are, and *where* you are. At that point in time you have a trial waiting for you, and charges to face, like kidnapping for starters."

"Good point, Tori dear. You always were bright."

"But if you sell Benjamin's paintings to the church, perhaps through Father Mario, your silence can be bought as well. For an even greater price."

Peter smiled widely, enjoying this moment of savoring his strategy, regardless that I had figured it out.

"And, you want to be sure Father Mario, or whomever else you deal with in the hierarchy of the church, understands exactly who Benjamin is, in case you need to use him as an embarrassing threat just prior to the appointing of Daniel in a few days. But it's too late Peter. They already know. I've just come from Father Mario. I told him I needed to see you and he gave me your address. He and everyone else at the cathedral knows I am here, as well as my American contacts." I didn't ellaborate, letting his imagination decide who all those contacts might be.

"Victoria," Peter began softly, with a seductive tone that made me cringe, "of all the women I have ever known, you are the one I wished most of all had come to me on your own. I loved you first, and still do. It isn't too late. We could become a team, a couple . . . do this together—orchestrate the selling of your brilliant prodigy son's artwork to the Catholic empire, for its safe keeping." He chuckled again, wickedly deep and twisted. It felt like a knife to my heart, which had begun beating significantly faster. I squeezed the only object, thrown into my bag last minute, that might protect me from this dispicable man should he try to overtake me physically.

Peter was leaning forward in his chair, hands folded, eyes focused on every part of me seemingly at once. "Worse things could happen, Victoria, than that you and I might become rich off the son you were forced to raise alone, thanks to Daniel's choosing God over the all-American family."

"Was I the first woman you drugged and raped, for not returning your feelings of love?" I asked, coldly, knowing Peter was incapable of love.

Peter sighed deeply. "Tori, Tori. Whatever makes you think I could do such a thing? It hurts me to hear you talk this way."

"How much money are you planning to make off Benjamin's gift for healing?" I asked. "Would you have him perform his miracles in the streets like a circus act, or hidden in back alleys—while taking money from whoever is most desperate to have their loved ones healed?"

I walked to the open window, focusing on the wisteria flooding over the window box. Its delicate beauty calmed me a little. I hoped Peter wouldn't notice my hands had become shaky. I couldn't believe I was alone in this room, in this foreign country, with the very man that had brought me more misery and grief than anyone should have to bear. I feared Peter sensing my fear more than anything, so I continued speaking boldly. "Or were you planning to barter with the church over the healing powers too . . . over Benjamin's future as a servant of God?"

"My, my, aren't we all worked up. I dare say, Victoria, you are quite charming when agitated."

"I have a proposal for you, Peter."

"You want to marry me? I'm okay with that." Peter grinned and winked.

I perched on the edge of the sofa and tried to appear calm. "No, that won't be necessary. I think we can come to an agreement about Benjamin, short of marriage."

"And what sort of an agreement would that be, exactly?" Peter was no longer smiling and I decided that the cheerful Peter was less scary.

"I will sign paternity papers, Peter, if you let me have Benjamin back. Then, you can be his own personal art dealer and do as you please with his work. Sell it to anyone you wish. Benjamin will never care. He doesn't paint for money anyway. He would cooperate happily to protect who his real father is."

"Why would that be preferable and more lucrative than bartering with the church for these paintings?"

"Because I am a sure thing, and the church isn't. If Daniel got wind of what you were doing he would come forward, confess, and put a stop to it."

I paused there and determined Peter was indeed listening.

"In all likelihood he *will* find out. Too many people know that Benjamin is his son. He practically knows himself. He is on the verge of discovering it, and if he does, then he will step down from his position, whatever it is, and you will have nothing. The church will not touch the paintings if the painter becomes controversial."

I studied my advisory and prayed he would believe me. In actuality I had no idea, at this point, if Daniel would ever choose to admit he was Benjamin's father. Perhaps he would deny the child was his and continue to claim Peter had impregnated me. His appointment to be bishop was much more important to him than he had ever verbalized. I could see it in his eyes, down by the creek at Jonathan's barbeque—his shock when realizing the truth of Benjamin's paternity, and then the denial, followed by absolute focus on his pious priorities. When all was said and done, Daniel might be willing to sacrifice everyone and everything in order to be bishop. But Peter wouldn't know that, and so I held my breath.

He stood and walked to the kitchen pantry. When he returned, Peter had a bottle of red wine and two stemmed glasses. He opened the bottle and poured the wine while looking at me in a way that said we did indeed have a deal.

"I will let you sign my paternity papers and give you back your bastard son if you agree to drink a toast to our arrangement," he offered up with a raised eyebrow. Then he began rummaging through his briefcase by the sofa, with his back to me.

Something caught my eye on the floor, and I reached down to pick it up. It was a vile of some sort, with a white powder in it. Immediately I knew it had fallen from Peter's overstuffed briefcase. I wondered if the contents were his drug of choice for rendering victims helpless, or lifeless, whichever the case may be.

"Damn, I know those papers are here somewhere," he muttered.

"Did you really drug all those women, Peter?" I asked, while fingereing the vile in my hand.

"Of course not," he answered, sounding rather iritated, obviously looking for something in his briefcase that was not there. The papers he sought had been extracted and placed on the beveled glass table beside his leather case.

"You have never possessed any dangerous concoction for causing someone to become unconscious, or even die?"

"Victoria, I know that bastard attorney of yours has planted such morbid thoughts in your head, but I am telling you they are completely untrue." He said it while staring at his briefcase as if he could will it to produce whatever he was looking for. "Excuse me, I need to use the restroom," he said, looking at me just as I folded my hand around the tiny vile and squeezed it shut from view. "I won't be long. Here, read these," he said, handing me the papers from the beveled glass table. Then he disappeared down the short hall.

Without hesitation I opeded the vile and poured the contents into the wine glass across from the one set in front of me. Strangely, my heart was calm and my breathing steady. My hands were not shaky, clammy, or awkward. With the deftness of a snake charmer I closed the vile and slid it into my oversized bag. It clinked against the letter opener, reminding me that my sanity was either fully present or completely gone.

I tried to concentrate on the words of the document, while waiting for him to return, which he did shortly, looking unhappy I would say, by his furrowed brows.

Peter handed me a pen. My head was throbbing, and had been ever since I'd left the cathedral. But only now did it seem excruciating enough to take notice of. The letters were scrambled on the document before me, and I wondered if I were even capable of signing my name. The room began to spin as I fingered the cold shiny pen in my hand. Cold and shiny like the weapon in my bag. But perhaps I had found an even better weapon against Peter.

"Sign this, and we can drink to a partnership that hopefully will last a lifetime, despite it not being sweet matrimony, *my love.*" Peter didn't seem to be relishing this golden opportunity to get what he wanted as much as he had earlier.

"These papers are from the paternity suit," I acknowledged. "They claim you are the father, and there is false documentation here as to your DNA, and Benjamin's."

"That is correct. If you sign these, then I have every right, as a father, to be Benjamin's personal art dealer and money manager," Peter winked. "And of course, it clearly states that you have full custody. But if you try to have that attorney friend of yours interfere, well, then I might just decide otherwise. These things can get very ugly in court, who belongs to whom, who is lying and who is not."

"It's almost as if you knew I was coming, Peter. And what I would want when I arrived." Sweat began trickling down my back. Having him so near was stifling. I stared at the glasses of wine, observing them to look equally innocent. Thankfully no residue appeared in either one.

"Perhaps I know you better than you know yourself, Vicotria." He chuckled, deeply from his gut as if he hadn't been this amused for quite some time. "My false documentation is so fool proof it is extremely doubtful anyone would ever question it. Not the DNA samples, or how many witnesses saw you officially sign this," Peter snickered. He reached out to move a piece of damp hair off my forehead, causing me to shiver.

We stared at each other for a few seconds. Then I opened the pen and signed in my best longhand, *Victoria Winslow Agostini.* I couldn't help as I looked at my name but wonder as to whom the real victor would be. Peter obviously had a plan B. His frustration at not finding the vile seemed to have evaporated into thin air. Did he find a second vile? How many were in his possession at any given time? I suddenly wished I'd paid more attention to him since returning from the bathroom. Perhaps we were in double jeapordy of non-redemption.

Peter took the papers from me before the ink was dry, and placed them back into his briefcase. In that few seconds while his back was turned I stared into the wine again, but the red vino revealed nothing other than allowing me to become painfully aware that we had sealed our fate—Peter and I—whatever that fate was to be.

Peter returned promptly and didn't hesitate to pick up the glasses and hand me the one closest to me. My heart began racing, my hands began shaking, my body was wringing with sweat. I couldn't think clearly. I had no idea if I had beaten Peter at his own game or played nicely into it. Based on our history together, the odds were not in my favor. I could only hope that God *was.*

"Let's drink a toast to our new partnership," he said, smiling.

"Yes, let's do," I added staring at him blankly.

We gently clinked our warfare, and drank in silence, both of us thirsty and seemingly confident we had won this game of chance.

CHAPTER THIRTY-SIX

My heart had slowed to a snail's pace
and I couldn't decide which of us was drunk or dying.

Peter poured us each another glass and sat down in the chair by the window. We had consumed the first glass rather quickly. Either from nerves or the relief of knowing we each had gotten what we wanted. I had custody of Benjamin, or did I? He had all the money from Benjamin's art. Or did he? And more importantly, which of us would live to tell about it?

"Victoria, I lied to you. I must confess." Peter looked serious, sitting there holding the stemmed glass. He took a sip and continued to stare at me.

"Lied about what?" I asked, knowing that he probably had never told the truth about anything, so therefore everything that ever passed through his lips was a lie. I leaned back against the sofa, feeling drained suddenly. Exhausted . . . more than just weary.

"Well, technically you do not have custody of Benjamin, in as much as you won't be around to collect him." Peter didn't smile. He either wasn't joking or didn't find his own humor amusing.

I was beginning to wonder if I had indeed consumed the drug he was so fond of dispensing in women's beverages. Could I be that easy to trick? I wanted to believe not. I wanted to believe God was on my side. I know He doesn't allow everything to turn out peachy just because we have finally admitted we trust in Him, but so many things were riding against Peter. He knew I had told everyone where I was going and who I'd be with, and he was already treading thin ice with this hobby of drugging women. Miranda's lawsuit was proof of that. Even if he dumped my body somewhere and convinced everyone he hadn't seen me since he left the States, it wouldn't add up well for him.

"And why not?" I asked. "Why won't I be around to live in peace with my son?"

Peter twirled the wine left in his glass. He looked from it to me and shrugged. "I think you will be far, far away, my sweet. Where some of the beautiful women go after I love them."

"And where is that, Peter?" I asked, observing him carefully, thinking wildly. Surely he would not poison a drink placed squarely before me, knowing I was fully aware of this rather bad habit of his. It was impossible to believe he had slipped something into my glass when returning from the bathroom, even knowing it would be uncharacteristic of him not to. Yet I could barely focus on him, barely hold a coherent thought as he poured the rest of the wine into his glass.

"Tori, darling. You aren't drinking your wine. Was one glass enough to quench your thirst?"

"Did you do it?" I asked.

"Do what?"

"Kill Claire?"

Peter grinned. "Why would you ask about Claire, and not yourself? Don't you want to know if I plan to kill *you*, my love? But certainly not until I've *made love* to you, at least once more."

I finished my second glass of wine, realizing it had calmed my nerves but would not help keep my wits about me, if indeed I wasn't dying. "Peter, at least give me the satisfaction of answering my question. What can it hurt? Who can I tell if I am dead?" I asked, trying to focus on him, sitting there in the chair, a blur with shiny hair gel glistening in sunlight.

"I suppose I could grant you one last request. You will, after all, soon be fulfilling all my desires as I make passionate love to you." Peter chuckled. "Okay then, let's play true confessions for a moment." He finished his wine, and sat the stemmed glass on the floor. Then he leaned back, resting his arms on either side of the chair and I thought it a perfect position to be electrocuted, if only I had some restraining belts and a live current handy.

Staring straight ahead rather than in my direction, Peter began to speak without the lightheartedness he had been maintaining thus far. He sighed heavily before beginning his true confession. "I would love to have killed Claire. The satisfaction of doing-in Robert's wife would have been reason enough. But she was such an enjoyable lover, at least, heavily drugged. It would have been fun to have her die in the act. But it was too risky, especially with that idiot friend of yours having my every move watched, or most of them. Too many of them for me to attempt such a delightful experience."

Peter paused there and I wanted him to finish quickly before I either passed out, or worse. On the other hand, he didn't look at all affected by whatever was in his vile I had added to his drink. Perhaps my skittish fragmented thoughts and throbbing head had caused me to create drama where there was none. Perhaps the vile was filled with nothing more than artificial coffee sweetener.

"Crazy Claire took her own life, damn her. In my office, of all places, the stupid bitch. I can't believe she did that. The woman was so pathetic, who ever would have thought she could be that vindictive? And I mistakenly assumed that she worshipped me. I was the only doctor who got rid of her symptoms, consistently at least, with my hypnotic treatments. Lots of doctors tried lots of meds, and they all worked for a time. But then Claire had allergic reactions to them sooner or later, or the side effects drove her even crazier than she already was."

Peter's speech had slowed and his words were slurring. Of course, he'd consumed three glasses of wine in less than thirty minutes. He sat quietly, and stared at the lace sheers still moving in the breeze. I could feel it on my face and its coolness was welcome, but my heart had slowed to a snail's pace and I couldn't decide which of us was drunk or dying.

"And what about the others, Peter? Did you kill all of them?" I asked, without enough energy to sound angry.

"Only the ones that woke up before I had finished with them, or figured it out and went tattling to the authorities." Peter sighed deeply again and was quiet. I stood up and began walking around—touching the framed art on the walls, running my hands down the heavy velvet curtains that adorned each window—hoping to regain some strength by moving about.

"Peter, I thought you told me you hadn't drugged anyone—ever." I looked into his dull eyes.

"Yes, of course I did, my love. I'm only confessing because you won't live to tell anyone." He laughed without enthusiasm. "And of course, with these papers you've signed, Benjamin will automatically be mine after your death, unless Daniel suddenly gets a conscience."

He tried to laugh again but it came out as a choking gasp. "That is so unlikely—Daniel getting a conscience—it is the least of my concerns," he nearly whispered, his voice raspy and strained. "I shouldn't have drank my wine so quickly," he added, while shakily standing. And then like a hawk he reached forward in one fell swoop and grabbed onto my arms. I tried to scream but he quickly placed a hand across my face while forcing me onto the sofa. I squirmed as he held me there, but my strength had been drained from wine and fear, and hopefully from nothing else.

Peter removed his hand and I gasped for air as he spoke. "You stupid little whore. Did you really think I would let you leave? Whatever were you thinking?" He played with my hair and stroked my cheek. I thought about the letter opener in my bag. It was useless at this point. False security. Like everything with Peter. You could never come out on top. Never have the upper hand. Never have any control over him whatsoever. How crazy had I been to try and win against him? Beat the odds? How crazy indeed. I wouldn't be here had my sanity not slipped from my grasp the minute Sarah told me Satan Himself had taken Benjamin from me.

I considered screaming again but decided to think my situation through instead. *Think. Think. Think* . . . is all I could think. My mind was thick and my thoughts bogged down under a cloud somewhere as I lay there beneath the weight of Peter. He began to run his hand down my neck and onto my blouse, fumbling to open the first button and then the second. When he reached the third all I could think to do was *talk*. "Peter, did you drug . . . my wine? When you returned . . . from the bathroom?" I gasped, his heavy body constricting my lungs.

"No, Tori darling. I would have, but I lost the vile, damn it all. Your death will have to be something a bit more physical . . . like strangling." His hands slithered up my unbuttoned blouse and folded around my neck.

"I found it . . ." I whispered, barely able to speak at all as he tightened his grip.

We stared into each other's eyes.

His were filled with fear. I'd never seen fear in Peter's eyes before. It gave me renewed strength. Pushing his hands from my neck I bolted upright, shoving him onto the floor, where he fell hard. Peter's fearful eyes became quite large and he couldn't seem to move.

"Vic . . . toria. You must call . . . for help."

I looked down at him, not more than an arms length away from where I stood shaking. Awkwardly I stumbled to the open window where I sucked in mouthfuls of fresh air. Inhaling the scent of sweet wisteria flowers brought back my sense of purpose.

"Who would I call, Peter? I don't know anything about how to report an accidental poisoning in Italy. It is accidental if you lie to the person doing the poisoning, isn't it? By telling them you've never had any in your possession. I mean, had you told me, Peter, that you keep poison lying around, I would have thought twice about pouring it into your wine. Perhaps you should consider telling the truth once in a while?" I turned to look at him sprawled out on the floor.

Peter tried to move, but he couldn't. "You are not . . . a murderer. Call for help. There is time . . ." Peter fumbled around, trying to rise from the floor but then his body became limp and his breathing shallow.

I pulled the little vile from my bag and turned it over in my hands. Carefully I wiped my prints from the bottle and squeezed it firmly into Peter's palm. It fell between his leg and the floor. I left it there, and looked into his face. His eyes opened partially. "Tell them . . ." he choked in a cracking whisper, ". . . what I took."

His dull eyes were pleading with me as I stood in front of him. I looked away, glancing out the window at the sunny day and the white wisteria, almost too bright to admire with the glare of the sun.

"It's over, Peter." I looked into those haunting eyes again. "The drugging, the raping, the killing . . . the kidnapping and greed. Lording power over others because you were powerless to make others love you. All it would have taken is a little kindness, Peter—a little empathy and compassion. All the things you felt you never got would have been yours, had you chosen to give them to someone else."

Still his eyes were half open, staring at me. His chest was moving up and down and so I knew he was not dead, but I had no idea if he could hear me, or understand me until he tried to speak.

"I beg you, Tori . . . please call."

"Peter, assuming that I let you lie here and die as you well deserve, do you want to make peace with God? Confess your sins?" I asked coldly.

"There is . . . no God," Peter choked out, gasping for air, and I almost believed that he actually sneered. Although the drug somewhat obliterated facial expressions, as far as I had observed thus far.

"Fine. Hell is a suitable place for you anyway," I replied, while gathering my purse and sticking my wine glass in it. I extracted the papers I had signed from Peter's briefcase, and carefully opened the door with the sleeve of my blouse. I nearly broke into a run while covering the short distance back to the cathedral, slowing my pace only enough as to not draw undue attention to myself.

Once inside the church I stood in the vestibule and tried to slow my breathing. A nun who happened to be near looked at me and asked if I was okay—first in Italian, and then in broken English.

"Someone needs to . . . check on this man," I said, pushing the crumpled paper into her hands with Peter's name and address on it. I could only hope the Italian nun understood English well enough to know what I was saying. "He does not . . . answer his door and I know he is inside . . . maybe hurt." We shared eye contact and the nun nodded, indicating she understood. Then she left abruptly, I assumed to make a phone call to an ambulance.

Entering the sanctuary I felt as if in a daze. I slid into a back pew, and kneeled to pray. Fortunately there were no other worshipers there at that moment, because I soon fell completely apart and began to sob uncontrollably. I begged God's forgiveness and asked for his mercy. I had only begun to calm down when Father Mario appeared from the front of the sanctuary and joined me in the pew.

"Ms. Agostini, did you see Dr. Cairns?"

"Yes."

"Tell me what happened?"

I slid back into the pew from the kneeling bench and looked at the worried priest.

"Father Mario, Peter is dead."

His eyes became large as he studied my expression. "How can that be?"

"The not-so-good doctor has had a taste of his own medicine."

"Did you see this happen?" Father Mario asked, the color draining from his face.

"I was there, yes."

"You are so pale, and shaking." He reached out and touched my shoulder, just as the nun returned. She began to speak in Italian to Father Mario. In the distance I heard sirens. Then he answered her and she was gone. We were alone again. The sirens stopped.

"Father Mario, where is Benjamin?"

"He is painting. I was just with him, before Sister Agnes told me of your return. He is worried about you."

I nodded but did not say anything. My thoughts were scattered and confused. I wondered if I should take a little blue pill. What would Miranda want me to do? I had wished she'd been there so that I might ask her.

"Ms. Agostini, tell me exactly what happened. *Exactly.*" Father Mario took my hand and folded it into his, firmly. I looked into his face, into his eyes. He was so reverent, so genuinely concerned.

"I knocked on the door . . . and Peter answered. He was . . . surprised to see me. I thought he seemed . . . taller . . . than I had remembered. I was afraid. I didn't want to be . . . alone with him, to enter his parlor. *Come into my parlor, said the spider to the fly,*" I whispered under my breath. I didn't think Father Mario heard this, or at least, he didn't acknowledge it. Then I was silent.

"Continue, please. What happened next?" He patted my hand to encourage me, but all I could think of was the rest of the poem. It had been one of my favorites as a child. The poem kept running through my head, line for line, over and over. I did not recite it to Father Mario, I am sure. Or did I? I couldn't actually remember. I couldn't focus on anything else Father Mario said, but his voice was kind and soothing. I truly liked him. He was a very good man. A nice man. Sister Agnes came to sit beside me, not long after he had left. She smiled but did not look cheerful.

All I could think about was Peter. I wondered if the ambulance came soon enough to save him. I wondered if I wished it had or wished it hadn't. I hated the thought that he might have lived, but I also hated the thought that I might have saved him, and didn't. It occurred to me I might be spending a lot of time in a foreign prison. At least if that happened, surely they would let Daniel and Benjamin visit. Would they stay in Rome, to serve God here instead of back in the States, for my sake? And then I remembered that Daniel was due to arrive any minute now to prepare for becoming bishop in just a few days. I smiled to myself. The last several hours would have been worth it if I had silenced Peter from preventing that ceremony, and from ever exploiting Benjamin again. I suddenly felt an anxiety attack coming on at the thought of Peter *not* dying.

Why had I asked the nun to make that phone call?

CHAPTER THIRTY-SEVEN

"Then who is his father, Tori. For the love of God I need to know."

"Tori, is it true? Is Peter really . . . dead?"

I looked at the person next to me with the deep, enchanting voice. It was Jonathan. Where had Sister Agnes gone?

"Tori, honey, speak to me."

Jonathan looked very serious. Where had he come from? "Where is Daniel?" I asked, glancing about, wondering. For hadn't Anda Panda said they were coming together?

"He's with Father Ralph and Father Mario. They all go back a long way, to when he was just Benjamin's age, and Father Mario was his best friend. Father Ralph was his mentor."

"Benjamin! Where's Benjamin?" I was suddenly dismayed that I had completely forgotten about my son. How could I do that? Just forget about him when he is all I have, and I am all he has, and he is why I am here. And then I thought of Father Mario, and yes, he did look about Daniel's age, whereas Father Ralph was quite ancient. He was slow and bent over, with a full head of white hair and kind, knowing eyes. What would any of them say if they knew I had killed Peter?

"Tori, Benjamin is fine. Daniel is fine. But you aren't. Tell me what happened with Peter." He took me in his arms and hugged me, not letting me go so that I could see into his face, see if he knew I had killed Peter. Or had I? It didn't matter. It felt good to have him hold me.

"Father Mario said Peter let you in, when you knocked on the door. What happened then?" he asked, whispering into my hair.

"Yes. He let me in. I sat in his front room on a blue sofa. And he sat in a blue chair. The sheer lace curtains were blowing in the breeze from the window," I whispered into his neck. He smelled nice. It made me want to kiss him. When was the last time I kissed him? "And the wisteria. You should have seen the wisteria, Jonathan, poking their little heads over the window box, peeking in at me. It was beautiful. *Tis the prettiest little parlor that ever could you spy."* There was that poem again, barely audible as I whispered it under my breath.

Jonathan pulled away and looked into my eyes, his hands on my shoulders. "Tori, listen to me. You have to remember what happened. Can you tell me?"

"Yes, of course I can. What do you want to know?" I asked, focusing on his handsome face. "Is Peter dead?" I added, for I really had no idea.

"I don't know," Jonathan answered somberly. "Why would he be dead, Tori? What happened in that apartment?"

"He drank his own poison."

"Why would he do that?"

My mind suddenly wandered to Peter sprawled out on the floor. "He didn't know his wine was drugged."

"Tori, what exactly was put in the glass?"

"Wine, of course. Red wine. We were drinking a toast to our partnership. He should have known I would never drink wine with him unless . . ." I looked away from Jonathan and stared at the altar. There were fewer candles burning than yesterday. I thought maybe I should light one for poor wretched Peter.

"Unless what?" Jonathan put his hand on my chin and turned my face back to his.

"Unless I knew he was getting the poison."

"Tori, listen to me carefully. Did you pour the wine?"

"No."

"Did you open the bottle?"

"No."

"Did you put the poison in the glass?"

"Peter told me he had none in his possession, poison. Not *ever*. And that he'd never poisoned anyone." I stared at Jonathan, into his clear intelligent eyes and added, "I guess it was silly of me to believe him." It was a non-answer, really, but the best I could do, and then I found myself adding, *"The way into my parlor is up a winding stair, and I've a many curious thing to show when you are there . . ."* while Jonathan kissed my forehead and held me to him, whispering, "Thank God you are okay."

We both looked up as Daniel appeared in the doorway. He appeared very priestly in his black robes, only much too handsome for a priest.

"Peter Cairns is dead," he announced. "Apparently he committed suicide, but there was no note."

We both stared at Daniel, neither of us finding words to respond. He walked over and sat in the pew in front of us, near the end so he could sit sideways and easily look into both our faces, which he studied intently. "Father Mario tells me you went to see Peter earlier. Is that true?" he asked, looking directly at me.

"Yes."

"Did you actually see him alive?"

"What did Father Mario say?" I asked.

"He said you did. At least, that's what you told him."

"Has he told anyone else that Tori saw Peter alive, except you?" Jonathan asked Daniel.

"Only Father Ralph," Daniel replied.

We all fell silent, and watched Sister Agnes enter by the altar door, genuflect, make the sign of the cross and then approach us. "Come, please," she said, gesturing for us to follow, which we did. Daniel led the way and Jonathan walked beside me, his hand lightly on my arm. She led us to Father Mario's study and knocked on the door for us, opening it without waiting for a response.

We entered and Daniel sat in a chair beside a table full of old and worn-looking books while Jonathan and I sat in the ladderback chairs facing Father Mario, looking quite serious behind his massive desk.

"Who is going to tell Benjamin about Peter?" Father Mario asked, looking first at me and then at Jonathan.

Jonathan volunteered and so it was decided that he would explain what had happened, without indicating my part in Peter's death. Then all three men spoke among themselves as if I were not there, and truthfully, I felt as if somewhere else, observing from above perhaps. All I could think about was Benjamin. I had not seen him for what seemed like an eternity since arriving at the cathedral this morning. I wanted to go look for my son, but I just sat in the chair and listened to men's voices surrounding me, deep and assertive, every one of them, and they were disagreeing.

"I think we should not tell the authorities anything," Father Mario said.

"I disagree. Not coming forward would only make things worse for Tori in the long run, if they figure out that she saw Peter alive, shortly before his death," Daniel replied. "Don't do or say anything to anyone until I come back," Jonathan added, and then left—I presumed to go see Benjamin. I wanted to see Benjamin too, but I didn't have the energy to follow Jonathan.

"Tori, we have put the luggage you left here in one of our guest rooms, where visiting priests stay from time to time. Sister Agnes is going to take you there. She will bring you some nice hot tea, and something to eat. You can spend the night. We wouldn't have it any other way." Father Mario smiled at me. It was warm and sincere but filled with worry and concern.

I nodded my head and then Sister Agnes was there and I left with her. She held onto my arm carefully and ushered me down the long hall, opposite of where Jonathan had gone to see Benjamin. I envisioned him painting in the old study, undistracted and unaware of all that was happening. Lost in his little world, as he could so easily do for hours on end when being creative. I missed him so much I ached for him. But Jonathan was with Benjamin and he would reassure my son that I was fine and that Peter, well Peter was no real loss to the world.

Before I knew it we were in a small cozy room with a feather bed covered by a quilt in shades of sunny gold and soft aqua, like the sea. I sat on the bed and stared at the beautiful quilt. Running my hand across the material I wished that I were on a bright sunny beach somewhere, with the gently rushing tide lapping at my toes.

Sister Agnes smiled from the door and told me she would soon return with a pot of tea. I laid back and closed my eyes, and wondered if I should call Miranda. *Peter's dead, Andi. He can't ever hurt you again. I have seen to that. I have made sure, with God as my witness, that he will never hurt anyone again.*

When I awoke there was a tray on the table by the bed. It was the first thing I saw when I opened my eyes. There was a silver teapot and a china cup with pink flowers. I sat up and saw a plate of sandwiches beside the teapot, cut into little squares on dark rye bread. There was also a bowl of fruit—one big yellow apple, two little green pears, and some dark purple grapes hanging over the side in a clump. A light was dimly lit on the table at the foot of the bed, and I knew it must be late, for the sun had set and it was dark outside the window over the bed.

I nibbled on the food and savored the sweetened tea after freshening up in the adjoining bathroom. Just as I became anxious to search the corridor for Benjamin I heard a knock at the door and Jonathan popped his head in. He smiled and said I looked much better than I had earlier, and there was someone important here to see me. Benjamin came bounding into the room and onto the bed where we hugged and fell back against the pillows.

There we lay, talking about Rome and the works of art scattered around the city. Father Ralph had taken Benjamin on a tour to see as many paintings, statues, and fountains as possible.

"I can't wait to show you, Mom. It's such a beautiful place."

"There is no one I'd rather have for a tour guide," I confessed, already feeling so much better now that Benjamin was there. The cloud over me seemed to lift.

Benjamin beamed and I smiled at him. It was the first time I could remember smiling since embracing Benjamin early that morning, which felt like an eternity ago.

In the hour or so that Jonathan left us alone together we covered many subjects but not the kidnapping, Peter's death, or Daniel's upcoming appointment to be bishop. Perhaps Benj had been instructed to avoid these subjects, or maybe he just didn't want to address them. I was grateful not to have to speak about any of it.

When Jonathan returned he informed Benjamin that Sister Agnes had dinner for him in the kitchen. We hugged and then my son was gone as quickly as he had come. Jonathan sat on the bed beside me and we looked quietly at one another.

"Jonathan, what is it?" I asked, for I could feel there was something he wished to discuss with me, hiding there beneath the silence.

"Tori, you did not kill Peter Cairns. I have been to the hospital, and I can tell you there was plenty of time to save him from his own poison, if only anyone knew exactly what that drug was in the amber bottle. Even if you had called the minute he drank the wine, it wouldn't have mattered.

They still hadn't figured out what was in the vile when I left there just a little while ago."

I stared at him, into his eyes. But all I saw was reassurance, no doubt or disapproval. I could only hope God would be so understanding and forgiving.

"I didn't have to let him drink it at all, Jonathan, and then we wouldn't have needed to know what it was."

We both looked up as Daniel stood in the doorway. "You *did* take part in Peter's death, then, didn't you?" Daniel entered the room and sat in a hard leather chair across from the bed, beside the tallest chest of drawers I had ever seen.

"Her actions were strictly self-defense. She was helpless to do anything but watch it happen," Jonathan argued, somewhat agitated.

"It is not self-defense to watch someone drink poisoned wine and then do nothing about it." Daniel was answering Jonathan, but looking at me.

"Does it matter that the poison was intended for Tori? That she sat there knowing he wanted to harm her again? Perhaps rape her again? And certainly kill her, in the end, as he had no doubt killed others. What choice did she have, Daniel, alone with this murderer? Should she have said please, don't drink that and die? So he could then manually force it down her throat?"

"Why didn't you call from the room, Tori, after Peter was no longer coherent and able to harm you?" Daniel asked me this gently, not really accusatorily—more like he were my mentor, or my parish priest. "It is not our place to decide who deserves to live and who should die," he added. "It is not our place to play God, Tori."

I looked into his eyes and all I saw there was love and concern, but not for any legal complications this might cause, which were Jonathan's priority. No, Daniel clearly did not care about legalities. It was my ethics and moral obligations that weighed heavy on his mind. It was partly what I loved about him. Daniel was so pure and good. He saw the best in everyone. He was so aligned with God's principals. Surely Christ himself was not more conscientious or compassionate.

"Daniel, even God tells us somewhere in scripture that we can defend ourselves. Why can't you see that her actions were justifiable? What is the matter with you?" Jonathan asked angrily.

"Was Peter Benjamin's father?" Daniel inquired, ignoring his friend. He looked away from me, as if he could not look at me and ask such a question. Perhaps he knew his expression would show that he never really believed Peter might have been Benjamin's father. Perhaps he knew it would show clearly on his face exactly who the father of Benjamin was.

"No, Daniel. He was not. I have never lied to you about that. Do you honestly believe that something so good and pure could come from something so inherently evil?"

Daniel ran his hands through those flaxen curls and terror crossed his face. "Then who is his father, Tori. *For the love of God I need to know*."

He looked at me, into my eyes, and I could not answer. I could only stare back at him. But then Jonathan lost it completely and said his peace to the undoing of Daniel's.

"What she is saying, Daniel, is that you are the father of that boy. And you are in denial because you want to be bishop. Open your eyes, my friend! Who are we kidding? Do you think God is in the dark about this? At least confess your sins and ask for forgiveness. At the very least, Daniel, ask Tori to forgive you for playing God with the lives of others while accusing *her* of doing that very thing."

Daniel stared at Jonathan, his face ashen, and then he looked at me. His usually sparkling eyes were clouded by thoughts that seemed to cause a storm in his very soul. Daniel's body was trembling, I thought, as he stood there speechless, and then he was gone from the doorway. I turned to Jonathan beside me on the bed and asked, "What now? How will he sort it all out? What will he do?"

"I don't know," Jonathan replied. "The cards are his to play, but at least the whole hand has been dealt."

CHAPTER THIRTY-EIGHT

Benjamin was our one true link to each other, a testimony to our love,
but still a love never really meant to be, or was it?

I looked down into the ruins and saw cats, lots of cats, hundreds of them. You had to look closely. They were hidden behind old clay pots and long spindly ferns and some lay stretched out in the sun, right in the middle of a small patch of grass. They were the hardest to see of all, the cats in the open where you least expected them. I couldn't believe these old ruins were here, in the middle of the city, one story down from where I stood on the sidewalk. Partially crumbled columns and other fragments of a civilization long ago. Now it was a refuge for the homeless felines, looking quite proud of their historic dwelling place.

It had been a perfect day after the disastrous one before it. Jonathan, Benjamin, and I had toured the city. Father Mario gave us a private showing of the Sistine Chapel, and the art museum housed within St. Peter's. We had seen the Pope's cats, lounging on the cathedral grounds looking much fatter than the ones here in the ruins. Benjamin was beside himself with the art everywhere, fashioned either in clay, marble, or oils. We had gelato and I thought of Bronwin and Emma enjoying the Italian ice cream last summer with their mother.

I decided to climb down into the ruins and see the cats a little closer, as I waited for Jonathan. He was returning Benjamin to the cathedral in Campo di fiore. Father Ralph and Father Mario had graciously insisted we stay there during our time in Rome.

Sitting on a marble bench beside a sleek gray tabby, I felt the warmth of the sun and closed my eyes to bask in it, feeling as fully appreciative as the cat. But then I was startled by a voice and the tabby meowed, jumping down and running off.

Daniel took the tabby's place on the bench.

"I'm sorry. I didn't mean to frighten you and your friend there," he said, nodding at the cat, now beneath a fern washing her paws.

I smiled at him. "It was an honor to give an impending bishop her seat."

Daniel ignored my comment. He seemed to have a lot on his mind.

"Jonathan told me you were here, when he returned with Benjamin. Father Mario has taken the boy on a surprise visit to meet the Pope, who is fascinated by Benjamin's paintings of Vincent Gianni's doves. I guess he has read about Benjamin in the London art magazine," Daniel offered up. There was something entirely different about his mood than I had ever sensed in the past, but what it was exactly, I could not be sure.

"I knew he was going. I'm glad he has such a wonderful opportunity. I'm sure he'll never forget it," I replied.

We looked at one another and time seemed to stand still for us. He wore a white button-down shirt and gray trousers. He didn't look priestly. Quite the opposite, Daniel looked in need of a priest. I wanted to reach over and touch him, feel his troubled face, so like his mother in shape and form, only more masculine. The white curls moved gently in the breeze and his eyes were as clear as the Rogue had been all those years ago when we rafted it. What Daniel's eyes and that scenic river had in common was a mysterious untamed beauty that drew you into its depth.

"Tori, I've been thinking. All night. I haven't slept. I haven't eaten. I need to tell you what's on my mind, if you will only hear me out."

Daniel looked more than nervous, he looked desperate.

"Of course. Please say what's on your mind." I laid my hand on top of his and it felt warm from the sun.

"Tori, you know I love you. But more than that, I love Benjamin." He picked my hand up and held it in both of his. "Even when I refused to believe that he was mine. In my heart I always knew, ever since that first time I laid eyes on him. But I couldn't admit it to myself, admit I had left you out there on your own to deal with a pregnancy and supporting a child by yourself, while struggling to go back to school and build a career. Me, of all people, dedicating my life to helping others while derailing yours."

"No, that's not true," I interrupted. "Benjamin was never a derailment. He was a surprise stop along the route that I would never take back. Benjamin has been nothing but a blessing. He has only enriched my life. We all have our struggles. I was fortunate that my struggles were never without family and friends on this train of life, if you will, to help me through."

"Tori, listen to me. I know I have no right to ask, but I want to be part of your family, too. I want to be Benjamin's father. What I am trying to say is, *I want to marry you.*"

I studied him sitting there and tried to determine if this was truly his heart's desire or just his desire to try and do what was right. I couldn't decide. "Daniel, bishops cannot be married."

"I don't need to be bishop. But I need you. And Benjamin."

"You may not *need* to be bishop, but you *want* to be bishop more than anything. And you will make a great one. The best."

"I want you more than I want the appointment." He looked sincere, and I believed at that moment, he did think he wanted me more than the church.

"Daniel, what about your commitment to God? You can't just turn your back on Him. You have an amazing gift, Daniel, and it needs to be shared with the world."

"I can still help those in need. No one has to choose between God's work and a family, Tori. It's possible to have both a strong marriage and a strong commitment to God, and God's work." He smiled at me and his face lit up. The troubled look was gone. As if spilling his heart's desire was a huge relief.

"How would you earn a living? You don't know how to do anything but be a priest," I said. I lifted my hands from his and touched his cheek. I couldn't help myself. I had to feel the warmth of his beautiful face, with those angelic eyes that seemed to reflect the very soul of God.

"Tori, I can actually do a lot of things. I could teach at the college in Portland."

"That's not the point, Daniel. None of this is the point," I replied. I took several deep breaths, and then looked boldly into those cyan eyes. "Daniel, the point is, I don't want to marry you. I love you, to be sure. But I love another more. And I have already agreed to marry him," I lied. For I hadn't told Jonathan I would marry him, not yet. Truthfully, I didn't know until then how much I wanted Jonathan. Knowing that I could have Daniel and that he wanted me more than his precious church suddenly dissolved my need to possess him. I felt ashamed at that realization.

"Then you really do love Jonathan?" Daniel didn't look surprised, only disappointed.

"Yes, I really do. Very much." We were both quiet for a few seconds, absorbing the heavy weight of my words. "I'm sorry, Daniel, but please, tell me you'll still be bishop."

"Well, Victoria," Daniel sighed, "I suppose if you don't want me, then there is nothing left for me but to be bishop."

"Daniel, it isn't a matter of what's left. The privilege of being bishop has never been something you've taken lightly. You know in your heart it is a great calling."

We didn't speak again for a while, but watched several cats nearest us. One rather large white cat jumped into Daniel's lap and he petted it absent-mindedly.

"Daniel, do you think I will burn in hell for letting Peter die?" I asked, remembering yesterday and his disapproval of my intentions.

"Of course not. God will forgive you. He already has, if you have asked him to."

"Do you think I was wrong, I mean to watch him suffer, and not do anything, not call anyone?"

"If this man threatened you in any way, then you were under no moral obligation to help him while there in his presence. And when you returned to the cathedral, you had the nun call for help. No one could have been any more conscientious than that, under the circumstances." The cat jumped down and he folded his hands in his lap.

"But Daniel, I wanted him to die. It was almost enjoyable watching him suffer. I feel as if in a way that makes me as evil as he was."

"No, you are not evil. This man hurt you, and until the moment he died he posed a very real threat to you. He kidnapped your son, Tori. You would not be human to feel any other way about his death."

I stood up, knowing Jonathan would return soon, knowing he only gave Daniel so much time alone with me to make his plea. It must have been difficult for Jonathan, not knowing what I would say, for surely Daniel had told him what he planned to do. At least now Jonathan would know that, given the choice, I chose *him*.

Daniel stood up, too, and we faced one another, our eyes reflecting the sadness we felt at this very different parting from any before it. It seemed as if Daniel and I were always parting, and never meant to come together except for a fleeting affair by the Rogue, that haunted us still for its depth and power over each of our lives.

"Daniel, Benjamin loves you. Please spend however much time with him that you wish. He would like that. He needs you, needs to know exactly who he is, and only you can help him discover the things about himself that make him unique."

Daniel didn't respond, other than to nod. Tears were forming in his eyes, and then in mine as we stood there, nearly touching, saying our last good-bye before he would be bishop. Benjamin was our one true link to each other, a testimony to our love, both past and present, but still a love never really meant to be, or was it? We came together in a kiss and an embrace that was long, tender, tortured, and so very bittersweet for all that it said and all that we were and would never be. When we finally tore ourselves apart, Daniel struggled to speak.

"I love Benjamin, as I love you. I will look forward to spending time with him. Tell him that for me, will you?"

"Of course." I glanced up and saw Jonathan standing against the rail, watching. He was probably thinking, if he'd been there long, that he had lost.

"Daniel, will you marry us? Jonathan and I? On the Rogue in the spring? Can bishops do that, marry someone by the side of the Rogue?"

Daniel smiled and wiped away a tear. "Of course."

We took one last look at each other and my memories flooded back to those nights by the rushing river. I felt sure, by the expression on Daniel's face, that he was there with me, in my arms again, beneath the stars.

"Tori, do you remember on the very first night of our trip when Jonathan asked you about your name and you said it was short for Victoria? You said it was easier to go by the middle of your name, because there was less pressure of what to live up to."

"Yes, I remember that," I replied.

"Well, Victoria, I believe that you have lived up to your name quite nicely."

I smiled. "Perhaps I have," I admitted.

And it was true. I had indeed gone the distance. I had given birth to Benjamin and loved him as much as Grams had wished for me to. In the process I had found someone to love me in the same way, a mere mortal with nothing to stand between us. He was right there waiting for me at the top of the crumbling haphazard stairs that connected these ruins to the rebuilt city of Rome.

I hugged Daniel again tightly and told him we would all be at the ceremony in St. Peter's and that I was very proud of him, and all he had accomplished and would yet accomplish for God's people. Then I left him standing there alone, except for the white cat that had jumped upon the bench behind him.

When I reached the top of the ruins I faced Jonathan, standing there with a questioning look on his face. Without a word I took his hand in mine and we walked away. It felt as if an enormous weight had been lifted from me, as if the guardian angels of a world somewhere between this one and the next had suddenly dispersed from the shadows of my every step. I felt inexplicable joy, knowing that whatever Daniel and my Benjamin were or were not, no one—now that Peter had met his demise—would ever be the wiser.

The ceremony at St. Peter's *was* beautiful and I cried the entire time, but Jonathan managed to only tear up once. He did cry, however, on the side of the Rogue when Daniel married us in the spring. Robert stood up for Jonathan and Rachel for me. Bronwin, Emma, and Sarah were flower girls. Benjamin was ring bearer. Miranda, Wil and Paige, Vincent and Maggie, Jonathan's partners, and a few other friends and family were also present. Daniel, with his special appointment as bishop, an honor given to him by the Pope himself, looked quite majestic in all his special attire and with his personal entourage to escort him.

With obvious mixed emotions of joy and love for Jonathan and I both, and perhaps a hint of sadness for himself, Daniel sealed forever a fate born long ago, that first night on the Rogue when Jonathan had inquired about my name. And here I was, suddenly feeling quite victorious. Perhaps God had meant for it all to happen in just this way. Who could know? I only knew that Benjamin needed to be born. Looking out at his beautiful face framed by flaxen curls, standing there next to Sarah, Bronwin, and Emma,

I couldn't help but wonder what his future held, indeed, what all their futures held.

I could only wish for them that it would be a tale to tell as rich as mine.

ACKNOWLEDGMENT

I would like to thank my father,
who has always encouraged me to follow my dreams.

ABOUT THE AUTHOR

Kathryn Mattingly has always had a passion for writing. Her short fiction pieces have received recognition for excellence in *Writer's Digest Award Winning Stories, Mind Trips Unlimited, Beacons of Tomorrow* and *Internationally Yours: Prize Winning Stories.* Her work has appeared in *Dark Discoveries* magazine and she is a feature writer for *Leading Possibilities* e-magazine, where her short fiction is also featured. Kathryn is inspired by real-life events and places she has lived or traveled. She currently resides in the foothills of Northern California.

Follow Kathryn:
Website: penpublishpromote.com
Facebook - facebook.com/kathrynwriter
Twitter - twitter.com/KathrynWriter

CPSIA information can be obtained at www.ICGtesting.com
Printed in the USA
BVOW031251290513

321873BV00001B/8/P